Mellichampe

*Available from the Simms Initiatives and the
University of South Carolina Press*

The Army Correspondence of
Colonel John Laurens, ed.

As Good as a Comedy
and Paddy McGann

Beauchampe

Border Beagles

Carl Werner, 2 vols.

The Cassique of Kiawah

Castle Dismal

Charlemont

The Charleston Book, ed.

Confession

Count Julian

The Damsel of Darien, 2 vols.

Dramas: Norman Maurice, Michael
Bonham, and Benedict Arnold

Egeria

Eutaw

The Forayers

The Geography of South Carolina

The Golden Christmas

Guy Rivers

Helen Halsey

Historical and Political Poems (*which
includes* Monody, The Vision of Cortes,
The Tri-Color, Donna Florida, and
Charleston and Her Satirists)

The History of South Carolina

Joscelyn

Katharine Walton

The Letters of
William Gilmore Simms, Vol. 1

The Letters of
William Gilmore Simms, Vol. 2

The Letters of
William Gilmore Simms, Vol. 3

The Letters of
William Gilmore Simms, Vol. 4

The Letters of
William Gilmore Simms, Vol. 5

The Letters of
William Gilmore Simms, Vol. 6 (exp. ed.)

The Life of Captain John Smith

The Life of the Chevalier Bayard

The Life of Francis Marion

The Lily and the Totem

Marie de Berniere

Martin Faber and
Other Tales, 2 vols.

Mellichampe

The Partisan

Pelayo, 2 vols.

Poems, Descriptive, Dramatic,
Legendary, and Contemplative, 2 vols.

The Remains of
Maynard Davis Richardson

Richard Hurdis

Sack and Destruction of
the City of Columbia

The Scout

Selections from the
Letters and Speeches of the
Hon. James H. Hammond, ed.

Simms's Poems Areytos

Social and Political Prose:
Slavery in America/Father Abbot

South Carolina in the
Revolutionary War

Southward Ho!

Stories and Tales

A Supplement to the Plays
of William Shakespeare

Vasconselos

Views and Reviews in
American Literature,
History and Fiction, 2 vols.

Voltmeier

War Poetry of the South

The Wigwam and the Cabin

Woodcraft

The Yemassee

Mellichampe

A Legend of the Santee

William Gilmore Simms

*Critical Introduction and
Biographical Overview by David Moltke-Hansen
and Explanatory Notes by Leland Cox*

The University of South Carolina Press

New material © 2014 University of South Carolina

Cloth original published by Redfield, 1854
Paperback published by the University of South Carolina Press
Columbia, South Carolina 29208

www.sc.edu/uscpress

Manufactured in the United States of America

22 21 20 19 18 17 16 15 14
10 9 8 7 6 5 4 3 2 1

ISBN 978-1-61117-062-7 (pbk)

Published in cooperation with the Simms Initiatives, a project of the University of South Carolina Libraries with the generous support of the Watson-Brown Foundation. Thanks are also due to the Institute for Southern Studies at the University of South Carolina for permission to reprint the end notes.

William Gilmore Simms: A Biographical Overview

David Moltke-Hansen

Introduction

Harper's Weekly put it succinctly in its July 2, 1870, issue: "In the death of Mr. Simms, on the 11th of June, at Charleston, the country has lost one more of its time-honored band of authors, and the South the most consistent and devoted of her literary sons" (qtd. In Butterworth and Kibler 125–26). Indeed no mid-nineteenth-century writer and editor did more than William Gilmore Simms to frame white southern self-identity and nationalism, shape southern historical consciousness, or foster the South's participation and recognition in the broader American literary culture. No southern writer enjoyed more contemporary esteem and attention, at least after Edgar Allan Poe moved north. Among American romancers (or writers of prose epics), only New Yorker James Fenimore Cooper was as successful by the 1840s. In those same years, Simms was the South's most influential editor of cultural journals. He also was the region's most prolific cultural journalist and poet, publishing an average of one book review and one poem per week for forty-five years.

Before his death Simms saw his national reputation fall along with the Confederacy he had vigorously supported and with the slave regime that many in the North had come to despise. Nevertheless reprints of most of the twenty titles in the selected edition of his works, first published between 1853 and 1860, appeared up until World War I. Thereafter only *The Yemassee*, an early romance about an Indian war in South Carolina, continued in print. The tide began to turn in the 1950s, when five volumes of Simms's letters appeared and a growing number of his works were issued in new editions. Publication in 1992 of the first literary biography, by John C. Guilds, and establishment of the William Gilmore Simms Society and the *Simms Review* the next year at once reflected and fostered this revived interest. Yet not until the 2011 launch of the digital Simms edition of the South Caroliniana Library of the University of South Carolina did scholars of southern, American, and nineteenth-century culture have the prospect of ready access to all of Simms's separately published works. With the University of South Carolina Press's cooperation, readers also will have access to sixty works in paperback editions by the end of 2014. Simms himself never saw nearly so many of his works in print at one time.

Clearly the decline in the critical standing of, and historical attention to, Simms and his oeuvre in the century after his death has reversed in the years since. The last three decades of the twentieth century saw more published on Simms than the previous hundred years (Butterworth and Kibler 126–200; MLA International). The last decade of the twentieth and first decade of the twenty-first centuries saw more dissertations and theses on him (forty-one) than had appeared in all the years before. This is not to say that Simms is yet given the attention directed to some of his contemporaries. For the first decade of the twenty-first century, the Modern Language Association International Bibliography lists roughly four times as many scholarly publications on James Fenimore Cooper, more than ten times as many on Nathaniel Hawthorne, and sixteen times as many on Edgar Allan Poe. Not surprisingly, therefore, Simms is not yet included in most anthologies of American literature, although he is a subject or a source in an expanding and ever more diverse body of scholarship.

To prepare to read Simms, it is important to see his writings in multiple contexts. He rarely wrote about himself outside of his more personal poems and his letters (some fifteen hundred of the many thousands of which survive). Yet he systematically drew on his background, personal experience, and relationships in his work. He also shaped that work through a progressively developed poetics and philosophy of life, history, and art. He did so in the context of his very broad reading of both contemporary and earlier Western literature and in the midst of multiple professional engagements and responsibilities. The richness and variety of these writings and involvements make Simms a key figure for future understanding of the literary culture, issues, and networks in mid-nineteenth-century America.

Background

Simms's family history reflected the dynamics that fueled the spread southward and westward of the populations, plantation economy, and society of the South Atlantic states. Simms's ancestry also reflected the Scots-Irish and English roots of what became identified as southern culture by the 1830s, a generation after the end of most immigration to the region. Two of Simms's grandparents, William and Elisabeth Sims, were Scots-Irish and migrated to South Carolina from Ulster. One, John Singleton, was an American-born son of putatively English immigrants, who had come to South Carolina from Virginia. The fourth, Jane Miller, was daughter of two Scots-Irish and Irish descended people—John Miller, of North and then South Carolina, and Jane Ross. Ross's family also migrated to South Carolina from western Virginia, where members lived cheek by jowl with other Scots-Irish families, who migrated to the Carolinas (White, *Ross*). Simms's father and Uncle James migrated in 1808 from Charleston to Tennessee, then to Mississippi. This was after the bankruptcy of the elder William's business and the deaths of his wife and their other two sons. Following the last of these losses, the elder Simms's hair turned white in a week. To his anguished eyes, Charleston appeared "a place of tombs" (qtd. in Guilds 6, 12).

For the son, however, Charleston was home—so much so that he refused to leave his maternal grandmother and move to Mississippi when his uncle came to get him in 1816. Then the fifth largest and by far the wealthiest city, as well as one of the greatest ports, in America, Charleston was at the peak of its influence (Moltke-Hansen, "Expansion" 25-31; Rogers). Cotton culture on the sea islands to the south, begun in 1790, and rice culture in impounded lowcountry tidal marshes meant that the port was filled not only with sailors of many lands and languages, but also with enslaved people of many African and Creole cultures and speech ways (slaves continued to be imported legally in large numbers until 1808). This street life made vivid the transnational nature of plantation agriculture and the fact that the developing region's dramatically expanding borders "were not just geographic; they also were human, historical, and intellectual" (Moltke-Hansen, "Southern" 19).

Even more important for the future author, the expanding region's borders and nature were taking imaginative shape. The West of the senior William Gilmore Simms and the first Creek War in which he fought, the Revolutionary War of the young Simms's maternal grandfather, the backcountry of many related Scots-Irish settlers, all these became grist for a lonely, energetic boy, who spent as much time with books as he could (Simms, *Letters* 1:161). The possibilities of such settings, incidents, and characters were not confined to history alone. Simms reported that he "used to glow and shiver in turn over 'The Pilgrim's Progress,'" while "Moses' adventures in 'The Vicar of Wakefield' threw [him] into paroxysms of laughter" (Hayne 261–62). Sir Walter Scott's Border and medieval romances and James Fenimore Cooper's Leatherstocking tales also deeply colored his imagination (Simms, *Views* 1:248, and Moltke-Hansen, "Southern" 6–15). As affecting were the ghost stories and Revolutionary War tales of his grandmother and the verses sent, and tales told, by his father.

These diverse tales became reasons to explore—in books, but also on the ground. As a boy, Simms ranged through the city and along the banks of the Ashley River, which fed into Charleston Harbor. He did so in search of scenes of colonial and Revolutionary battles and incidents (*Letters* 1:lxii). He first heard his uncle's and father's many Irish and frontier stories when they visited in Charleston in 1816 and 1818, respectively. He heard more on his trips to Mississippi during the winter of 1824 through the spring of 1825 and again in 1826. The first trip took him through Georgia and Alabama, where he saw elements of the Creek and Cherokee nations. At the time, Simms later reported, he was a boy "cumbered with fragmentary materials of thought, . . . choked by the tangled vines of erroneous speculation, and haunted by passions, which, like so many wolves, lurked, in ready waiting, for their unsuspecting prey" (*Social* 6). When he first got to Mississippi, traveling partly by stage, partly by riverboat, and partly by horse, Simms learned that his father had just come back from "a trip of three hundred miles into the heart of the Indian country" (Trent 15). Later father and son "rode together on horseback to various settlements on the frontier of Alabama and Mississippi" (Guilds 10-11, 17-18). Simms recalled as well "having traveled 150 miles beyond the Mississippi" (Shillingsburg, "Literary Grist" 120). The next year he returned to the Southwest by ship. "During this [second] trip he carried a 'note book.'" There he jotted episodes, encounters, stories heard, characters seen, and descriptions of the landscapes unfolding around him. He also wrote "at least sixteen poems" (Kibler, "First"; Shillingsburg, "Literary Grist" 123).

Simms took a third western trip five years later, writing letters back to the newspaper that by then he was editing (*Letters* 1:10-38). Together these three trips provided materials for his writings over more than forty years. "The first . . . produced mainly short fiction; the second inspired much poetry; . . . the first and third . . . yielded three novels written in the 1830s" (Shillingsburg, "Literary Grist" 119). This was, in part, because of the trips' timing. Sixteen years after the first trip, Simms told students at the University of Alabama that in the interval their world had changed from a howling wilderness into a place of growing civilization (Simms, *Social* 5-6). Had he not gone when he did, he would have been too late to see the frontier. Later travels took him many other places and also provided much grist for his writing. Never again, however, did he experience the frontier firsthand. Furthermore, on these later trips Simms was a practiced professional writer, no longer that boy haunted by passions.

Personal Life

After the ten-year-old boy's momentous refusal to leave Charleston, his grandmother sent Simms for two years to the grammar school taught on the campus and by the faculty of the nearly moribund College of Charleston. By then he already was "versifying the events of the war [of 1812]," just concluded, publishing "doggerel" in the local papers, and learning to read in several languages (*Letters* 1:285). His trip west a decade later helped him decide to pursue both literature and a career in law, but back in Charleston—this despite his father's urging that he stay in Mississippi. Upon his return home, he began to read law and also launched a literary weekly, the *Album*, which ran for a year. He became engaged as well to Anna Malcolm Giles, daughter of a grocer and former state coroner.

A year later the young couple married. This was six months before Simms was admitted to the South Carolina bar, on his twenty-first birthday, not long before he was appointed as a city magistrate. Although living up the Ashley River in the more healthful, less expensive village of Summerville, Simms kept a law office in the city. Shortly after using his maternal inheritance to buy the *City Gazette* at the end of 1829 and moving down to Charleston Neck, just north of the city limits where he had lived as a boy, Simms lost both his father and his maternal grandmother. He also found himself attacked because of his Unionist stance in the Nullification crisis resulting from South Carolina's rejection of a federal tariff. Then, in early 1832, Simms's wife died. Soon after, he took his four-year-old daughter back to Summerville to live and determined to sell his newspaper and leave the state for a literary life in the North.

Fueling his ambition was the correspondence Simms had begun several years earlier with an accountant whom he had published in his *City Gazette* but not yet met—Scots immigrant James Lawson. At the time Lawson, seven years Simms's senior, edited a New York City newspaper and, in addition to writing plays and poetry, was a friend (and, later, informal literary agent) to a wide circle (McHaney, "An Early"). Simms's trip north in the summer of 1832 saw the two begin a lifelong friendship, cemented as they squired ladies about and interacted with Lawson's literary circle. In subsequent years Simms multiplied the number of his friendships, in both the North and the South, making them in some measure a replacement for the family that he had lost. Lawson remained the closest of his northern friends, while James Henry Hammond, a future governor and U.S. senator, became his closest friend in South Carolina.

Late in 1833, after his Summerville house burned, Simms wrote Lawson to say that he was enamored of "a certain fair one" (*Letters* 1:73). Seventeen-year-old Chevillette Eliza Roach was the daughter of "a literary-minded aristocrat of English descent" with two plantations on the banks of the Edisto River in Barnwell District (later County) (Guilds 70). The courtship was protracted, as Simms felt it necessary first to clear debts that friends had bought up on his behalf. He also was determined "to marry no woman" before he was "perfectly independent of her resources, and her friends" (*Letters* 1:78). Therefore he did not propose until the spring of 1836. The nuptials took place seven months later, and as a result, Simms came to call the four thousand acres of Woodlands Plantation, with its seventy slaves, home. It was twenty years, however, before he took over management of the plantation and, then, only in the wake of his father-in-law's final sickness and death. Five years after that, he lost his wife, the mother of fourteen of his fifteen children. Nine of the children Chevillette bore him had already died, devastating Simms repeatedly. Five were still living (three sons and two daughters), as was Simms's daughter by his first marriage, who helped raise the youngest of her siblings. Those remaining children — even Gilly, who fought in the Confederate army — all outlived their father. Gilly and a brother-in-law ran Woodlands after the war, when Simms, though dying of cancer, was earning what he could by writing again for publications in the North and editing one or another South Carolina newspaper.

Career

The trip north in 1832 did not result in Simms moving there. Except during the Civil War, however, he returned almost every year. This was because the contacts he made, and the exposure to literary culture that he enjoyed, helped him define his future as an author. Earlier he had written fiction and criticism as well as journalism, filling the pages of several short-lived cultural journals and his newspaper, but between the ages of nine and twenty-six Simms had focused his literary efforts primarily on poetry. Beginning with his first book of verse in 1825, he had published five small volumes in Charleston. A couple had received positive notice in New York, and in the fall of 1832, J. & J. Harper issued the sixth anonymously from there, *Atalantis: A Story of the Sea*. Coming back the following summer, Simms had in hand for the Harpers a gothic novella, *Martin Faber,* and after his return south, he also would send the manuscript of his first two-volume border romance, *Guy Rivers: A Tale of Georgia*.

The reception of these and the romances and short stories that followed quickly made Simms one of the nation's most successful fictionists. He continued to issue poetry as well — roughly a collection every three years over the thirty-seven years that he worked as a professional author. But this output was dwarfed by the fiction — on average a title every year (counting several serialized works but not counting the many revised editions). Then there were the two dozen separately published orations, histories, and biographies as well as edited collections of documents and dramas and a geography of South Carolina. Add to these the revised editions and the further printings and issues of his own works and it appears that Simms saw a title coming off the presses at the rate of one every three months or so. Making that figure all the more astounding is the fact that, during more than a dozen of those years (the early-to-mid 1840s, the late 1840s-to-early 1850s, and the mid-to-late 1860s), he also was editing a cultural journal or newspaper. Furthermore he contributed reams of reviews and poems, hundreds of op-ed pieces and columns, and dozens of short stories and public addresses, which were never collected and published in volume form.

His career mapped an arc. It ascended meteorically in the 1830s and peaked in the early-to-mid 1840s, before beginning to descend. One reason was the popularity of the historical fiction that Simms began to write. When he left behind the law, his first newspaper, and the Nullification controversy, as well as his sadness, historical fiction was all the rage. Sir Walter Scott had fueled the craze, beginning with the publication of his first Border romance in 1814. He died in September 1832. Seventeen years Simms's senior, James Fenimore Cooper, the closest America had to a Scott at the time, was at the peak of his reputation and success, having started publishing his romances in 1820. Thus the way had been prepared for a writer of Simms's historical imagination and preoccupations. Within five years of his first trip north, moreover, Lawson's (and now his) circle became loosely affiliated with a nationalistic and Democratic group, self-styled Young America, this after Young Italy and similar ethnic, nationalist, European, cultural and political movements (Moltke-Hansen, "Southern"). Edgar Allan Poe and other members gave Simms's first fictions positive, if not uncritical, attention.

By the end of the 1830s, paradoxically, Simms, like Cooper, found his success attracting unauthorized editions of his works because Britain and America did not have an international copyright agreement. Further, in the wake of the panic of 1837, Americans bought fewer books. Simms's response was to diversify his portfolio. He turned to biography and history, including his hugely successful *Life of Francis Marion* (1844). He also returned to the editor's chair, overseeing one and then another cultural journal. These were unlike the ones he had edited in the 1820s: they included contributions by numerous authors, not just those from Charleston, but from the region and also the North. The ambition motivating the journals was to connect and promote Charleston intellectually. Consequently the journals more closely resembled metropolitan quarterly reviews in their offerings.

The mid-1840s saw Simms involved in politics, even serving a term in the South Carolina legislature. By the middle of the Mexican-American War in 1847, he had concluded that the South needed to become an independent nation. Thereafter, although he maintained ties with many in the Young America circle, he no longer promoted his writings as fostering Americanism in literature (*Views*). Instead he increasingly emphasized the ways in which his three romance series—the colonial, the Revolutionary, and the border—were making tangible and meaningful the origins and development of the future southern nation and the sad but inevitable consequences for Native Americans (Watson, *From Nationalism*; compare Nakamura).

Sectional politics colored more and more of Simms's perceptions, speeches, and private communications. The rising tide of abolitionism had him aghast. It also fed his growing sense that his position in American letters was slipping. He returned to editing, and his poetry, which was more often explicitly about the South, became increasingly patriotic in tone. Although his first biographer, William Peterfield Trent, insisted that Simms's declining standing reflected the change in literary fashion from historical romances to realistic novels, Simms in fact wrote more and more as a social realist in the 1850s (Wimsatt, "Realism").

The Civil War consumed Simms. As he wrote Lawson, "Literature, especially poetry, is effectually overwhelmed by the drums, & the cavalry, and the shouting" (*Letters* 4:369-70). He did manage to editorialize often and to rework and finish things long on his desk, including poems, a novel, and a dramatic treatment of Benedict Arnold, the northern traitor in the Revolutionary War. Then, in the wake of the Confederacy's loss and the failure of his vision for the South, he found himself recording the loss in a new newspaper, dealing with the trauma in his poetry, and becoming more existential and psychological in his fictional treatments. Simms's old New York friends tried to help. He did edit and see through publication a volume of Confederate war poetry. Yet it is a measure of his reduced stature that the several new romances he published appeared only in serial form. In part this may have been because he was in a sense competing with himself. Publishers were beginning to reprint volumes out of the selected edition of his writings. Many of Simms's works were available in book form, just not new works.

Associations

As the *Letters* testify, Simms had complex, overlapping networks of friends and colleagues. As a boy and young man, he received the friendship, patronage, and commendation of a variety of well-placed people in Charleston, including Charles Rivers Carroll. It was Carroll with whom he read law, to whom he dedicated his first romance, and after whom he named a son. Both men were Unionists during the Nullification controversy. So were Hugh Swinton Legare (later U.S. attorney general) and the considerably older William Drayton, as well as lawyer and editor Richard Yeadon and Greenville, South Carolina, newspaper editor Benjamin Franklin Perry. Also considerably older was James Wright Simmons, who had joined with Simms to launch the *Southern Literary Gazette* in 1828, when Simms was twenty-two. Through him Simms had direct contact with such British literary figures as Leigh Hunt and Byron (Kibler, *Poetry* 15).

The next group of influential friends and collaborators that Simms acquired were members of the Lawson circle and included such figures as Edwin

Forrest, the Shakespearean actor, and Evert Duyckinck, who published several of Simms's volumes in Wiley and Putnam's series Library of American Books, which he edited. Among the many others were poets and editors William Cullen Bryant and Fitz-Greene Halleck. Simms also made nonliterary friends in New York and Philadelphia, such as John Jacob Bockee and William Hawkins Ferris, the cashier at the U.S. Treasury office in New York who, after the war, helped Simms, Henry Timrod (poet laureate of the Confederacy), and others.

As a Barnwell planter, Simms met a widening circle of South Carolina's leaders and literati. For instance his acquaintance with James Henry Hammond began in the late 1830s and deepened into a friendship in the early 1840s. It was in the early 1840s, too, when he again was editing cultural journals, that Simms became friends with many southern writers. He regarded several of them, including Virginians George Frederick Holmes, Edmund Ruffin, and Nathaniel Beverley Tucker as members, together with Hammond and himself, in a "sacred circle." Uniting the circle were members' devotion to the South and a shared sense of the marginal status and critical importance of the life of the mind in a largely rural and unintellectual region (Faust, *Sacred*). Others of Simms's wide connections in the region did not interact as much with each other, but Simms long corresponded with Maryland novelist and lawyer John Pendleton Kennedy, Irish-born Georgia poet Richard Henry Wilde, Alabama lawyer and writer Alexander Beaufort Meek, and Louisiana historian and assistant attorney general Charles Gayarré, among others. By the 1850s, when Simms once more returned to editing a cultural journal, many of the writers whom he recruited were members of a younger generation. Poets Paul Hamilton Hayne and Henry Timrod were two. Often they and a half dozen others of Simms's and their generations met in John Russell's Charleston Book Shop and adjourned to dinner at Simms's Smith Street home, "dubbed 'The Wigwam'" (*Letters* 1:cxxxvi). Shortly before his death fifteen or so years later, Simms wrote Hayne, "I am rapidly passing from the stage, where you young men are to succeed me" (*Letters* 5:287).

Thought

The welter of Simms's works disguises unities and dynamics of the thought underlying them. From early on Simms was convinced that art ennobles or transforms, as well as gives voice to individuals and societies; therefore it must be cultivated assiduously. Without the potential for high artistic attainment, he insisted, societies are not ready for the independence and regard of free peoples. This is where Simms the historian joined Simms the poet. Societies develop, he argued (using the stadialism of the Scottish historical school), from imitation through self-assertion to achievement and also from savagery through strife to settled agricultural communities and, ultimately, to a hierarchical civilization supporting a rich artistic life. It was the job of the artist to help envision the goal, inspire the pursuit, and inform the process. That process was at once progressive and dialectical. Order, without dynamism, stifled development, as did the obverse—the dominance by ungoverned impulses or uncontrolled license. This was true in the individual, but also in societies as a whole. War was necessary for civilization, but its success was measured in the securities of the home, the center of cultural production and reproduction.

Whether in the public or in the domestic arena, "the true governor, as [Thomas] Carlyle call[ed] him—the king man—" guided rather than impeded the forces of change and progress (Simms, "Guizot's" 122). There were few such men with the capacity to lead. The same was true of nations. Neither all people nor all peoples were equal in either capacity or attainment. That was why Native Americans were overrun and Africans had been enslaved by European peoples in the New World. Indeed, Simms argued, "slavery in all ages has been found the greatest and most admirable agent of Civilization," giving education and examples to less evolved peoples (*Letters* 3:174). The degree to which a people had evolved mattered. That was why, he held, Americans had won independence from the most powerful empire in the world. They had done so through their Revolution, led by an elite that felt correctly its time had come (Simms, "Ellet's" 328). By mid-1847 that also was Simms's judgment for the South: the region had evolved enough to become independent (*Letters* 2:332). The hope inspired and then failed him and the people he sought to lead.

While not all men could rise to the highest rank, they all had the same responsibility at home. There the father was patriarch, protector, and head, while the mother was nurturer, moral instructor, and heart. There, too, children's characters and minds were formed by age twelve ("Ellet's"). Children's upbringing was critical to citizenship, and it was through her sons and the support of her husband, father, and brothers that a woman shaped the public sphere. The culture and character instilled in the child expressed and informed not just the household, but the larger society—the people.

"The history of peoples and their embodiments in institutions, states, and artistic productions—these were the great subjects" in Simms's view (Moltke-Hansen, "Southern" 120). Yet "poets were the only class of philosophers who had recognized" this until his own day, when at last "we now read human histories. We now ask after the affections as well as the ceremonies of society" ("Ellet's" 319-20). Peoples or races—that is, ethnic groups—were not unchanging any more than were their politics and their cultures. They either advanced or were overrun by history. Further, new peoples emerged, and old identities were submerged. The Spanish conquistadors were the creation of centuries of conflict with the Moors: their motivation was the glory of conquest, not the routine of trade or the plow. On the other hand, the English settlements in North America reflected the impulse to transform the wilderness into verdant farms and build society (*Views* 64, 178–85; *Social* 8). The same impulse drove Americans westward in Simms's own day and gave Americans their Manifest Destiny.

To explore these facts of the South's settlement and its place in international conflicts, Simms wrote all together, between 1833 and 1863, two romances set in eighth-century Spain, two set during the Spanish exploration and conquest of the Americas and two during the later English colonization of South Carolina, seven set during the American Revolution, and—depending on how one counts—perhaps eight set on the borders of the nineteenth-century South. After the war he published one more Revolutionary romance and two more that, like it, were set beyond the boundaries of civilization. He also left two unfinished romances, also set beyond society's normal reach. These late works, however, no longer had as their framing justification the cultivation of the South's future and civilization.

White southerners had their independence foreclosed by the war. In his last works, therefore, Simms found himself exploring the psychological, philosophical, and historical impulses that led to the Confederacy's demise and what, in the aftermath, it meant to be a good man and to build for the future, however impoverished. On the first score, he argued that the impulse to idealism behind abolitionism ignored historical realities, becoming inhuman in its consequences. On the latter score, he affirmed responsibility for one's dependents and the virtues of stoicism, as well as a continued commitment to the beauty and truth of art and the impulses to the cultivated life and fields. Therefore, in the face of the burning of his Woodlands home and library in February 1865—during Sherman's march and in the midst of desperate circumstances—he insisted that home, or the ideals and past characterizing its potential, still was at the center of true civilization, but only if elevated by art (*Sense* 8, 17). It was wrong to measure civilization by the getting, spending, and mad dashing, or material progress and utilitarianism, characteristic of both a capitalistic North and also many southerners. These traits he often had attacked even before the war, insisting that "the work of the Imagination, which is the Genius of a race, is only begun when its material progress is supposed to be complete" (*Poetry* 12).

Writings

Simms expressed many of his ideas most personally in letters and most cogently in essays, speeches, and occasional introductions to his books. But he illustrated them most fully in his fiction and poetry. By the time he arrived in New

York in 1832, he had formed many of the core ideals and beliefs that would shape his work. His application of them, however, modified his understanding over time. Growing as a writer and growing in knowledge and experience, he also grew as a thinker.

In his hierarchy of values, poetry came first. It was a prophetic calling as well as evocative of the deeply felt (or, sometimes, the fleeting) and thus testimony to the perdurance and transcendence of the beautiful and the human spirit. Yet, as Simms often ruefully reflected, prose spoke to many more people. That was a principal reason why he turned to writing prose epics or romances. He gave his most concerted consideration of poetry's value and roles in three lectures in Charleston in 1854. Over the prior three years he had given portions of them in Augusta, Georgia, Washington, D.C., and Richmond and Petersburg, Virginia. Entitled *Poetry and the Practical*, they did not see print until 1996, as Simms never found the time to expand them as he wanted. On the other hand, his last address on the same themes, *The Sense of the Beautiful*, was issued soon after he delivered it, also in Charleston.

Many of his important reviews have not yet been gathered, but Simms collected some in 1845–46, and *Views and Reviews in American Literature, History and Fiction* came out in 1846 and 1847 in two "series." Beginning with a consideration of "Americanism" in literature, the first series explored the themes and periods of American history for treatment by the novelist. Simms argued there, and in forewords to several of his romances, that fiction rendered the past more truthfully, interestingly, and tellingly than histories and biographies could because fiction—like poetry—required imagination to look beyond what is not known or expressed. The second series examined additional American writers and what distinguished them, for instance, in their humor.

Despite their early success, Simms's romances, novellas, and stories provoked mixed reviews. Poe eventually concluded that Simms had become "the best novelist which this country has, on the whole, produced" but also insisted that "he should never have written 'The Partisan,' nor 'The Yemassee.'" This was in a review of *Confession*. That novel, like the gothic *Martin Faber*, demonstrated, Poe contended, that Simms's "genius [did] not lie in the outward so much as in the inner world." Yet he nevertheless wrote of Simms's short-story collection *The Wigwam and the Cabin* that "in invention, in vigor, in movement, in the power of exciting interest, and in the artistical management of his themes, he has surpassed, we think, any of his countrymen." Other critics, especially in the genteel and Whiggish Knickerbocker circle, joined Poe in condemning what they considered to be the excessively graphic and vulgar qualities of many characters and scenes, and Simms's prolixity and sententiousness, in his romances (Butterworth and Kibler 64, 50).

The violent realism and earthiness of the romances did not result in realistic novels. Although Simms received early praise for his characterizations (particularly of women), he used the romance formula, with its stereotypic heroes and heroines, predictable themes, and conventional polarities. People were on quests or had lost their way or were fighting long odds or were carrying forward the banner of (and modeling) civilization or were mired in the slough of despond or were resisting all the claims of civilized society and behavior or were pursuing love interests. Deceitfulness, selfishness, and greed opposed honor, high-mindedness, and honesty against the backdrop of the South's development from the earliest days of Spanish exploration to the westward movement in Simms's own youth.

It was only gradually that Simms married the psychological acuity of some of his portraits of the interior struggles of his gothic characters and fiction to the historical romance. Helping him think through how to do so were the biographies he wrote in the mid-1840s, but also the incidents on which he focused particular fictions, such as the murder in *Beauchampe; or, The Kentucky Tragedy* (1842). However incomplete the blending of realism and romanticism or of stereotypical and socially individuated renderings through the 1840s, by the 1850s Simms fundamentally had made the transition to social realism in such works as *Woodcraft* and *The Cassique of Kiawah*. Indeed some scholars have considered *Woodcraft* the first realistic novel in America (Bakker; Wimsatt, "Realism").

In some sense disguising the transition is the fact that Simms also increasingly wrote as a humorist and, in so doing, often rendered his late narratives fabulistically, when not writing social comedy or stories of manners. This dimension of Simms's work was largely hidden, however, until the 1974 publication of *Stories and Tales,* volume 5 in the Centennial Simms edition. There, for the first time, readers had access in print to "Bald-Head Bill Bauldy." There, too, for the first time one could read together that story, "Legend of the Hunter's Camp," and "How Sharp Snaffles Got His Capital and Wife," which was published posthumously in *Harper's Magazine* in October 1870. These and other stories and tales made it clear that Simms was a fecund contributor to southern and American humor.

Humor let Simms take up issues that he could not otherwise address in print and still expect to be well received. He did so both during and after the war. The war also pushed Simms past the emerging fashion of social realism. Having destroyed the familiar, the preoccupation of much realistic fiction, the war made the liminal central (Shillingsburg, "Cub"). While his romances and tales had often explored life on the edge or in extreme circumstances, whether in war or on the frontier or on the verge of madness or in fanciful realms, it had done so against a backdrop of, and with the goal of affirming, social norms and development. In the war's wake that goal seemed absurd. Mythologized memories of a healthy past might nurture a sense of the beautiful but could not help one deal with the present. Thus Simms's conclusion, in a March 1869 letter to Paul Hamilton Hayne: "Let us bury the Past lest it buries us!" (*Letters* 5:214). Fifteen months later he lay dead in the 13 Society Street, Charleston, home of his oldest daughter, with the shell holes in the walls of the bedroom he had shared with several children.

Posthumous Reputation

The twenty years after Simms's death saw him often respectfully treated, first in obituaries, later in memoirs and columns, and also in literary dictionaries and encyclopedias. Yet Charles Richardson's 1887 *American Literature: 1607–1885* proved a harbinger of a shift: Simms, Richardson observed, was "more respected than read," having "won considerable note because he was so sectional" and then having "lost it because he was not sectional enough," although he showed "silly contempt for his Northern betters" (qtd. in Butterworth and Kibler 130). Five years later Trent's biography of Simms appeared. It was the first full-length, scholarly treatment. Its central thesis was that Simms's environment frustrated his abilities: the South was inimical to art and the life of the mind, and Charleston high society's hauteur marginalized Simms despite his talent and character. Trent's second thesis was that Simms's commitment to the romance and his romanticism meant that his works had become largely unreadable in an age of literary realism. Although Vernon Parrington and later scholars recognized Simms's impulses to realism, the two theses long shaped Simms criticism and, indeed, also helped frame study of antebellum southern literature and intellectual life (Parrington 119–30).

A Virginian born in 1862, Trent was a progressive who wanted a New South radically different from the old. He saw his pioneering study of Simms as an opportunity to criticize what the Civil War had made untenable. From his perspective the Old South was not the expanding and rapidly developing environment, with a deep history, that Simms portrayed, but a place where slavery stultified and stunted the growth and progress displayed by the North. Southern—especially South Carolinian—writers occasionally challenged Trent's agenda and conclusions, but those critiques had little impact. Not until after publication of the Simms letters in the 1950s did scholars begin to consider the author in the historical and contemporary contexts that he had rendered in his poetry and fiction. And not until after the centennial of his death did a growing number of scholars, having concluded that southern intellectual history was not an oxymoron, begin to study in detail the culture in which Simms participated and to which he contributed so voluminously and variously.

Some of these scholars also have had agendas: they have wanted to see Simms included in the American literary canon, for instance, or they have wanted to defend the heritage that in their view Trent, and so many others, inappropriately belittled or ignorantly dismissed. More fruitfully, other scholars have begun to reframe the understanding of nineteenth-century American intellectual life by stripping away preconceptions that characterized earlier evaluations of Simms and his contemporaries. They are closely examining the historical record and transatlantic and other contemporary contexts and developments in the process. Although the pursuit of canonical status in a post-canonical age seems quixotic at this point, the explosion of the canon is leading to more varied fare being offered and may, therefore, mean that Simms, once his work is widely available, will be more often anthologized as well as studied. Defensiveness about Simms and the antebellum South may warm the hearts of like-minded people, just as critics of the Old South have been encouraged by shared presuppositions and disdain. Yet dueling cultural ideologies do not advance comity and may only reinforce mutual incomprehensions. Continued, deep research in original sources and the theoretical reframing that Atlantic history, the history of the book, and other perspectives offer — these approaches promise most for further study of Simms, his works, and his world.

Works Cited

For amplified readings by and on Simms and on his world, go to http://simms.library.sc.edu/bibliography.php.

Bakker, Jan. "Simms on the Literary Frontier; or, So Long Miss Ravenel and Hello Captain Porgy: *Woodcraft* Is the First 'Realistic' Novel in America." In *William Gilmore Simms and the American Frontier*, edited by John Caldwell Guilds and Caroline Collins, 64-78. Athens: University of Georgia Press, 1997.

Butterworth, Keen, and James E. Kibler Jr. *William Gilmore Simms: A Definitive Guide*. Boston: G. K. Hall, 1980.

Faust, Drew Gilpin. *A Sacred Circle: The Dilemma of the Intellectual in the Old South, 1840-1860*. Baltimore: Johns Hopkins University Press, 1977.

Guilds, John C. *Simms: A Literary Life*. Fayetteville: University of Arkansas Press, 1992.

Hayne, Paul Hamilton. "Ante-Bellum Charleston." *Southern Bivouac* 1 (October 1885): 257-68.

Kibler, James E. "The First Simms Letters: 'Letters from the West' (1826)." *Southern Literary Journal* 19 (Spring 1987): 81-91.

———. *The Poetry of William Gilmore Simms: An Introduction and Bibliography*. Columbia: Southern Studies Program, University of South Carolina, 1979.

McHaney, Thomas L. "An Early 19th-Century Literary Agent: James Lawson of New York." *Publications of the Bibliographical Society of America* 64 (Spring 1970): 177–92.

Moltke-Hansen, David. "The Expansion of Intellectual Life: A Prospectus." In *Intellectual Life in Antebellum Charleston*, edited by Michael O'Brien and David Moltke-Hansen, 3–44. Knoxville: University of Tennessee Press, 1986.

———. "Southern Literary Horizons in Young America: Imaginative Development of a Regional Geography." *Studies in the Literary Imagination* 42, no. 1 (2009): 1–31.

Nakamura, Masahiro. *Visions of Order in William Gilmore Simms: Southern Conservatism and the Other American Romance*. Columbia: University of South Carolina Press, 2009.

Parrington, Vernon L. *The Romantic Revolution in America, 1800–1860*. Vol. 2 of *Main Currents in American Thought*. New York: Harcourt, Brace and Company, 1927.

Rogers, George C., Jr. *Charleston in the Age of the Pinckneys*. Columbia: University South Carolina Press, 1980.

Shillingsburg, Miriam J. "The Cub of the Panther: A New Frontier." In *William Gilmore Simms and the American Frontier*, edited by John Caldwell Guilds and Caroline Collins, 221–36. Athens: University of Georgia Press, 1997.

———. "Literary Grist: Simms's Trips to Mississippi." *Southern Quarterly* 41, no. 2 (2003): 119–34.

Simms, William Gilmore. *Atalantis: A Story of the Sea: In Three Parts*. New York: J. & J. Harper, 1832.

———. *Beauchampe; or, The Kentucky Tragedy*. 2 vols. Philadelphia: Lea and Blanchard, 1842.

———. *The Cassique of Kiawah: A Colonial Romance*. New York: Redfield, 1859.

———. *Confession; or, The Blind Heart. A Domestic Story*. 2 vols. Philadelphia: Lea and Blanchard, 1841.

———. "Ellet's 'Women of the Revolution.'" *Southern Quarterly Review*, n.s. 1 (July 1850): 314–54.

———. "Guizot's Democracy in France." *Southern Quarterly Review* 15, no.29 (1849): 114–65.

———. *Guy Rivers: A Tale of Georgia*. 2 vols. New York: Harper & Brothers, 1834.

———. *The Letters of William Gilmore Simms*. Edited by Mary C. Simms Oliphant, Alfred Taylor Odell, and T. C. Duncan. 6 vols. Columbia: University of South Carolina Press, 1952–82.

———. *The Life of Francis Marion*. New York: Henry G. Langley, 1844.

———. *Martin Faber, the Story of a Criminal; and Other Tales*. 2 vols. New York: Harper & Brothers, 1837.

———. *Poetry and the Practical*. Edited by James E. Kibler. Fayetteville: University of Arkansas Press, 1996.

———. *The Sense of the Beautiful: An Address . . . before the Charleston County Agricultural and Horticultural Association, May 3, 1870*. Charleston: Charleston County Agricultural and Horticultural Association, 1870.

———. *The Social Principle: The Source of National Permanence. An Oration, Delivered before the Erosophic Society of the University of Alabama . . . December 13, 1842.* Tuscaloosa: Erosophic Society, University of Alabama, 1843.

———. *Stories and Tales.* Vol. 5 of *The Writings of William Gilmore Simms.* Centennial edition; introductions, explanatory notes, and texts established by John Caldwell Guilds. Columbia: University of South Carolina Press, 1974.

———. *Views and Reviews in American Literature, History and Fiction.* 2 vols. New York: Wiley and Putnam, 1845 (1846).

———. *The Wigwam and the Cabin.* 2 vols. New York: Wiley and Putnam, 1845–46.

———. *Woodcraft, or Hawks about the Dovecote: A Story of the South, at the Close of the Revolution.* New York: Redfield, 1854.

Trent, William Peterfield. *William Gilmore Simms.* Boston: Houghton, Mifflin, 1892.

Wakelyn, Jon L. *The Politics of a Literary Man: William Gilmore Simms.* Westport, Conn.: Greenwood Press, 1973.

Watson, Charles S. *From Nationalism to Secessionism: The Changing Fiction of William Gilmore Simms.* Westport, Conn.: Greenwood Press, 1993.

White, William B., Jr. *The Ross-Chesnut-Sutton Family of South Carolina.* Franklin, N.C.: Privately printed, 2002.

Wimsatt, Mary Ann. "Realism and Romance in Simms's Midcentury Fiction." *Southern Literary Journal* 12, no. 2 (1980): 29–48.

Critical Introduction

THE REVOLUTIONARY ROMANCES

David Moltke-Hansen

William Gilmore Simms, preeminent mid-nineteenth-century southern author, wrote eight novels set during the American Revolution and its immediate aftermath. This introduction provides an overview. Although it covers all eight works, one volume—*Woodcraft*—has a separate introduction in this edition from the University of South Carolina Press and the William Gilmore Simms Initiatives. This is because it is the single work that has attracted the most attention from twentieth- and twenty-first-century critics.

From the outset the American Revolution compelled attention from writers and artists. Yet fictionists were slow to follow advocates like Thomas Paine, poets like Philip Freneau, and painters like Jonathan Trumbull. When novelists finally did, Simms proved the most prolific. His contributions remained unrivalled in their extent long after his death. It was only in the wake of World War I, when the Revolution's sesquicentennial approached, that other novelists began to treat more or less as fully as had Simms the subject of the War for Independence. Notably, in most of eight historical novels with characters from his native Maine, Kenneth Roberts turned to the subject, or the years just before and after, again and again. Van Wyck Mason did the same in the six volumes of his "American Revolution" series.

Still later writers followed suit as the war's bicentennial approached. Often this was in multi-generational family chronicles that included the Revolution but ranged much earlier or later. Among the most popular are Inglis Fletcher's "Carolina Chronicles" (12 vols.), John Jakes' "Kent Family Chronicles" (8 vols.), and Elswyth Thane's "Williamsburg" series (7 vols.). Several recent series with a more military focus treat just the Revolution. They include Edward Cline's "Sparrowhawk" (6 vols.), James Nelson's "Revolution at Sea Saga" (5 vols.), and Adam Rutledge's "Patriots" (6 vols.).

Simms paved the way for all these series, though not many authors have known their debt. At one level, his accomplishment was to give narrative form and force to the complicated ebb and flow of the Revolution in his native South Carolina. By doing so over a third of a century, starting just after the conclusion of the war's semi-centennial, he also helped claim the Revolution for

America's imaginative life. Before considering his individual titles, their publication and reception, and their later, critical standing, it is important to understand what motivated him. Then one can assess the series as a whole and ask its value to twenty-first-century readers.

The Revolution's Changing Significance, 1815-45

To a remarkable degree, the Revolution framed Simms's boyhood. The future author was nine years old when America's so-called second revolution, the War of 1812, finished. During the conflict, his immigrant father fought under General Andrew Jackson in the Red Stick or First Creek War. That conflict led the budding poet to effuse in verse. Inspired as well by his Charleston, S. C. grandmother's tales of his mother's family in the Revolution, the young Simms was in the habit of scouting old war sites in the surrounding countryside (Simms, *The Partisan* [1835] vii-viii; Guilds, *Simms* 7, 11).

This enthusiasm was further stoked by the fact that the American Revolution was gaining literary purchase. First came the hagiographies, memoirs, and historical accounts of the founders, together with reams of verse and documentary compilations. Then the story tellers started. Washington Irving's *The Sketchbook of Geoffrey Crayon, Gent.* appeared in 1820 and contained "The Legend of Sleepy Hollow" and "Rip Van Winkle," tales set immediately before and after the war. James Fenimore Cooper's *The Spy* came out in 1821 and his *The Pilot: A Tale of the Sea* two years later. Both these novels had Revolutionary settings — in the one case upstate New York (Irving's setting as well) and in the other the English coast and seas. It was in this latter environment that American naval hero John Paul Jones preyed on British shipping with storied success. Inspired by *the Spy* and by work editing a two-volume history of the Revolution, Mainer John Neal penned *Seventy-Six; or, Love and Battle* in just under a month in 1822.

At the time the sixteen-year old Simms thought of himself as a poet, not a fictionist. Despite his subsequent work as a journalist during the early 1830s, he did not shift his primary literary production from poetry to prose until after his 1832 trip to New York to launch a national literary career (Kibler, *The Poetry*; Brennan). He published his first gothic novella, *Martin Faber*, the next year. Then, over the course of two years, he wrote three romances. These commenced the three series that occupied him much of the rest of his life. He began the Border series in 1834 with *Guy Rivers: A Tale of Georgia*, set during the gold rush that started in 1828 in the northern corner of the state. The series ultimately treated the westering edge of southern settlement, from Georgia to Texas, as well as the southern backwoods, from the mountains of North Carolina to the swamps of Florida, in Simms's own life time.

The other series quickly followed. Simms started the Colonial in 1835 with *The Yemassee. A Romance of Carolina*, about a 1715-16 conflict between Native Americans and British colonists and their African slaves. The wider series broadly treated the periods of European exploration and colonization in the Americas from the 16th through the early 18th centuries. The third series, the Revolutionary, focused on that war in South Carolina. Simms delivered *The Partisan: A Tale of the Revolution* to Harper & Brothers, his publishers, just six months after the publication of John Pendleton Kennedy's Revolutionary novel *Horseshoe Robinson: A Tale of the Tory Ascendency*, set as well in the backcountry of South Carolina (Kennedy viii).

Simms subsequently wrote poetry, short stories, and novellas, as well as biographies and essays, in each of the subject areas of his series. Yet the majority of his output in all three was in long-form fiction—what he called romances. In making the move from poetry to romance, he followed the example of Sir Walter Scott. Scott died just as Simms's sixth volume of verse and first New York-published book, the 1832 dramatic poem *Atalantis*, was coming off the press to national critical acclaim. It was nearly 40 years earlier that the Scottish author began collecting and publishing the ballads of his country. Then, in 1814, he started his prolific and successful career as a novelist or romancer.

Scott judged fiction more accessible to broad readerships than poetry, and it was important to him to influence as many as possible. This was especially so in light of his goal of fostering a shared sense of British nationality among the Scots and the English—people of fraught histories, diverse origins, and deep antipathies. To this end, he examined not only the interactions of these ethnicities, which he did in *his* Border romances, set on the English-Scottish border. He also treated the earlier conflicts of Highlanders and Lowlanders in Scotland and of Anglo-Saxons and Normans in England. He did this to help people understand how Scottish and English identities had arisen out of the clashes and mixing of earlier ethnicities (Simms, *Views and Reviews. First Series* 40-41; Moltke-Hansen, "Southern Literary Horizons" 6-13).

The reason for such fictional narratives, Scott contended, was that ballads and other traditional lays do not have the same sweep as, for instance, *The Iliad*. A people's rise, conflicts, and conquests, myths, heroes, and villains, he concluded, need to be set and narrated on a large scale. Ancient bards did this formerly in epics chanted across generations. In a later and literate age, however, the surest way to provide people with a sense of their stirring past and mythic memories was in print. In type, prose carried the individual reader more effectively than poetry. The latter was supremely an oral and aural art.

Consequently, Scott, with others, developed the romance to tell epic stories in prose (Lukacs). It was different from the novel in both its purpose and its subject. As Simms put it in his "Advertisement" to *The Yemassee*, "the domestic novel [of Fielding and Richardson] ..., confined to the felicitous narrative of common and daily occurring events, is altogether a different sort of composition." Its standards are not "those of the epic," but the romance's are. That is why, Simms also insisted, "the modern romance is a poem in every sense of the word" (vi).

Though deploying Scott's formula, Simms was not a copycat (Holman, *The Roots* 50-60). His subjects were American (*The Yemassee* [1835] vii). As Scott wrote of the ethnogenesis of the Scots, the English, and the British, Simms treated Americans' emergence as a people out of their diverse origins and historical experiences. He and Scott shared a genre, because it was the necessary and appropriate form for the subject matter and purposes of each. In time, Simms would have an elaborate understanding of what that meant. Yet, despite his clarity about the genre, he did not start with a grand plan to fictionalize Americans' rise and spread westward. His initial intention for the Revolutionary series was just a trilogy "devoted to the illustration of the war of the Revolution in South Carolina" (Simms, *The Partisan* [1854] v).

While feeling his way toward a larger vision, Simms alternated among his three series. In the subset of his American-focused review essays and lectures, gathered in *Views and Reviews in American Literature, History and Fiction* and issued in 1846-47, he laid out his rationale for the three. The case he made was one trumpeted by his friends in the informal association of nationalist, Democratic writers centered in New York—the Young America circle (Widmer). Although adumbrated already in his 1835 preface to *The Yemassee* and elaborated over the next months in both his first two Revolutionary romances, *The Partisan* and *Mellichampe*, the argument he advanced was in a sense his *ex post facto* justification of his practice. He claimed that he was writing what the Alabama poet and politician Alexander B. Meek came to call, in an 1844 oration, *Americanism in Literature* (*Views and Reviews. First Series* 1-19).

Anticipating Meek, Simms lectured in 1842 on "The Epochs and Events of American History, as Suited to the Purposes of Art in Fiction." He explained that he saw American history divided into four epochs—that of initial European exploration and conquest in the three-quarters of a century or so after Columbus made landfall in the new world; the subsequent two centuries of British colonial settlement and continuing conflict with Native Americans and rival European powers; the two decades that saw the British American move from remonstrance to Revolution and independence; and the subsequent western expansion, self-development, and Manifest Destiny of the new nation and people (*Views and Reviews. First Series* 20-101). In treating each of these epochs in romances, Simms published at least two dozen long-form fictions—a third of them in the Revolutionary series.

While all three series shared common purposes, Simms had particular reasons to treat the Revolution as and when he did. A supporter of his father's old commander, President Andrew Jackson, and the Union during the bitter campaign of the early 1830s to have South Carolina unilaterally nullify federal tariffs, he was keen to assert the Palmetto State's role in the making of the American nation. The political passions of the nullification episode reminded him, too, that "the excesses of patriotism, when attaining power, have been but too frequently productive of a tyranny more dangerous in its exercise, and more lasting in its effects, than the despotism which it was invoked to overthrow" (*Mellichampe* [1836] v; Wakelyn 19-50). His early Revolutionary romances also "suggested clews [sic] to the historian ... and laid bare to other workers ... the veins of tradition which everywhere enrich" South Carolina. True, his "friends denounced [his] waste of time," but the result was that the Palmetto State had "furnished more materials for the use of art and fiction ... than half the states in the Union" (Simms, *Katherine Walton* [1854] 3).

These early Revolutionary romances reflected as well a commitment to realism. This was despite their conventional, romantic, chief protagonists. Indeed, many criticized Simms for the vulgarity and violence of his secondary characters. He answered the charge with a rhetorical question that reflected his dedication to historical verisimilitude: "Does the story profess to belong to a country and to a period of history which are alike known—and does it misrepresent either?" The implied answer to the first part of the question was "yes" and, to the second part, "no." Clearly, as he insisted, he had no desire "to make a fairy tale ... in which none but the colors of the rose and rainbow shall predominate" (*Mellichampe* [1836] ix).

Rather, Simms's "object usually [was] to adhere, as closely as possible, to the features and the attributes of real life." Further, it seemed to him obvious "that vulgarity and crime must always preponderate ... in the great majority during a period of war." Because, "to paint morally, the historic novelist must paint truly," Simms concluded that the fact that "the low characters predominate" should not surprise his readers (*Mellichampe* [1836] x-xii). The need to reiterate the point against a persistent strain in the criticism of his work may have been behind his observation in the historical overview with which he began his third Revolutionary romance, *The Kinsman: or The Black Riders of Congaree*: "That atrocious and reckless warfare between the whigs and the tories, which had deluged the fair plains of Carolina with native blood, was now at its height" (17). The romance that started there was his last in the series for almost a decade.

Southern Honor and the American Revolution

When Simms returned to writing Revolutionary romances in 1849, he still had these earlier motives and judgments. Yet, in the interval, his rationales for writing had shifted. He had developed new intellectual and political priorities. He addressed these initially in review essays penned between 1845 and 1852. He published three of the essays as *South-Carolina in the Revolutionary War: Being a Reply to Certain Misrepresentations and Mistakes of Recent Writers, in Relation to the Course and Conduct of This State* (1853) (Moltke-Hansen, "Why History Mattered"; Simms, *Letters* 6: 328 n. 8). There he argued that novelists, editors, biographers, and historians were mischaracterizing the course and conduct of the Revolution and of the Revolutionaries in the South—especially South Carolina. Even such an eminent southern writer as John Pendleton Kennedy had made material errors in his *Horse-Shoe Robinson*. These were not justified by the demands of his story or the faulty memory of the real Horse-Shoe Robinson. The consequence of such mistakes was to make the patriots appear less, and the British more, effective than they were (Simms, *South Carolina in the Revolutionary War* 60-72).

Even more galling was the critique of the patriots for excesses against the loyalists. Simms early acknowledged both the fact and, in particular instances, the unfortunate consequences. Yet he vehemently resisted reading those instances as normative (*Mellichampe* [1836] iv-v; Moltke-Hansen, "Why History Mattered"). Many loyalists earned the vigor of the actions against them. Many patriots were sorely provoked. The civil warfare between para-military forces of both sides inevitably produced violent interactions. To take the viewpoint of "the Descendants of the loyalists," as did Ann Pamela Cunningham, granddaughter of an up country South Carolina tory colonel, was to use "about the worst authorities ... on the subject of the Revolution"; for those descendants were seeking to assuage their "mortification" and to meet the need "to make out a case" for their own families (*Letters* 6: 330; Moltke-Hansen, "Why History Mattered").

Simms argued the point so strongly because it was part of a larger debate about the role of the South in the Revolution. Northern editors and writers contended increasingly that it took northern troops to drive the British army from Georgia and South Carolina to Yorktown and surrender. This was because the South's population was divided in the conflict and, indeed, often resisted the patriot forces. To the contrary, Simms insisted, local partisans in South Carolina repeatedly saved the American army. Moreover, they did this while also fighting "all the tories who infested [the state], though these were mostly *refugees from all the States south of New York*, who had taken refuge in

[British] Florida, & who followed in the wake of the British when they penetrated Geo. & S. C." (*Letters* 6: 330).

Simms contended that the South's leadership largely supported the Revolution but that the many recent Scottish and German immigrants tended to loyalism. Unlike the Irish and Scots-Irish, who often hated the English and also unlike the descendants of Huguenot immigrants, they owed too much to the British Crown ("Ellet's"). Further, at least in South Carolina, they made up "nearly half of [the colony's] population" and "had not been in the country 10 years" (*Letters* 6: 330). At the time, by contrast, New England was overwhelmingly settled by descendants of people who had arrived before the English Civil War over a century and a quarter before. The populations of the two regions therefore were very different in their make ups.

New Englanders, according to Simms, mostly were local patriots, not active on behalf of the larger cause of American independence. Consequently, South Carolina "sent, in proportion, more troops into the war than any other colony" (*Letters* 6: 330). Moreover, had it not been for southern leaders such as George Washington, the light of liberty would have been snuffed out. "You assailed my country ... unjustly," Simms wrote New England historian Lorenzo Sabine. He then lamented Sabine's "abuse of partial facts; and the evident purpose which it betrayed, rather to goad, sting, wound & disparage, than to be historically just & true" (*Letters* 6: 328-29).

These points mattered not only because of the importance of historical accuracy. They had political ramifications. Charles Sumner of Massachusetts used the introduction to the 1847 edition of Sabine's *The American Loyalists, or Biographical Sketches of Adherents to the British Crown in the War of the Revolution* in his attack in a speech in the United States Senate on South Carolina and one of its senators, Andrew Butler. He characterized the Palmetto State as stained by "its imbecility from Slavery, confessed through the Revolution," and then "made the state out to be unpatriotic and un-American, not only in 1856 but at least as far back as the Revolutionary War," three quarters of a century and more before (Shillingsburg, "Simms's Failed Lecture Tour" 185). That attack, Simms maintained, was what provoked the notorious "cudgelling" [sic] of Sumner on the Senate floor by Congressman Preston Brooks, Butler's South Carolina relation. Sabine "also misled Mr. [Daniel] Webster, who fell into a good deal of spoken blundering, in [his address to the New England Society of] Charleston, touching the vast number of New Englanders who perished in our battles" (*Letters* 6: 331).

Simms intended his fall 1856 lecture tour of the North, just months after Brooks used his gutta percha cane on Sumner, to set the record straight and to maintain the honor of South Carolina's role in the Revolution. Not surprisingly, given those intentions, the tour was a disaster and had to be cut short. His references to "Sumner's attack on S.C. as that of a deliberate & wanton malignant" antagonized his audiences (Shillingsburg, "Simms's Failed Lecture Tour" 191). The newspapers replied in kind, claiming that Simms was "seeking to do, in the historical field, what Brooks had done in the physical" (194). The next year Simms lectured on his northern reception for a southern audience. Northerners, he insisted, were morally incapable of listening to southern viewpoints, because the "politico-social relations of the two great sections" were "in absolute and direct antagonism" (188; Hagstette, "Private vs. Public" 52-58).

These intellectual and political conclusions were not the only developments that shaped Simms's return to his Revolutionary romance series. He formed new aesthetic goals as well. Although an early advocate of realism in fiction, he did not begin as a literary realist. Instead he regarded everyday life as being in the scope of the novelist; he was rather an epic writer of romances. Then it occurred to him that he could fuse these approaches, creatively using the tensions and differences between them (Ackerman 165).

Simms's fourth Revolutionary romance, *Katherine Walton*, reflected the change. Its purpose was "the delineation of the social world of Charleston, during the Revolutionary period" (*Katherine Walton* [1854] 3). Simms still considered the work a romance but used its social realism to attack aristocratic prejudice in the manner of William Makepeace Thackeray (Watson, *From Nationalism* 92-93). According to Mary Ann Wimsatt, "the Loyalists, who controlled government, churches, and clubs, continued the city's glittering amusements—a fact that made [the city] ripe for treatment in the novel of manners vein" (*The Major Fiction* 179). Consequently, "for the first time in the Revolutionary War series, ... Simms [made] social hostilities rather than military maneuvers the backbone of a book" (179-80).

Because *Katherine Walton* was the first novel serialized in *Godey's Lady's Book*, the most widely circulated American cultural journal of the day, it presumably had more readers than any other of Simms's Revolutionary romances. Yet many scholars consider Simms's next his best. *The Sword and the Distaff; or, "Fair, Fat and Forty," A Story of the South, at the Close of the Revolution* appeared in serial form, too, but in Charleston. Publication started in February 1852. The book came out that fall—also in Charleston—before the conclusion of the serialization and its Philadelphia publication from the same plates the next year. Subsequently it became known by the title of its revised, 1854, Redfield edition: *Woodcraft; or, Hawks about the Dovecote. A Story of the South at the Close of the Revolution* (Bakker).

In its serial form, Simms's work overlapped with the last segments of the serialization of Harriet Beecher Stowe's famous abolitionist novel *Uncle Tom's*

Cabin, which ran for 40 weeks between 5 June 1851 and 4 March 1852. Simms contended shortly afterwards that his romance was the best answer to Stowe's work (*Letters* 3: 222). He did not mean that he wrote to reply to Stowe, as many others in fact eventually did. After all, he initially published for a largely southern audience—the only time he did so in his Revolutionary series. Moreover, he could not have been writing in reply because of the near simultaneity of the publications of his and Stowe's works.

Rather, scholars understand Simms to have meant either of two things. One is that the social world and relations conveyed in his domestic romance gave a radically more accurate and positive picture of slavery and the plantation South than did Stowe's sentimental domestic novel. Both works were critical of failings of the institution, but to different ends (Watson, "Simms's Answer"). Social order wins in the one, and moral order loses in the other. The second reading of Simms's assertion is that his melding of sentimental domestic fiction with the romance was radically more effective than Stowe's appropriation of the romance structure for her work. In making this case, Zeno Ackerman argues that Simms and Stowe both dealt with responses to the disruption of the plantation idyll—by war in one case, by progressive, capitalist alienation in the other case (165). Whatever Simms meant, it aggrieved him that Stowe's book sold hugely, while his did not, published as it initially was in a small circulation journal and then in a North becoming more and more abolitionist in sentiment.

As James Kibler argues in his introduction to *Woodcraft*, Simms did not believe that the success of South Carolina plantation society was guaranteed. Rather, it had to be achieved again and again (xxviii-xxxi). To survive it also had to be protected from hostile influences. Yet historically the social order did carry forward. Once carved out of the wilderness and later restored after the disruptions and devastation of the Revolution, plantations remained the epitome of patriarchal order, and, under the guiding hand of plantation mistresses, the big house served as their moral centers. This ideal, Simms understood, was not always the reality, but it was, he maintained, the cultural, social, and ethical norm.

Modern critics argue that Simms's patriarchal plantation purveyed a fantasy. Like other slave owners, Simms deceived himself about the bonds between slaves and masters. Most slaves did not happily think of themselves as members of their masters' families, black and white. Neither did they believe they owned their masters as much as their masters owned them. Nor did slaves all love their owners or, as happened repeatedly in Simms's romances, reject the chance of freedom (Genovese and Fox-Genovese; Foley; King 140; Shelton 77). At the same time as scholars criticize, however, they praise the verisimilitude of the details of Simms's renderings—not just in *Woodcraft*, but in all the Revolutionary romances.

Simms scoured the written record available to him in manuscript as well as print, conducted oral history interviews, sought out informants about incidents and places he did not know, and weighed the relative merits of his evidence. He began as a boy, musing about the stories implicit "in "the local tradition, which, unconsciously, [his] mind began to throw together, and to combine in form." As he explained in the revised and expanded introduction to the 1854 edition of *The Partisan*, "even where the written history has not been found, tradition and the local chronicles, preserved as family records, have furnished adequate authorities." He concluded: "a sober desire for history—the unwritten, the unconsidered, but veracious history—has been with me, in this labour, a sort of principle" (vii-ix).

Even when he originally wrote *The Partisan*, Simms understood, as he rephrased the point in 1854, that "History ... is quite too apt to overlook the best essentials of society—such as constitute the moving impulses of men to action—in order to dilate on great events,—scenes in which men are merely massed, while a single favourite overtops all the rest, the Hero rising to the Myth, and absorbing within himself all the consideration which a more veracious and philosophical mode of writing would distribute over states and communities, and the humblest walks of life." Although in his romance "the persons of the Drama, many of them, are names of the nation, familiar to our daily reading," the focus of *The Partisan* was not on them, but on "the little nucleus of the Partisan squad ... first formed in the recesses of the swamp" (*The Partisan* xi).

That preoccupation let Simms show "how the personal wrong ... goaded the indifferent into patriotism ... [and] the submissive into rebellion" (*The Partisan* [1835] ix, viii). In doing so, he was explaining why things happened as and when they did. His purpose, as he observed in his 1835 introduction, was to "give a story of events, rather than of persons"(x). Events moved men and moved history forward. The treatment of events gave one the opportunity to explore history's unfolding and the consequences (Holman, *The Roots* 35). The why of history, nevertheless, was different than the what.

Literary Realism, Sectionalism, and the Postbellum Turn

Simms's sense of the "what" of history shifted between the early 1840s and the '50s. The fundamental question in *Woodcraft* is not about the motivations and actions of the Revolution, which is finished, but about the restoration of a moral order and economy in the face of the war's social dislocations. Those disruptions challenged the character of both individuals and the community. In the process of shifting to this focus, Simms turned the historical romance into a novel of social realism and manners or a domestic romance (Dale). Indeed, Jan Bakker argues that *Woodcraft* is "the First 'Realistic' Novel in America" (64-78). That may slight *Katherine Walton* (Wimsatt, "Realism and Romance"). In any event, the post-*Woodcraft* Revolutionary novels, although set in war-time, carried forward this social critical emphasis. Conservative, low country aristocrats continued to be objects of attack, as were the unworthy low-born, twisted by greed and hate.

Individuals of these castes at opposite ends of the social spectrum were too often tories. "Unable to lead themselves," according to Simms, they "threw themselves, as so many dead weights, about the car of *movement* [sic]; and it is no reproach to those who did lead, that they were passed over, or flung off, by the wheels" ("*Civil Warfare*" 260-61). "The language he used to describe the tyranny of the tories in 1780 was the same as he used to describe the tyranny of the nullifiers ... and [also] the tyranny of Northern interests in the 1850s" (Moltke-Hansen, "Ordered Progress" 138). Tory forces and their partisan opposition figure centrally in the last two of his antebellum Revolutionary romances, published in 1855-56. There they play key roles in the run up to, and the ultimate outcome of, the Battle of Eutaw Springs. This engagement is the event around which *The Forayers; or The Raid of the Dog-Days* and *Eutaw: A Sequel to The Forayers, or the Raid of the Dog-Days. A Tale of the Revolution* revolve.

The critique of the failures of leadership and allegiance in these romances grew out of deep frustration. Starting in the mid-'40s, Simms first ramped up this criticism in other writings. Like the tory elite, too many of the antebellum South's leading citizens were temporizing about the region's political future. Increasing Simms's sense of urgency was his apprehension about capitalism's growing and coercive influence. It infected not just politics, but also cultural life and other spheres. Avarice and the new, socially destructive methods of wealth's generation were undermining political resolve and corrupting arts'—and thought's—producers, productions, and consumers as well as social relations. His Revolutionary romances of the '50s all show this process. In doing so, they reflect what Amy Kaplan argues literary realism is: a "strategy for imagining and managing the threats of social change" (ix).

The disease of capitalism, Simms believed, had been at work longer and had infected more people and more of life in the industrializing and urbanizing North and Britain of his day than in his region. Yet, as his Colonial and Revolutionary romances show, the South was not immune. Moreover, capitalism progressively compromised the social, cultural, and political health of the region as the nineteenth century advanced (Minguera; Pearce). At least slavery, he contended, isolated the South from some of the worst consequences of the disease (Ackerman 165).

This belief was in part why Simms proposed the extension of the South's slave regime over countries on the Caribbean littoral. That goal, in Simms's view, was southerners' manifest destiny. Besides, Mexicans and others needed to be disciplined and civilized by the institution (*Self-Development* 22-23). This aggrandizing vision was part of Simms's design to protect southern rights against an overweening North. The South would do so by augmenting its influence and political power ("The Southern Convention"). Simms's ambitions became greater still: establishment of the sovereignty and nationhood of the southern people. Only in this way, he eventually concluded, could the extension and preservation of his people's way of life and independence be assured. In his eyes as well, these were fundamentally the same motivations and objectives as those which animated America's Revolutionary founders.

The study of the Revolution, then, revealed the way forward, not just the heroics and necessities of an earlier age. History was about the future—until, that is, the Civil War created a chasm between the slave regime and its aftermath. In the process, the war turned the burgeoning South of Simms's Border Romance series, westward expansion, and Manifest Destiny into the Old South of beguiling and fading memories, timeless tradition, and social order. It also proved that the reasoning undergirding Simms's antebellum historical thought was wrong. The South was not destined for independence; white southerners would not become their own nation, and slavery was not the future of a Caribbean basin dominated by them (Moltke-Hansen, "When History Failed" 27-30).

Yet even after Confederate defeat Simms continued the fight against capitalism. Shortly before his death in 1870, he told the ladies of the Charleston Horticultural Society that they must be resolute in their efforts to stem capitalism's corrupting and debasing influence. They needed to do this to preserve the South's distinction, culture, and values. The remembered patriarchal order of the antebellum plantation, centered on the big house run by the plantation mistress, might be no more; nonetheless it offered a model to inform his auditors' sense of a healthy society. At the same time, the sacrifices of the Civil War in defense of the southern way of life required the continuing commitment to that life (*The Sense of the Beautiful*; Georgini; John Miller). Sadly, in Simms's view, what that defense could not do was free the South from Yankeedom.

The last of his Revolutionary romances, *Joscelyn*, serially published in 1867, reflected the shift in historical perspective and reality with which Simms had to deal after defeat. The chief protagonist, Stephen Joscelyn, is unlike earlier leading men of the series: he is a cripple, physically and psychologically. He is driven to fight against his demons as well as for the patriot cause. War is an inner tumult as much as an outward conflict. The notorious tory Thomas Browne, based on a historical figure, in effect loses himself and the last battle of the story in his parallel struggle. Joscelyn, though, finally affirms his manhood, his honor, and his sanity. His concluding victory is as much personal as military or political.

War's fortunes are uncertain, but a man can be responsible for himself. In the end, the inference seems to be, character is achieved (or lost), not simply a birthright and an example, as it was for Simms's early romance heroes. One's conduct is all one can control in the face of chaotic military and political conflict and social upheaval. Indeed, character is the fundamental measure of success and the chief bulwark against disorder and dissolution. Simms went on to suggest to the ladies of the Horticultural Society that, by this measure, the conquering Yankees had failed. This was because of how they behaved not only in the winning, but also in the aftermath of victory (*The Sense of the Beautiful*; Georgini; John Miller). Morally and aesthetically, therefore, victory should still go to the South.

Joscelyn's story revealed Simms shifting from a social to a psychological understanding of war and literary realism. The move shaped all three of his last published romances, including two in the Border series—*Voltmeier, or The Mountain Men* and *The Cub of the Panther; A Mountain Legend*, both serially issued in 1869. The move reflected as well Simms's preoccupation with states of mind back to his early days as a writer of gothic tales (Hagstette, "Screams from the South"). Unlike his late romances, however, those tales did not—could not—use the intellectual and aesthetic tools of the psychological realism just beginning to emerge in literature at mid-century. Furthermore, even among his last long fictions only *Joscelyn* and the unpublished and incomplete pirate romance "The Brothers of the Coast" deal with the impact of war on the individual or use war as a metaphor, as well as an occasion, for the inner conflicts and moral dilemmas of their protagonists (Meriwether). Some scholars even consider *Joscelyn* a proto-existentialist work (Moltke-Hansen, "When History Failed" 29-30).

The Eight Revolutionary Romances

Joscelyn is the last written but the first in its chronological setting, treating as it does the Revolution's beginnings in the backcountry along the Georgia-South Carolina border in 1775. Before going back to the beginning, Simms thought of *The Partisan* as his opening, as well as his first, work in the series. He explained the relations of his earlier Revolutionary romances in the "Historical Summary" with which he introduced *The Forayers*. "The 'Partisan'," he observed there, closed with the melancholy defeat of the first southern continental army under [General Horatio] Gates, at Camden. "Mellichampe" illustrated the interval between this event and the arrival of [General Nathanael] Greene, with the rude material for the organization of a second army; and was more particularly intended to do honor to the resolute and hardy patriotism of the scattered bands of patriots, who still maintained a predatory warfare against the foe among the swamps and thickets, rather keeping alive the spirit of the country, than operating decisively for its rescue. "The Scout," originally published under the name of "The Kinsmen," occupied a third period, when the wary policy of Greene began to make itself felt, in the gradual isolation and overthrow of the detached posts and fortresses which the enemy had established with the view to overawe the people in the leading precincts of the state; while "Katherine Walton," closing the career of certain parties, introduced to the reader by the "Partisan," and making complete the trilogy begun in that work, was designed to show the fluctuations of the contest, the spirit with which it was carried on, and to embody certain events of great individual interest, connected with the fortunes of persons not less distinguished by their individual worth of character, and their influence upon the general history, than by the romantic circumstances growing out of their career.

This narrative brought down the record to a period, when, for the first time, the British were made to understand that the conflict was doubtful; that their conquests were insecure, and that, so far from extending their arms over the interior, it became a question with them whether they should be able to maintain their hold upon the strong places of which they had so long held possession. ... To maintain themselves in Charleston and Savannah, the necessity was pressing that they should contract their powers and concentrate their forces. Reinforcements from Europe were hardly to be expected. The British empire was in a state of exhaustion, and the army of the invader was now half made up of the provincial loyalists (4-5).

At that point Simms resumed the historical narrative in *The Forayers* and its sequel, *Eutaw*. In doing so, he continued to "seek to illustrate the social condition of the country, under the influence of those strifes and trials which give vivacity to ordinary circumstances, and mark with deeper hues, and stronger colors, and sterner tones, the otherwise common progress of human hopes and fears, passions and necessities" (5). *Woodcraft* followed chronologically, although appearing right after *Katherine Walton* and, so, before *The Forayers*. Together, the seven antebellum Revolutionary romances treat the period "from the fall of the city of Charleston, in 1780," to the months after "the provisional articles of peace, between the King of Great Britain, and the revolted colonies of America, were signed at Paris, on the 13th November, 1782" (*The Partisan* [1854] vii; *Woodcraft* 5). At his death, Simms had plans for at least one additional romance for the series, presumably to help fill in the four-plus year gap between the action of *Joscelyn* and that of *The Partisan* (*Letters* 4: 625-26).

It only became possible to read all eight of the works in the series in book form during the bicentennial of the Revolution. Until the University of South Carolina Press issued *Joscelyn* in the Centennial Simms edition in 1975, that work had been available just in serial form. The next year, for the bicentennial, the Southern Studies Program of the University issued all eight romances. For the first time, they also were available with annotations explaining historical and literary references. It is with the permission of the program's successor, the Institute for Southern Studies, that those annotations and texts are made available here.

To recap, drawing on the introduction to the bicentennial edition, the eight novels of Simms's Revolutionary series first appeared in the following order:

The Partisan: A Tale of the Revolution. 2 volumes. (1835) New York: Harper & Brothers. Revised edition, entitled *The Partisan: A Romance of the Revolution*, New York: Redfield, 1854. Simms began this first novel in his Revolutionary War series early in 1835. He had a dozen chapters finished by June, and the book was published in November. He revised it extensively for publication, in January 1854, in the Redfield selected edition of his works. It deals with the 1780 Battle of Camden and its aftermath, especially the guerilla warfare by partisan forces under Francis Marion and other militia commanders. Like most of the other titles in the series, it was many times reprinted, first by Redfield and later by other publishers, but without further revision or correction by the author.

Mellichampe: A Legend of the Santee. 2 volumes. (1836) New York: Harper & Brothers. Revised edition, New York: Redfield, 1854. Simms's second novel of the Revolution was begun soon after publication of *The Partisan* and was issued apparently in October the next year. Revised for publication in March 1854 in the Redfield edition, it was many times reprinted but, as in the case of other volume in the series, without further revision or correction by the author. The story follows the fictional band of Francis Marion's partisans in their conflicts with loyalist and British forces in the wake of the Battle of Camden.

The Kinsmen; or the Black Riders of Congaree: A Tale. 2 volumes. (1841) Philadelphia: Lea and Blanchard. Revised edition, entitled *The Scout; or The Black*

Riders of Congaree, New York: Redfield, 1854. Simms began writing his third novel of the Revolution early in 1840, and it was published in February 1841. Revised extensively for inclusion in September 1854 in the Redfield edition of his works, with its new title, the novel was many times reprinted in that form. It opens shortly after the Battle of Hobkirk's Hill, or the second Battle of Camden, in May 1781. The action ends with the British departure from the Star Fort at Ninety-Six, S. C. the following month. A good brother is a partisan leader and chief protagonist; a bad brother is secretly the tory head of the Black Riders and a rival in love. Allied with the partisan leader is Supple Jack Bannister, the "authentic voice of the liberty-loving frontiersman," a recurrent figure in all three of Simms's romance series and also the Scout of the retitled and revised version of the novel (5).

Katherine Walton; or, the Rebel of Dorchester: An Historical Romance of the Revolution in Carolina. (1850-51) A shorter version was the first novel to appear serially in *Godey's Lady's Book* (February-December 1850), under the title "Katherine Walton; or, the Rebel's Daughter: A Tale of the Revolution." The initial book publication was by A. Hart in Philadelphia in 1851. The revised edition, entitled *Katherine Walton; or, The Rebel of Dorchester*, was included in the Redfield edition in 1854 and many times reprinted in that form. Although the work had been planned much earlier, the actual writing of this fourth novel of the Revolution apparently was not begun until the fall of 1849. Set in Charleston, the novel examines the social world there under British occupation and, because of this setting, has more unity of action and scene than other novels in the series. Simms called it the "most *symmetrical & truthful* of all my Revolutionary novels" (*Letters* 6: 120).

The Sword and the Distaff; or, "Fair, Fat and Forty," A Story of the South, at the Close of the Revolution. (1852) Charleston: Walker, Richards & Co. Retitled issue, entitled *Woodcraft; or, Hawks about the Dovecote: A Story of the South at the Close of the Revolution*, New York: Redfield, 1854. First published serially in semi-monthly supplements to the *Southern Literary Gazette* (February-November, 1852) and reprinted often from the Redfield edition, this fifth of the Revolutionary novels is set during the chaotic close and aftermath of the war, beginning with the British evacuation of Charleston in December 1782 and moving to Glen-Eberley plantation on the Ashepoo River south of the city, where the plantation community is striving to reestablish relative civil order and comity. Because the plates of the serialized version were used for the first Charleston printing of the book, that was called the second edition. Lippincott, Grambo of Philadelphia reissued the work from the same plates and with the same title in 1853. The Redfield edition was stereotyped by C. C. Savage of New York with modest emendations.

The Forayers; or, The Raid of the Dog-Days. (1855) New York: Redfield. This novel covers the British retreat from Ninety-Six and the lead up to the Battle of Eutaw Springs. Simms started the composition in November 1854, while finalizing the revisions for the Redfield edition of *Guy Rivers.* In February 1855, he claimed to be half finished. The novel appeared nine months later. In the interval, Simms staged his play *Michael Bonham,* gave an oration "On the Choice of a Profession" at the College of Charleston, revised *Border Beagles, Confession,* and *Beauchampe* for the Redfield edition of his selected works, and read proof on *Guy Rivers.* Like the other romances in the Redfield edition, *The Forayers* was reprinted many times.

Eutaw: A Sequel to The Forayers, or the Dog-Days. A Tale of the Revolution. (1856) New York: Redfield. This sequel completes the story of the British withdrawal from their outpost at Ninety-Six, including the Battle of Eutaw Springs, the last major engagement of the Carolina theatre, and that battle's aftermath. First reprinted by Redfield in 1858, the novel saw many subsequent reprintings.

Joscelyn: A Tale of the Revolution. (1867) Columbia, S. C.: University of South Carolina Press, 1975. First published serially in *The Old Guard* (January-December 1867), a copperhead (northern Democratic) journal. The serial publication stopped with several installments still to come. Consequently this last of the Revolutionary romances is not quite complete. Simms conceived the work as early as March 1858, when he was making plans to visit Augusta, Ga. to familiarize himself with the setting (*Letters* 4: 41, 72, 82). Afraid of how he would treat the tories in their history, the local media reacted negatively, and Simms determined not to return (83-4). Nevertheless, he intended to resume work on the book in 1860, before family issues, health, financial problems, and the secession crisis intervened. By October 1866 he had written 120 pages. The serialization of the work over the next year meant he was writing to deadline just ahead of the printers.

Critical Reception and Subsequent Reappraisal

The initial receptions of these eight novels reflected more than changing standards and tastes or the increase in sectional animosities. In the mid-1830s, when Simms began producing long fiction, the historical romance was a widely approved genre. By 1850, after Simms returned to romance writing, it was still popular among readers but becoming passé among the *literati.* In the English-speaking world Dickens was supplanting Scott as the dominant writer, while the novel was supplanting the romance, and literary realism was transforming Romanticism. Simms responded to these changes, incorporating social and then psychological realism in his fiction and appreciatively reading Dickens (Moltke-Hansen, "A Revolutionary Critic"). Nevertheless, his continued adherence to the romance form made him appear increasingly as a member of an older literary generation (Holman, *The Roots* 75-86; Wimsatt, *The Major Fiction* 8-9).

The diminishment of Simms's currency is shown by the fact that, after 1860, the only new works he published in book form were three collections that he edited: one of Confederate poetry, one of his friend James Henry Hammond's speeches and writings, and one an edition of the Revolutionary War letters of Col. John Laurens of South Carolina. He also produced a couple of pamphlets: an account of the *Sack and Destruction of the City of Columbia, S.C.*, in 1865, issued by his own press, and his final address, *The Sense of the Beautiful*, which was locally published as well. His last romances appeared just in periodicals despite his efforts to see them issued in book form. Neither did he have success with the ideas for other books that he floated to his publishers (Moltke-Hansen, "When History Failed" 14-19).

In effect, the Civil War ended Simms's career as an American author. The fact that the selected Redfield edition of his writings, including the first seven of his Revolutionary romances, continued to be reprinted emphasized all the more that Simms was an antebellum figure. He was regarded as a representative of the Old South, not the New. His world and slavery were in the past in the eyes of most postbellum publishers and readers. Yet, while true so far as it goes, this narrative is too simple.

After all, it was Simms's 1850 romance *Katherine Walton* that had the widest readership of all the works in the Revolutionary series. Furthermore, Simms always got mixed reviews even from his admirers, such as Edgar Allan Poe. Too, his sometime enemies, such as those in the *Knickerbocker* circle, did not review him in exclusively negative terms (Moltke-Hansen, Introduction, *Views and Reviews*). Indeed, the *Knickerbocker* praised *The Partisan* shortly after its 1835 publication, saying, "of all of the efforts of the author, we esteem this, in many respects, the best" (6 [Dec. 1835], 577). Yet it was just over a year later that Poe, in the *Southern Literary Messenger*, excoriated its "blunders," "bad taste," and "shockingly bad" English (2 [Jan. 1837], 117-21).

The next romance, *Mellichampe*, had the *Knickerbocker* thinking that Simms would "soon be at the front rank of American writers" (8 [Dec. 1836], 735-37). Upon publication of the third in the series, *The Kinsmen*, five years later, Poe concluded in *Graham's* that, "since the publication of the Pathfinder [by James

Fenimore Cooper], we have seen nothing equal to" this newest work by Simms (18 [Mar. 1841] 143). In the interval, however, Simms had a falling out with the editor of the *Knickerbocker*, and that journal was becoming increasingly—though not consistently—dismissive (Butterworth and Kibler 39-54). In turn, Simms was becoming more vociferous about nationalism in literature.

The dyspeptic conclusion of the *Knickerbocker* in 1842 was that Simms's nationalism was a "device to secure an extrinsic and undue consideration for flimsy novels" (20 [Aug. 1842]), 199-200). Yet Poe's judgment in the *Broadway Journal* three years later was that Simms was "the best novelist which this country has, upon the whole, produced" (2 [4 Oct. 1845], 190-91). As if this were not confusing enough, Charleston poet, editor, and young Simms protégé Paul Hamilton Hayne maintained, in his 1854 Charleston *Weekly News* reviews of the new Redfield edition of the early Revolutionary romances, first that *The Partisan* was "the nearest perfection," then, months later, that *Mellichampe* was (47 [4 Feb. 1854], 2; n. s. 4 [6 Apr. 1854], 2). Fifteen years after Simms's death, however, Hayne called *Eutaw* the best ("Antebellum Charleston" 257-68).

Also approving of *Eutaw*, *Godey's* nevertheless was rueful at the time of the romance's publication nearly thirty years before. This was because Simms's "commemoration of events" of the Revolution did not evoke "pleasant recollection" among the British (53 [July 1856], 84). His choice of subject did him honor, then, but hurt his trans-Atlantic sales and standing. Writing in 1856 as well, Simms's friend James Henry Hammond, U. S. Senator from South Carolina, went so far as to urge Simms to "cease to write novels." In his view his literary friend could not "better these last"—*The Forayers* and *Eutaw* (*Letters* 3: 425 n).

On balance, the later Revolutionary romances were esteemed more and read less than the first four. This was despite the perception of both contemporary critics and subsequent scholars that the 1850s saw Simms at the height of his power as a fictionist (Guilds, *Simms* 191-233). His youthful enthusiasm was tempered and to some extent disciplined by experience. Shaping his works as well, as David Newton observes, was the fact that by then "Simms had spent more than a decade [as an editor and contributor] on a succession of failed Southern literary journals." Consequently, he was deeply frustrated "over the lack of an intellectually engaged readership in the South" (Afterword 496-97). This led him, Newton argues, to focus in his later Revolutionary romances "on acts of reading—both literal and imaginative" (497).

By reading, Simms did not mean only the consumption of and response to literature or print. Woodcraft was a form of reading, and society and the political realm required reading every bit as much as the forest and books. Yet the need for and value of reading ran deeper. "The novels interrogate a culture," Newton continues, "where education possesses a marginal value at best, where economic, political, and material priorities overshadow the importance of a morally and spiritually informed imagination" (Afterword 497-98). That imagination was necessary for the creation of a country and advance of a people. "The reader's ability to recognize the signs and traces, both natural and human, thus become essential in making appropriate moral and imaginative judgments and in understanding the social and human complexities that are presented" (500). As the motto on the crest that Simms designed for himself read, "*video volans*" — I see soaring.

The revolution advocated in these later romances is much deeper, therefore, than the pursuit of independence by bold and desperate bands of partisans. It is the achievement of self-worth, cultural independence, and moral and spiritual progress. The fruits of the political and military revolution were the civilization that Simms was helping to create and the character and community that he was helping to inspire, shape, and preserve. The artist made fully meaningful the promise of America's founding. Nationalism was not just the formation and perpetuation of a polity, but the expression and the achievement of a rising people and culture. That is why Simms insisted on nationalism in literature. It also is why the suppression of his new nation through the Confederacy's defeat meant the necessary re-imagination of both self-worth and cultural independence — the work he sought to advance in the last of his Revolutionary romances, *Joscelyn*.

The generally high regard accorded the later Revolutionary romances at the time of their publication did not carry forward after the Civil War. To judge by the number of reprints of the Redfield edition, Simms's works continued to sell for almost half a century. Yet, enthralled by modernism, postbellum critics were increasingly derogatory of Simms's historical romances. An early case in point is Simms's first academic biographer, William Peterfield Trent. His 1892 assessment was that, in contrast to Edgar Allan Poe, whom he later championed, Simms was too enmeshed in his slave society and in the romance tradition to write successfully according to modernism's aesthetic criteria (Trent, *William Gilmore Simms*; Trent *et al.*, *Edgar Allan Poe*). Although in some respects admiring, Vernon Parrington later also judged Simms as "essentially a failed realist," at once constrained and compromised by his literary and social environment (Parrington 2: 119-30; Wimsatt, *The Major Fiction* 8).

It was not until after World War II that Hugh Holman suggested that Simms's literary substance might be "of minor importance in terms of [its] intrinsic value today" but "of major importance in terms of the degree to which [Simms] embodied the attitudes and formalized the assumptions of a region" (Holman, "Status" 181). Holman subsequently called attention to the ways that the first seven Revolutionary romances explored the civil war of the early

1780s. What fascinated him was how Simms portrayed the war as a class conflict. Of the 98 characters, 30 were upper class—seven of them tories. Of the 21 poor whites, 18 were tories. Of the 25 middle class representatives, seven also were. Of the dozen slaves, only one was (*The Roots* 35-47).

What Holman did not do in his essay, but others have done, is consider the impact of Simms's own times on his historical portrayals. It mattered that Simms was writing after the Palmetto State first was riven by the nullification controversy and then as it moved toward Civil War (Higham; Taylor; Wakelyn; Watson). While acknowledging the point, other scholars have contended that such readings have missed critical literary dimensions. After all, these later writers have insisted, Simms self-consciously used literary forms to literary ends. Moreover, his standing among his contemporaries put him at the forefront of American literature up through the so-called American renaissance of the early 1850s (Guilds, *Simms* 191-233; Wimsatt, *The Major Fiction* 156-210).

Yet the only work in the Revolutionary series to receive substantial literary analysis from these recent critics is *Woodcraft*. Generally it is read alone rather than in tandem with other romances. There are three principal exceptions. Some scholars compare or assume differences between northern and southern romances (Simpson; Nakamura; Taylor). Some look for themes uniting Simms's different romance series or consider tropes, such as that of the hero, common to Simms and other antebellum southern writers (Grammer; Kolodny; Kreyling, *Figures* 30-51; Nakamura). Finally, there are those who ask how the changing politics of Simms's day shaped his writing (Higham; Kreyling, *Inventing* 93-104; Taylor; Wakelyn; Watson).

Despite these inquiries, many aspects of Simms's Revolutionary series have not been substantially considered. No effort has gone into comparison of more recent Revolutionary series with it. No one has juxtaposed Simms's historical romances with those of nineteenth-century European romantic nationalists. Indeed, American critics who have treated Simms have shown little awareness, beyond Sir Walter Scott, of the trans-Atlantic national romantic tradition. Instead they have privileged a different romantic strain, embodied in the romantic genius at odds with or critical of society (Rubin). The one book-length study of Simms's historical thought focuses on the non-fiction (Busick). Shrewd and deeply learned readings of historicism and historical thought in antebellum southern culture do not dwell on the theoretical and practical concomitants of Simms's historicist preoccupations and pursuits (O'Brien 2:591-682; Fox-Genovese and Genovese 125-248).

The scholarly neglect is even greater for Simms's Revolutionary fictions than for his Border and Colonial romances. This is despite the relatively high regard given several of the Revolutionary works. One reason is that Simms's treatment of Native Americans has claimed much of the attention given to him since the 1835 publication of *The Yemassee*, the only one of his works always to have remained in print (Guilds and Hudson; Frye; Moltke-Hansen, Introduction, *The Yemassee*). The frontier themes, characters, language, and humor of the Border romances in turn fit into the study of the realism of Mark Twain and those in the southern and frontier humor tradition who influenced, or were influenced by, him (Parks; Wimsatt, "The Evolution"; Wimsatt, "Simms and Southwest Humor"). Too, these topics have shaped treatments of and courses in American exceptionalism, Manifest Destiny, and their literary refractions (Guilds and Collins).

Yet these same issues and elements occur in the Revolutionary romances. That fact, however, has not claimed attention except, in passing, from Mary Ann Wimsatt and John C. Guilds (Wimsatt, *The Major Fiction* 57-84, 156-95; Guilds, *Simms*). Rather than accept the point, Masahiro Nakamura argues that, on the one hand, the Revolutionary romances are about the construction of an ordered society, based on the plantation. On the other hand, the Border romances are about the challenge of the frontier and disorder to that society (*Visions of Order*). The counter argument is that Simms insistently explored the relationship of order to those conditions and developments that both threatened to undermine and made necessary social and cultural progress (Moltke-Hansen, "Ordered Progress").

Future Study

These debates may serve as background to the future study of the Revolutionary series. Yet those investigations will engage issues that earlier treatments did not: the relationship of colonialism to post-colonialism; the impact of the Revolution on gender, race, and class relations; the antebellum constructions and perceptions of these relationships and their rationales. Behind these sorts of questions are others about the purposes and original standing of such literature as Simms wrote and about the purposes of reading such works more than a century and a half after their production.

Holman did not emphasize part of the fascination of Simms's portrait of Revolutionary South Carolina society: that picture reveals a world dramatically at odds with the received view of the plantation South. Contrary to the stereotype, that world is not old, even though the environs of Charleston may be. Many of the characters there are recent arrivals rather than exemplars of ancient traditions. They also are multi-cultural. Class and other divisions fissure the society, as well as destabilize conventional understandings of it. Some elite men are afraid to lead or incapable of leadership. When failed by men, women sometimes take matters into their own hands. Greed is a prime motivator and especially destructive of poor whites. So is willful ignorance. The frontier is close at hand, as is violence. America's birth pangs are dreadful. And yet liberty is won, and social order in the end is advanced, if only provisionally.

How did these awarenesses frame the thinking, by Simms and others, of developments in their own day? How and why did these white southerners decide that America's fragility could become the South's strength? In the end, the Revolutionary romances are about much more than their subject matter or the series' place in either Simms's *oeuvre* or the (former) American canon. Read with Simms's 16-plus other long fictions, they reflect a more insistent and influential epic vision of the American South than that of any other author. None of the twentieth- and twenty-first-century Revolutionary War series, even those set in the South, has had a comparable impact, although many of these later titles have sold much more than any of Simms's ever did.

The epic vision and ambition that came to shape Simms's work had historical consequences. More than a century later, Faulkner implicitly critiqued it in his Yoknapatawpha series, turning his southern vision into an anti-epic. The writing of the historical Revolution as an epic conflict meant that Simms and many of his readers came to see war as an instrument of progress, at least up until the Civil War (Moltke-Hansen, "When History Failed" 5-10). Given Simms's complex understanding of the Revolution's divisions, course, and consequences, this was not simply the result of jingoistic pride. Compelling all the same, his epic reading and orientation made the Civil War in effect a reprise and a continuation of the Revolution (Watson, "Simms and the American Revolution").

This belief helped shape and color Simms's enthusiasm for secession and the conflict that followed. During that conflict he continued his research and writing on the Revolution, completing his drama on Benedict Arnold as a meditation on the requirements of citizenship and patriotism (Moltke-Hansen, "When History Failed" 10-14). This commitment to literature as a patriotic act and evocation had earlier, and has had later, American advocates. It fueled Confederate literature, as recent scholarship has shown (Bernath; Hutchison 18-98). It also was especially strong in parts of the Europe of Simms's day and later, a point that has long engaged students of nationalism (Moltke-Hansen, "Identity Politics").

In a post-modern and multi-cultural era, it is difficult to recover the intensity of the nationalist impulse in cultural production. Focusing on the epoch of America's political emergence, Simms's Revolutionary romances provide an opportunity to assess the impulse in his time and place. More, they invite consideration of the roles of history and art in framing identity. Because Simms privileged nationalism, he made it a political weapon. In his hierarchy of values, nationalism trumped racial, ethnic, and class interests that challenged its success. Simms confronted these conflicts by showing elements of them—for instance, the clashes between tories and patriots—while denying others—for instance, the African American impulse to freedom.

Simms used nationalism as well to perpetuate patriarchal authority and gendered roles, while critiquing those men who failed their responsibility in these roles (Simms, "Ellet's"). Treating history providentially, furthermore, he eventually made American liberty a basis to argue for southern independence. In doing so, he pointed to the path he believed the region's leaders should take in that pursuit. The complex negotiation of these multiple priorities and goals through his Revolutionary romances make those works rich sites for the recovery and critique of a long lost but once regnant artistic and political ambition. Simms did more to frame and to promote that ambition than did any other southern man of letters.

Works Cited

Ackerman, Zeno. *Messing with Romance: American Poetics and Antebellum Southern Fiction*. Frankfurt: Peter Lang, 2012.

Bakker, Jan. "Simms on the Literary Frontier; or, So Long Miss Ravenel and Hello Captain Porgy: *Woodcraft* Is the First 'Realistic' Novel in America." *William Gilmore Simms and the American Frontier*. Ed. John C. Guilds and Carolina Collins. Athens.: U of Georgia P, 1988. 64-78.

Bernath, Michael T. *Confederate Minds: The Struggle for Intellectual Independence in the Civil War South*. Chapel Hill: U of North Carolina P, 2010.

Brennan, Matthew C. *The Poet's Holy Craft: William Gilmore Simms and Romantic verse Traditions*. Columbia: U of South Carolina P, 2010.

Busick, Sean R. *A Sober Desire for History: William Gilmore Simms as Historian*. Columbia: U of South Carolina P, 2005.

Butterworth, Keen, and James E. Kibler. *William Gilmore Simms: A Reference Guide*. Boston: G. K. Hall & Co., 1980.

Dale, Corinne. "William Gilmore Simms's Porgy as a Domestic Hero," *Southern Literary Journal* 13.1 (1980): 55-71.

"Editor's Table." *Knickerbocker* 20 (Aug. 1842): 199-200.

Foley, Ehren. "Isaac Nimmons and the Burning of Woodlands: Power, Paternalism, and the Performance of Manhood in William Gilmore Simms's Civil War South." *William Gilmore Simms's Unfinished Civil War: Consequences for a Southern Man of Letters*. Ed. David Moltke-Hansen. Columbia: U of South Carolina P, 2013. 89-111.

Fox-Genovese, Elizabeth, and Eugene Genovese. *The Mind of the Master Class: History and Faith in the Southern Slaveholders' Worldview*. Cambridge and New York: Cambridge UP, 2005.

Frye, Steven. "Simms's *The Yemassee*, American Progressivism and the Dialogue of History." *Southern Quarterly* 35.3 (1997): 83-89.

Genovese, Eugene, and Elizabeth Fox-Genovese. *Fatal Self-Deception: Slaveholding Paternalism in the Old South*. Cambridge and New York: Cambridge UP, 2011.

Georgini, Sara. "The Angel and the Animal." *William Gilmore Simms's Unfinished Civil War: Consequences for a Southern Man of Letters*. Columbia: U of South Carolina P, 2013. 212-23.

Grammer, John M. *Pastoral and Politics in the Old South*. Baton Rouge: Louisiana State UP, 1996.

Greenspan, Ezra. "Evert Duyckinck and the History of Wiley and Putnam's Library of American Books, 1845-1847." *American Literature* 64.4 (1992): 677-93.

Guilds, John C. *Simms: A Literary Life*. Fayetteville: U of Arkansas P, 1992.

—— and Caroline Collins, eds. *William Gilmore Simms and the American Frontier*. Athens: U of Georgia P, 1997.

—— and Charles Hudson, eds. *An Early and Strong Sympathy: The Indian Writings of William Gilmore Simms*. Columbia: U of South Carolina P, 2003.

Hagstette, Todd. "Private vs. Public Honor in Wartime South Carolina: William Gilmore Simms in Lecture, Letter, and History." *William Gilmore Simms's Unfinished Civil War: Consequences for a Southern Man of Letters*. Ed. David Moltke-Hansen. Columbia: U of South Carolina P, 2013. 48-67.

——. "Screams from the South: The Southern Psycho-gothic Novels of William Gilmore Simms." MA thesis. College of Charleston, 1998.

Hayne, Paul Hamilton. "Ante-Bellum Charleston." *Southern Bivouac* 1 (Oct. 1885): 257-68.

——. Rev. of *Mellichampe*. By William Gilmore Simms. Charleston *Weekly News* n.s. 4 (6 Apr. 1854): 2.

——. Rev. of *The Partisan*. By William Gilmore Simms. Charleston *Weekly News* n.s. 3 (7 Jan. 1854): 2.

Higham, John. "The Changing Loyalties of William Gilmore Simms." *Journal of Southern History* 9.2 (1943): 210-23

Holman, C. Hugh. *The Roots of Southern Writing: Essays on the Literature of the American South*. Athens: U of Georgia P, 1972.

——. "The Status of Simms." *American Quarterly* 10 (Summer 1958): 181-85.

Holt, Keri. "Reading Regionalism across the War: Simms and the Literary Imagination of Post-Bellum Literary Magazines." *William Gilmore Simms's Unfinished Civil War: Consequences for a Southern Man of Letters*. Ed. David Moltke-Hansen. Columbia: U of South Carolina P, 2013. 159-82.

Hutchison, Coleman. *Apples & Ashes: Literature, Nationalism, and the Confederate States of America*. Athens: U of Georgia P, 2012.

Justus, James. *Fetching the Old Southwest: Humorous Writing from Longstreet to Twain*. Columbia: U of Missouri P, 2004.

Kaplan, Amy. *Social Construction of American Realism*. Chicago: U of Chicago P, 1988.

Kennedy, John Pendleton. *Horse Shoe Robinson; A Tale of the Tory Ascendency*. 2 vols. Philadelphia: Carey, Lea and Blanchard, 1835.

Kibler, James Everett. Introduction. *Woodcraft; or, Hawks about the Dovecote*. By William Gilmore Simms. Columbia: U of South Carolina P, 2012. xxiii-xxxvi.

———. *The Poetry of William Gilmore Simms: An Introduction and Bibliography*. Columbia: Southern Studies Program, 1979.

King, Vincent. "'Foolish Talk 'Bout Freedom': Simms's Vision of America in *The Yemassee*." *Studies in the Novel* 35.2 (2003): 139-48.

Kolodny, Annette. "The Unchanging Landscape: The Pastoral Impulse in Simms's Revolutionary Romances." *Southern Literary Journal* 5 (Fall 1972): 46-67.

Kreyling, Michael. *Figures of the Hero in Southern Narrative*. Baton Rouge: Louisiana State UP, 1987.

———. *Inventing Southern Literature*. Jackson: UP of Mississippi, 1998.

"Literary Notices." *Godey's* 53 (July 1856): 84.

Lukacs, Georg. *The Historical Novel*. Trans. Hannah Mitchell and Stanley Mitchell. London: Merlin P, 1962. Trans. of *Der historische Roman*, 1937.

Meriwether, Nicholas G. "An Unfinished Reconstruction: Simms's 'The Brothers of the Coast.'" *William Gilmore Simms's Unfinished Civil War: Consequences for a Southern Man of Letters*. Ed. David Moltke-Hansen. Columbia: U of South Carolina P, 2013. 185-201.

Miller, John D. "The Sense of Things to Come: Redefining Gender and Promoting the Lost Cause in *The Sense of the Beautiful*." *William Gilmore Simms's Unfinished Civil War: Consequences for a Southern Man of Letters*. Ed. David Moltke-Hansen. Columbia: U of South Carolina P, 2013. 224-38.

Miller, Perry. *The Raven and the Whale: The War of Words and Wits in the Era of Poe and Melville*. New York: Harcourt, Brace and Co., 1956.

Minguera, Corey Don. "'Cash Is Conqueror': The Critique of Capitalism in Simms's 'The Western Emigrants' and 'Sonnet—The Age of Gold.'" *Simms Review* 17.1-2 (2009): 87-96.

Moltke-Hansen, David. "A Critical Revolution and a Revolutionary Critic." *William Gilmore Simms's Selected Reviews on Literature and Civilization*. Ed. James Everett Kibler and David Moltke-Hansen. Columbia: U of South Carolina P, 2014: forthcoming.

———. "Identity Politics and the Civil War: The Transformation of South Carolina's Public History, 1862-2012." *Historically Speaking* 14.1 (2013): forthcoming.

———. Introduction. *Views and Reviews in American Literature, History and Fiction. First and Second Series*. By William Gilmore Simms. Columbia: U of South Carolina P, 2013. Forthcoming.

———. Introduction. *The Yemassee: A Romance of Carolina*. 1854. Columbia: U of South Carolina P, 2013.

———. "Ordered Progress: The Historical Philosophy of William Gilmore Simms." *"Long Years of Neglect": The Work and Reputation of William Gilmore Simms*. Ed. John Caldwell Guilds. Fayetteville: U of Arkansas P, 1988. 126-47.

———. "Southern Literary Horizons in Young America: Imaginative Development of a Regional Geography." *Studies in the Literary Imagination* 42.1 (2009): 1-31.

———. "When History Failed: William Gilmore Simms's Artistic Negotiation of the Civil War's Consequences." *William Gilmore Simms's Unfinished Civil War: Consequences for a Southern Man of Letters*. Columbia: U of South Carolina P, 2013. 3-31.

———. "Why History Mattered: The Background of Ann Pamela Cunningham's Interest in the Preservation of Mount Vernon," *Furman Studies* n. s. 26 (Dec. 1980): 34-42.

Nakamura, Masahiro. *Visions of Order in William Gilmore Simms: Southern Conservatism and the Other American Romance*. Columbia: U of South Carolina P, 2009.

Newton, David W. Afterword. *Eutaw: A Sequel to* The Forayers, or The Raid of the Dog Days. By William Gilmore Simms. Ed. David W. Newton. Fayetteville: U of Arkansas P, 2007. 495-511.

O'Brien, Michael. *Conjectures of Order: Intellectual Life and the American South, 1810-1860*. 2 vols. Chapel Hill: U North Carolina P, 2004.

Parks, Edd Winfield. "The Three Streams of Southern Humor." *Georgia Review* 9 (Summer 1955): 147-59.

Parrington, Vernon L. *Main Currents in American Thought*. 3 vols. New York: Harcourt, Brace and Co., 1927-30. [The chapter on Simms, "William Gilmore Simms: Charleston Romancer," appears in Vol. 2: 119-30.]

Pearce, Colin D. "All Aboard! 'The Philosophy of the Omnibus' and the Problem of Progress in William Gilmore Simms." *Simms Review* 18.1-2 (2010): 71-91.

Poe, Edgar Allan. Rev. of *The Kinsmen*. By William Gilmore Simms. *Graham's* 18 (Mar. 1841): 143

———. Rev. of *The Partisan*. By William Gilmore Simms. *Southern Literary Messenger* 2 (Jan. 1836): 117-21.

———. Rev. of *The Wigwam and the Cabin*. By William Gilmore Simms. *Broadway Journal* 2 (4 Oct. 1845): 190-91.

Rev. *Mellichampe*. By William Gilmore Simms. *Knickerbocker* 8 (Dec. 1836): 735-37.

Rev. *The Partisan*. By William Gilmore Simms. *Knickerbocker* 6 (Dec. 1835): 577.

Rubin, Louis D. *The Edge of the Swamp: A Study of Literature and Society of the Old South*. Baton Rouge: Louisiana State UP, 1989.

Shelton, Austin J. "African Realistic Commentary on Culture Hierarchy and Racistic Sentimentalism in *The Yemassee*." *Phylon* 25.1 (1964): 72-8.

Simms, William Gilmore. "The Civil Warfare in the Carolinas and Georgia, during the Revolution." *Southern Literary Messenger* 12.5-7 (1846): 257-65, 321-36, 385-400.

———. "Ellet's 'Women of the Revolution.'" In *William Gilmore Simms's Selected Reviews on Literature and Civilization*. Ed. James Everett Kibler and David Moltke-Hansen. Columbia: U of South Carolina P, 2014: forthcoming.

———. *Eutaw: A Sequel to* The Forayers, or The Raid of the Dog-Days. A Tale of the Revolution. 1856. Columbia: U of South Carolina P, 2013.

———. *The Forayers: or The Raid of the Dog-Days*, 1855. Columbia: U of South Carolina P, 2013.

———. *Joscelyn. A Tale of the Revolution*. Columbia: U of South Carolina P, 2013.

———. *Katherine Walton: or The Rebel of Dorchester*. Rev. ed. 1854. Columbia: U of South Carolina P, 2013.

——. *The Kinsmen: or The Black Riders of Congaree. A Tale.* 2 vols. Philadelphia: Lea and Blanchard, 1841.
——. *The Letters of William Gilmore Simms.* 6 vols. Ed. Mary C. Simms Oliphant *et al.* Columbia: U of South Carolina P, 1952-2012.
——. *Mellichampe. A Legend of the Santee.* 2 vols. New York: Harper & Brothers, 1836.
——. *Mellichampe: A Legend of the Santee.* Rev. ed. 1854. Columbia: U of South Carolina P, 2013.
——. *The Partisan: A Tale of the Revolution.* 2 vols. New York: Harper and Brothers, 1835.
——. *The Partisan: A Romance of the Revolution.* Rev. ed. 1854. Columbia: U of South Carolina P, 2013.
——. *The Scout: or The Black Riders of Congaree.* Rev. ed. of *The Kinsmen.* 1854. Columbia: U of South Carolina P, 2013.
——. *The Sense of the Beautiful. An Address.* Charleston: Charleston County Agricultural and Horticultural Association, 1870.
——. *Self-Development. An Oration Delivered before the Literary Societies of Oglethorpe University; Georgia; November 10, 1847.* Milledgeville.: Thalian Society, 1847.
——. *South-Carolina in the Revolutionary War: Being a Reply to Certain Misrepresentations and Mistakes of Recent Writers, in Relation to the Course and Conduct of This State.* Charleston: Walker and Evans, 1853.
——. "The Southern Convention." *William Gilmore Simms's Selected Reviews on Literature and Civilization.* Ed. James Everett Kibler and David Moltke-Hansen. Columbia: U of South Carolina P, 2014: forthcoming.
——. *The Sword and the Distaff; or, "Fair, Fat and Forty," A Story of the South at the Close of the Revolution.* Charleston: Walker, Richards, and Co., 1852.
——. *Views and Reviews in American Literature, History and Fiction. First and Second Series.* 1845 [1846-47]. Columbia: U of South Carolina P, 2013.
——. *Woodcraft: or, Hawks about the Dovecote. A Story of the South at the Close of the Revolution.* 1854. Columbia: U of South Carolina P, 2012.
——. *The Yemassee: A Romance of Carolina.* 2 vols. New York: Harper & Brothers, 1835.
Simpson, Lewis P. *The Dispossessed Garden: Pastoral and History in Southern Literature.* Athens.: U of Georgia P., 1975.
Smith, Steven D. "Imagining the Swamp Fox: William Gilmore Simms and the National Memory of Francis Marion." *William Gilmore Simms's Unfinished Civil War: Consequences for a Southern Man of Letters.* Ed. David Moltke-Hansen. Columbia: U of South Carolina P, 2013. 32-47.
Stafford, John. *The Literary Criticism of "Young America": A Study in the Relationship of Politics and Literature, 1837-1850.* Berkeley and Los Angeles: U of California P, 1952.
Taylor, William R. *Cavalier and Yankee: The Old South and American National Character.* Cambridge: Harvard UP, 1961.
Trent, William P. *William Gilmore Simms.* Boston: Houghton Mifflin, 1892.
Wakelyn, Jon L. *The Politics of a Literary Man: William Gilmore Simms.* Westport., CT: Greenwood P, 1973.

Watson, Charles S. *From Nationalism to Secessionism: The Changing Fiction of William Gilmore Simms*. Westport, CT: Greenwood P, 1993.

———. "Simms and the American Revolution." *Mississippi Quarterly* 29 (1976): 76-89.

———. "Simms's Answer to *Uncle Tom's Cabin*: Criticism of the South in *Woodcraft*." *Southern Literary Journal* 9.1 (1976): 78-90.

Widmer, Edward L. *Young America: The Flowering of Democracy in New York City*. New York: Oxford UP, 1999.

Wimsatt, Mary Ann. "The Evolution of Simms's Backwoods Humor." In *"Long Years of Neglect": The Work and Reputation of William Gilmore Simms*. Ed. John C. Guilds. Fayetteville: U of Arkansas P, 1988. 148-65.

———. *The Major Fiction of William Gilmore Simms*. Baton Rouge: Louisiana State UP, 1989.

———. "Realism and Romance in Simms's Midcentury Fiction." *Southern Literary Journal* 12.2 (1980): 29-48.

———. "Simms and Southwest Humor." *Studies in American Humor* 3 (Nov. 1979): 118-30.

MELLICHAMPE

A LEGEND OF THE SANTEE

By W. GILMORE SIMMS, Esq.
AUTHOR OF "THE PARTISAN," "THE YEMASSEE," "KATHERINE WALTON,"
"THE SCOUT," "WOODCRAFT," "GUY RIVERS," ETC.

NEW AND REVISED EDITION

REDFIELD
110 AND 112 NASSAU STREET, NEW YORK.
1854.

Entered, according to Act of Congress, in the year 1854,
By J. S. REDFIELD,
in the Clerk's Office of the District Court of the United States, in and for the Southern District of New York.

STEREOTYPED BY C. C. SAVAGE,
13 Chambers Street, N. Y.

TO

COLONEL M. C. M. HAMMOND,

OF SOUTH CAROLINA.

———◆———

My Dear Col.—

WHILE you are, probably, all abroad, chasing the deer, at this very moment, in some of the swamps and thickets of Georgia; and bringing together, with a blast of the horn, a whole host of friends; I look up from the accumulated sheets before me, and, in "my mind's eye," survey the scene, with no small appetite to share. I behold you, towering like Saul, head and shoulders above the joyous circle, the silver drinking cup in hand, and all hands elevated and waiting for the pledge. It is given, and the words reach me as certainly as if I were present. I feel that I am remembered, and I requite you with like remembrance. Revising the last pages of "Mellichampe," I resolve, beaker in hand,—

——"The instant impulse of the thought,
Having twin action,"—

that the book—which has hitherto gone without a sponsor—shall be honored with your name. You will read it, I trust, as well for my sake as its own; and, yourself a soldier, famous as a military critic, you will probably find frequent provocation to a savage military review, while going over my experiences and studies in partisan warfare. But you must remember,that our rangers of the Revolution were no *West-Pointers.* But they were *Pointers,* nevertheless, and could *set* as well as *set-to.* If they wallopped the enemy without first satisfying themselves that the operation was *selon les régles,* still, it must be admitted, that the thing *was done;* and we must not be too strict, when the end has been gained, in asking after the fashion of the performance. That our backwoods boys bungled frequently in winning their victories, may afford a surly fireside satisfaction to the beaten party; as the Austrians are said to have consoled themselves, after their successive defeats, at the hands of Napoleon, by the reflection that, according to all the laws of war, to say nothing of the Great Frederick, he should have been drubbed, on every one of these occasions, out of his regimental breeches. We may leave our enemies this satisfaction surely. For my part, I could never find much consolation, with my eyes utterly darkened by the awkward usage of a *rough and tumble* operator, in the conviction that I had, nevertheless, all the science to myself. The *laws* of war are, no doubt, very admirable and wholesome provisions; but I confess, with other politicians, that I prefer the *spoils.* Our rangers knew but little of the one, but they had an instinctive appreciation of the other; and contrived to get them, by hook and by crook, at periods when Science herself had no measures to offer. "Mellichampe" will help to show some of the processes by which they worked, awkwardly preferring the spoils to the laws of war; and when you put on your critical military spectacles, to study their *modus operandi* with me, be pleased to let the glasses be of the fashion which was worn between the years 1754 and 1783, when the rangers were getting their education—when it was not found easy to persuade them to exchange the long rifle for the musket, and when the argument which sought to convince them that the cover of a tree, or any dodge from a bullet, reflected somewhat upon the valor of a soldier, would have been laughed at as the wildest folly. Nay, in those days, the idea of embracing a bayonet with the naked bosom, only served to inform the ranger of the true uses of his legs, and to run well, when there was no farther chance from fight, was supposed to be a very becoming military accomplishment. For my part, I shall be very sorry that the day should ever arrive when the good sense of this doctrine shall be subjected to dispute. These, and other heresies in the practice of war, such as are doubtlessly to be discovered in these pages, must be excused therefore, my dear colonel, in deference to the homely education of our rangers, who seem to have been always singularly regardless of rules, but who were never wanting to their rations; and whose art, while it lacked science, yet enabled them to execute a great many pretty little operations, by which to turn the sharp edge of a bullet, escape all direct collision with a plunging bayonet, feed without a commissariat, and fight with a reasonable chance of being able to fight again.

But a truce with this trifling, which is with me a sign of sadness. To our muttons. I commend "Mellichampe" to your favor, and if it find it not, I have taken your name in vain. For the plan of the story, and all which it may be necessary to read before beginning it, I refer you to the original preface, which I retain without alteration. This will suffice for readers in general, as well as for you. To them, and to you, my friend, I say—Father Chrystmasse, being at the door and crying, "cheer" for admission—"Waes Hael! Drink Hael! and the dawning of a yet brighter day upon ye, with the opening of the New Year."

Very faithfully, &c.

W. GILMORE SIMMS.

WOODLANDS, S. C., *December* 20, 1853.

ADVERTISEMENT.

The story which follows is rather an episode in the progress of the "Partisan," than a continuation of that romance. It has no necessary connection with the previous story, nor does it form any portion of that series originally contemplated by the author, with the view to an illustration of the several prominent periods in the history of the revolution in South Carolina; although it employs similar events, and disposes of some of the personages first introduced to the reader by that initial publication. The action of "Mellichampe" begins, it is true, where the "Partisan" left off; and the story opens by a resumption of one of the suspended threads of that narrative. Beyond this, there is no connection between the two works; and the reader will perceive that even this degree of affinity has been maintained simply to indicate that the stories belong to the same family, and to prevent the necessity of breaking ground anew. Much preliminary narrative has thus been avoided; and I have been enabled to obey the good old, popular, but seldom-practised maxim, of plunging at once into the bowels of my subject. The "Partisan" was projected as a sort of ground-plan, of sufficient extent to admit of the subsequent erection of any fabric upon it which the caprice of the author, or the quantity of his material, might seem to warrant and encourage.

The two works which I projected to follow the "Partisan," and to complete the series, were intended to comprise events more strictly historical than those which have been employed in this "Santee legend." The reader must not, however, on hearing this, be less inclined to accept "Mellichampe" as an historical romance. It is truly and legitimately such. It is imbued with the facts, and, I believe, so far as I myself may be admitted as a judge, it portrays truly the condition of the time. The events made use of are all historical; and scarcely a page of the work, certainly not a chapter of it, is wanting in the evidence which must support the assertion. The career of Marion, as here described during the precise period occupied by the narrative, is correct to the very letter of the written history. The story of Barsfield, so far as it relates to public events, is not less so. The account which the latter gives of himself to Janet Berkeley—occurring in the thirty-seventh chapter—is related of him by tradition, and bears a close resemblance to the recorded history of the notorious Colonel Brown, of Augusta, one of the most malignant and vindictive among the southern loyalists, and one who is said to have become so solely from the illegal and unjustifiable means which were employed by the patriots to make him otherwise. The whole history is one of curious interest, and, if studied, of great public value. It shows strikingly the evils to a whole nation, and through successive years, of a single act of popular injustice. Certainly, as the ebullitions of popular justice, shown in the movements of revolution, are of most terrible effect, and of most imposing consequence; so the commission of a crime by the same hands, must, in like degree, revolt the sensibilities of the freeman, and inspire him with a hatred which, as it is well-founded, and sanctioned by humanity itself, must be unforgiving and extreme. The excesses of patriotism, when attaining power, have been but too frequently productive of a tyranny more dangerous in its exercise, and more lasting in its effects, than the despotism which it was invoked to overthrow.

The death of Gabriel Marion, the nephew of the general, varies somewhat, in the romance, from the account given of the same event by history; but the story is supported by tradition. The pursuit of the "swamp fox" by Colonel Tarleton—a pursuit dwelt upon with much satisfaction by our historians, as an admirable specimen of partisan ingenuity on both sides, follows closely the several authorities, which it abridges. The character of Tarleton, and his deeds at this period, present a singular contrast, in some respects, to what was known of him before. His popularity waned with his own party, and his former enemies began to esteem him more favorably. We have, in Carolina, several little stories, such as that in "Mellichampe," in which his human feelings are allowed to appear, at brief moments, in opposition to his wonted practices, and quite at variance with his general character. Nor do I see that there is any inconsistency between these several characteristics. The sensibilities are more active at one moment than at another; and he whose mood is usually merciless and unsparing, may now and then be permitted the blessing of a tear, and the indulgence of a tenderness, under the influence of an old and hallowed memory, kept alive and sacred in some little corner of the heart when all is ossified around it.

The destruction of the mansion-house at "Piney Grove" by Major Singleton, and the means employed to effect this object, will be recognised by the readers of Carolina history, and the lover of female patriotism, as of true occurrence in every point of view; the names of persons alone being altered, and a slight variation made in the locality. Indeed, to sum up all in brief, the entire materials of "Mellichampe"—the leading events—every general action—and the main characteristics, have been taken from the unquestionable records of history, and—in the regard of the novelist—the scarcely less credible testimonies of that venerable and moss-mantled Druid, Tradition. I have simply forborne to call it an historical romance, as it contained nothing which made an era in the time—nothing which, in its character and importance, had a visible effect upon the progress of the revolution. Let us now pass to other topics.

It is in bad taste, and of very doubtful policy, for an author to quarrel with his critics: the laugh is most usually against him when he does so. I shall not commit this error, and hope not to incur this penalty; nor, indeed, have I any good cause to justify me in the language of complaint. My critics have usually been indulgent to me far beyond my merits; and I can see a thousand imperfections in my own books which they have either failed to discover, or forborne, in tenderness, to dwell upon. Farther, I may confess—and I find no shame in doing so—whenever they have dwelt upon deficiencies and defects, I am persuaded that, in most cases, they have done so with perfect justice. In many instances I have availed myself of their opinions, and subsequent editions of my stories have always borne testimony to the readiness with which, whenever this has been the case, I have adopted their suggestions. Sometimes, it is true, an occasional personal and unfriendly reference—perhaps a show of feelings even more equivocal in the case of some random reviewer—has grazed harshly upon sensibilities which are not legitimate topics of critical examination; but even these evidences of unjust assumption and false position have been more than counteracted by the considerate indulgence of the vast majority—the kindness of the reader having more than neutralized the asperities of the reviewer.

But while, in general, the opinions of the critic are acknowledged with respect and held in regard, there are one or two topics upon which I would willingly be justified with him. One friendly reviewer—a gentleman whose praise has usually been of the most generous and least qualified character—one whose taste and genius are alike unquestionable, and whose own achievements in this department give him a perfect right to be heard on all matters of romance—has made some few objections to portions of the "Partisan," and—with all deference to his good judgment, and after the most cautious consideration—I am persuaded, with injustice. He objects to that story, in the first place, as abrupt and incomplete. That it is *unfinished*—that the nice hand has been wanting to smooth down and subdue its rude outlines into grace and softness in many parts—I doubt not—I deny not. The work was too rapidly prepared for that; and the finish of art can only be claimed by a people with whom art is a leading object. No other people are well able to pay for it—no other people are *willing* to pay for it; and, under the necessity of haste, the arts in our country must continue to struggle on, until the wealth of the people so accumulates as to enable the interior to react upon the Atlantic cities. When the forests shall cease to be attractive, we may look for society to become stationary; and, until that is the case, we shall look in vain for the perfection of any of the graceful and refining influences of a nation. But the objection of my friend was one of more narrowing compass: it was simply to the story, *as a story*, that he urged its want of finish — its incompleteness. This objection is readily answered by a reference to the plan of the "Partisan," as set forth in the preface to that work. The story was proposed as one of a series, the events mutually depending upon each other for development, and the fortunes of the personages in the one narrative providing the action and the interest of all. This plan rendered abruptness unavoidable; and nobody who read the preface, and recognised the right of an author to lay down his own standards and prescribe his own plans, could possibly utter these objections. The design may have been unhappy, and in that my error may have lain; but, surely, no objection can possibly lie to the incompleteness or abruptness of the one and introductory story, if no exception was taken to the plan at first.

Another, and, perhaps, more serious cause of issue lies between us. My friend objects to the preponderance of low and vulgar personages in my narrative. The question first occurs, "Does the story profess to belong to a country and to a period of history which are alike known — and does it misrepresent either?" If it does not, the objection will not lie. In all other respects it is the objection of a romanticist — of one who is willing to behold in the progress of society none but its most lofty and elevated attributes — who will not look at the materials which make the million, but who picks out from their number the man who should *rule*, not the men who should *represent* — who requires every second person to be a demigod, or hero, at the least — and who scorns all conditions, that only excepted which is the ideal of a pure mind and delicate imagination. To make a fairy tale, or a tale in which none but the colors of the rose and rainbow shall predominate, is a very different, and, let me add, a far less difficult matter, than to depict life as we discover it — man in all his phases, as he is modified by circumstance, and moulded by education — and man as the optimist would have, and as the dreamer about inane perfectibility delights to paint him. My object usually has been to adhere, as closely as possible, to the features and the attributes of real life, as it is to be found in the precise scenes, and under the governing circumstances — some of them extraordinary and romantic, because new — in which my narrative has followed it. In this pursuit, I feel confident that I have "nothing extenuated, nor set down aught in malice." I certainly feel that, in bringing the vulgar and the vicious mind into exceeding activity in a story of the borders, I have done mankind no injustice; and while I walk the streets of the crowded city, and where laws are said to exist, and in periods which, by a strange courtesy, are considered civilized, I am still less disposed to admit that my delineations of the species in the wilds of our country, and during the strifes of foreign and intestine warfare, are drawn in harsh colors and by a heavy hand. I am persuaded that vulgarity and crime must always preponderate — dreadfully preponderate — in the great majority during a period of war; and no argument would seem necessary to sustain the assertion, when we look at the insolence and brutality of crime, as it shows itself among us in a time of peace. Certainly, if argument be needed, we shall not have to look far from our great cities for the evidence in either case.

It is true that the novelist is, or should be, an *artist*, and his taste and judgment are alike required to *select* from his materials, and choose, for his personages, judicious lights. An undue preponderance of *dark* will not do in a picture, unless to produce some such pyrotechnic performances as John Martin delights in — vast dashes of glare and gloom, alternately shifting, and an explosion of fireworks in a conspicuous centre. The discriminating eye will require that the light and shadow be so distributed that the one shall not be oppressive nor the other dense. These are general principles to be observed, not less by the poet than the painter—not less by the novelist of real life that the romancer who seeks only for extraordinary material.

But it is not merely as an artist that the historical novelist is to regulate his performances. He is required to have regard to those moral objects which should be in the eye of the painter also—though not to the same extent—since both these arts, along with those of poetry and the drama, are never so legitimately exercised as when they aim to refine the manners, soften the heart, and elevate the general standards of society and man. To paint morally, the historic novelist must paint truly; and vice was never yet painted truly, that it did not revolt the mind. One error of our time is, not to paint it truly. If we tell of the thousand crimes, we dwell with such emphasis upon the solitary virtue, that they only serve as a shadowy foil to its exceeding loveliness and light. It is curious to perceive how completely this sort of error has found its way into all our habits, not merely those of thought and taste, but those of expression. With what tenderness, nowadays, we speak of every form of vice! A drunkard, unless he is very poor and destitute, is seldom or never called a drunkard: he is only a little excited. A debauchee and gambler is simply a gay man; and a forger for millions is only guilty of a sad mistake. We become wonderfully soon reconciled to vice, when we mince the epithets which we apply to it: the vice soon ceases to be held such when we call it by a milder name.

The low characters predominate in the "Partisan," and they predominate in all warfare, and in all times of warfare, foreign and domestic. They predominate in all imbodied armies that the world has ever known. War itself is a vice, though sometimes an unavoidable one. The novelist would not draw truly, according to the facts, if he did not show that there are but few men calculated, by ability and force of character, to lead the many; and this truth is of universal application. It belongs to the million always, and will apply to every existing nation on the surface of the globe.

The question which propriety may ask, having the good of

man for its object, is—"Has the novelist made vice attractive, commendable, successful, in his story? Is virtue sacrificed — are the humanities of life and society endangered, by the employment of such agents as the low and vulgar? Is there anything in the progress of the vicious to make us sympathize with them—to make us seek for them? These are the proper questions, and they are such as the "Partisan" must answer for itself. Some of our critics and novelists, wanting though they may be in most standards of discrimination, have, nevertheless, sympathies and tastes in common; and, perhaps, if, instead of naked vulgarity and barefaced crime, I had robed my villains in broadcloth, adorned their fingers with costly gems, provided them liberally with eau-de-Cologne, and made them sentimental, I should have escaped all objections of this nature. It is too much the fashion to conceal the impurities which we should seek to cleanse, as some people employ the chloride of lime to sprinkle the nuisance which propriety would instantly remove.

W. G. S.

Le Roy Place, New York,
September 1, 1836.

MELLICHAMPE.

CHAPTER I.

THE CURTAIN RISES.

The battle of Dorchester was over; the victorious partisans, successful in their object, and bearing away with them the prisoner whom they had rescued from the felon's death, were already beyond the reach of their enemies, when Major Proctor, the commander of the British post, sallied forth from his station in the hope to retrieve, if possible, the fortunes of the day. A feeling of delicacy, and a genuine sense of pain, had prompted him to depute to a subordinate officer the duty of attending Colonel Walton to the place of execution. The rescue of the prisoner had the effect of inducing in his mind a feeling of bitter self-reproach. The mortified pride of the soldier, tenacious of his honor, and scrupulous on the subject of his trust, succeeded to every feeling of mere human forbearance; and, burning with shame and indignation, the moment he heard a vague account of the defeat of the guard and the rescue of Walton, he led forth the entire force at his command, resolute to recover the fugitive or redeem his forfeited credit by his blood. He had not been prepared for such an event as that which has been already narrated in the last pages of "The Partisan," and was scarcely less surprised, though more resolute and ready, than the astounded soldiers under his command. How should he have looked for the presence of any force of the rebels at such a moment, when the defeat and destruction of Gates's army, so complete as it had been, had paralyzed, in the minds of all, the last hope of the Americans? With an audacity that seemed little less than madness, and was desperation, a feeble but sleepless enemy had darted in between the fowler and his prey — had wrested the victim of the conqueror from his talons, even in the moment of his fierce repast; and, with a wild courage and planned impetuosity, had rushed into the very jaws of danger, without shrinking, and with the most complete impunity.

The reader of the work of which the present is offered as a continuation, will perhaps remember the manner in which we found it necessary to close that story. It was from a scene of bloody strife that we hurried the chief personages of the narrative; and, only solicitous for their safety, paused not to consider the condition of the field, or of the other parties who remained behind. To that field we will now return, and at a moment which leaves it almost doubtful whether, in reality, the strife be ended. The cry of men in their last agony — the panting prayer for a drop of water from the gasping wretch, through whose distended mouth the life-blood pours forth more freely than the accents that implore Heaven and man alike for succor and relief — the continued flight of the affrighted survivors, and the approaching rush of Proctor's troop — these speak as loudly for the dreadful conflict as the shrill blast of the hurrying trumpet, or the sharp clashing of conflicting steel. The beautiful town of Dorchester, in a bright flame at several points, illumined with an unnatural glare the surrounding fields and foliage, and, with the shrieks of flying women and children, still more contributed to the terrible force of the picture. The ruddy light bathed and enveloped for miles around, with a brilliancy deeper than that of the sun, the high tops of the towering pines, while the thick dense smoke, ascending over all, hung sluggishly and dark in the slumberous sky of August, like some of those black masses of storm that usually come in the train, and burst in ruin over the southern cities, with the flight of the sister month of September.

The hurry of Major Proctor was in vain. He came too late to retrieve the fortunes of the fight. The partisans had melted away like so many shadows. Vain were all his efforts, and idle his chagrin. He could only gaze in stupid wonderment upon the condition of the field, admiring and deploring that valor which had eluded his own, and set at naught all his precautions. Never had surprise been more complete; never had enterprise been better planned or more perfectly executed, with so much hazard, and with so little loss. The whole affair was one to annoy the British commander beyond all calculation. There was nothing to remedy — there was no hope of redress. The rebels were beyond his reach; and, even were they not, the force under Proctor was quite too small, and the condition of his trust, in and about Dorchester, of too much hazard and importance, to permit of his pursuing them. Convinced of this, he turned his attention to the field of battle, every step in the examination of which only contributed the more to his mortification and regret. Several of his best soldiers lay around him in the last agonies or the final slumbers of death; several were maimed or wounded, and the few who survived and had fled from the unlooked-for combat, had not, in every instance, escaped unhurt. But few of the partisans had fallen, and their wounds had all been fatal. They were no longer at the mercy of any human conqueror. There was none upon whom the mortified commander, had he been so disposed, could wreak his vengeance, and punish for the audacity of his rebel leader. The bitterness of his mood increased with the conviction that there was no victim upon whom to pour it forth. Revenge and regret were alike unavailing.

While thus he mused upon the gloomy prospect and the bloody field, the soldiers, who, meanwhile, had been dispersed about in the inspection of the adjoining woods and scene of strife, came before him, bringing an individual whom they had found, the only one who seemed to have escaped unhurt in the combat. Yet he was found where the strife appeared to have been hottest. A pile of dead bodies was around him, and, when discovered, he was employed in turning over the senseless carcases and dragging them apart, as if searching for some particular object. The British major started when he beheld him; and, as he gazed upon the bronzed, sinister, and well-known features, and saw with what calm indifference the blear eye of the half-breed Blonay met his own, a doubt of his fidelity grew active, at the expense of one whose character had always been too equivocal to be held above the commission of the basest treachery. The brow of the Briton put on new terrors as he surveyed him; and, glad of any victim, even though not the most odious, he addressed the reckless savage in the sternest language of distrust.

"What do you here, Blonay? Speak quickly, and without evasion, or you shall swing, by heaven, on that gallows, instead of him whom you have helped from it. Tell out the whole story of this traitorous scheme—unfold the share you had in it, and who were your abettors—who rescued the prisoner—by whom were they commanded—how many—and where are they gone? Answer, fellow; answer, and without delay; speak out!"

Proctor could scarcely articulate his own requisitions, so intense were his anxiety and passion. The person addressed seemed almost totally unmoved by an exhortation so earnestly made, or only moved to defiance. His swarthy cheek grew even darker in its depth of hue, and his lips were now resolutely fastened together, as he listened to the language of his superior. His air, full of scornful indifference, and his position, lounging and listless, might have provoked Proctor to an act of violence, had they been maintained much longer. But, as if moved by more prudent counsels from within, the half-breed, in a moment after, changed his posture to one of more respectful attention. The rigidity passed away from his muscles—his high cheek-bones seemed to shrink—his eyes were lowered—and his head, which had been elevated before into an unwonted loftiness, was now suffered, in compliance with his usual habit, to fall upon one shoulder. His mood grew more conciliatory as he proceeded to reply to one, at least, of the several questions which Proctor had asked him, almost in a breath. Siill, however, the reply of the half-breed was found rather to accord with the first than the last expression of his air and attitude.

"And if you was to hang me up, major, you wouldn't be any the wiser, and would hear much less than if you was to let me run."

"No trifling, sirrah, but speak to the point, and quickly: I am in no mood for jest. Speak out, and say what is the part you have taken in this business. The truth, sirrah—the truth only will serve you."

"I'm no rebel, major, as you ought to know by this time. As for the truth, I'm sure I can tell it, if you'd ax me one thing at a time. I a'n't sparing of the truth when I've got it."

"I do know you, sirrah, and know you too well to trust you much. Briefly, then, and without prevarication, do you know the parties who rescued Colonel Walton? What do you know of the matter? The whole truth; for I have the means of knowing whether you speak falsely or not."

"Well, now, major, I knows no great deal; but what I knows is the truth, and that I'll tell. The men who *fout* here were Marion's men, I reckon. I looked out from the bay-bushes there; I was doubled up in a heap, and I seed the whole business, from the very first jump."

"Relate the matter."

"Relate—oh, ay—tell it, you mean. Why, then, sir, the rebels came down the trace, from out the cypress, I reckon, and ——"

"Who led them?" demanded Proctor, impatiently.

"Why I reckon 'twas Major Singleton."

"Reckon! Do you not know, sir?"

"Well, yes, major, I may say I do, seeing that I seed him myself."

"And why, sirrah, did you not shoot him down? You knew he was a rebel—that a price was set upon his head—that you could have rendered no better service to your king and to yourself, than by bringing in the ears of a traitor so troublesome! Had you not your rifle, sirrah? Why, unless you are a rebel like himself, did you not use it?"

"Adrat it, major, it did go agin me not to pull trigger; but you see, major, 'twould ha' been mighty foolish now. More than once I had the drop on both of 'em, and could easy enough ha' brought down one or t'other with a wink; but there was no fun in it, to think of afterward. I was only one shot, you see, sir, and quite too close to get away. They were all round me, and I had to lie mighty snug, or they'd ha' soon mounted through the brush upon me like so many varmints; and the swamp's a good mile off—too far off for a man that wants to hide his head in a hurry. It's no use, major, you know, to lose one for one, when one's all you've got."

"Miserable coward!" exclaimed Proctor, with indignation. "Miserable coward, to count chances at such a moment; throwing away so good an opportunity. But who was the other person? You spoke of another with Singleton."

"Eh?—what?" was the vacant and seemingly unconscious reply of Blonay. The impatience of Proctor appeared to increase.

"The other—the person beside Singleton. You said that your aim was upon both of them."

A quick, restless, dissatisfied movement followed on the part of the half-breed; and, before he replied, he drew himself up to his fullest height, while a darker red seemed to overshadow his features. His answer was hurried, as if he desired to dismiss the subject from his mind.

"T'other was Bill Humphries."

"And why have you named him, in particular, with Singleton?"

"'Cause I only seed him."

"What! you do not mean to say that these two men beat the guard and rescued the prisoner?" demanded the Briton, with astonishment.

"Adrat it, major, no—I don't say so. There was a matter of twenty on 'em and more; but I didn't stop to look after the rest. I took sight at them two—first one and then t'other; and, more than once, when they were chopping right and left among the red-coats, I could ha' dropped one or t'other for certain, and would ha' done so if 'twan't for the old woman. She would go on the hill, you see."

"Who?" asked the officer.

"Why, sir, the old woman. Jist when I was going to pull trigger upon that skunk Humphries, as he came riding down the road so big, I heard her cry out, and I couldn't help seeing her. She did try hard to get out of the way of the horses, but old people, major, you know, can't move fast like young ones, and I couldn't help her, no how."

"Of whom do you speak now?" demanded Proctor. "What old woman are you talking of?"

Blonay simply lifted his finger, without changing countenance or position, while he pointed to a mangled carcass lying a few paces from the place of their conference, It was there, indeed, that the soldiers of Proctor, on their coming up, had discovered him; and the eye of the British major followed the direction of Blonay's finger only to turn away in horror and disgust. The miserable features were battered by the hoofs of the plunging horses out of all shape of humanity, yet Proctor was not slow to comprehend the connection between the vagrant before him and his hag-like mother. Turning away from the spectacle, he gave directions to the men to assist in removing the carcass, under the direction of the son, whom he however proceeded to examine still farther, and from whom, after innumerable questions, he obtained all the leading particulars of the fray. It seemed evident to Proctor, when his first feeling of exasperation had subsided, that the bereaved wretch before him was innocent of any participation in the assault of the partisans, and he soon dismissed him to the performance of those solemn offices of duty, the last which were to be required at his hands for the parent he had lost.

Obedient to the commands of their superior, the soldiers drew nigh, and proceeded to transfer the corpse to one of the carts, which they had now already filled in part with the bodies of some of those who had been slain. The son resisted them.

"You a'n't going to have her to Dorchester burying-ground —eh?"

"To be sure — where else?" was the gruff reply of the soldier having charge of the proceeding.

"Adrat it — she won't go there," replied Blonay.

"And how the,d—l can she help herself? She's as dead, poor old creature, as a door-nail, and she's been hammered much harder. See — her head's all mashed to a mummy."

He raised the lifeless mass, and allowed it to fall heavily in the cart, as if to convince the hearer, however unnecessarily, that she no longer possessed a will in the transaction. Blonay did not seem to heed the soldier, but explained his own meaning in the following words:—

"There's a place nearer home the old woman wants to be buried in. She a'n't guine to sleep quiet in the churchyard, with all them people round her. If you wants to help me, now, you must give me a cart on purpose, and then I'll show you where to dig for her. She marked it out herself long time ago."

His wish was at once complied with, as the orders of Major Proctor had been peremptory. An additional cart was procured, into which the mangled remains were transferred by the soldiers. In doing this, Blonay lent no manner of assistance. On the contrary, his thoughts and person were entirely given to another office which seemed to call for much more than his customary consideration. Bending carefully, in all directions, over the scene of strife, even as a hungry hound gathering up from the tainted earth the scent of his selected victim, he noted all the appearance of the field of combat, and with the earnest search of one looking for the ruined form of a lost but still remembered and loved affection, he turned over the unconscious carcasses of those who had fallen, and narrowly examined every several countenance.

"He a'n't here," he muttered to himself; and an air of satisfaction seemed to overspread his face. "I thought so — I seed him go to the cart, and he warn't hurt then. I'll chaw the bullet for him yet."

Thus saying, his search seemed to take another direction, and he now proceeded to inspect the ground on which the battle had taken place. In particular, he traced out upon the soft red clay, which had retained every impression, the various marks made by the hoofs of the shodden horses. One of these he heedfully regarded, and pursued with an air of intense satisfaction. The impression was that of a very small shoe—a deer like hoof-trace—quite unlike, and much smaller than those made by the other horses. There was another peculiarity in the shoe which may be noted. That of the right forefoot seemed in one place to be defective. It had the appearance of being either completely snapped in twain, and the parts slightly separated directly in the centre, or by a stroke of the hammer, while the metal was yet malleable, it had been depressed by a straight narrow line evenly across. Whatever may have been the cause, the impression of the shoe upon the earth left this appearance of defect, making the track of its owner sufficiently conspicuous to one having a knowledge of, and on the look-out for, it. Having once satisfied himself of the continued presence of the shoe, with which he seemed to have been previously familiar, he gave over his examination; and, as the cart was now ready, and all preparations completed for the return of the party to the village, he gathered up his rifle, drew the 'coon-skin cap over his eyes, and, without a word, at once fell in procession with the rest, following close behind the body of his mother. Passing through the village of Dorchester, where they only paused to procure a coffin, which was furnished by the garrison, they proceeded directly to the miserable cabin a few miles beyond, which she had hitherto inhabited. Here, under a stunted cedar, in a little hollow of the woods behind her dwelling, a stake, already driven at head and foot, designated the spot which she had chosen for her burial-place. The spade soon scooped out a space for her reception, and in a few moments the miserable and battered hulk of a vexed and violent spirit was deposited in silence. The son lingered but a little while after the burial was over. He turned away soon after the rest; and, without much show of sympathy, and with none of its feeling, those who had thus far assisted left him to his own mood in the now desolate abiding-place of his mother.

CHAPTER II.

INDIAN BLOOD.

To estimate the solitude of such a creature as Blonay under the present loss of his parent, by any of those finer standards of humanity which belong to a higher class and better habits, would be manifestly idle and erroneous. But that his isolation previously from all others, and his close dependence for sympathy upon the one relative whom he had just lost, added largely to his degree of suffering now, is equally unquestionable. Supposing his mere human feelings to have been few and feeble, they were yet undivided. Concentrating upon the one object as they had done for so long a period, they had grown steady and unwavering; and, if not very strong or very active at any time, they were at least sufficiently tenacious in their hold to make the sudden wrenching of their bands asunder to be felt sensibly by the survivor. But he did full justice in his deportment to the Indian blood which predominated in his veins. He had no uttered griefs; no tears found their way to his cheeks, and his eyes wore their wonted expression, as he took his seat upon the floor of his lonely cabin, and, stirring the embers upon the hearth, proceeded, with the aid of the rich lightwood which lay plentifully at hand, to kindle up his evening fire.

But, if grief were wanting to the expression of his countenance, it did not lack in other essentials of expression. Having kindled his fire, he sat for some time before it in manifest contemplation. His brow was knitted, his eyes fixed upon the struggling blaze, his lips closely compressed, and a general earnestness of look indicated a laboring industry of thought, which, were he in the presence of another person, would never have been suffered so plainly to appear. For some time he sat in this manner without change of position, and during all this period it would seem that he was working out in his mind some particular plan of conduct, in the pursuit of an object of no less difficulty than importance. Of that object we can only conjecture the nature from a reference to events, and to his actual condition. The vindictive blood within him — his irresponsible position in society — the severity of the treatment to which, justly or not, he had been subjected by one of the parties between whom the province was divided — and the recent dispensation which had deprived him of the companionship of one, who, however despicable and disgusting to all others, was at least a mother to him — were circumstances well calculated to arouse the savage desire of vengeance upon those to whom any of his sufferings might be attributed.

That such were his thoughts, and such the object of his deliberations, may safely be inferred from the few words of muttered declamation which fell from his lips at intervals while thus rapt in his contemplations. It would be to no purpose to record these words, since they do little more than afford a brief and passing sanction to the opinion we have thus ventured to entertain, and prove, at the same time, the character of a mood seemingly hostile to humankind in general. They were bitter and comprehensive, and summed up, to the cost of humanity, all the wrongs to which he had been subjected, and many others, wrongs in his sight only, of which he but complained. Yet an attentive listener might have observed, that in what he said there was an occasional reference to one individual in particular, who was yet nameless; which reference, whenever made, called up to his black, penetrating, but blear eyes, their most malignant expression. All their fires seemed to collect and to expand with a new supply of fuel at such moments, and his swarthy skin glowed upon his cheeks, as if partaking with them a kindred intensity of blaze.

He remained in this state of feeling and reflection for some hours, indulging his usual listnessness of habit while pursuing the thought which his mood had prompted; when, at length, as if he had arrived at a full and satisfactory conclusion, he arose from his place, supplied the fire with new brands, and, as night had now set in, proceeded to bring forth his supper from the little cupboard where it usually stood. His fare was simple, and soon despatched. When this duty had been performed, he next proceeded to such arrangements as seemed to indicate his preparation for a long journey. He brought forth from the recess which had supplied him with his evening repast a small sack of corn-meal, possibly a quart or more, and a paper containing at least a pound of common brown sugar. A huge hoe, such as is used in the corn-field, was then placed by him before the blazing fire — the flour and sugar, previously stirred together, were spread thickly over it, and, carefully watching the action of the heat upon his mixture, he took due heed to remove it at that period when he perceived the flour to grow slightly brown, and the sugar to granulate and form in common particles along with it. It was then withdrawn from the fire, exposed for an hour to the air, and afterward poured into a sack made of the deerskin, which seemed to have been employed frequently for a like purpose. To this, in another skin, the remnant of a smoked venison ham was added, and the two parcels, with one or two other items in the shape of hoe-cake and fried bacon, were deposited in a coarse sack of cloth, opening in the centre like a purse, and so filled as to be worn across the saddle after the fashion of the common meal-bag. This done, he proceeded to what appeared a general overhaul of the hovel. Various articles, seemingly of value, were drawn out from their secret recesses; these were carefully packed away in a box, and, when ready for removal, their proprietor, honestly so or not, proceeded to secure them after his own manner. Leaving the cabin for an instant, he went forth, and soon returned bearing in his hands a spade, with which, in a brief space, he dug a hole in the centre of the apartment sufficiently large to receive and conceal his deposite. Here he buried it, carefully covering it over, and treading down the earth with his feet until it became as hard as that which had been undisturbed around it. Placing everything which he was to remove ready for the moment of departure, he threw himself upon the miserable pallet of his hut, and soon fell into unbroken slumbers.

The stars were yet shining, and it lacked a good hour of the daylight, when he arose from his couch and began to bestir himself in preparations for departure. Emerging from the hovel with his bundles, as we have seen them prepared the night before, he placed them under a neighboring tree, and, undoing the string from the neck of the hungry cur that kept watch in his kennel immediately beside the hovel's entrance, he left him in charge of the deposite, while he took his way to the margin of a little canebrake a few hundred yards off. There, with a shrill whistle and a brief cry two or three times repeated, he called up from its recesses a shaggy pony — a creature of the swamps — a hardy, tough, uncouth, and unclean little animal, which followed him like a dog to the hovel which he had left. The hollow of a cypress yielded him saddle and bridle, and the little goat-like steed was soon equipped, and ready for his rider. This done, Blonay fastened him to a tree near his dog, and, without a word, proceeded to apply the torch to several parts of the building. It was not long before the flames rose around it in every quarter; and, lingering long enough to perceive that the conflagration must now be effectual, the half breed at length grasped his rifle, mounted his tacky, and, followed by his ill-looking dog, once more took his way to the village of Dorchester.

Moving slowly, he did not reach the village until the day had fully dawned. He then proceeded at once to the garrison, and claimed to be admitted to the presence of the commander. Proctor was too good a soldier, and one too heedful of his duty, to suffer annoyance from a visit at so early an hour; and, though not yet risen, he gave orders at once for the admission of the applicant, and immediately addressed himself to the arrangement of his toilet. With a subdued but calm air of humility, Blonay stood before the Briton — his countenance as immovable and impassive as if he had sustained no loss, and was altogether unconscious of privation. Regarding him with more indulgence than had hitherto been his custom,

Proctor demanded of him, first, if the soldiers had properly assisted him in the last offices to his mother; and next, his present business. Blonay had few words, and his reply was brief.

"The old woman didn't want much help, and we soon put her away. About what I want now, major, it a'n't much, and it'll be a smart bit of time 'fore I come back to trouble you agin."

"Why, where do you propose to go?" demanded the Briton.

"I'm thinking to go up along by Black river, and so up into Williamsburgh, and perhaps clear away to old Kaddipah—Lynch's creek, as they calls it now. I don't know how long I may be gone, and it's to get a paper from you that I'm come."

"To Black river and Lynch's creek—why, know you not that the rebels are as thick as hops in that quarter? What carries you there?"

"There's a chap in that quarter stands indebted to me, and I wants he should settle, seeing pay-day's come and gone long ago. I a'n't 'fear'd of the rebels, for I'm used to the woods and swamps, and 'taint often I'll be in their company. I'll keep out of harm's way, major, as long as I can; and when I can't keep out any longer, why, then I'll stand a shot, and have done with it."

"And what sort of paper is it that you desire from me?" asked Proctor.

"Why, sir—a little protection like, that'll be good agin our own people, and stand up for my loyalty. You can say I'm a true friend to his majesty, and how you knows me; and that'll be enough, when you put your own name to it in black and white."

"But to show that to a rebel will be fatal to you. How will you determine between them?"

"Every man has his own mark, major, same as every tree; and where the mark don't come up clear to the eye, it will to the feel or the hearing. I'm a born hunter, major, and must take my chance. I a'n't afear'd."

"And yet, Blonay, I should rather not give you a passport to go in that quarter. Can you not wait until Lord Cornwallis takes that route? Is your claim so very considerable?"

"'Taint so much, major, but I can't do so well without it. I've been in want of it long enough, and I'm dubous him that owes me will clear away and go into North Carolina, and so I'll lose it. You needn't be scared for me, major; I'm not going to put my head in the bull's mouth because his hide has a price in market; and I think, by the time I get up there, Marion's men will be all off. I a'n't afeard."

Proctor, after several efforts to dissuade him from his purpose, finding all his efforts unavailing, gave him the required passport, which he carefully concealed from sight, and with many acknowledgments and professions of loyalty, took his departure. From Dorchester, proceeding to the battle-ground, he again carefully noted the tracks of the one shoe, which he followed with the keen eye of a hunter, from side to side of the road, in its progress upward to the cypress swamp. Sometimes losing it, he turned to the bushes on either hand, and where they seemed disordered or broken, he continued the trail, until, again emerging from the cover, he would find, and resume the more distinct impression, as it was made upon the clay or sandy road. In this way he reached the broken ground of the swamp, and there he lost it. Alighting, therefore, he concealed his pony in a clump of bushes, and with his rifle primed and ready for any emergency, he pursued his farther search into the bosom of the swamp on foot. Here he still thought that he might find the partisans—if not the entire troop of Singleton, a least a portion of it; probably—though on this head he was not sanguine—the very object of his search. From point to point, with unrelaxing vigilance and caution, he stole along until he reached the little creek which surrounded and made an island of the spot where Singleton had held his temporary camp.

The place was silent as the grave. He crossed the narrow stream, and carefully inspected the ground. It bore traces enough of recent occupation. The ashes of several fires, still retaining a slight degree of warmth—the fresh track of horses, that of the broken shoe among them—hacked trees and torn bushes—all told of the presence there, within a brief space, of the very persons whom he now sought. The search of Blonay, worthy of that of the ablest Indian hunter, was thorough and complete. From the one island, he took his way to sundry others which lay in its neighborhood, susceptible of occupation, in all of which he found traces of men and horses, encouraging him to proceed farther and with continued caution. At length he passed an oozy bog, and stood upon a little hummock, which seemed formed for a place of refuge and repose. An awful silence rested over the spot, and the exceeding height of the cypresses, and the dense volume of undergrowth which surrounded and darkened the wide intervals between them, seemed almost too solid to admit of his progress. The gloom of the region had all the intensity of night, and appeared to impress itself upon the feelings of one even so habitually wanting in reverence as the half-breeds. He stopped for an instant, then moving forward by a route which he seemed to adopt with confidence, he rounded the natural obstruction of woods and thicket, and an amphitheatre opened before him, not so spacious as it was perfect.

He paused suddenly—he heard a footstep—there was evidently a rustling in the woods. He stole behind a tree for an instant, sank upon his knee, lifted his rifle, which he cocked with caution, and watched the quarter intently from which the sound had arisen. A shrill scream rose upon the air, and in the next instant he beheld a monstrous wildcat, startled like himself, and by him, bound forward to an opposite point of the area, and leap into the extending arms of a rotten tree, that shook under its pressure. Perching upon the very edge of a broken limb which jutted considerably out, it looked down with threatening glance upon his approach. He rose from his knees and advanced to the spot whence the animal had fled and over which it still continued to brood with flaming eyes and an aroused appetite. It was not long before Blonay discovered the occasion of its presence.

The figure of a man, huge in frame, seemingly powerless, lay stretched upon the ground. The half-breed soon recognised the person of the maniac Frampton. He lay upon the little mound which covered the remains of his wife. To this he seemed to have crawled with the latest efforts of his strength.

That strength was now nigh exhausted. His clothes were in tatters, and covered with traces of blood and mire. His bloodshot eyes were glazing fast. The curtain of death was nearly drawn over them, but his feeble hand was uplifted occasionally to the tree where the wildcat sat watching hungrily for the moment when the restless but feeble motion of the dying man should cease. Blonay approached, and, as his eye glanced from man to beast, he lifted his rifle, intending to shoot the monster. The action seemed to irritate the creature, whose half-suppressed scream, as Blonay advanced his foot toward him in the act to fire, appeared to defy and threaten him.

"The varmint!" exclaimed the half-breed, "I could shoot him now easy enough, but it's no use. There's plenty more on 'em in the swamp to come after him, and I don't love them any better than him. There's no reason why I should keep the meat from him only for them. It's the natur of the beast to want its fill, and what the wild-cat don't eat the buzzards must. The varmint won't touch him so long as he can move a finger, and when he can't he won't mind much how many of 'em get at him."

So speaking, he turned from the animal to the maniac. The hand was uplifted no longer. The eye had nothing of life's language in it. The last lingering consciousness had departed for ever; and Blonay looked up to the watching wild-cat, as he turned the body with his foot, muttering aloud as he did so — "Adrat it, you may soon come down to dinner."

The animal uttered a short, shrill cry, two or three times repeated, and with a rising of its bristles, and such a flashing of its eyes, that Blonay half determined to shoot it where it stood, for what appeared to him its determined insolence. Once, indeed, he did lift his rifle, but, with the thought of a moment, he again dropped it.

"It's only a waste," he muttered to himself, "and can do no good. Besides, it's a chawed bullet. It's of no use to bite lead when a wildcat's to be killed. Smooth bullet and smooth bore will do well enough, and them I ha'n't."

Such were his words as he turned away from the spot, and departed for the place where his horse was fastened — such was his philosophy. The bullet, marked for vengeance by the impression of his teeth, was not to be thrown away upon mere pastime; and, though feeling a strong desire to destroy the cat, he was yet able to forbear. He hurried through the quagmire, but had not gone far when the repeated screams of the animal, calling probably to its fellows, announced to the half-breed that he had already begun to exult in the enjoyment of his long-withheld and human banquet.

CHAPTER III.

THE COMPANIONS.

BLONAY emerged from the swamp only to commence a journey of new difficulties, the termination of which he could not foresee. Leaving him upon the road for a while, we will now change the scene to that beautiful tract of country lying close along the borders of the Santee, and stretching thence, in a northwardly direction, across the present district of Williamsburgh to the river Kaddipah — a stream which, according to modern usage, has shared the fate of most of our Indian waters, and, exchanging that more euphonious title conferred upon it by the red man, is now generally known to us as Lynch's creek. With a patriotic hardihood, that will be admitted to have its excuse if not its necessity, we choose to preserve in our narrative the original Indian cognomen whenever we may find it necessary to refer to it; and the reader, whose geographical knowledge might otherwise become confused, will henceforward be pleased to hold the two names as identical, if not synonymous.

To the Santee, extending from point to point in every direction leading to the Kaddipah, the action of the Carolina partisans was for a long time limited. Our narrative will be confined within a like circuit. The entire region for nearly two hundred miles on every hand, was in the temporary and occasional occupation of Marion and his little band. With the commission of the state, conferring upon him the rank of a brigadier in its service, Governor Rutledge had assigned to the brave partisan the entire charge in and over all that immense tract comprehended within a line drawn from Charleston along the Atlantic to Georgetown, inclusive — thence in a westerly direction to Camden, and thence in another line, including the Santee river, again to Charleston. This circuit comprehended the most wealthy and populous portion of the state, and could not, under existing circumstances, have been intrusted to better hands. And yet, not a foot of it but was in actual possession and under the sway of the invader. His forts and garrisons at moderate intervals, covered its surface, and his cavalry, made up chiefly of foreign and native mercenaries, constantly traversed the entire space lying between them.

The worthy governor of South Carolina, thus liberal in appropriating this extensive province to the care of the partisan, dared not himself set foot upon it unless under cover of the night; and the brave man to whom he gave it availed himself of the privileges of his trust only by stratagem and stealth. Fortunately, the physical nature of the country so bestowed was well susceptible of employment in the hands of such a warrior as Marion. It afforded a thousand natural and almost inaccessible retreats, with the uses of which the partisan had been long familiar. The fastnesses of river and forest, impervious to the uninitiated stranger, were yet a home to the "swamp fox." He doubled through them, night and day, to the continual discomfiture and mortification of his pursuers. From the Santee to the Black river, from the Black river the two Peedees, through the Kaddipah, to thence to Waccamah, and back again to the Santee, he led his enemies a long chase, which wearied out their patience, defied their valor, and eluded all their vigilance. Availing himself of their exhaustion, he would then suddenly turn upon the pursuing parties, watch their movements, await the moment of their neglect or separation, and cut them up in detail by an unlooked-for blow, which would amply compensate by its consequences for all the previous annoyance to which he might have been subjected in the pursuit.

It was to his favorite retreat at Snow's island that Major Singleton followed his commander, after the successful onslaught at Dorchester. Himself familiar with the usual hiding-places, he had traced his general with as much directness as was possible in following one so habitually cautious as Marion.

He had succeeded in uniting with him, though after much difficulty ; and, as the partisan studiously avoided remaining very long in any one place, the union had scarcely been effected before the warriors were all again in motion for the upper Santee. This river, bold, broad, rapid, and full of intricacies, afforded the finest theatre for the sort of warfare which they carried on. Its course, too, was such as necessarily made it one of the great leading thoroughfares of the state. Detachments of the enemy's troops were continually passing and repassing it, in their progress either for the seacoast or the interior. Supplies and recruits to Cornwallis — then in North Carolina — despatches and prisoners in return from him to the Charleston garrison, made the region one of continual life, and, to Marion, of continual opportunity. Hanging around its various crossing-places, like some vigilant and vengeful hawk in confident expectation of his prey, he kept an unsleeping watch, an untiring wing, an unerring weapon. In its intricacies we shall find him now — the swamps not less his home than the element of his peculiar genius. His scouts are dispersed around him in all directions, and in all disguises — lying in the bush by the wayside — crouching in the oozy mire in close neighborhood with the reptile — watchful above, and buried in the thick overhanging branches of the tree — crawling around the cottage enclosure, in readiness and waiting for the foe.

The scene to which we would now direct the eye of our reader is sufficiently attractive of itself to secure his attention. The country undulates prettily around us, for miles, in every direction: now rising gently into slopes, that spread themselves away in ridges and winding lines, until the sight fails to discover the valleys in which they lose themselves — and now sinking abruptly into deepening hollows and the quietest dells, whose recesses and sudden windings, thickly covered with the massive and umbrageous natural growth of the region, terminate at last, as by a solid wall, the long and variously-shadowed prospect. On the one hand a forest of the loftiest pines, thousands upon thousands in number, lies in the deep majesty of unappropriated silence. In the twilight of their dense and sheltered abodes, the meditative and melancholy mind might fitly seek, and readily obtain, security from all obtrusion of uncongenial objects. Even the subtile and oppressive beams of the August sun come as it were by stealth, and tremblingly, into their solemn and sweet recesses. Their tops, gently waving beneath the pressure of the slight breeze as it hurries over them, yield a strain of murmuring song like the faint notes of some spirit mourner, which accords harmoniously with the sad influence of their dusky forms. The struggling and stray glance of sunlight, gliding along their prostrated vistas, rather contributes to increase than remove the sweet gloom of these deep abodes. The dim ray, like an intrusive presence, flickering between their huge figures with every movement of the declining sun, played, as it were, by stealth, among the brown leaves and over the gray bosom of the earth below. Far as the eye can extend, these vistas, so visited, spread themselves away in fanciful sinuosities, until the mind becomes unconsciously and immeasurably uplifted in the contemplation of the scene, and we feel both humbled and elevated as we gaze upon the innumerable forms of majesty before us, rising up, it would seem, without a purpose, from the bosom of earth — living without notice and without employ — uncurbed in their growth — untroubled in their abodes — and perishing away in season only to give place to succeeding myriads having a like fortune.

On the other hand, as it were, to relieve the mind of the spectator from the monotonous influence of such a survey, how different is the woods — how various the other features of the scene around us. Directly opposed to the pine-groves on the one hand, we behold the wildest and most various growth of the richest southern region rising up, spreading and swelling around in the most tangled intricacy — in the most luxurious strength. There the hickory and gum among the trees attest the presence of a better soil for cultivation, and delight the experienced eye of the planter. With these, clambering over their branches, come the wild vines, with their thorny arms and glowing vegetation. Shrubs gather in the common way; dwarf trees and plants, choked, and overcome, yet living still, attest the fruitfulness of a land which yields nutriment but denies place; and innumerable species of fungi, the yellow and the purple fringes of the swamps, the various mosses, as various in hue as in form and texture—parasites that have no root, and, like unselfish affections, only claim an object upon which to bestow themselves—these, crowding about and clustering in gay confusion along the dense mass, swelling like a fortress before the eye, seem intended to form a labyrinthine retreat for the most coy of all selfish creations.

Immediately beyond this dense and natural thicket, the scene—still the same—presents us with another aspect. A broken and dismantled fence, the rails half rotten and decaying fast on all sides, seems to indicate the ancient employment of the place by man. The period must have been remote, however, as the former product of the spot thus enclosed had been superseded by the small-leafed or field pine-tree, in sufficient size and number almost to emulate the neighboring and original forest. There was little here of undergrowth, and yet, as the pine thus occupying it is of inferior and frequently of dwarf size, the thicket was sufficiently dense for temporary concealment. It had a farther advantage in this respect, as it sunk rapidly in sundry places into hollows, that lay like so many cups in the bosom of crowding hills, and had for their growth, like the original wood we have just passed over, a tangled covering of vines and shrubbery.

It was on the side of one of these descents, about noon, on the third day after Blonay's departure from Dorchester, that we find two persons reclining, sheltered by a clump of the smaller pines of which we have spoken, and sufficiently concealed by them and the shrubbery around, to remain unconcerned by the near proximity of the highway. The road ran along, and within rifle distance, to the south, below them. The elder of the two was a man somewhere between thirty and forty years of age. His bulky form, as it lay extended along the grass, denoted the possession of prodigious strength; though the position in which he lay, with his face to the ground, and only supported by his palms, borne up by his elbows resting upon the earth, would incline the spectator to conceive him one not often disposed for its exercise. An air of sluggish inertness marked his manner, and seemed to single him out as one of the mere beef-eaters—the good citizens, who, so long as they get wherewithal to satisfy the animal, are not apt to take umbrage at any of the doings of the world about them. His face, however, had an expression of its own; and the sanguine flush which overspread the full cheeks, and the quick, restless movement of his blue eye, spoke of an active spirit, and one prompt enough at all times to govern and set in motion the huge bulk of that body, now so inert and sluggish. His forehead, though good, was not large; his chin was full, and his nose one of length and character. He was habited in the common blue and white homespun of the country. A sort of hunting-shirt, rather short, like a doublet, came over his hips, and was bound about his waist by a belt of the same material. A cone-crowned hat, the rim of which, by some mischance, had been torn away, lay beside him, and formed another portion of his habiliments. Instead of shoes, he wore a rude pair of buckskin moccasins, made after the Indian manner, though not with their usual skill, and which lacked here and there the aid of the needle. His shirt-collar lay open, without cravat or covering of any kind; and, by the deeply-bronzed color of the skin beneath, told of habitual exposure to the elements. A rifle lay beside him—a long instrument,—and in his belt a black leather case was stuck conveniently, the huge knife which it protected lying beside him, as it had just before been made subservient to his midday meat.

His companion was a youth scarcely more than twenty years of age, who differed greatly in appearance from him we have attempted to describe. His eye was black and fiery, his cheek brown and thin, his hair of a raven black like his eye, his chin full, his nose finely Roman, and his forehead imposingly high. His person was slender, of middle height, and seemed to indicate great activity. His movements were feverishly restless—he seemed passionate and impatient, and his thin, but deeply red lips, quivered and colored with every word, and at every movement. There was more of pretension in his dress than in that of his companion, though they were not unlike in general structure and equipment. Like him he wore a hunting-shirt, but of a dark green, and it could be seen at a glance that its material had been of the most costly kind. A thick fringe edged the skirts, which came lower, in proportion to his person, than those of his companion. Loops of green cord fastened the coat to his neck in front, and a belt of black polished leather confined it to his waist. He also carried a rifle — a Spanish dirk, with a broken handle of ivory, was stuck in his belt, a pouch of some native fur, hanging from his neck by a green cord, contained his mould and bullets. This dress formed the uniform of a native company. His powder-horn had been well chosen, and was exceedingly and curiously beautiful. It had been ingeniously wrought in scraping down, so as to represent a rude but clear sketch of the deer in full leap, a hound at his heels, and a close thicket in the perspective, ready to receive and shelter the fugitive. These were all left in relief upon the horn, while every other part was so transparent that the several grains of powder were distinctly visible within to the eye without.

The youth was partially reclining, with his back against a tree, and looking toward his elder companion. His face was flushed, and a burning spot upon both cheeks told of some vexing cause of thought which had been recently the subject of conversation between them. The features of the elder indicated care and a deep concern in the subject, whatever it may have been, but his eye was mild in its expression, and his countenance unruffled. He had been evidently laboring to sooth his more youthful comrade; and though he did not seem to have been as yet very successful, he did not forego his efforts in his disappointment. The conversation which followed may help us somewhat in arriving at a knowledge of the difficulty before them.

"I am not more quick or impatient," said the youth to his companion, as if in reply to some remark from the other, "than a man should be in such a case. Not to be quick when one is wronged, is to invite injustice; and I am not so young, Thumbscrew, as not to have found that out by my own experience. I know no good that comes of submission, except to make tyrants and slaves; and I tell you, Thumbscrew, that so long as my name is Ernest Mellichampe, I shall never submit to the one, nor be the other."

"A mighty fine spirit, Airnest; and to speak what's gospel true, I likes it myself," was the reply of the other, who addressed the first speaker with an air of respectful deference, as naturally as if he had been taught to regard him as a superior. "I'm not," he continued, "I'm not a man myself to let another play tantrums with me; and, for sartain, I sha'n't find fault with them that's most like myself in that partic'lar. If a man says he's for fight, I'll lick him if I can; if I can't —that's to say, if I think I can't—I'll think longer about it. I don't see no use in fighting where it's ten to one — where, indeed, it's main sartain I'm to be licked; and so, as I says, I'll take time to think about the fighting."

"What! until you're kicked?" replied the other, impetuously.

"No, no, Airnest — not so bad as that comes to neither. My idee is, that fighting is the part of a beast-brute, and not for a true-born man, that has a respect for himself, and knows what's good-breeding; and I only fights when there's brutes standing waiting for it. Soon as a man squints at me as if he was going to play beast with me, by the eternal splinters, I'll mount him, lick or no lick, and do my best, tooth, tusk, and grinders, to astonish him. But, afore that, I'm peaceable as a pine stump, lying quiet in my own bush."

"Well, but when you're trodden upon?" said the other.

"Why then, you see, Airnest, there's another question — who's atop of me? If it's a dozen, I'll lie snug until they're gone over: I see nothing onreasonable or onbecoming in that — and that, you see, Airnest, is jist what I ax of you to do. They a'n't treading on you 'xactly, tho' I do confess they've been mighty nigh to it; but then, you see, there's quite too many on 'em for you to handle with, onless you play 'possum a little. There's no use to run plump into danger, like a blind bull into a thick fence, to stick fast there and be hobbled; when, if you keep your eyes open, and a keen scent, you can track all your enemies, one by one, to his own kennel, and smoke 'em out, one after another, like a rabbit in a dry hollow. Hear to my words, Airnest, and don't be vexed now. Dang my buttons, you know, boy, I love you the same as if you was my own blood and bone, though I knows my place to you, and know you're come of better kin, and are better taught in book-larning; but, by God! Airnest, you hav'n't larned, in all your larning, to love anybody better than I love you."

"I know it, Thumby, I know it—I feel it," said the other, moved by the earnestness of his companion, and extending his hand toward him, while his eyes filled with ready tears.—"I know it, I feel it, my friend; forgive me if I have said anything to vex you. But my heart is full, and my blood is on fire, and I must have utterance in some way."

"Never cry, Airnest—don't, I tell you—'taint right—it's onbecoming, Airnest; but—dang it!" he exclaimed, dashing a drop from his own eye as he spoke, " dang it! I do believe I've been about to do the same thing. But it's all the fault of one's mother, as larns it to us so strong when we're taking suck, that we 'member it for ever after. A man that's got a-fighting, and in the wars with tories one day and British the next, it's onbecoming for him to cry; and, Airnest, though things are black enough about home, it's not black enough to cry for. It'll come light again before long, I'm sartain. I've never seed the time yet when there wasn't some leetle speck of light on the edge of the cloud somewhere—it mought be ever so leetle, or ever so fur off, but it was there somewhere; it mought be in the east, and that showed the clearing away was further off; or it mought be in the northward, and that wasn't the best place either for it to break in, but it was somewhere for certain—that leetle speck of white; jist like a sort of promise from God, that airth should have sunshine again."

"Would I could behold it now," responded the other, gloomily, to the cheering speech of his companion, "would I could behold it now! But I see nothing of this promise—there is no bright speck in the dark cloud which now hangs about my fortunes."

"You're but young, yet, Airnest, and it a'n't time yet for you to talk so. You haven't had a full trial yet, and you're only at the beginning—as one may say, jist at the threshold of the world, and ha'n't quite taken your first step into it. Wait a little; and if you've had a little nonplush at the beginning, why, man, I tell you, larn from it—for it's a sort of lesson, which, if you larn it well, will make you so much the wiser to get on afterward, and so much the happier when the storm blows over. Now, I don't think it so bad for them that has misfortunes from the jump. They are always the best people after all; but them that has sunshine always at first, I never yet knew one that could stand a shower. They're always worried at everything and everybody—quarrelling with this weather, and quarrelling with that, and never able to make the most of what comes up to 'em. Hold on, Airnest—shut your teeth, and keep in your breath, and stand to it a leetle longer. That's my way; and, when I keep to it, I'm always sure to see that leetle white speck I've been telling about, wearing away all round, till it comes right before my eyes, and there it sticks, and don't move till the sunlight comes out again."

"You may be right in your philosophy," responded the youth, "and I would that I could adopt it for my own; but my experience rejects, and my heart does not feel it. These evils have come too fast and too suddenly upon me. My father cruelly murdered—my mother driven away from the home of my ancestors—that home confiscated, and given to the murderer—and I, a hunted, and, if taken, a doomed man! It is too much for my contemplation. My blood boils, my brain burns—I can not think, and when I do it is only to madden."

The speaker paused in deepest emotion. His hand clasped his forehead, and he sank forward, with his face prone to the earth upon which he had been reclining. His companion lifted his hand, which he took into his own, and, with a deep solicitude of manner, endeavored, after his own humble fashion of argument and speech, to exhort his youthful and almost despairing associate to better thoughts and renewed energy.

"Look up, Airnest, my dear boy, look up, and listen to me,

Airnest. It's unbecoming to be cast down like a woman, because trouble presses upon the heart. I know what trouble is, and, dang my buttons, Airnest, I feel for you all over; but I don't like to see you cast down, because then I think you a'n't able to turn out to have satisfaction upon the enemy for what they've done to you. Now, though I do say you're to keep quiet, and lie snug at the present, that isn't to say that you're to do nothing. No, no — you're to get in readiness for what's to come, and not be wanting when you have a chance to turn your enemy upon his back. It a'n't revenge, but it's justice, and my lawful, natural right, that I fights for; and you mustn't be cast down, Airnest, seeing that then you mought'n be ready to take the benefit of a good opportunity."

"It's revenge not less than justice," said the youth, impatiently. "I must have the one, whether the other be obtained or not. I will have it — I will not sleep in its pursuit; and yet, Thumbscrew, I will take your advice — I will be prudent in order to be successful — I will pause in order to proceed. Do not fear me now — I shall do nothing which will risk my adventure or myself; but I will temper my mood with caution, and seek for that vengeance, which shall be the white speck among the clouds of which you have spoken."

"Well, now, that's what I call becoming, and straight-forward right. I'm for — but hush! don't you hear something like a critter? and — that was the bark of a cur, I'll be sworn to it."

The sturdy woodman thrust his ear to the earth, and the sound grew more distinct.

"Keep close, Airnest, now, and I'll look out, and make an examination. There's only one horse, I reckon, from the sound; but I'll see before I leave the bush. I'll whistle should I want you to lend a hand in the business."

Seizing his rifle as he spoke, with an alacrity which seemed incompatible with his huge limbs, and must have surprised one who had only beheld him as he lay supine before, he bounded quickly but circumspectly up the hill, and through the copse toward the highway whence the sounds that had startled them appeared to proceed. The cause of the disturbance may very well be reserved for explanations in another chapter.

CHAPTER IV.

YORKSHIRE VERSUS YORKSHIRE.

BEFORE reaching the road the sturdy woodman became yet more cautious, and, stealing from cover to cover, thus eluded any eye that might be approaching upon it. He gained the cover of a little hedge, formed of the tallow-bush and myrtle, and crouched cautiously and silently out of sight, as he perceived, from the short, quick cry of the cur, that he was advancing rapidly. He had scarcely done so, and arranged an aperture in the copse through which he might observe the road, when he beheld the cause of the uproar which the dog was making. Leaping in irregular bounds, and evidently nearly exhausted, a frightened rabbit came down the trace, inclining from the opposite and open ground of pine forest, to the close bushes in which he was himself concealed.

"Poor Bon," exclaimed the woodman, "it's a bad chance for her this time. I only hope she won't pop into this quarter, or it will be a bad chance for some of her friends."

The muttered apprehensions of the woodman were realized. His eye had scarcely noted the pursuing dog which emerged from the wood closely upon the rabbit's heels, when the poor thing rushed to the very shelter in which he stood, and, darting between his legs, was there secured by their involuntary pressure together. He stooped to the earth, and took up the trembling animal, which lay quivering in his grasp, preferring, by the natural prompting of its instinct, to trust the humanity of man rather than the well-known nature of the enemy which had pursued it.

"Poor Bonny," said the woodman, soothingly, as he caressed it. "Poor Bon—you could'nt help it, Bonny—you were too mighty frightened to know the mischief you're a-doing. Ten to one you've got us into a hobble, now; but there's nothing to be done but to see it out."

The dog by this time rushed into the brush, and recoiled instantly as he beheld the stranger. The quick, rapid cry with which he had pursued the rabbit, was exchanged for the protracted bark with which he precedes his assault upon the man. His white teeth were displayed, and, as if conscious of approaching support, he advanced boldly enough to the attack. The woodman grew a little angry, and lifting his rifle in one hand, while maintaining the terrified but quiet rabbit in the other, he made an exhibition of it which prompted the cur to give back. It was then that, through the bushes, he saw a person approaching along the road whom he readily took to be the owner of the dog. He dropped his rifle instantly, which he suffered to rest, out of sight, against a tree which stood behind him; and, hallooing to the new-comer, he advanced without hesitation from his place of concealment into the road.

Blonay — for it was he — drew up his tacky, and the rifle which he carried across the saddle, in his hand, was grasped firmly, and, at the first moment, was partially uplifted; but seeing that the stranger was unarmed, he released his hold, and saluted him with an appearance of as much good-humor as he could possibly put on. Thumbscrew advanced to him with the trembling rabbit which he made the subject of his first address.

"How are you, stranger? I reckon this is some of your property that I've got here — seeing as how your dog started it. I cotched it 'twixt my legs — the poor thing was so scared, it did'nt know — not it — that 'twas going out of the frying-pan into the fire. It's your'n now; though, dang it, stranger, if so be you don't want it much, I'd rether now you'd tell me to put it down in the bush and let it run, while you make your dog hold in. It's so scared, you see, and it's a pity to hurt anything in natur when you see it scared."

He patted the feeble and trembling animal encouragingly as he spoke, and Blonay was surprised that so large a man should be so gently inclined. He himself cared little, at any time, about the feelings and the fears of yet larger objects. His reply to the application for mercy was favorable, however.

"Well, if you choose, my friend, you can let it go. I don't want it. The dog only started it for his own fun, seeing that it's the nature of the beast. Here, Hitch'em, Hitch'em! lie down, nigger—and shut up. You can let her go now, my friend."

Blonay quieted his dog, and Thumbscrew took his way into cover, watched his moment, and, with a parting pat upon its back, and a cheering "Hurrah, Bon! run for it with your best legs," dismissed the little captive, once more in safety, to its forest habitations. He then returned to the spot where Blonay remained in waiting, and, in his blunt, good-humored way, at once proceeded to commence a conversation with him, after the manner of the country, with a direct question.

"Well, now, stranger, you've been travelling a bit—can you tell me, now, if you've seed anywhere in your travels a man or boy that looks very much like a thief, riding upon a fine, dark-bay nag, that looks like he was stolen?"

"No, that I haven't, friend; I'm much obliged to you, but I haven't seen any," was the reply of Blonay.

"Well, you needn't be obliged to me, stranger, seeing it's no sarvice to you, the question I ax'd you. But if it a'n't axing you too much, I should like to know which road you come."

"Well to say truth, now, my friend, I don't know the name it goes by; it's a main bad road, you see."

"I ax, you see, because, when you tells me you a'n't seed the nag and them that's riding him on the road you come, it's a clear chance they've gone t'other. So, now, if you'll only but say which road you tuk, I'll take the contrary."

The reasoning was so just, and the air of simplicity so complete, which the inquirer had put on, that Blonay saw no necessity for keeping concealed so unimportant a matter as the mere route which he had been travelling; so, without any further scruple, he gave the required information.

"Well, then, I reckon, stranger, you're all the way from

the big city, clear down to the salt seas. There's a power of people there now, a'n't there?"

"I a'n't from Charleston," coldly replied the half-breed.

"Oh, you a'n't! but, do tell—you hear'd about a man that was hung at Dorchester—reckon you seed it?"

"He worn't hung; he got off."

"What! they pardoned him—and so many people as was guine to see him dance upon nothing? What a disappointment! I was a-guine down myself, but, you see, I lost my critter, and so I couldn't; and now I'm glad I didn't, if so be, as you say, he worn't hung."

"No, he worn't hung: there was a fight, and he got away. But this is only what they tell me; I don't know myself."

"Who tell'd you?"

"The people."

"What, them that seed it? Perhaps them that did it—eh?"

This was pushing the matter quite too far, and Blonay began to be uneasy under so leading a question. He replied quickly, after the evasive manner which was adopted between them—

"No! I don't know; they told me they heard it, and I didn't ax much about it, for it worn't my business, you see."

"Oh! that's right—everybody to his own business, says I; and, where people's a-fighting, clean hands and long distance is always best for a poor man and a stranger. They gits a-fighting every now and then in these here parts, and they do say they're a-mustering now above, the sodgers."

"What soldiers?" demanded Blonay, with an air of interest.

"Eh! what sodgers? Them that carries guns and swords, and shoots people, to be sure: them's sodgers, a'n't they?"

"Yes; but have they got on uniforms, or is it only them that carries a rifle, or a knife, or perhaps a rusty sword, or a hatchet? Some soldiers, you know, has fine boots and shoes, with shining buttons, and high caps and feathers; and some ha'n't got shoes, and hardly breeches."

Blonay had become the examiner, and had begun with a leading question also. He had fairly described the British and tory troops in his enumeration of the one, and the rebels, or whigs, in the description of the latter class. The former were usually well provided with arms, ammunition, and every necessary warlike equipment; the whigs were simply riflemen, half the time without powder and lead, and, during the greater part of the war, without necessary clothing. To tell Blonay which of these two classes was in the neighborhood, was no part of Thumbscrew's policy; and his reply, though unsatisfactory, was yet given with the most off-handed simplicity.

"They're all the same to me, stranger, breeches or no breeches, boots or no boots, high caps and feathers, or a ragged steeple like mine—they're all the same to me. A sodger's a sodger; any man that can put a bullet into my gizzard, or cut me a slash over my cheek, up and down, without any marcy for my jawbone—he's a sodger for me, and I gits out of his way mighty soon, now, when I hear of his coming. It's a bad business that, stranger, and I hope you don't deal in it. I say I hope so, for I don't like to see a man I may say I know, chopped up and down, and bored through his head, or his belly, without any axing, and perhaps onbeknown to him."

No interest could be seemingly so earnest as that which Thumbscrew manifested, as he thus expressed his anxiety on the score of Goggle's connection with the military. He put his hand warmly, as he spoke, upon the neck of the little tacky which the other bestrode—a movement which the rider did not seem very greatly to approve, as he contrived, in the next moment, by a sudden jerk, to wheel the animal away from the grasp of the stranger, and to present himself once more in front of him. Thumbscrew did not appear to charge the movement so much upon the rider as the horse.

"Well, now, stranger, your nag is mighty skittish. It's a stout pony that, and smells, for all the world, as if it had fed on cane-tops and salt-marsh all its life. Talking about horses, now, I've heard say that they were getting mighty scarce down in your parts, where the troops harry them with hard riding. Some say that they were buying and stealing all they could, to bring troops up into this quarter. You a'n't hear'd any say about it, I reckon?"

The inquiry was adroitly insinuated, but Blonay was not to be caught, even had he been in possession of the desired information. He availed himself of the question, however, to suggest another, by which, had his companion been less guarded, he might have discovered to which party he belonged.

"What troops?" he asked, carelessly.

"Why, them that fights, to be sure. Troops, if I'm rightly told, is them men that rides on horseback, and fights with swords and pistols, and the big cannon."

"Yes, troopers," said Blonay, tired, seemingly, of putting questions so unprofitably answered.

"Ay — troopers, is it? — I always called them troops. But you a'n't tell'd me if they're coming in these parts. You a'n't seed any on the road, I reckon? — for you a'n't hurt, that I can see. But, may be you out-travelled 'em; they shot at you, though?"

The volubility of Thumbscrew carried him so rapidly on in his assumptions, that it was with difficulty Blonay kept himself sufficiently reserved in his communications. He was at some pains, however, to assure him that he had neither seen any troops, nor been pursued, nor shot at by them; that his whole journey hitherto had been unmarked by any other adventure of more importance than the catching of the single rabbit, in which Thumbscrew had himself so largely assisted. This reference drew the attention of Thumbscrew to the ragged and mean-looking cur that followed the stranger. He admired him exceedingly, and at length proceeded to ask —
"Won't you trade him, now, stranger? I want a hunting-dog mightily."

Blonay declined, and was so pleased and satisfied with the simplicity of his new acquaintance, that he ventured to ask some direct questions; taking care, however, that none of them should convey any committal of his sentiments. He stated, for himself, that he was on his way to Black river and the Santee; that he was looking after a person who was indebted to him; that he was a peaceable man, and wanted to get on without fighting, and he was therefore desirous of avoiding all combatants. In order to do this, he would like to know where Gainey's men were (tories), and Marion's men — if they were likely to lie in his way by pursuing such and such routes, all of which he named, and seemed to know, and how he should best avoid them. In making these inquiries, Blonay had well adopted the manner of one solicitous for peace, and only desirous of getting to the end of his journey without difficulty or adventure. In referring to the different leaders of the two parties in that section of country, he took especial care, at the same time, to utter no word, and exhibit no look or gesture, which could convey the slightest feeling of partiality or preference, on his part, for either; and all that Thumbscrew could conjecture from the inquiry, supposing that the traveller was disguising the truth, was, that, so far from his wishing to avoid all of these parties, by obtaining a knowledge of their lurking-places, he was rather in search of one or the other of them. His scrutiny failed uttered when he strove to find out which. He did not long delay to answer these inquiries, which he did in the unsatisfactory fashion of all the rest.

"Well, now, stranger, you ax a great deal more than I have to answer. These here people that you talk about, I hear, every day, something or other said of them, but nothing very good, now, either way. It's now one, and now another of them that shoots the poor folk's cattle, and maybe shoots them too, and there's no help for it. Sometimes Gainey's people run over the country, burning and plundering — then Marion's men comes after, burning and plundering what's left. So that, between the two, honest, quiet, good-natured sort of people, like you and me, stranger — we get the worst of it, and must cut strap and take the brush, rather than lose life with property. It's a sad time, now, stranger, I tell you."

"But you ha'n't heard of either of 'em in these parts lately, have you?" inquired Blonay.

"Dang it, stranger, they're here, there, and everywhere: they're never long missing from any one place, and — dang my buttons! — I think I hear some of them coming now."

Thumbscrew turned as he spoke, and appeared to listen. Sounds, as of horses' feet, were certainly approaching, and perceptible to Blonay not less than to his dog. With the confirmation of his conjecture, the woodman turned quickly to the forest cover, and, shaking his head, cried to his companion, as he bounded into its depth —

"Look to yourself, stranger, for, as sure as a gun, some of them sodgers is a-coming. They'll shoot you through the body, and chop you into short meat, if you don't cut for it."

He disappeared on the instant, but not in flight. His purpose was to mislead Blonay, and it was sufficient for this that he simply removed himself from sight. Keeping the edge of the forest, as close to the road as he well might, to avoid discovery from it, he now chose himself a station from which he might observe the approaching horsemen, and, at the same time, remain in safety. This done, he awaited patiently their approach. His late companion, in the meanwhile, whose policy was a like caution, quickly followed the suggestion and example of the woodman, and sank into the forest immediately opposite that which the latter had chosen for his shelter. Here he imbowered himself in the woods sufficiently far for concealment, and, hiding his horse, and placing his dog in watch over him, he advanced on foot within a stone's cast from the road, to a spot commanding a good view of everything upon it. Here, in deep silence, he also stood — a range of trees between his person and that of the approaching horsemen, and his form more immediately covered by the huge body of a pine, from behind which he occasionally looked forth in scrutinizing watchfulness.

CHAPTER V.

THE TORY SQUAD.

THE two watchers had not long to wait in their several places of concealment. The sound which had disturbed their conference, and sent them into shelter, drew nigher momentarily, and a small body of mounted men, emerging at length from a bend in the irregular road over which they came, appeared in sight. They were clothed in the rich, gorgeous uniform of the British army, and were well-mounted. Their number, however, did not exceed thirty, and their general form of advance and movement announced them to be less thoughtful, at that moment, of the dangers of ambuscade and battle, than of the pleasant cheer and well-filled larder of the neighboring gentry. Two officers rode together, in advance of them some little distance, and the free style of their conversation, the loud, careless tones of their voices, and the lounging, indifferent manner in which they sat upon their horses, showed them to be, if not neglectful of proper precautions, at least perfectly unapprehensive of any enemy. A couple of large military wagons, drawn each by four able-bodied horses, appeared in the centre of the cavalcade, the contents of which, no doubt, were of sufficient importance to call for such a guard. Yet there was little or nothing of a proper military discipline preserved in the ranks of the troop. Following the example of the officers who commanded them, and who seemed, from their unrestrained mirth, to be engaged in the discussion of some topic particularly agreeable to both, the soldiers gave a loose to the playfullest moods—wild jest and free remark passed from mouth to mouth, and they spoke, and looked, and laughed, as if their trade was not suffering, and its probable termination a bloody death. Their merriment, however, as it was subdued, in comparison with that of the officers, did not provoke their notice or rebuke. The whole party, in all respects, seemed one fitted out for the purposes of pleasure rather than of war. Elated by the recent victories of Cornwallis over Gates, and Tarleton over Sumter, together with the supposed flight of Marion into North Carolina, and the dispersion of his partisans, the British officers had foregone much of that severe, but proper discipline, through which alone they had already been able to achieve so much. The commander of the little troop before us moved on with as much indifference as if enemies had ceased to exist, and as if his whole business now was the triumph and the pageant which should follow successes so complete.

"Gimini!" exclaimed Thumbscrew, as he beheld, at a distance, their irregular approach. "Gimini! if the major was only here now, jist with twenty lads only — twenty would do — maybe he wouldn't roll them redjackets in the mud!"

The close approach of the troop silenced the further speculations of the woodman, and he crouched among the shrubbery, silent as death, but watchful of every movement. The person of the captain who commanded them was rather remarkable for its strength than symmetry. He was a man of brawn and muscle — of broad shoulders and considerable height. His figure was unwieldy, however, and, though a good, he was not a graceful horseman. His features were fine, but inexpressive, and his skin brown with frequent exposure. There was something savage rather than brave in the expression of his mouth, and his nose, in addition to its exceeding feebleness, had an ugly bend upward at its termination, which spoke of a vexing and querulous disposition. His companion was something slenderer in his person, and considerably more youthful. There was nothing worthy of remark in his appearance, unless it be that he was greatly given to laughter — an unprofitable habit, which seemed to be irresistible and confirmed in him, and which was not often found to await the proper time and provocation. He appeared of a thoughtless temper — one who was content with the surfaces of things, and did not disturb the waters with a discontented spirit, seeking for more pleasure than the surface gave him. At the moment of their approach the good-humor of the two was equally shared between them. The subject upon which they had been conversing appeared to have been productive of no small degree of merriment to both, and of much undisguised satisfaction to the elder. He chuckled with uncontrollable complacency, and, long after the laugh of his companion had ceased, a lurking smile hung upon his lips, that amply denoted the still lingering thought of pleasure in his mind. Though ignorant of the occasion of their mirth before, we may now, as they approach, hear something of the dialogue, which was renewed after a brief pause between them; and which, though it may not unfold to us the secret of their satisfaction, may at least inform us, in some degree, of much that is not less necessary for us to know. The pause was broken by the younger of the two, whose deferential and conciliatory manner, while it spoke the inferior, was, at the same time, dashed with a phrase of fireside familiarity, which marked the intimacy of the boon companion.

"And now, Barsfield, you may laugh at fortune for ever after. You have certainly given her your defiance, and have triumphed over her aversion. You have beaten your enemy, won your commission, found favor in the sight of your commander, and can now sit down to the performance of a nominal duty, with a fine plantation, and a stout force of negroes, all at your command and calling you master. By St. George and the old dragon himself, I should be willing that these rebels should denounce me too as a tory, and by any other nickname, for rewards like these."

"They may call me so if they think proper," said the other, to whom the last portion of his comrade's remark seemed to be scarcely welcome; "but, by God! they will be wise not to let me hear them. I have had that name given me once already by that insolent boy, and I did not strike him down for it — he may thank his good fortune and the interposition of that fellow Witherspoon, that I did not — but it will be dangerous for any living man to repeat the affront."

"And why should you mind it, Barsfield?" responded his companion. "It can do you no mischief — the term is perfectly innocuous. It breaks no skin — it takes away no fortune."

"No! but it sticks to a man like a tick, and worries him all his life," said the other.

"Only with your thin-skinned gentry. For such an estate as yours, Barsfield, they might be licensed to call me by any nickname which they please."

"I am not so indulgent, Lieutenant Clayton," replied the other; "and, let me tell you that you don't know the power of a nickname among enemies. A nickname is an argument, and one of that sort too, that, after once hearing it, the vulgar are sure never to listen to any other. It has been of no small influence already in this same war — and it will be of greater effect toward the conclusion, if it should ever so happen that the war should terminate unfavorably to the arms of his majesty."

"But you don't think any such result possible?" was the immediate reply of Clayton.

"No — not now. This last licking of Sumter, and the wholesale defeat of Gates, have pretty well done up the rebels in this quarter. Georgia has been long shut up, and North Carolina will only wake up to find her legs fastened. As for Virginia, if Cornwallis goes on at the present rate, he'll straddle her quite in two weeks more. No! I think that rebellion is pretty nigh wound up; and, if we can catch the 'swamp fox,' or find out where he hides, I'll contrive that we shall have no more difficulty from him."

"Let that once take place," replied his companion, "and you may then retire comfortably, in the enjoyment of the *otium cum dignitate*, the reward of hard fighting and good generalship, to the shady retreats of 'Kaddipah.' By-the-way, Barsfield, you must change that name to something modern — something English. I hate these abominable Indian names — they are so uncouth, and so utterly harsh and foreign in an English ear. We must look up a good name for your settlement."

"You mistake. I would not change the name for the

3

world. I have always known the place by that name, long before I ever thought to call it mine; and the name sounds sweet in my ears. Besides I like these Indian names, of which you so much complain. They sound well, and are always musical."

"They are always harsh to me, and then they have no meaning—none that we know anything about."

"And those we employ have as little. They are generally borrowed from individuals who were their proprietors, and this is the case with our Indian names, which have the advantage in softness and emphasis. No! 'Kaddipah Thicket' shall not lose its old name in gaining a new owner. It wouldn't look to me half so beautiful if I were to give it any other. I have rambled over its woods when a boy, and hunted through them when a man, man and boy, for thirty years—known all its people, and the name seems to me a history, and brings to me a whole world of recollections, which I should be apt to lose were I to change it."

"Some of them, Barsfield, it appears to me that you should prefer to lose. The insult of old Mellichampe, for example."

"I revenged it!" was the reply, quickly and gloomily uttered. "I revenged it in his blood, and the debt is paid."

"But the son? did you not, only now, complain of him also? did he not call you——"

"Tory! I'll finish the sentence for you, as I would rather, if the word is to be repeated in my ears, have the utterance to myself. You are an Englishman, and the name does not, and can not be made to apply to you here, and you can not understand, therefore, the force of its application from one American to another! He called me a tory! denounced, defied, and struck at me, and I would have slain him—ay, even in the halls which are henceforward to call me master—but that I was held back by others, whose prudence, perhaps, saved the lives of both of us; for the strife would have been pell-mell, and that fellow Witherspoon, who was the overseer of old Mellichampe, had a drawn knife ready over my shoulder, at the moment that mine was lifted at the breast of the insolent youngster. But this is a long story, and you already know it.

I have been revenged on the father, and have my debt against the son. That shall be cancelled also, in due course of time."

"And where is the youngster now, Barsfield? Have you any knowledge of his movements?"

"None. His mother has fled to the Santee, where she is sheltered by Watson. But of the son I know nothing. He is not with her, that's certain; for Evans, whom I sent off in that direction as a sort of scout and watch over her, reports that he has not yet made his appearance."

"He must be out with Marion, then?" was the suggestion of the other.

"We shall soon see that, for our loyalists are all ready and earnest for a drive after the 'fox;' and it will be a close swamp that will keep him away from hunters such as ours. These arms will provide two hundred of them, and we have full that number ready to volunteer. In a week more I hope to give a good account of his den, and all in it."

While this dialogue was going on, the speakers continued to approach the spot where Thumbscrew lay in hiding. It was not long, as they drew nigh, before he distinguished the person of Barsfield, and a fierce emotion kindled in his eye as he looked out from his shelter upon the advancing figure of the successful tory. His whole frame seemed agitated with the quickening rush of the warm blood through his veins—his teeth were gnashed for a moment fiercely, and, freeing a way through the bushes for his rifle-muzzle, in the first gush of his excited feelings, he lifted the deadly weapon to his eye, brought back the cock with the utmost precaution, avoiding any unnecessary click, and prepared to plant the fatal bullet in the head of the unconscious victim. But the tory rode by unharmed. A gentler, or, at least, a more prudent feeling, got the better of the woodman's momentary mood of passion; and, letting the weapon fall quietly into the hollow of his arm, he muttered in a low tone to himself—

"Not yet, not yet—let him pass—let him git on as he can. It ain't time yet—he must have a little more swing for it before I bring him, for 'tain't God's pleasure that I should drop him now. I don't feel like it, and so I know it can't be right. It's a cold-blooded thing, and looks too much like murder; and, God help me, it ain't come to that yet, for Jack Witherspoon to take it out of his enemy's hide without giving him fair play for it. Let him go — let him go. Ride on, Barsfield; the bullet's to be run yet that bothers you."

And, thus muttering to himself, the woodman beheld his victim pass by him in safety, his troop and wagons following. He was about to turn away and seek his comrade in the wood, when he saw his travelling acquaintance, Blonay, emerge from the opposite quarter, and place himself before the British officers. This movement at once satisfied the doubts of Thumbscrew as to the politics of the low-countryman.

"As I thought," said he to himself, "the fellow's a skunk, and a monstrous sly one. He knows how to badger, and can beat the bush like a true scout. It's a God's pity that a fellow that has good qualities like that, shouldn't have soul enough to be an honest man. But no matter — pay-day will come for all; and Truth will have to wait in the swamp till Cunning can go help her out."

Thus moralizing, the woodman went back from his hiding-place, and soon joined his now impatient companion.

Blonay, in the meanwhile, had made the acquaintance of the British party. Confirmed by their uniform, he boldly advanced, and presented himself before the captain.

"Who the devil are you?" was the uncourteous salutation.

A grin and a bow, with a few mumbled words, was the sort of reply manifested by the half-breed, who followed up this overture by the presentation of the passport furnished by Proctor. Barsfield read the scroll, and threw it back to him.

"And so you are going our way, I see by your paper. It is well — you will prefer, then, falling in with us, and taking our protection?"

Blonay bowed assent, and muttered his acknowledgments.

"And, perhaps," continued the tory captain, "as you are a true friend to his majesty's cause, you will not object to a drive into the swamps along with us after these men of Marion, who are thought to be lurking about here?"

The half-breed gave his ready assurance of a perfect willingness to do so.

"Well said, my friend; and now tell us, Mr. Blonay, what have been your adventures upon the road? What have you seen deserving of attention since you came into this neighborhood?"

The person addressed did not fail to relate all the particulars of his meeting, but a little before, with the woodman, as the reader has already witnessed it. Barsfield listened with some show of attention, and only interrupted the narrator to ask for a description of the stranger's person. This was given, and had the effect of producing an expression of earnest thought in the countenance of the listener.

"Very large, you say—broad about the shoulders? And you say he went into this wood?"

"Off there, cappin, close on to them bays, and in them bushes?"

Barsfield looked over into the thick-set and seemingly impervious forest, and saw at a glance how doubtful and difficult would be the pursuit, in such a place, even were the object important, of a single man. After a momentary pause of action and speech, he gave orders suddenly to move on in the path they were pursuing. Taking the direction of his finger, Blonay fell behind, and was soon mingled in with the party that followed.

"You shall see, my fair neighbor," said the tory captain to his companion, when the party resumed its progress, as if in continuation of the previous discourse; "she is as beautiful and young, Clayton, as she is pure and intellectual. She is the prize, dearer and richer than all of my previous attainment, for which I would freely sacrifice them all. You shall see her, and swear to what I have said."

"You will make her your own soon, then, I imagine," said the other, "esteeming her so highly."

"If I can—be sure of it," responded Barsfield. "I will try devilish hard for it, I assure you; and it will be devilish hard, indeed, if, with a fine plantation, and no little power—with a person which, though not superb, is at least passable"

—and the speaker looked down upon his own bulky frame with some complacency—" it will be devilish hard, I say, if I do not try successfully. Her old father, too, will back me to the utmost, for he is devilish scary, and, being a good loyalist, is very anxious to have a son-in-law who can protect his cattle from the men of Marion. They have half frightened him already into consent, and have thus done me much more service than they ever intended."

"But your maiden herself, the party chiefly concerned?" said Clayton, inquiringly.

"She fights shy, and does not seem over-earnest to listen to my courtier speeches; but she is neither stern nor unapproachable, and, when she replies to me, it is always gently and sweetly."

"Then she is safe, be sure of it," was the sanguine response of the other.

"Not so," said the more sagacious Barsfield, "not so. I am not so well satisfied that because she is gentle she will be yielding. She can not be otherwise than gentle — she can not speak otherwise than sweetly, even though her words be those of denial. I would rather a cursed sight that she should wince a little, and tremble when I talk to her; for then I should know that she was moved with an interest one way or the other. Your cool, composed sort of woman, is not to be surprised into any foolish weakness. They must listen long, and like to listen, before you can do anything with them. But you shall see her soon, for here her father's fields commence. A fine clearing, you see, and the old buck is tolerably well off — works some eighty hands, and has a stock that would fit out a dozen Scotch graziers."

Thus discussing the hopes and expectations which make the aim and being of the dissolute adventurer, they pricked their way onward with all speed, to the dwelling of those who were to be the anticipated victims.

CHAPTER VI.

THE PLOT THICKENS.

Slowly, and with an expression of sorrow in his countenance, corresponding with the unelastic and measured movement of his body, Thumbscrew took his way back to the hollow where he had left his more youthful companion.

"Well, what have you seen to keep you so long, Thumbscrew?" was the impatient inquiry of the youth. The answer of the woodman to this interrogatory was hesitatingly uttered, and he first deliberately told of his encounter with Blonay, and the nature of the unsatisfactory dialogue which had taken place between them. He dwelt upon the cunning with which the other had kept his secret during the conference; "but I found him out at last," said he, "and now I knows him to be a skunk — a reg'lar built tory, as I mought ha' known from the first moment I laid eyes on him."

"Well — and where is he now, and how did you discover this?" was the inquiry of the other.

This inquiry necessarily unfolded the intelligence concerning the troop of horse, whose number, wagons, and equipments, he gave with all the circumspectness and fidelity of an able scout; and this done, he was silent; with the air, however, of one who has yet something to unfold.

"But who commanded them, Thumbscrew?" asked the other, "and what appeared to be their object? You are strangely limited in your intelligence, and, at this rate, will hardly justify the eulogy of Major Singleton, who considers you the very best scout in the brigade. Can you tell us nothing more? What sort of captain had they?"

"A stout fellow, quite as broad, but not so tall as me, with a skin brown, like mine, as a berry; a hook nose, and a mouth more like the chop of a broad-axe than anything else."

He paused, and the eyes of the scout and those of his young comrade met. There was a quickening apprehension of the truth in those of Mellichampe, which made them kindle with successive flashes, while his mouth, partaking of the same influence, quivered convulsively, as, bending forward to his more sedate companion, he demanded, with a stern, brief manner—

"You are not speaking of Barsfield, surely?"

"I am — that's the critter, or I'm no Christian."

The youth seized his rifle as he replied — "And you shot him not down! you suffered him to pass you in safety! my father's blood yet upon his hands — unavenged — and he going now, doubtless, to reap the reward of his crime and perfidy! But he can not have gone far. He must be yet within reach, and, by the Eternal! he shall not escape me now. Hold me not back, Thumbscrew — hold me not back! I deem you no friend of mine that suffered the wretch to pass on in safety, and I shall deem you still less my friend if you labor to restrain me now. Hold me not, I tell you, Witherspoon, or it will be worse for you."

The youth, as he spoke, leaped upon his feet in a convulsion of passion, that seemed to set at defiance all restraint. His eyes, that before had sent forth only irregular flashes of light and impulse, were now fixed in a steady, unmitigated flame, that underwent no change. Not so his lips, which quivered and paled more fitfully than ever. He strove earnestly with his strong-limbed comrade, who had grasped him firmly with the first ebullition of that passion which he seemed to have anticipated.

"What would you do, Airnest? don't be foolish now, I beg you; running your head agin a pine knot that you can't swallow. It's all foolishness to go on so, and can do no good. As to shooting that skunk, I couldn't and wouldn't do it, though I had the muzzle up, and it was a sore temptation, Airnest; for I remembered the old man, and his white hair, and it stood before my eyes jist like a picture, as I seed it last when it was thickened together with his own blood."

"Yet you could remember all this, and suffer his murderer to escape?" reiterated the other.

"Yes! for it goes agin the natur of an honest man to bite a man with cold bullet, when the t'other a'n't on his guard agin it. I'll take a shot any day with Barsfield, man to man, or where a fight's going on with a hundred, but, by dogs! I can't lie at the roadside, under a sapling, and send a bullet at him onawares, as he's riding down the trace. It's an Injen'way, and it's jist as bad as any murder I've ever hearn tell of their doing. No, no, Airnest; there's a time coming! as I may say, the day of judging them's at hand; for here, you see, is this chap, going down now, snug and easy, with a small handful of troops, to take possession of Kaddipah. Let him set down quietly till the 'fox' gets up his men, and I'll lay you what you please we git our satisfaction out of him by fair fight. We'll smoke him out of his hole 'fore Sunday next, if I'm not monstrous wide in my calkilation."

"And where is the difference between shooting him now and shooting him then? I see none. Release me, Mr. Witherspoon," cried the other, his anger now beginning to turn upon the tenacious Thumbscrew, who held upon his body with a grasp that set at defiance all his efforts. In the next moment he was released, as he had desired, and, with a deference of manner, a subdued and even sadder visage, the countryman addressed the youth:—

"You're gitting into a mighty passion, Airnest, and, what's worse, you're gitting in a passion with me, that was your friend and your father's friend, ever since I know'd you both, though, to be sure, I never could do much for either of you in the way of friendship."

"I am not angry with you, Witherspoon; only, I am no child, to be restrained after this fashion. I know you are my friend, and God knows I have too few now to desire the loss of any one of them—and particularly of one who, like yourself, has clung to me in all trials; but there is a certain boundary beyond which one's best friend has no right to go."

" Oh, yes! I understand all that, Airnest. I'm your friend so long as I don't think or act contrary to your thinking and acting. Now, to my thinking, that's a bargain that will only answer for one side, and I never yet made a bargain in my life under them sort of tarms. If I sells a horse or buys one, I does it because I thinks there'll be some sort of benefit or gain to myself. I don't want to take ondue advantage of the other man, but I expects to git as good as I gives. That's the trade for me; whether it be a horse that I trades, or my good word and the heart, rough or gentle, all the same, that I bring to barter with my friend. When I makes sich a trade, I can't stand and see the man I trade with making light of the article I gives him. If it's my friendship and good word, he mustn't make them a sort of plaything, to sport which way he pleases; and, so long as I say I'm his friend, he sha'n't butt a tree if I can keep his head from it, though I have to take main force to hold him in. On them same tarms, Airnest, I stood by the old 'squire, your father, when he got into difficulties about the line of his land with Hitchingham; when the two got all their friends together, and *fout*, as one may say, like so many tiger-cats, along the rice-dam, for two long hours by sun. You've hearn tell of that excursion, I'm thinking. That was a hard brush, and I didn't skulk like a skunk then, as they will all tell you that seed it. But that worn't the only time; there was others, more than a dozen beside that, and all jist as tough, when Thumbscrew hung on to the 'squire, as if he was two other legs and arms of the same body, and nobody could touch the one without touching the other. Then came that scrape with Barsfield; and now I tell you, Airnest, it worn't a murder, as you calls it, but a fair fight, for both the parties was fairly out; and, though the old 'squire, your father, was surprised, and not on his proper guard, yet it was a fair-play fight, and sich as comes about, as I may say, naturally, in all our skrimmages with the tories. They licked us soundly, to be sure, 'cause they had the most men; but we fout 'em to the last, and 'twas a fair fight from the jump."

"And what of all this, now — why do you repeat this to me here?" said the other, with no little imperiousness.

"Why, you see, only to show you, Airnest, as a sort of excuse and apology for what I did in trying to keep you from going after Barsfield —"

"Apology, Witherspoon!" exclaimed the other.

"Yes, Airnest, apology — that's the very word I makes use of. I jist wanted to show you the reason why I tuk the liberty of trying to keep an old friend's son out of harm's way, that's all. I promise you, Airnest, I won't make you angry agin, though I don't see yet the harm of liking a body so much as to do the best for 'em."

The woodman turned away as he spoke, lifted his rifle, and seemed busy in rubbing the stock of it with the sleeve of his hunting-shirt. The youth seemed touched by this simple exhortation. Without a word he approached his unsophisticated companion, whose face was turned from him, and placing his hand affectionately, with a gentle pressure, upon his shoulder, thus addressed him :—

"Forgive me, Jack — I was wrong. Forgive me, and forget it. I am rash, foolish, obstinate — it's my fault, I know, to be so, and I try to control my disposition, always, when I'm with you. You know I would'nt hurt your feelings for the world. I know you love me, Jack, as if I were your own brother; and believe me, my old friend — my father's friend — believe me, I love you fully as much. Say, now, that you forgive me — do say!"

"Dang my eyes! Airnest, but, by the powers! you put it to me too hard sometimes. Jist when I'm doing the best, or trying to do the best, you plump head over heels into my teeth, and I'm forced to swallow my own doings. It a'n't right — it a'n't kind of you, Airnest; and, dang it, boy, I don't see why I should keep trying to do for you, to git no thanks, and little better than curses for it. I'm sure I gits nothing by sticking to you through thick and thin."

Half relenting, and prefacing his yielding mood only by this outward coating of obduracy, the woodman thus received the overtures of his companion, who was as ready to melt with generous emotion as he was to seek for strife under a fierce and impetuous one. The youth half turned away as the latter reply met his ears, and, removing his hand from the shoulder where it had rested, with a freezing tone and proud manner, he replied, while appearing to withdraw—

"It is indeed time, Mr. Witherspoon, that company should part, when one reproaches the other with his poverty. You certainly have said truly, that you have nothing to gain by clinging to me and mine."

"Oh, Airnest, boy—but that's too much," he cried, leaping round and seizing the youth's hands, while he pressed his eyes, now freely suffused, down upon them. "I didn't mean that, Airnest, I'm all over foolish to-day, and done nothing but harm. It was so from morning's first jump; I've been fooling and blundering like a squalling hen in an old woman's cupboard. Push me on one side, I'm sure to plump clear to the other end, break all the cups and dishes, and fly in the old wife's face, before I can git out. It's your turn to forgive me, Airnest, and don't say that we must cut each other. God help me, Airnest, if I was to dream of sich a thing, I'm sure your father's sperrit would haunt me, with his white hair sticking all fast with blood, and—"

"No more, Jack, old fellow, let us talk no more of that, but sit down here, and say what we are to do now about that reptile, Barsfield."

"Bless you, Airnest, what can we do till the 'fox' whistles? We'll have news for him to-morrow, and must only see where Barsfield goes to-night, and larn what we can of what he's going to do. I suspect that them wagons have got a plenty of guns and bagnets, shot and powder for the tories; and if so, there'll be a gathering of them mighty soon in this neighborhood. We shall see some of the boys to-morrow—Humphries and 'Roaring Dick' ride on this range, and we may hear their whistle in the 'Bear Brake' before morning."

"We must meet them there, then, one or other of us certainly. In the meantime, as you say, we must trail this Barsfield closely, and look where he sleeps, since you will not let me shoot him."

"And where's the use? I could ha' put the bullet through his skull to-day, but the next moment the dragoons would have made small work of a large man. They'd ha' chopped me into mince-meat. There's no difficulty in killing one, but small chance to git away after it, when there's so many of them upon you; and, as I said afore, this shooting a man from the bush onawares, when he's travelling in quiet, looks too much like cold-blooded Ingin murder. It's like scalping and tomahawk. Give the enemy a fair field, says I, though it be but a bow-legged nigger that's running from you in the swamp."

And, thus conferring, the two followed the route pursued by Barsfield and his party, until the shades of evening gathered heavily around them.

CHAPTER VII.

PINEY GROVE.

The British troopers, meanwhile, pursued their journey. With an humility that knew its place, Blonay followed with the hindmost, and showed no annoyance. though exposed to the continual and coarse jests of those about him. He was becomingly indifferent, as he seemed perfectly insensible. The termination of the day's journey was at length at hand. The zigzag fences rose upon both sides of the road. The negro settlement, some thirty or forty log-dwellings, forming a square to themselves, and each with its little enclosure, well stocked with pigs, poultry, and the like, came in sight; and beyond, the eager eye of Barsfield distinguished, while his hand pointed out to his companion, the fine old avenue, long, overgrown, and beautifully winding, which led to the mansion-house of the Berkeley family.

"There," said he, "is 'Piney Grove'—such is the name of the estate; a name which it properly takes from the avenue which leads to it, the chief growth of which, as you will see, is the field-pine. You will not see many like it in the country."

The troop halted at the entrance, which was soon thrown open; and, narrowing the form of their advance, they were in a moment after hurrying along the shady passage which led to the hospitable dwelling. Barsfield had said rightly to his companion: there were not many avenues in the country like that which they now pursued. A beautiful and popular feature, generally, in all the old country-estates of Carolina, the avenue in question was yet of peculiar design. In the lower regions, where the spreading and ponderous live-oak presents itself vigorously and freely, and seems by its magnificence and shade expressly intended for such a purpose, no other sort of tree can well be employed. Here, however, in the region which we now tread, wanting in that patriarchal tree, the field-pine had been chosen as the substitute, and nothing surely could have been more truly beautiful than the one in question. A waving and double line, carried on in sweeping and curious windings for two thirds of a mile, described by these trim and tidy trees, enclosed the party, and formed a barrier on either hand, over which no obtrusive vine or misplaced scion of some foreign stock was ever permitted to gad or wander. Some idea may be formed of the pains and care which had been taken in thus bending the free forests in subservience to the will of man, when we know that, though naturally a hardy tree of the most vigorous growth, the pine is yet not readily transplanted with success, and is so exceedingly sensitive in a strange place, as in half the number of instances to perish from such a transfer. A narrow but deep ditch formed an inner parallel line with the high trees along the avenue; and the earth, thus thrown up into a bank beneath the trees, gave ample room and nutriment to a crowded hedge of greenbrier and gathering vines, interspersed, during a long season, with a thousand various and beautiful flowers.

Emerging from the avenue, the vista opened upon a lovely park, which spread away upon either hand, and was tastefully sprinkled here and there, singly and in groups, with a fine collection of massive and commanding water-oaks, from around the base of which everything in the guise of shrubbery and undergrowth, the thick, long grass excepted, had been carefully pruned away. A few young horses were permitted to ramble about and crop the verdure on one side of the entrance, while on the other a little knot of ruminating milch-cows, to which a like privilege had been given, started up in alarm, and fled at the approach of strangers so numerous and so gorgeously arrayed. Throwing aside the heavy, swinging gate before them, the troopers passed through a trace leading forward directly to the dwelling. On either side of this passage a fence of light scantling, which had once been whitewashed, proved a barrier against any trespass of the cattle upon a province not their own.

The dwelling of Mr. Berkeley lay centrally before this passage, and at a little distance in the rear of the park. It was an ancient mansion, of huge and clumsy brick, square and heavy in its design, though evidently well constructed. It was built about the time of the Yemassee war, after the fashion of that period, and was meant to answer the purposes of a fortress against the savage, not less than a dwelling for the civilized man. On one occasion the Edistohs had besieged it with a force of nearly two hundred warriors; but the stout planter who held it at the time, old Marmaduke Berkeley, with the aid of his neighbors, and a few trusty Irish workmen, who had been employed upon the estate, made a sturdy defence, until the friendly Indians, who were the allies of the whites, and, consequently, foes to the Edistohs, came to their relief, and beat off the invaders. The external aspect of the edifice bore sufficient testimony of its antiquity. The bricks were dark and mouldy in appearance, and the walls in several places had begun to crumble and crack beneath their own cumbrousness. Clambering parasites on the northern side had run at liberty over its surface, still holding on, even in corresponding ruin, when half withered and sapless themselves. Little tufts of dank moss protruded here and there from dusty apertures; and a close eye might even find an insidious and lurking decay thriving fast in the yielding frame which sustained this or that creaking shutter. The mansion attested, not merely its own, but the decline of its proprietor. A man of energy, character, and due reflection, would have found little difficulty in maintaining a resolute and successful defence against the bold assault of the tempest, or the insidious gnawings and sappings of time. The present owner, unhappily, was not this sort of man. He was prematurely old, as he had been constitutionally timid and habitually nervous. His life, so far, had passed in a feverish and trembling indecision, which defeated all steady thought and prompt action. He was one of those who, having the essentials of manhood, has yet always been a child. He had tottered through life with no confidence in his arms, and as if his legs had been crutches, borrowed from a neighboring tree, rather than limbs of a native growth, and destined to the performance of his will. Gladly, at all times, would he prefer to lean upon the shoulders of his neighbor rather than trust independently to his own thews and sinews. In politics he could be none other than the truckler to the existing authority, having preferences, however, which he dared not speak, vacillating between extremes, temporizing with every party, yet buffeted by all.

The appearance of the troop brought the old gentleman down his steps to receive them. Barsfield only advanced, leaving Clayton to quarter the troop on the edge and within the enclosure of the park. Mr. Berkeley's manner was courteous and cordial enough, but marked by trepidation. His welcome, however, was unconstrained, and seemed habitual. Like the major part of the class of which he was a member, the duties of hospitality never suffered neglect at his hands. Like them, he delighted in society, and was at all times ready and pleased at the appearance of a guest. Nor did the perilous nature of events at the period of which we write, his own timidity, and the doubtful character of the new-comer, tend, in any great degree, to chill the freedom and check the tendency of his habit in this respect. Accustomed always to wealth and influence, to the familiar association with strangers, and to a free intercourse with a once thickly-settled and pleasant neighborhood, a frank, open-hearted demeanor became as much his characteristic as his jealous apprehensions. This was also his misfortune, since, without doubt, it increased the natural dependence of his mind. The habit of giving a due consideration to the claims of others, though a good one, doubtless, has yet its limits, which to pass, though for a moment only, is to stimulate injustice, and to encourage the growth of a tyranny to our own injury. In his connection with those around him, and at the period of which we write, when laws were nominal, and were administered only at the caprice of power, the virtue of Mr. Berkeley became a weakness; and he was accordingly preyed upon by the profligate, and defied by the daring—compelled to be silent under wrong, or, if he resented it, only provoking thereby its frequent repetition. His mild blue eye spoke his feelings; his nervousness amply announced his own consciousness of imbecility; while his pale cheek and prematurely white hair told of afflictions deeply felt, and of vexing and frequent strifes, injuries, and discontent.

On the present occasion he received his guest with a kindly air of welcome, which was most probably sincere. He was quite too feeble not to be glad of the presence of those who could afford him protection; and there was no little truth in the boast of the tory captain to his companion, when he said that the timidity of Berkeley would be one of the probable influences which might facilitate his progress in the courtship of his daughter. The manner of Barsfield was influenced somewhat by his knowledge of the weakness of Mr. Berkeley, not less than by his own habitual audacity. He met the old gentleman with an air of ancient intimacy, grasped the proffered hand with a hearty and confident action, and, in tones rather louder than ordinary, congratulated him upon his health and good looks.

"I have not waited, you see, Mr. Berkeley, for an invitation. I have ridden in and taken possession without a word, as if I was perfectly assured that no visiter could be more certainly welcome to a good loyalist like yourself, than one who was in arms for his majesty."

"None, sir—none, Captain Barsfield—you do me nothing more than justice. You are welcome—his majesty's officers and troops are always welcome to my poor dwelling," was the reply of the old man, uttered without restraint, and seemingly with cordiality; and yet, a close observer might have seen that there was an air of abstraction indicative of a wandering and dissatisfied mood, in the disturbed and changing expression of his features. A few moments elapsed, which they employed in mutual inquiries, when Lieutenant Clayton, having bestowed his men, their baggage, and wagons, agreeably to the directions given him, now joined them upon the steps of the dwelling, and was introduced by Barsfield, in character, to his host. Clayton reported to his captain what he had done with the troop, their disposition, and the general plan of their arrangement, in obedience to orders; turning to Mr. Berkeley at the conclusion, and politely apologizing for the unavoidable disturbance which such an arrangement must necessarily occasion in his grounds. The old man smiled faintly, and murmured out words of approbation; but, though he strove to be and to appear satisfied, he was evidently ill at ease. The invasion of his beautiful park by a prancing and wheeling troop of horse — its quiet broken by the oaths, the clamor, and the confusion common to turbulent soldiers, and the utter dispersion of his fine young horses, which had leaped the barrier in their fright, and were now flying in all directions over the plantation, brought to his bosom no small pang, as they spoke strongly for the extent of his submission. He controlled his dissatisfaction, however, as well as he could, and now urged his guests, with frequent entreaties, to enter his mansion for refreshment. They followed him from the piazza into a large hall, such as might have answered the purposes of a room of state, calculated for the deliberations of a thousand men. It was thus that our ancestors built, as it were, with a standard drawn from the spacious wilds and woods around them. They seemed also to have built for posterity. Huge beams, unenclosed, ran along above, supporting the upper chambers, which were huge enough to sustain the weight of a palace. The walls were covered with the dark and durable cypress, wrought in panels, which gave a rich, artist-like air to the apartment. Two huge fireplaces at opposite ends of the hall attested its great size, in one of which, even in the month of September, a few broken brands might be seen still burning upon the hearth. A dozen faded family pictures, in massive black frames, hung around — quaint, rigid, puritanical faces, seemingly cut out of board, after the fashion of Sir Peter Lely, with glaring Flemish drapery, and that vulgar style of coloring which makes of red and yellow primary principles, from the contagion of which neither land, sea, nor sky, is suffered in any climate to be properly exempt, The furniture was heavy and massive like the rest — suitable to the apartment, and solid, like the dwellings and desires of the people of the bygone days.

Seats were drawn, the troopers at ease, and the good old

Madeira of the planter soon made its appearance, to which they did ample justice. The generous liquor soon produced freedom of discourse; and, after a few courteous and usual overtures, consisting of mutual inquiries after the health of the several parties present, their relations, friends, and so forth, the conversation grew more general, and, perhaps, more important, as it touched upon the condition of the country.

"You have quiet now, Mr. Berkeley," said Barsfield. "The rousing defeats which the rebels have recently sustained have pretty well done them up on every side. The game is very nigh over, and we shall soon have little else to do than gather up the winnings. The drubbing which Cornwallis gave that conceited fellow, Gates, and the surprise of Sumter, both events so complete and conclusive, will go very far toward bringing the country back to its loyalty."

"God grant it, sir," was the ardent response of Mr. Berkeley, "for we shall then have peace. These have been four miserable years to the country, since the beginning of this war. Neighbor against neighbor, friend against friend, and sometimes even brother arming and going out to battle with his brother. It has been an awful time, and Heaven grant, sir, it may be as you say. Heaven restore us the quiet and the peace which have been for so long strangers in the land."

"You shall have it, sir, I promise you, after this; though I should think, by this time, you have been perfectly freed from the incursions of that skulking fellow, Marion. The report is that he has disbanded his men, and has fled into North Carolina. If so, I shall have little use for mine; and these arms which I have brought for distribution among your loyal neighbors, will scarcely be necessary to them. Have you any intelligence on this subject, Mr. Berkeley?"

"No, sir—no, none! I am not in the way, Captain Barsfield, of hearing intelligence of this nature. I know nothing of the movements of either party."

This reply was uttered with some little trepidation; and, as the old gentleman spoke, he looked apprehensively around the apartment, as if he dreaded to see the redoubtable "swamp fox" and all his crew, "Roaring Dick," "Thumbscrew," and the rest, fast gathering at his elbow. Barsfield smiled at the movement, and crossing one leg over another, and slapping his thigh with an air of unmitigated self-complaisance as he spoke, he thus replied, rather to the look and manner than the language of his host:—

"Well, sir, I hope soon to rid you of any apprehensions on the subject of that marauding rebel. I am about to become your near neighbor, Mr. Berkeley."

The old gentleman bowed in token of his satisfaction at the intelligence. Barsfield continued—

"You have heard, doubtlessly, that I am now the proprietor of the noble estate of 'Kaddipah,' formerly the seat of Max Mellichampe, and confiscated to his majesty's uses on account of that arch-traitor's defection. Having had the good fortune to slay the rebel with my own hand, his majesty has been pleased to bestow upon me the estate which he so justly forfeited."

There was some emotion of an equivocal sort visible in the countenance of Berkeley, as he listened to this communication. A shade of melancholy overspread his face, as if some painful memory had suddenly grown active; and a slight suffusion of his eyelashes was not entirely undistinguished by his guests. Struggling with his feelings, however, whatever may have been their source, the old man recovered himself sufficiently to reply, though in a thick voice, which left his language but half intelligible.

"Yes—yes, sir—I did hear—I'm glad, sir—I shall be happy—"

And here he paused in the imperfect speech which Barsfield did not leave him time to finish.

"There will be nothing then, sir, that any of us will have to fear from these outliers in the swamps; when that takes place, 'Kaddipah,' sir, so long as the war continues, will be a place of defence, sufficiently well-guarded as a post to resist any present force of Marion; and, as I shall have charge of it, I think it safe to say, from what they know of me, they will not often venture even within scouting distance. Talking of scouts, now, Clayton, where's the fellow we picked up to-day, having a pass from Proctor? He looks as if he would make an admirable one. If his eyes only see as far as they seem willing to go, he is certainly a very valuable acquisition.

A distinct hem from another quarter of the hall attracted all eyes in that direction, and there, squat upon the hearth of one of the fireplaces, sat the form of Blonay. He had piled the dismembered brands together, and sat enjoying the fire, unperceived and certainly unenvied. At what time he had so secretly effected his entrance, was utterly unknown to any of the party. Barsfield started as he beheld him, and, seeming to forget his host, hastily addressed him:—

"Why, how now, fellow? you seem to make yourself at home. Why are you here? why did you not remain with the troop?"

"Why, cause I an't one of them, you see, cappin, and they all pokes fun at me."

The simplicity of this reply disarmed Barsfield of his anger, and his presence gave him a new subject upon which to enjoy himself. The half-breed was now made to undergo another examination, conducted by both the officers, who mingled freely with their inquiries sundry poor jests at his infirmity, all of which fell upon the seemingly sterile sense of the subject as if he had been so much marble. While thus engaged an inner door was thrown open, and the guests started involuntarily to their feet.

"My daughter, gentlemen, Miss Berkeley—my niece, Miss Duncan," were the words of the old man, uttered with an air of greater elevation than was his wont. The two ladies were provided with seats, and in the momentary silence which followed their first appearance, we may be permitted to take a passing glance at their persons. Our opinions may well be reserved for another chapter.

CHAPTER VIII.

JANET BERKELEY.

The appearance of Janet Berkeley fully justified the high encomium which Barsfield had passed upon her beauties; yet nothing could be more unassuming than her deportment — nothing more unimposing than her entire carriage. A quiet ease, a natural and seemingly effortless movement, placed her before you, and, like all perfect things, her loveliness was to be studied before it could be perceived. It did not affront you by an obtrusion of anything remarkable. Her features were all too much in unison with one another — too symmetrically unique, to strike abruptly; they seemed rather to fill and to absorb the mind of the spectator than to strike his eye.

Her person was rather small and slender: her features, though marked by health, were all soft and delicate. A pale, high forehead, from beneath which a pair of large black eyes flashed out a subdued, dewy, but rich, transparent light — a nose finely Grecian — cheeks rather too pale, perhaps, for expression — and a mouth which was sweetly small and delicately full — were the distinguishing features of her face. Her chin, though not prominent, did not retreat; and her neck was white and smoothly round, as if a nice artist had spent a life in working it to perfection. Her hair, which was long and dark, was gathered up and secured by a white fillet, without study, yet with a disposition of grace that seemed to denote the highest efforts of study. It was the art which concealed the art — the fine taste of the woman naturally employed in adorning the loveliest object in creation — herself. It was the fashion of the time to pile the hair in successive layers upon the crown, until it rose into a huge tower, Babel-like and toppling. Janet was superior to any such sacrifice of good sense and good taste, simply in compliance with a vulgar rage. Her long tresses, simply secured from annoyance, were left free to wander where they would about her neck, to the marble whiteness of which they proved an admirable foil; while the volume was so distributed about the head as to prevent that uncouth exhibition of its bulk in one quarter, which is too much the sin of taste in the sex generally. So admirably did the features, the dress, and the deportment, of Janet Berkeley blend in their proper effects together, that the dullest sense must have felt their united force, even though the eye might not have paused to dwell upon any one individual beauty. Her carriage denoted a consciousness of her own strength, which spoke forcibly in contrast with the equally obvious feebleness of her father's spirit. Perhaps, indeed, it was the imbecility and weakness of his which had given strength and character to hers. It is not uncommon for the good natural mind to exercise itself in those attributes which, in others, they perceive inactive and wanting to their owners. She had seen too many evil results from her father's indecision and imbecility, not to strive sternly in the attainment of the faculty in which he was so lamentably deficient; and she had not striven in vain. Though yet unenforced to open exercise and exhibition of its strength by controlling and overcoming dangers, the heart of Janet Berkeley was strong in her, and would not have been unprepared for their encounter. Her untroubled composure of glance, her equanimity of manner, her unshrinking address, and the singular ease with which, without tremor or hesitation, her parting lips gave way to the utterance of the language she might deem necessary to the occasion — were all so many proofs of that strength of soul which, associated as it was with all the grace and susceptibility of woman, made her a creature of moral, not less than of physical symmetry — the very ideal of a just conception of the noblest nature and the gentlest sex. The deportment of Mr. Berkeley was unconsciously elevated as he surveyed hers: such is the influence of the pure heart and perfect character. His pride grew lifted in the contemplation; and, timid and tame, and without a manly spirit, as he was, he felt that he could willingly die to serve and to preserve her.

"She is indeed a jewel, Barsfield!" said Clayton, in a whisper, aside to his superior; "she is a jewel — you are a lucky man."

"A goddess!" was the quick reply, in similar tones — "a goddess! — she will make Kaddipah a very heaven in my sight."

"Let it be a Christian heaven, then, I pray you, by dropping that abominable heathen name."

The other maiden, whom we have seen introduced as Miss Duncan, was an orphan, a niece of Mr. Berkeley, and for the present, residing with her cousin. She was pretty, and her eyes danced with a lively play of light, that spoke a gay heart and cloudless disposition. Perhaps, at the first glance, she would have been found more imposing than Janet; there was more to strike the eye in her features and deportment, as there was more inequality — more that was irregular — none of that perfect symmetry, which so harmonizes with the observer's glance and spirit, as not often to arrest, at first, his particular attention. A study of her face, however, would soon disenthral, though it would not offend, the observer. It wanted depth — profundity — character. At a glance you beheld its resources. There was nothing more to see; and you would turn away to her more quiet companion, and find at every look, in every passing shade of expression, every transition of mood, that there was more hidden than revealed — that the casket was rich within — that there was a treasure and a mystery, though it might demand a power of the purest and the highest to unlock its spells, and to remove the sacred seal that was upon it.

A few moments had elapsed after the entrance of the ladies, when a servant announced the supper to be in readiness, after the wholesome fashion of the country. A table was spread in an adjoining apartment, and now awaited the guests. Barsfield would have offered his arm to Janet, but she had already possessed herself of her father's. Lieutenant Clayton had already secured the company of Miss Duncan; and they were soon seated round the hospitable board. But where was Blonay— the despised—the deformed—the desolate? Miss Berkeley, presiding at the head of the table, remarked his absence, and her eye at once addressed her father.

"The other gentleman, father?" she said inquiringly.

"Gentleman, indeed!" was the exclamation of Barsfield, accompanied by a rude laugh, which was slightly echoed by his companions; "Gentleman, indeed! give yourself no manner of concern on his account, Miss Berkeley. He is some miserable overseer—a sand-lapper from Goose Creek, of whom we know nothing, except that Proctor, the commandant at Dorchester, has thought proper to give him a passport to go where he pleases."

"He is my father's guest, sir," was the dignified and rebuking reply; "and we can take no exception to his poverty, or his occupation, or the place from which he comes. We have not heretofore been accustomed to do so, and it would be far less than good policy now, when the vicissitudes of the times are such, that even a person such as you describe him to be may become not only our neighbor but our superior, to-morrow."

Mr. Berkeley started from his chair in some little confusion. He felt the truth of what his daughter said, yet he saw that her speech had touched Barsfield to the quick. The red spot was on the cheek of the tory, and his lips quivered for an instant.

"Janet is right, Captain Barsfield; the hospitality of Piney Grove must not be impeached. Its doors must be open to the poor as well as the rich; we can not discriminate between them:" and, so speaking, he hurried out to look after the half-breed. He had not far to look. To the great surprise of the old man, he found Blonay a listener at the door of the apartment. He must have heard every syllable that had been spoken. He had been practising after his Indian nature, and was not sensible of any impropriety in the act. Revolting at the task before him, Mr. Berkeley, with as good a grace as possible, invited the scout into the apartment—an invitation accepted without scruple, and as soon as given; and he sidled into a seat, much to the annoyance of Barsfield, directly in front of him. This little occurrence did not take place without greatly disquieting the host. He saw that Barsfield felt the force of the sarcasm which his daughter had uttered, and he strove, by the most unwearied attentions on his own part, to do away with all unpleasant feelings on the part of the tory captain. Janet, however, exhibited no manner of change in her deportment. She did not seem conscious of any departure from prudence, as she certainly had been guilty of no departure from propriety; but, when she saw the indefatigable and humiliating industry, with which her father strove to conciliate a man whom she had good reason to despise as well as hate, the warm color stole into her cheeks with a flash-like indignation, and her upper lip took its expression from the bitter scorn in her bosom, and curled into very haughtiness as she surveyed the scene. The expression passed away in an instant, however; and when, a little more composed himself, Barsfield ventured to cast a sidelong glance at the maiden, and saw how subdued, how gentle, how utterly wanting in malignity, were her features, he dismissed from his mind the thought that what she had said, so directly applying as it did to himself — he having sprung from the dregs of the people, and such having been his fortunes — was intended for any such application.

The angry scowl with which the tory might have regarded the maiden, was turned, however, upon the half-breed; who, as he beheld its threatening expression, would have been glad to have taken to his heels, and to have hidden his disquiet in the surrounding woods. But the kind look of Janet reassured him, and he turned his frightful and blear eyes in no other direction. His mind, probably for the first time, seemed to take in a new sentiment of the loveliness of virtue. Though blear-eyed, he was not blind; and, as she did not seem to behold his deformity, he was able to examine her beauty. In morals, the German theory of the senses is more than half right. The odor and the color are in us, rather than in the objects of our survey; and yet, unless acted upon by external influences, the latent capacity might never expand into energy and consciousness. To bring out this capacity is the office of education, and this art had never so far acted upon the half-breed, as to show him how much there was of a good nature dormant, and silent, and mingled up with the evil within him. His education, in a leading respect, was yet to begin.

CHAPTER IX.

OWLS ABROAD.

LET us back to the woods and their wild inhabitants. We have seen the success of the woodman in dissuading his young companion from the idle and rash demonstration which he sought to make upon the person of the tory captain. Prevented from any attempt upon the life of Barsfield, Mellichampe nevertheless determined upon watching his footsteps. In this design he was readily seconded by Witherspoon. This, indeed, was a duty with them both. They were then playing the part of scouts to Marion. Taking their way on foot, immediately after their enemies, they kept the cover of the forest, with the caution of experienced woodmen, venturing only now and then upon the skirts of the road, in such contiguity as to enable them to command a full view, for some distance on either hand, of everything that took place upon it. Familiar with the neighborhood, they availed themselves of each by-way and foot-path to shorten the distance; and thus, gaining ground at every step, they were readily and soon enabled to come in sight of the persons they pursued.

The fierce spirit of the youthful Mellichampe could scarcely be restrained by a wholesome prudence, while he saw, at moments, through the leaves, the person of his enemy. It was with no small increase of vexation, when they came in sight of Piney Grove, that he saw the troop of the tory turning into the avenue. Could he have listened to the dialogue between the tory captain and his lieutenant at this time, his fury would scarce have been restrainable. It would have been a far more difficult matter for his companion then to have kept him from his meditated rashness. A passing remark of

Thumbscrew, as the course of Barsfield grew obvious, seemed to add new fuel to the fire already burning in his bosom.

"So ho! he's for Piney Grove to-night! Well, Airnest, that knocks up your business. There's no gitting to see Miss Janet while Barsfield's there, I reckon."

"And why not?" was the fierce demand, "why not? I will see her to-night, by Heaven, though I die for it! I have promised her, and God help me, as I shall keep that and every promise that I have made, or shall ever make, to her! Do you think, Thumbscrew, that I fear this scoundrel? Do you think that I would not the rather go, if I thought that it was possible to encounter him alone? I have prayed for such a chance, and I would pray for it now, even were the odds more numerously against me."

"Don't be rash, Airnest — don't be headstrong and contrary, boy. It'll be mighty onwise and redic'lous for you to go to Piney Grove to-night, though you did make a promise: there's no use for it, and it's like going into the lion's den, as a body may say. Barsfield, you may be sure, will put out his sentries; and them tories, like the smallpox they have in Charleston now, are mighty catching. You can't go there with any chance of clearing the bush; and if that chap gets you in his gripe, it'll go monstrous hard with you. He knows you've got no reason to love him; and he's hearn, long ago, how you've sworn agin him; and he'd like nothing better now, do you see, than to set finger upon you. You can't think how pleasant it would make him feel to put a grape-vine round your neck: so you must keep quiet, and not think of seeing Miss Janet to-night."

"But I must and will think of it. I will see her at every hazard, and you need say nothing more on the subject, Thumbscrew, unless you change very greatly the burden of what you say. This caution — caution — caution — nothing but caution — is the dullest music; it sickens me to the soul. You are too careful of me by half, Thumbscrew; I can't move but you follow and counsel me — striving to guard me against a thousand dangers and difficulties which nobody ever dreams of but yourself."

"That's because I loves you, Airnest, much better than anybody else, and much better, when the truth's spoken, than you loves yourself," replied the woodman, affectionately putting his arms around the neck of his youthful companion: " I loves you, Airnest, and I watches you like an old hen that's got but one chicken left, and I clucks and scratches twice as much for that very reason. If there was a dozen to look after, now, the case would be different; I wouldn't make half the fuss that I make about the one: but, you see, when it so happens that the things a man's got to love gits fewer and smaller, they gits more valuable, Airnest, in his sight; for he knows mighty well, if he loses them, that he's jist like an old bird that comes back to the tree when the blossoms and the flowers have all dropped off, and are rotting under it. It's mighty nigh to winter in his heart then, Airnest—mighty nigh—and the sooner he begins to look out for a place to sleep in, the wiser man you may take him to be. But, Airnest, 'taint altogither that I loves you so that makes me agin your going to-night to see the gal——"

"Stop, Thumbscrew, if you please," were the words of interruption sternly uttered by the youth; "you will change your mode of speech in speaking of Miss Berkeley, and, when you refer to her in my hearing, you will please do so with becoming respect."

"Swounds, Airnest, don't I respect her? Don't you know that I respects her? Don't I love her, I ax you, a-most as much as I loves you? and wouldn't I do anything for you both, that wasn't a mean, cowardly thing? You know I doesn't mean to be disrespectful in what I says consarning her; and you mustn't talk so as if you thought I did. I says I'm agin your going to see her, or anybody at Piney Grove, not because it's you that's going, but because I wouldn't have anybody go, that b'longs to Marion's men, into the clutches of them there thieves and murderers. It'll be as much as your neck's worth to go there, for Barsfield is something of a soger, and will be sure to put out scouts and sentries all round the house. If he don't he's no better than a nigger, and desarves to be cashiered."

"Danger or no danger, Thumbscrew, I'll go to Piney Grove this night, as I have promised. You may spare yourself all farther exhortation. I keep my word, though death be in the way."

"Well, now, Airnest, that's what I call pervarsion and mere foolishness. She won't look for you, Airnest. She's a lady of sense and understanding, and won't so much as dream to see you after Barsfield's coming."

"Say no more," said the youth, decisively; "I will go. Let us now return to our horses, and you can then go on to Broom Hollow, where I'll meet you by midnight."

The youth turned away while speaking, and the woodman followed him, though slowly, and with looks of deepest concern.

"You wants to see her, Airnest, that's it; it ain't so much because you promised, as because you wants to keep your promise. Ah, Airnest, this love in young people—it ain't sensible, and I say it ain't strong and lasting. No love is strong and lasting if it ain't sensible. This what you has now is only a sulky autumn fever, Airnest; it'll burn like old vengeance for a month or so, and everybody that don't know anything about it might reckon it hot enough to set the woods a-fire; but it goes off monstrous quick after that, for you see it burns its substance all away, and then comes on the shaking ague, and it sticks to you, God only knows, there's no telling how long!"

The youth smiled, not less at the earnestness of his companion's manner, than at the grotesqueness of his comparisons. He contented himself as they pursued their way back to the cover which they had left, by insisting upon the superior nature of his affecton to that which he had described.

"Not so with me, Thumbscrew; I know myself too well; and, if I did not, I certainly know Janet too well ever to love her less than now, unless some change of which I dream not, and which I believe impossible—some strange change—shall come over both of us. But no more of this; let us see to our horses, and with the dark you can go on to Broom Hollow, where I will seek you as soon after I leave 'Piney Grove' as I can."

The woodman shook his head and muttered to himself, with an air not less of decision than of dissent. If his companion was fixed in his determination, Thumbscrew was not less resolved in his; but of this he said nothing. Quietly enough, and with the composure and intimacy of two relying friends, they sought out their retreat, behind which, some hundred yards, a close bay gave shelter to their horses—two noble animals, well caparisoned, which bounded away beneath them with a free step and a graceful movement, though the darkness already covered the highway, making the path doubtful, if not dangerous, in some places, to riders less experienced and bold than themselves. They retraced the ground which they had just left, and when they had reached the avenue leading to "Piney Grove," they sunk into the contiguous woods, and there Mellichampe, alighting, prepared himself for that visit to his mistress from which his comrade had so earnestly endeavored to dissuade him. Nor did he now forbear his solicitations to the same effect. He urged his objections more gently, yet with his former earnestness, only to meet with same stern decision.

"Well, now, Airnest," said the faithful woodman, "sence you're bent to go, like a wilful fox that's still got a tail worth docking, suppose you let me go along with you? You'd better, now; I can keep watch—"

"Pshaw! Thumbscrew, what nonsense! I need no watch, and certainly would not permit your presence at such a time. You know I go to meet with a lady."

"Swounds, Airnest! but she sha'n't see me."

"Why, man, of what do you speak? Would you have me guilty of a meanness, Thumbscrew?"

"Dang it, Airnest!" I see it's no use to talk. You're on your high horse to-day, and nobody can take you down. I'll leave you; but, Airnest, boy, keep a bright look-out, and stick to the bush close as a blind 'possum that's lame of a fore-paw. You're going among sharp woodmen, them same tories; and they'll give you a hard drive if they once sets foot on your trail. When do you say you'll come?"

"About midnight—but don't wait for me. Go to sleep, old fellow, for I know you need it."

"Good-by, Airnest! God bless you!"

"Good-by."

"And, Airnest—"

"What now, Thumby?"

"Keep snug, that's all, and don't burn daylight; that's to say, don't waste time. Good-by."

The youth, leaving his horse carefully concealed and fastened in a well-chosen spot, hurriedly plunged forward, into the woods with a precipitation seemingly intended to free him from the anxieties of his companion, who watched his progress for a few moments as he divided the bushes in his flight. Thumbscrew looked after him with all the concern of a parent in a time of trying emergency. He shook his head apprehensively, as, leading his own steed forth toward the highway, he seemed to prepare for his departure in the direction assigned him.

He had scarcely reached the road, however, when the approach of a driving horseman struck his senses and arrested his progress. The scout drew back instantly into the cover of the bush, and, placing himself in a position which would enable him to retreat at advantage, should the horseman prove other than he wished, he whistled thrice in a manner peculiar to the men of Marion. He was instantly answered in the same manner by the horseman who drew up his steed with the exchange of signals. Thumbscrew at once emerged from the copse, and was addressed by the stranger in a dialect adopted among the partisans for greater security. Thumbscrew replied by what would seem a question.

"Owls abroad?"

"Owls at home!" was the immediate response of the stranger, by which the calling in of the scouts to the main body was at once signified to his comrade. He continued, as they approached each other—

"What owl hoots?"

"Thumbscrew," was the reply of Witherspoon, giving the familiar name by which his companions generally knew him.

"Ah, Witherspoon," said the other, who proved to be Humphries, "is that you?"

"A piece of me — I ain't altogether myself, seeing that I ain't in a good humor quite."

"Well, stir up, for you're wanted. The boys have work on hand, and the 'fox' has got news of a tory gathering, so he's gone to drinking vinegar, and that's sign enough to show us that we must have a brush. Major Singleton has ordered in our squad, and looks out for a squall. So there's news for you."

"I reckon I've got quite as much, Humphries, to give you back for it in return. What would you say, now, if I tell you that Barsfield is here, within five hundred yards of us, with a smart company of red-jackets, and two big wagons of baggage?"

"No!"

"But I say yes!" and the scout then proceeded to inform his comrade of those matters in reference to Barsfield's arrival at Piney Grove with which the reader has already been made acquainted.

Humphries listened attentively, then exclaimed —

"I see it, Thumby; Barsfield is to meet these same tories, and probably take the lead of them. We heard from a boy that they were to gather, but he could not say who was to command 'em; and the general thought he could dash in among 'em before they could get arms and ammunition for a start. He'll have more work now than he thought for."

"Well, and where are you bent now, Humphries? a'n't you going back with this news, I tell you?"

"Yes, to be sure; but you must go in yourself at once. I am pushing on for Davis, and Baxter, and little Gwinn: they are all out on your line. We want all the muzzles we can muster. Where's Mister Mellichampe?"

The scout answered this question gloomily, as he told of the adventurous movement of the youth in visiting the "Piney Grove" while it was in the possession of the enemy, and of his own urgent entreaties to prevent it.

"It's an ugly risk he's taking," said Humphries; "but what can you do — you can't help it now?"

"Why, yes, I think I can," said the other, quickly. "I can't find it in my heart to leave the boy in the hand of them Philistines, and so, you see, Humphries, soon as I can hide my horse in the hollow, I'm going back after him. I won't let him see me, for he's mighty ticklish and passionate, and may get in a bad humor; but I can keep close on his skirts, and say nothing — only, if harm comes, I can lend him a helping hand, you see, when he don't look for it."

"Well, you've little time, and, soon as you let him know that he's wanted, you must both push off for the swamp. There's a branch broke across the road at 'My Lady's Fancy' — the butt-end points to the right track; and, on the same line, after you get into the bush, you'll see another broken branch just before you; go to the bush-end, and keep ahead — that'll lead you down to the first sentry, and that's M'Donald, I think. But the two branches a'n't thirty yards from each other; so that, if the one in the road should be changed by anybody, you'll only have to look round in the woods till you find the other."

Having given these directions, he stooped and whispered the camp password for the night in the ears of his attentive comrade: —

"Moultrie!"

Putting spurs to his steed, in another instant he had left the place of conference far behind him. Thumbscrew, then, returning to the wood, carefully placed his horse in hiding, and proceeded, according to the silent determination which he had made, upon the path taken by his young companion. He was soon in the thicket adjoining the plantation, and resolute to do his best to save the youth, over whom he kept a watch so paternal, from any of the evil consequences which he feared might follow from his rashness.

CHAPTER X.

THUNDER IN A CLEAR SKY.

At the hospitable board of Mr. Berkeley, to which we now return, the parties appear seated precisely as we left them. Their condition is not the same, however. They have done full justice, during our absence, to the repast, and to their own appetites, rendered more acute from their active travel of the day. The first rude demands of hunger had been satisfied; the urgent business of the table was fairly over; and nothing now remained to prevent the tory captain from playing the double part of social guest and earnest lover. His position might well have prompted him to an unwonted effort in the presence of one whose favor he sought to win. Not so, however. Barsfield, though bold and insolent enough with a rude troop and in the forest, was yet abashed in the presence of the beautiful and innocent Janet. He was one of those instances, so frequently to be met with, of a man possessed of energies of mind calculated to reach distinction, but wanting in that delicacy of feeling and demeanor, the result only of polished society, which alone can sustain him there unembarrassed and at ease. Too harsh in his habits to conciliate without an effort, he was, at the same time, too little familiar with the nice delicacies and acute sensibilities of the female heart to make the attempt with judgment; and we find him, accordingly, the well-dressed boor, in a strange circle, endeavoring to disguise his own consciousness of inadequacy by a dashing and forward demeanor, which had all the aspect of impertinence. He made sundry efforts to engage the maiden and her young companion in the toils of conversation, but proved far less successful than his second in command, who led the way in the suggestion of topics, caught up the falling ends of chit-chat, and, with all the adroitness of an old practitioner, knotted them together as fast as his superior, in his clumsy efforts to do likewise, tore them asunder.

Clayton was a lively, brisk, ready youth, not over well-informed, but with just sufficient reading and experience to while away a dull hour with a thoughtless maiden. Janet heard him with respect, but said little. Rose Duncan, however, had few restraints — certainly none like those restraining the former — and she chatted on with as thoughtless a spirit as if there had been no suffering in the land. Barsfield envied his lieutenant the immense gift of the gab which the latter possessed, and his envy grew into a feeling of bitter mortification, when every effort of his own to engage Janet in dialogue failed utterly, and, evidently, quite as often from his own inefficiency, as from the maiden's reluctance, to maintain it. A quiet "Yes" or "No" was the only response which she appeared to find necessary in answer to all his suggestions; and these, too, were uttered so coldly and so calmly, as to discourage the otherwise sanguine tory in the hope that maiden bashfulness alone, and not indifference, was the true cause of her taciturnity. The old man, her father, as he saw the anxiety of Barsfield to fix his daughter's attention, and, as he hoped to conciliate one having a useful influence, strove to second his efforts, by so directing the course of the conversation as to bring out the resources of the maiden; but even his efforts proved in a great degree unsuccessful. Her mind seemed not at home in all the scene, and exhibited but little sympathy with those around her. To those who looked closely, and could read so mysterious a language as that of a young maiden's eye, it might be seen that, in addition to her reluctance to converse with Barsfield, there was also a creeping fear in her bosom, which chilled and fevered all its elasticity. As the hour advanced, this feeling showed itself by occasional unquiet movements of her eye, which glanced its sweet fires fitfully around, as if in searching for some object which it yet dreaded to encounter.

This state of disquietude did not fail to strike the keen watchfulness of Barsfield, whose own imperfect success only made him the more jealously observant. Though unable to win the heart of a fair lady, he was yet not altogether incapable of perceiving its movements; and he soon discovered that, in addition to the dislike which Janet entertained for his pretensions, there was ground enough to imagine that she had far less aversion to those of another. He watched her the more closely from this reflection, and soon had assurance doubly sure on the subject of his conjecture.

In the meanwhile the supper things had undergone removal; the several persons of the party were dispersed about the room, the two ladies occupying the sofa, at one arm of which, and immediately beside Rose Duncan, sat Lieutenant Clayton, bending forward, and exchanging with her a free supply of chit-chat, sentimental and capricious. Barsfield, on the other hand, addressed his regards only to Janet, who sat, statue-like and pale, seemingly unmoved by all she heard, and with that air of abstraction and anxiety which shows the thought to be far distant. There was a dash of apprehension also in her air, such as the young fawn, skirting the roadside for the first time, might be supposed to exhibit, under the suggestion of its own timid spirit, rather than of any real danger from the approach of the hunter. This expression of countenance, however the maiden might labor for its concealment, was yet sufficiently evident to one so jealously aroused and suspicious as the tory captain; and he could not forbear, at length, as he found that all other topics failed to bring about a regular conversation with her, to insinuate his own doubts of that perfect composure of her mind which, in reply to his inquiry, her language had expressed, but which he did not think, at the same time, that she really entertained.

"Something surely has occurred to trouble you, Miss Berkeley — some unlucky disaster, no doubt? Your favorite nonpareil has broken bonds, perhaps — your mocking-bird has sung his last song before strangling himself between his wires — something equally, if not more sad, has fastened itself upon your spirits, and taken the wonted color from your cheeks. Let me sympathize with you in your misfortune, I pray you; let me know the extent and the cause of your affliction."

How bitterly ironical was the glance which accompanied this speech.

"Rather say," replied the laughing Rose, quickly and archly, as she beheld the annoyance which the words of the tory had brought to her cousin, "rather say that she dreads some danger to her favorite—that she has seen some threatening hawk hovering over her dovecot, and dreads momently that he will pounce upon the covey, and—"

"Rose! Rose Duncan!" hurriedly exclaimed Janet, with a most appealing glance of her eye, for she knew the playful character of her companion; "No more of this, Rose, I beg you. I am not in the humor for sport this evening. I beg that you will desist. I am not well."

"Oh, if you beg so prettily, and so humbly too, I have done, coz. I would not vex you for the world, particularly when you surrender so quietly at discretion. But, really, I have no other way to revenge myself for the sarcasms I am made to endure by Mr. Clayton; he is really so witty—so very excruciating."

She turned, as she spoke, with a full glance of her arch blue eye upon Clayton, and with an expression of face so comically sarcastic, that she even succeeded in diverting the glance of Barsfield from the face of her cousin to that of his lieutenant. Clayton laughed sillily in reply, and strove to meet the sarcasm with as much good-nature as would disarm it. He replied at the same time playfuly to Rose, and the conversation went on between them. This little episode—the allusion of Rose, though innocently made on her part, was calculated to increase as well the apprehensions of Janet, as the suspicions of Barsfield; and he determined not to yield the point, but, if possible, pressing it still more home, to see if he could not elicit some few more decided proofs of that disquiet of the heart under which Janet so evidently labored. He was not troubled with those gentlemanly scruples which should have produced a pause, if not a direct arrest, of such a determination. On the contrary, he knew of no principles but those which were subservient to the selfish purposes of a coarse, unpolished soul.

"This allegory of your fair friend, Miss Berkeley, would seem not altogether wanting in some direct application, if one may judge from the degree of annoyance which it occasions you. Is it true that some favorite dove is in danger—does the hawk really hang over head; and am I to trace in the likeness of the one, a wild rebel, an outlaw of the land—some sentimental robber of the swamp—and, in the other, the vigilant sentinel of an indulgent monarch, keeping watch over the fold and protecting it against the excursive marauder? If so, in which of these two shall I hold Miss Berkeley to be so greatly interested?"

Mr. Berkeley eagerly bent forward to hear the answer of his daughter; and even Blonay, who had withdrawn himself humbly into a corner of the room, seemed to comprehend something of the matter in hand, and stretched out his long neck, while his blear eyes peered into those which the maiden now fixed upon her questioner.

"I am not good, sir, at solving riddles," was her calm reply; "and really can not undertake to say to what your present remark should refer. Perhaps you are right, however, in comparing to the innocent bird, in danger from the lurking fowler, the outlaw whom you call the rebel. The hawk, sir, stands well enough for the pursuer. But, if these comparisons be true, there is no danger to us, I assure you, as I myself believe, even should the outlaw become the marauder."

And here she paused, and her eyes were withdrawn from the person to whom she had spoken. The tory bit his lip; and, though he strove with that object, failed to suppress the dissatisfaction which her speech had occasioned. Taking up her reply, which had been evidently left unfinished, he proceeded to carry out the sentence.

"But there is danger, you would say, from the latter. Let me remove your fears, Miss Berkeley. The hawk will watch over his charge without preying upon it, as you shall see. I am not unwilling to appear before you as one of the brood, and you and yours shall be secure in the protection I shall bring you against any lurking rebel in your swamps."

"I believe not that we have much to fear from that quarter,

Mr. Barsfield, provided none but Marion's men get into them. They never trouble us."

"But, my dear," said the old gentleman, " we are none the less indebted to Captain Barsfield for his aid and assistance. It is true, captain, we have not suffered much if any loss yet from the people who are out; but times may change, captain, and there's no knowing how soon your kind assistance may be of the utmost importance. We should not be ungrateful, Janet."

"I would not, father," responded the maiden, meekly; "Captain Barsfield has my thanks for the aid he has proffered us, though I still think we shall not find it necessary. Our home has always been a quiet one, and has been respected by all parties. My father," and here she turned to Barsfield with a free and fearless glance, "My father is an invalid, and can not take any part in the war which is going on; and while he extends his hospitality to all, without distinction, he may well hope to need little of the aid of either in defending him from any. It is as little, under these circumstances, as we can require, that our guests shall forbear the use of language which might either give us pain, as it refers contemptuously or unjustly to our friends and those whom we esteem, or must involve us in the controversy which we should better avoid. Captain Barsfield will forgive me if I am unwilling to listen to the abuse of my countrymen."

The manner of the maiden was so dignified as to silence farther controversy. Barsfield submitted with a very good grace, though inwardly extremely chafed at the resolute and unreserved manner in which she spoke of those whom he had denounced as rebels, and to whose patriotic conduct his own had been so unhappily opposed. He strove, however, not merely to subdue his ill-humor, but to prove to her that it had given way to better feelings; and, with a due increase of courtesy, he arose, and would have conducted her to the fine old harpsichord, which formed a most conspicuous article of the household furniture in the apartment. She declined, however, to perform, in spite of every compliment which he could bestow upon her skill and voice, with both of which he appeared to be familiar. Her father added his solicitations also; but she pleaded unpreparedness and her own indisposition so firmly, that the demand was at length given up. The lieutenant, however, was more successful with the inconsiderate and laughing girl who sat beside him. She offered no scruples — said she loved to play and sing of all things in the world; and, taking her seat in the midst of her own jest and laughter, touched the keys with a free finger, that seemed perfectly at home, while she sang the following little ditty, with a fine clear voice which filled the apartment:—

I.

Though grief assail thee, young heart,
 And doubt be there,
 And stone-eyed care,
And sickness ail thee, young heart,
 Love on — love on.

II.

A greater anguish, young heart,
 Than these can be,
 Should love, in thee,
For ever languish, young heart! —
 Love on — love on.

III.

Life's choicest pleasure, young heart,
 Can only wait
 On her whose fate
Makes love her treasure, young heart! —
 Love on — love on.

IV.

And know that sorrow, young heart,
 And wo, and strife,
 Belong to life,
And are love's horror, young heart! —
 Love on — love on.

V.

They fear his glances, young heart,
 And fleet away
 As night from day,
When he advances, young heart —
 Love on — love on.

VI.

A happy comer, young heart,
Love's earliest bird
May now be heard,
With voice of summer, young heart—
Love on — love on.

VII.

Around thee springing, young heart,
Bird, leaf, and flower,
That fill thy bower,
Are ever singing, young heart—
Love on — love on.

While the song of Rose was yet trilling in their ears, a faint but distinct whistle penetrated the apartment. The quick and jealous sense of Barsfield was the very first to hear it; and, from the corner where he sat crouching, the long neck of Blonay might have been seen suddenly thrust out, as his head leaned forward to listen. The eye of the tory captain involuntarily turned upon the face of Janet Berkeley: a deeper paleness had overshadowed it; and, though she did not, and dared not, look in the direction of her observer, she well knew that his gaze was fastened upon her, and this knowledge increased her confusion. The suspicions of Barsfield, always active, were doubly aroused at the present moment, though, with the policy of a practised soldier, he yet took especial care to conceal them.

It was curious to look on the half-breed all the while. The instinct of the scout had awakened into a degree of consciousness with that whistle, which all the sweet music of Rose Duncan, to which he had been listening, could never have provoked. His thought was already in the woods; and, like some keen hound, his mood began to grow impatient of restraint, and to hunger after the close chase and the bloody fray. The eye of Barsfield, turning from the face of the maiden, was fixed upon him; and, with his habitual caution, Blonay, as he saw himself observed, drew in his head, which now rested with his usual listnessness upon his shoulder, while he seemed to lapse away into his accustomed stupor.

The signal, if such it were, was again repeated, and closer at hand. A faint smile curled the lips of the tory captain, and his glance again settled upon the face of Janet. She strove to encounter that glance of inquisitive insolence, but her heart was too full of its fears. She could not—her eye sank away from the encounter, and the suspicions of the tory were confirmed.

"There's a signal for somebody," was his careless remark.

"A signal!" exclaimed Clayton and Rose, in the same breath.

"A signal!" said Mr. Berkeley, in alarm.

"Yes, a signal—and the signal of one of Marion's men," was the reply of Barsfield. "He has strayed this time into the wrong grounds, and will be laid by his heels if he heed not his footsteps."

The hands of Janet were clasped involuntarily, and a prayerful thought was rapidly springing in her mind, while her heart beat thick with its apprehensions.

"Why do you think it a signal of Marion's men, captain?" was the inquiry of Clayton; "may it not be the whistle of some idler among our own?"

"No; he might run some risk of a bullet if that were the case. Our loyalists know these sounds too well not to prick their ears when they hear them. That whistle is peculiar, and not so easily imitated. There—you hear it again! The enemy is daring, if he be an enemy; if a friend, he is not less so."

"It may be one of the negroes," was the timidly-expressed suggestion of Mr. Berkeley.

"Miss Berkeley will scarcely concur with you in that conjecture," was the sarcastic response of Barsfield, while his eye scrutinized closely and annoyingly the rapidly-changing color upon her cheeks. As he gazed, her emotion grew almost insupportable, and her anxiety became so intense as to be perceptible to all. Her eyes seemed not to regard the company, but were fixed and wild in their frozen stare upon a distant window of the apartment. That glance, so immoveable and so full of earnest terror, proved a guide to that of the tory.

He read, in its intensity of gaze, a further solution of the mystery; and, turning suddenly in the same direction, the secret was revealed. The distant but distinct and well-known features of Ernest Mellichampe were clearly seen through the pane, looking in over the head of Blonay, from the piazza to which he had ascended. The movement of Barsfield was instantaneous. With a fierce oath he dashed from his seat, and, seizing his sabre, which lay upon a neighboring table, rushed toward the entrance. The movement of Janet Berkeley was not less sudden. She darted with a wild cry, something between a shriek and a prayer, and stood directly in his pathway — her eye still fixed upon the window where her lover stood — her heart still pleading for his safety — her arm uplifted for his defence.

"Let me pass, Miss Berkeley!" were the hurried words and stern demand of the tory.

"Never — never — I will perish first!" she exclaimed, incoherently and unconsciously, in reply.

He extended his arm to put her aside, and by this time the whole party had arisen from their seats, wondering at what they saw, for they were ignorant of the knowledge possessed by the tory. The father of the maiden would have interposed, and Rose Duncan, surprised and terrified, also came forward; but Janet Berkeley heeded them not. Furious at the interruption, Barsfield cried out to Clayton to pursue.

"The rebel Mellichampe!" was his cry; "he is in the piazza now; he was but this instant at the window. Pursue him with all the men — cut him to pieces — give him no quarter — fly!"

The form of Janet filled the doorway: her arms were extended.

"Mercy!" she cried; "mercy, mercy! Fly not — pursue him not: he is gone — he is beyond your reach. Mercy — have mercy!"

They put her aside, and Barsfield hurried through the door. She caught his arm with a nervous grasp, and clung to him in the fervor of a desperation growing out of her accumulating terrors. He broke furiously away from her hold, and she sank, fainting and exhausted, but still conscious of her lover's danger, at full length along the floor. They were gone in the pursuit, the tory captain and his lieutenant; but Blonay, though he had risen with the rest, still remained in the apartment. The old father tottered to his daughter in consternation, and strove, with the assistance of Rose, to lift her from the ground. In his own rude way, and trembling, too, at the idea of his near approach to one so superior, Blonay proffered his assistance.

"The poor gal," he exclaimed in tones of unwonted pity, while lifting her to the sofa—"the poor gal, she's main frightened now, I tell you!"

"My child—my child!—speak to me, my Janet! Look upon me!—it is your father, Janet! Look up to me, my daughter!"

Her eyes unclosed, and her lips were moved in correspondence with the agonizing thoughts and apprehensions of her soul.

"Mellichampe—rash, rash Mellichampe! Oh, father, they will take—they will murder him!"

"Fear not, my child, fear not," was the father's reply, his own accents full of that very fear which he required that she should not feel. "Fear nothing; this is my house—these are my grounds. They shall not—no, my daughter, they dare not—touch a hair of the head of Mellichampe."

But the daughter knew better than her father his own weakness and the insecurity of her lover, and she shook her head mournfully, though listening patiently to all his efforts at consolation. In that moment the father's love of his child grew conspicuous. He hung over her, and sobbed freely like an infant. He said a thousand soothing things in her ears; predicted a long life of happiness with her lover; strove to reassure her on every topic of their mutual apprehension; and, on his own tottering frame, with the assistance of Rose Duncan, helped her to the chamber whose repose she seemed so imperatively to require.

CHAPTER XI.

SCIPIO.

The movement of Barsfield was almost as soon perceived by Mellichampe as it had been by Janet Berkeley. He saw, at a glance, the abrupt spring which the tory made from his chair; and, conjecturing the cause of his emotion, he prepared himself for flight. Though rash in the extreme, he was not so much of the madman as to dare the contest with such a force as Barsfield could bring against him: yet loath was he, indeed, to fly before so hated an enemy.

"Oh, could we but cross weapons alone in that deep forest, with no eye upon us but those heavenly watchers, and the grim spirits that hover around and exult in the good stroke which is struck for vengeance! Could we there meet, Barsfield— but this hour—I would ask nothing more from Heaven!"

This was the prayer of Mellichampe; these were his words, muttered through his clinched teeth, as, turning from the window, he placed his hands on the light railing of the balcony, and, heedless of the height—something over fifteen feet— leaped, with a fearless, yet bitter heart, into the yard below.

He had come, agreeably to his appointment with the maiden, and, as we have seen, in spite of all the solicitations of his friend and comrade. He had uttered his accustomed signals —they had been, of necessity, disregarded. Vexed and feverish, his blood grew more phrensied at every moment which he was compelled to wait; and, at no time blessed with patience, he had adopted the still more desperate resolution of penetrating to the very dwelling which contained the maiden whom he loved. What to him was the danger from an enemy at such a moment, and with feelings such as his? What were those feelings — what the fears which possessed him? Patient and reckless, his feelings and his thoughts did equal injustice to her and to himself.

"She forgets — she forswears me like all the rest. He seeks her, perhaps, and she — ha! what hope had the desperate and the desolate ever yet from woman, when pomp and prosperity approached as his rival?"

He little knew the maiden whom he so misjudged; but it was thus that he communed with his own bitter spirit, when he made the rash determination to penetrate to the dwelling, from the deep umbrageous garden in its rear, where, hitherto, the lovers had been accustomed to meet, in as sweet a bower as love could have chosen for a purpose so hallowed.

But, though rash almost to madness in coming to the dwelling, Mellichampe was not so heedless of his course as to forget the earnest warnings which Witherspoon had given him. In approaching the house he had taken the precaution to survey all the premises beforehand. The grounds were all well known to him, and he made a circuit around them, by which means he discovered the manner in which the encampment of the troop was made, and how, and where, the sentinels were posted. These he surveyed without exposure, and, though immediately contiguous on more than one occasion to the lounging guard, he escaped without challenge or suspicion. From the park he stole back into the garden. Emerging from its shelter, he advanced to the rear of the building, and, passing under the piazza which encompassed it, he stole silently up the steps, sought the window, looked in upon the company, and was compelled, as we have seen, to fly.

He was now in the court below; and, as the bustle went on above, he paused to listen and to meditate his course. Meanwhile the alarm was sounded from the bugle of the troop. The commotion of their movement distinctly reached his ears, and he leaped off fleetly but composedly among the trees, which concealed his flight toward the garden, just as the rush of Barsfield and Clayton down the steps of the piazza warned him of the necessity of farther precipitation. At that moment, darting forward, he encountered the person of one who was

5

advancing. He had drawn his knife in the first moment of his flight, and, looking now only for enemies, it had nearly found its sheath in the breast of the stranger, when the tones of his voice arrested the fugitive.

"Ha, Mass Arnest, dat you? Lord 'a massy, you 'most knock the breat out my body."

"Silence, Scip—not a word, villain. I am pursued by the tories. Would you betray me?" were the hurried and emphatic, but suppressed words of Mellichampe.

"'Tray you, Mass Arnest—how come you tink so? Enty da Sip—you truss Sip always, Mass Arnest—truss 'em now," was the prompt reply of the negro, uttered in tones similarly low.

"I will, Scip—I will trust you. Barsfield is upon me, and I must gain the garden."

"No go dere. Tory sodger jist run 'long by the garden fence."

"Where then, old fellow?"

The negro paused for a moment, and the clattering of the sabres was now heard distinctly.

"Drop, Mass Arnest, drop for dear life close behind dis tree. Hug 'em close, I yerry dem coming."

"I have it," said the youth, coolly, to the bewildered negro, as the sounds denoted the approach of the pursuers to that quarter of the area in which this brief conference had been carried on—

"I have it, Scip. I will lie close to this fallen tree, and do you take to your heels in the direction of the woods. To the right, Scip—and let them see you as you run."

"How den, Mass Arnest—wha de good ob dat?"

"Fly, fellow, they come—to the right, to the right."

With the words Mellichampe threw himself prostrate, close beside a huge tree that had been recently felled in the enclosure, while the faithful negro darted off without hesitation in the direction which had been pointed out to him. In another moment a body of the troopers was scattered around the tree, bounding over it in all directions. Barsfield led the pursuit, and animated it by his continual commands. The scene grew diversified by the rushing tumults and the wild cries of the pursuers, and it was not many minutes before the chase was encouraged by a glimpse which they caught of the flying negro. At once all feet were turned in the one direction. Soldier after soldier passed in emulous haste over the log where Mellichampe lay, and, when the clamor had sunk away in the distance, he rose quietly, and coolly listening for a few seconds to the distant uproar, he stole cautiously back into the garden, in the crowded shrubbery and thick umbrage of which he might have readily anticipated a tolerable concealment while the night lasted from all the troop which Barsfield could muster. Here he could distinguish the various sounds and stages of the pursuit; now spreading far away to the fields and on the borders of the park—and now, as the adroit Scipio doubled upon his pursuers, coming nigher to the original starting-place. But whether it was that Scip's heart failed him, or his legs first, may not be said. It is enough to know that he began to falter. His enemies gained ground rapidly upon him. He passed into a briar-copse, and lay close for a while, though torn by their thorns at every forward movement, in the hope to gain a temporary rest from the pursuit; but the chase tracked him out, and its thick recesses gave him no shelter. The sabres were thrust into the copse in several places, and, dreading their ungentle contact, the hunted negro once more took to his heels. He dashed forward and made for a little pine thicket that seemed to promise him a fair hope for concealment; but, when most sanguine, an obtrusive vine caught his uplifted foot as he sprang desperately forward, and, with a heavy squelch that nearly took the breath out of his body, he lay prostrate at the mercy of his enemy. Barsfield himself was upon him. With a fierce oath and a cry of triumph he shook his sabre over his head, and threatened instant death to the supposed Mellichampe. The poor negro, though not unwilling to risk his life for the youth, now thought it high time to speak; and, in real or affected terror, he cried aloud in language not to be mistaken,

"Don't you chop a nigger with your sword now, I tell you.

Gor A'mighty, Mass Cappin, you no guine kill a poor nigger da's doing nothing at all !"

Barsfield recoiled in astonishment, only to advance upon the crouching black with redoubled fury; and he might have used the uplifted weapon simply from the chagrin and disappointment, but that a stronger motive restrained him. With the strength and rage of a giant, he hurled the negro back to the ground whence he had now half risen, and fiercely demanded of him why he had fled from the pursuit.

"Ki! Mass Cappin, you ax a nigger wha' for he run, when you fuss run at 'em wid you' big sword, and want to chop 'em wid it. Da's 'nough to make a nigger run, I 'speck. No nigger nebber guine 'tand for dat."

"Scoundrel! do not trifle with me," was the fierce reply. "You have seen young Mellichampe."

"Who dat—Mass Arnest? No see 'em to-night Mass Cappin."

"Scoundrel! you are lying now. I know it. You have hidden him away. Lead us to the spot, or put us upon his track so that we find him, or, by the Eternal! I swing you up to these branches."

The negro solemnly declared his ignorance, but this did not satisfy the tory.

"Disperse your men over the grounds—the park—the garden—on all sides. The rebel must be hereabouts still. He can not have gone far. Leave me but a couple of stout fellows to manage this slave."

Clayton was about to go, when the words of Barsfield, uttered in a low, freezing zone of determination, reached his ear.

"And, hear you, Clayton—no quarter to the spy—hew him down without a word."

The lieutenant departed, leaving the two men whom his superior had required. One of those, in obedience to the command of Barsfield, produced a stout cord, which was conveniently at hand, from his pocket.

"Wha' you guine do now, Mass Cappin?" cried the negro, beginning to be somewhat alarmed at the cold-blooded sort of preparation which the soldier was making.

"You shall see, you black rascal, soon enough," was the reply.

"Noose it now, Drummond," was the order of the tory.

It was obeyed, and in another moment the cord encircled the neck of the terrified Scipio.

"Confess now, sir—confess all you have done—all that you know. Have you not seen the rebel to-night?"

"Which one, Mass Cappin?"

"No fooling, fellow. You know well enough who I mean—the rebel Mellichampe."

"Wha'—Mass Arnest?"

"Ay."

"No, sa, Mass Cappin. It's trute wha' I tell you now. I bery glad for see Mass Arnest, but I a'n't seen 'em dis tree day and seven week. He's gone, day say, high up the Santee, wib de rest."

"And you haven't seen him to-night?"

"Da's a trute—I no see'm to-night."

"A d——d lie, Scipio, which must be punished. Tuck him up, Drummond."

"Hab a pity on poor nigger, Mass Cappin! It's a nigger is no wort salt to be hom'ny. Hab a pity on poor nigger. Ah, Mass Barsfield, you no guine hang Scip? I make prayers for you, Mass Barsfield, you no hang Scip dis time."

The negro implored earnestly as the design appearèd more determinately urged by the tory. He was seriously terrified with the prospect before him, and his voice grew thick with horror and increasing alarm.

"Confess, then, or, by God! you swing on that tree. Tell all that you know, for nothing else can save you."

'I hab noting to tell, Mass Cappin. I berry good nigger, da's honest, sa, more dan all de rest of massa's niggers, only I will tief Bacon, Mass Cappin. I can't help tief bacon when I git a chance, massa. Da's all da's agen Scip, Mass Cappin."

There was so much of simplicity in Scipio's mode of defence, that Barsfield half inclined to believe that he was really ignorant of the place of Mellichampe's concealment; but, as he well knew that Scipio was a favorite family-servant, and remarkable for his fidelity, he did not doubt that he would keep a secret concerning one so long intimate with it as Mellichampe to the very last moment. This suggestion hastened his decision. With the utmost composure he bade the soldier execute his office, and looked on calmly, and heard without heeding the many adjurations, and prayers, and protestations of the negro, desperately urged, as they hurried him to the tree, over a projecting limb of which one end of the rope was already thrown.

"Will you tell now, Scipio?" demanded Barsfield of the slave, in a tone of voice absolutely frightful to him from its gentleness. "Tell me where Mellichampe ran — tell where you have concealed him, and I let you go; but, if you do not, you hang in a few moments on this very tree."

"I no see'm, Mass Cappin — he no run, he stan' in de same place. Hab a pity, Mass Cappin, 'pon Scipio, da's a good nigger for old massa, and da's doing noting for harm anybody."

"Once more, Scipio — where is the rebel? — where is Mellichampe?"

"Da trute, Mass Cappin, I don't know."

"Pull him up, men."

The cruel order was coolly given, and in tones that left no room in the minds of the soldiers to doubt that they were to execute the hurried sentence. Struggling, gasping, and laboring to speak, Scipio was lifted into air. He kicked desperately, sought to scream, and at length, as the agony of his increasing suffocation grew more and more oppressive, and in feeble and scarcely intelligible accents, he professed his willingness now to do all that was required of him.

"I tell — I tell ebbry ting, Mass Cappin — cut de rope, da's all. I tell — cut 'em fass — lose 'em quick. Oh — he da mash my head — I choke."

The cord was relaxed with the utterance of this promise. The victim was suffered to sink down upon the ground, where, for a few moments, he crouched, half sitting, half lying, almost exhausted with struggling, and seemingly in a stupor from the pain and fright he had undergone. But Barsfield did not much regard his sufferings. He took the negro at his word, and, impatient for his own revenge, hurried the movements of the poor creature. The rope was still twined about his neck, and thus, kept in continual fear of the doom which had been only suspended, he was required to lead the way, and put the pursuers upon the lost trail of the fugitive.

CHAPTER XII.

THE TRAIL LOST.

"Come, sir—away—put us on the track of the rebel. Show where he is hidden—and, hark you, Scipio—not a word—no noise to tell him we are coming, or—"

The threat was left unfinished, but it was nevertheless sufficiently well understood. The reply of the negro was characteristic.

"Gor A'mighty, Mass Barsfield, enty I guine? You no 'casion push a nigger so. Ef you was to hang me up agen, I couldn't go no more faster dan I does."

He led the way freely enough; but it was not the intention of Scipio to betray the trust of Mellichampe, even if it had been in his power to lead them to the place of his concealment. His object was simply to escape a present difficulty. He had no thought beyond the moment. With this object, with the natural cunning of the negro, and the integrity of the faithful slave, he framed in his mind a plan of search, which, while it should be urged on his part with all the earnestness of truth, should yet still more effectually mislead the pursuers. Scipio was one of those trusty slaves to be found in almost every native southern family, who, having grown up with the children of their owners, have acquired a certain correspondence of feeling with them. A personal attachment had strengthened the bonds which necessity imposed, and it was quite as much a principle in Scipio's mind to fight and die for his owners, as to work for them. Regarding his young mistress with a most unvarying devotion, he had been made acquainted at an early period with the nature of the tie which existed between herself and Mellichampe, and many were the billets and messages of love, which had been confided by the two to Scipio, during the unsophisticated courtship which had been carried on between them. Proud of the confidence reposed in him, and fond of the parties, the trust of Mellichampe was sacred in his keeping; and, at the moment of his greatest danger, when the rope was about his neck, and his life depended upon one whom he well knew to be merciless and unforgiving, he never once conceived the idea of effecting his escape by a revelation of any secret which might have compromised, in the slightest degree, either Mellichampe or the maiden. He now purposely led the tory from his object, trusting to his good fortune or his wit to relieve him from all subsequent emergencies.

It does not need that we should show how, in the prosecution of his scheme, the adroit negro contrived to baffle the vindictive Barsfield. He led him from place to place, to and fro, now here, now there, and through every little turn and winding of the enclosure in front of the dwelling, until the patience of the tory became exhausted, and he clearly saw that his guide had deceived him. For a moment his anger prompted him to prosecute the punishment with which he had sought at first to intimidate the negro. But a fear of the influence of such a proceeding upon the maiden induced a more gentle determination.

It was not, probably, the intention of Barsfield to carry into effect the threatened doom—his design was rather to procure the required intelligence by extorting a confession. He was now persuaded, so well had Scipio played his part, that the fellow was really ignorant. Finding that his long passages invariably led to nothing, he dismissed him with a hearty curse and kick, and hurried away to join Clayton, who, meanwhile, had been busied in the examination of the garden. The lieutenant had not been a whit more successful than his captain; for Mellichampe, the moment that he heard the pursuit tending in the quarter where he had concealed himself, simply moved away from his lair, and, leaping the little rail fence, which divided the garden from the forest, found himself almost immediately in the shelter of a dense body of woods, which would have called for five times the force of Barsfield to ferret him out in at night. Familiar of old with the region, which had been consecrated in the walks and worship of love, he strolled off to a favorite tree, not thirty yards from the fence, in an arm of which, sheltering himself snugly, he listened with scornful indifference to the clamors of that hot pursuit which the tory still continued. He saw the torches blazing in the groves where he had crouched but a little while before, and almost fancied that he could distinguish at intervals the features of those who bore them, and sometimes even the lineaments of that one deadliest enemy, whom of all the world he most desired on equal terms to encounter.

The chase was at length given over. Barsfield was too good a scout himself not to know that the woods in the rear of the garden must contain the fugitive. He was quite too familiar, however, with the nature of a Carolina thicket to hope for any successful result of pursuit and search in that quarter. And yet he still looked with straining eyes upon its dense and gloomy spots, as if longing to penetrate them. Had he been strong enough in men—could he even have spared the force which he had under his command for any such purpose, he would not have hesitated for an instant; but, under existing circumstances, the risk would have been rash and foolish, to have exposed so small a body of men to the possibility of contact with a lurking enemy. He little knew that the particular foe was alone—and that, even at the moment when these meditations were passing through his mind, his hated rival sat looking composedly down upon the unavailing toil of his long pursuit. How many circumstances were there in his past history to make him detest the fugitive! How many interests and feelings, active at the moment in his bosom, to make him doubly desire to rid himself of one so inimical— so greatly in his way! He turned from the garden in a bitter mood of disappointment. The fever of a vexing fear and of a sleepless discontent was goading him with every additional moment of thought, and kept him from all appreciation of the beauty of the rich flowers and those sweet walks which, in the intercourse of Mellichampe and Janet, had made a fitly associated scene. He felt nothing of the garden's beauties—its sweet solemnity of shade—its refreshing fragrance—its slender branches and twining shrubs, that quivered and murmured in the night breeze; or of that exquisite Art in the disposition of its groves and flowers, which, concealing herself in their clustering folds, peeps out only here and there, as if in childlike and innocent sport with her sister Nature.

Having made his camp arrangements for the night, Barsfield left Clayton in command of the troop, still occupying the park as at their coming, and proceeded once more to the dwelling. Mr. Berkeley awaited his approach at the entrance. The old gentleman was in no little tribulation. The presence of Mellichampe at such a time in his grounds, and under circumstances which seemed to indicate the privity of one or more of the household to his visits, was calculated, he well knew, to make Barsfield suspicious of his loyalty. It was his policy, and he was solicitous to prove to the tory that the youth received no manner of encouragement from him; that his presence was unlooked-for, and, if not contrary to his commands, was at least without his sanction. He also well knew the aim of Barsfield with reference to his daughter, and it was not less his object, on this account, to impress the tory with the idea of his own ignorance on all subjects which concerned the rebel. In tremulous accents, confusedly and timidly, he strove to win the ear of his sullen and dissatified guest.

"I am truly happy—Ah! I mean I am very sorry, Captain Barsfield—" and here he paused—the words were too contradictory, and his first blunder frightened him; but Barsfield, who also had his game to play, came to his relief by interrupting him in his speech.

"Sorry for what, Mr. Berkeley? What should make you sorry? You have nothing, that I can see, to be sorry for. Your house is haunted by a rebel, and, though you may not encourage him, and I suppose do not, I yet know that hitherto you have been unable to drive him thoroughly away. It is your misfortune, sir, but will not be a misfortune much longer. You will soon be relieved from this difficulty. My force in a short time will be adequate to clear the country in this quarter of the troop of outliers that haunt it; and this duty, sir, I have now in charge. Leave it to me to manage the youngster—I shall make my arrangements for his capture, and he can not long escape me. Once taken, he troubles neither of us again, He swings for it, sir, or there is no law in the land."

This discourse confounded the old gentleman. He was not unwilling to be thought free from any collusion with Mellichampe, but the youth was a favorite. The bitter speech of Barsfield, and the final threat, totally unmanned his hearer, and he exclaimed, in a voice made tremulous by his emotion—

"What! Ernest Mellichampe—hang Ernest Mellichampe, captain? Why, what has the poor youth done?"

"Done!" exclaimed the other; "done, Mr. Berkeley? Why, sir, is he not one of that traitorous brood of Max Mellichampe, who was so fierce an enemy of his king; so merciless in fight, and so uncompromising in whatever related to this struggle? I had the good fortune to serve my sovereign, as you know, by killing him; and, from what has been shown to me of this young man, I shall do my country no less a service by sending him after his father."

"Oh, ay, captain—but that was in fight. Of course Ernest, if he lifts arms against our sovereign, must take his chance like any other soldier in battle, but——"

"He has incurred another risk to-night, Mr. Berkeley—he has penetrated into my line of sentinels as a spy."

The tory silenced the well-intentioned speaker. They entered the hall, where Blonay still sat, alone, and in as perfect a condition of quiet as if there had not been the slightest uproar. Glancing his eye quickly around the apartment, and seeing that none other was present, Barsfield approached the half-breed with a look of stern severity, and, laying his hand upon his shoulder, he thus addressed him:—

"Hark'ee, fellow; you pretend to be a good loyalist—you have got Proctor's certificate to that effect—why did you not seek to take the rebel, when you were so much nigher the entrance than any one of the rest? Did you not see him?"

"Well, cappin, I reckon I did see him when he looked into

the glass, but I didn't know that he was a rebel. I didn't see no harm in his looking in the glass."

"But when I moved — when I pursued — did you not see that he was my enemy ?"

"That's true, cappin; but that was jist the reason, now, I didn't go for'ad. I seed from your eyes that he was your enemy, and I know'd from what you did you wanted to git a lick at him yourself, and so I wouldn't put in. Every man paddle his own canoe, says I; and, if I has an enemy, I shouldn't like to stand by and let another man dig at his throat to spile my sport, neither would you, I reckon. It's no satisfaction for one man to jump between and take away another man's pleasure, as I may say, out of his mouth."

The code of Blonay was new to Barsfield, though, from its expression, he at once well understood the prevailing character of the speaker. It was for Barsfield to desire that his enemy should perish, no matter by whose hands — the passion of Blonay prompted his own execution of every deed of personal vengeance, as a duty incumbent on himself. A few words farther passed between them, in which the tory hoped he had secured the services of the half-breed, of whose value he had conceived a somewhat higher idea from the strange reason which he had given for his quiescence in the pursuit of Mellichampe. This over, the tory captain signified his determination to retire, and, with a cordial "Good night!" to his host, he left the room, and was instantly conducted to his chamber.

Meanwhile, in the apartment of the two cousins, a far different scene had been going on. There, immersed in her own fears and apprehensions, Janet Berkeley listened in momently-increasing terror to every sound that marked the continued pursuit of her lover. As the clamor drew nigh or receded, her warm imagination depicted the strait of Mellichampe; and it was only when, after the departure of Barsfield for the night, when her father could seek her chamber, that she heard the pleasing intelligence of the tory's disappointment. It was then that the playful Rose, as she saw that the apprehensions of her cousin were now dissipated, gently reproached Janet for the want of confidence which she had shown in not unfolding to her the secret which the excitement of the preceding event had too fully developed.

"To carry on a game of hide-and-seek so slyly, Janet — to have a lover, yet no confidant — no friend, and I, too, so near at hand. I who have told you all, and kept nothing back, and would have locked up your secret so closely that no rival, no mama, no papa, should have been the wiser. And such a fine subject for talk, Janet, in these long, sweet summer nights — now, when all is quiet, and there is nothing of a cloud, dear, to be seen. Look, dearest, see what a beautiful night."

"I have no heart for it, Rose — none. I am very unhappy," was the sad response of the afflicted maiden.

"Serve you right; you deserve to be sad, Janet, if only for being so sly and silent. Why, I ask you again, why didn't you let me into the secret? I could have helped you."

"Alas, Rose, this secret has been too oppressive to me not to make me desire frequently to unfold it; but, as I have no hope with my love, I thought better to be silent."

"And why, dearest," exclaimed the other, "why should you have no hope? Why should your love never be realized? Think you that Mellichampe is the man to play you false?"

"No — oh no! He would not — he could not. He is too devoted — too earnest in all that he does and feels, ever to forget or deny. But it has been a sad engagement throughout — begun in sorrow, and strife, and privation, and carried on in defiance of all danger, and with an utter regardlessness of all counsel. God knows, I so misgive these visits, that I should rather he would be false to me than that he should come so frequently into danger of his life."

"Now out upon thee, cousin — how you talk! This danger is the very sweetness, and should not be a dampener of love. If the man be what he should be, he will not heed, but rather desire it, as in stimulating his adventure it will also stimulate his feeling and his flame. For my part, I vow that I would not have one of your tame, quiet, careful curs — your household husbands, who would neither do nor dare, but squat, purring like overgrown tabbies in the chimney corner, pass away a long life of tedium in a protracted and monotonous humming. If ever I get a lover, which, Heaven knows, seems but a doubtful prospect at this moment, I vow he should have no quiet—he should be required to do just what you fret that Mellichampe is now doing. He should scale fences and walls, ford creeks when there's a freshet, and regularly come to visit me through the swamp; and this he must prove to me that he has done, by a fair exhibition of his bespattered boots and garments. As for difficulties such as these frightening a lover from his purpose, I would not give my name for any lover who would not smile upon, while overcoming them."

In a sadder tone than ever, Janet replied to the playful girl, who continued to run on and interrupt her at intervals wherever her speech seemed more desponding than usual.

"It is not mere difficulties, Rose, but positive dangers, that I dread for Ernest; and, but that I know he will not heed my words in such a matter, I should utterly break with him, and for ever, if it were only to keep him away from the risk into which he plunges with little or no consideration. Twice or thrice has he nearly fallen a victim to this same man, Barsfield, who has a desperate hatred toward him——"

"And a desperate love for you," said the other.

"Which is quite as idle, Rose, as the other is rash," replied Janet, calmly, to the interruption. "Vainly have I implored him to desist—to forbear seeking or seeing me until the danger and the war are over; and, above all, to avoid our plantation, where my father is too timid and too feeble to serve him when there is danger, and where I am certain that spies of the tories are always on the watch to report against any of the whigs who may be stirring."

"And, like a good, stubborn, whole-hearted lover, Mellichampe heeds none of your exhortations that would keep him away. Heaven send me such a lover! He should come when he pleased, and, if I prayed him at all, it should be that he would only leave me when I pleased. I would not trouble him with frequent orders, I assure you."

"Ah, Rose! would I had your spirits!"

"Ah, Janet! would I had your lover! He is just the lover,

now, that I desire; and these perils that he seems to seek, and this rashness of which you complain, commend him warmly to my imagination. Poor fellow! I'm only sorry that he should have his labor for his pains to-night; and must go back the way he came, without getting what he came for."

"Heaven grant that he may, Rose!" said the other, earnestly; "but do you know that even this alarm will scarcely discourage Ernest Mellichampe? He has promised to come to-night, and exacted my promise to meet him under the great magnolia. I am persuaded that he will keep his word, in spite of all the dangers that beset him. He is bold to hardihood, and I look not to sleep to-night until I have heard his signal."

"Confess, confess, Janet, that you will sit up in the hope to hear it."

"Not in the hope to hear it, Rose, but I will sit up — at least for some time longer. I could not sleep were I to go to bed, under the anxiety which the belief that he will come must occasion in my mind. But you need not wait for me."

"I will not — I should be very peevish were I to hear a love-signal, and have no share in the proceedings. I am certainly a most unfortunate damsel, Janet, having a heart really so susceptible, so very much at the mercy of my neighbors, without having one neighbor kind enough to help me in its management." And thus, rattling on, the thoughtless girl threw herself upon her couch, and was soon wrapped in pleasant slumbers. Janet, sad and suffering, in the meanwhile turned to the open window, unconsciously watching the now rising moon, while meditating the many doubts and misgivings, the sad fears and the sweet hopes, of a true heart and a warmly-interested affection.

CHAPTER XIII.

SECRET PURPOSES.

Barsfield sought his chamber, but not to sleep. Some active thought was in possession of his mind, operating to exclude all sense of weariness, and, indeed, almost to make him forget, certainly entirely to overlook, the previous fatigues of the day. He paced his room impatiently for several minutes before he perceived that the servant was still in waiting. When he did so, he at once dismissed him; but, immediately after, called him back.

" Who's that — Tony ?"

" Yes, sa."

" Where does the traveller — the blear-eyed fellow — sleep to-night, Tony ?"

" In de little shed-room, Mass Cappin."

" Does it lock, Tony ?"

" He hab bolt inside, sir."

" 'Tis well; take this; you may go now."

He gave the negro, as he dismissed him, an English shilling, which called forth a grin of acknowledgment and a liberal scraping of feet. Alone the tory captain continued to pace up and down the apartment, absorbed seemingly in earnest meditation. But his thoughts did not make him forgetful of the objects around him. He went frequently to the windows, not to contemplate the loveliness of the night, but to see whether all was quiet in the little world below. His frequent approach to his own chamber-door, which he opened at intervals, and from which he now and then emerged, had a like object; and this practice was continued until all sounds had ceased; until all the family seemed buried in the profoundest slumber.

Cautiously, then, he took his way from his own apartment, and proceeding through the gallery, he soon reached the little shed-room to which Blonay had been assigned. He paused for a single instant at the entrance, then rapped lightly, and was instantly admitted. For a brief space the eyes of Blonay failed to distinguish the person of the intruder. A few embers in the fireplace, the remnants of the light-wood brands which had shown him his couch, yielded a blaze, but one too imperfect for any useful purpose. The voice of Barsfield, however, immediately enlightened the half-breed.

"A friend," said the tory, in a tone low, carefully low, and full of condescension. "A friend, and one who needs the services of a friend. I have sought you, Mr. Blonay, as I have reason to believe I can rely on you. You have the certificate of Major Proctor, a sufficient guaranty for your loyalty; but our brief conversation this evening has convinced me that you are able, as well as loyal, and just the man to serve my purposes."

The tory paused, as if in expectation of some answer; and Blonay, so esteeming it, proceeded in his own way to the utterance of many professions, which might have been unnecessarily protracted had not the impatience of his visiter interposed.

"Enough! I believe that you may be relied on, else I should not have sought you out to-night. And now to my business. You heard me say I had an enemy?"

The reply was affirmative.

"That enemy I would destroy—utterly annihilate—for several reasons, some of which are public, and others private. He is a rebel to the king, and a most malignant and unforgiving one. His father was such before him, and him I had the good fortune to slay. The family estate has become mine through the free grant of our monarch; in consideration of my good services in that act. Do you hear me, sir?"

"Reckon I do, cappin," was the reply of the half-breed.

"Then you will have little difficulty in understanding my desire. This son is the only man living who has any natural claim to that estate in the event of a change of political circumstances which shall throw back the power of our sovereign. In such an event, he would be the proper heir; and would, with reason, oppose his claim to mine. That claim would be valid and incontestable, most probably, under any change of circumstances, were he once put out of the way. For this reason, if for none other, I would destroy him."

"And reason enough," responded Blonay, "to kill a dozen rebels."

"True; but there are yet other reasons: he has aspersed me, denounced me to my face, on the commencement of this war, and under circumstances which prevented me from seeking any atonement. In arms I have never yet been able to encounter him; as, from his good knowledge of the swamp, he readily eludes my troop. He is, besides, attended by a fellow who watches over his safety, and follows and guards his every movement; and there are few men who manage with so much skill and adroitness as the man in question. He is only to be reached by one in a persevering search — one who would not turn an inch from his course, but, like the bloodhound, keep close upon the track without suffering anything, not even force, to divert him from his object. Such a man I hold you to be."

Blonay thanked the tory for his good opinion, and the latter proceeded.

"You are for killing your enemy with your own hand. I am indifferent who kills mine, so that he ceases to trouble me. The man who slays him for me is as much my instrument as the knife which, in your hand, does the good deed for you. Besides, even had I this desire, I could only pursue it at great sacrifice. I should be compelled to give up my public duties, which are paramount. I should be compelled to go single-handed, and play the part of an outlier in the swamps along with those whom I attempt to overreach. I am too well known by them all ever to hope to win their confidence; and the very nickname which they have conferred upon me for my adherence to my sovereign, if repeated in my ears, as it would be by this taunting youth in question, would only drive my blood into a more foolish and suicidal rebellion than is theirs.

Some other man — some single-hearted friend — must avenge and rid me of my enemy. Will you be that man?"

"Well, now, cappin, I should like to know more about this business; and the man — I should like to hear his name."

"Mellichampe — Ernest Mellichampe, the son of Colonel Max Mellichampe, killed at Monk's corner in January last."

"Why, I don't know the man, cappin. I never seed him, and shouldn't be able to make him out, even if I stumbled over him crossing a log."

"That is no difficulty. I will give you marks and signs by which you can not fail to know him under any circumstances. You saw his face to-night. He came here to see — and that is another reason for my hatred — he came here to see, not our troop, nor our disposition, nor with any reference to our warfare, but simply to see the young lady of the house."

"What, the gal in black — her that looks so grand and so sweet?" inquired Blonay, with some earnestness.

"The taller — the dark-eyed one — the daughter of the old man, Mr. Berkeley."

"And you reckon there's love atween them?" curiously inquired the half-breed.

"Ay, such love as I would not have between them," bitterly responded the other. "I know that Mellichampe has long loved her, and I fear that she requites him in kind. This is another reason why I should hate him for I too — but why should I tell you this? It is enough that I hate, and that I would destroy him. Here, Blonay, take this — it is gold — good British gold; and I give it as an earnest of what you shall have if you will bring me the ears of my enemy. Take the swamp after him — hunt him by day and by night; and when you can come and show me, to my satisfaction, that he troubles me no more, you shall have the sum doubled thrice. Say that you will serve me."

He put five guineas into the hand of the unreluctant half-breed, who at once deposited them from sight in a pocket of his garment; and yet, though he secured the money, Blonay paused before giving his answer.

"Why do you hesitate?" demanded the tory.

"Well," said the other, in his drawling fashion, "I don't know, cappin, how one business can go with the other. I have, you see, a little affair of my own to settle with one of the rebels in Marion's men, that's rather like the business you wants me to go upon for you. Now, one must be settled 'fore the other; and 'tan't in natur, when a man's blood's up, that he should turn away from his own enemy to go after another man's. I'm on trail of my enemy now, and I should be sorry to drop it, I tell you; and, 'deed, cappin, I can't, no how."

Barsfield was still prepared to meet the difficulties suggested by his proposed instrument.

"You need not give up one pursuit in taking up the other. It is fortunate for us that our enemies are both in the same drive. They are both men of Marion, and, in tracking one, the probability is that you can not be very far from the other. Indeed, for that matter, the one will be most likely to help you to the other, as the squad of Marion must now be greatly reduced, and he can not consequently venture to scatter them much. This is no difficulty, but rather an advantage."

Blonay was silenced, if not convinced on this point. He did not reply, but seemed for a few moments lost in deliberation; at length, breaking the silence abruptly, he spoke of another, and seemingly a foreign feature of the affair.

"And you say, cappin, that there's love atween him and the young gal of the house — Miss Janet, as they calls her?"

"Yes! but what is that to you?" replied the other, sternly. "It matters nothing whether they love or hate, so far as our business lies together. You are to labor to make that love fruitless, if so be there is love, but without troubling yourself to know or to inquire into the fact."

"Why, yes, that's true," responded the other; "it don't matter this way or that, and ——"

They were interrupted at this moment by a distinct and repeated whistle, — just such a signal sound as had preceded the appearance of Mellichampe at the window of the hall. The tory put his hand upon the wrist of Blonay, while he bent forward his ear to the entrance — muttering to himself a moment after, as he again heard the signal: —

"Now, by Heaven! but this is audacious beyond example. The rebel is back again; a scare has no effect upon him, and nothing but shot will. Stay!" he exclaimed; "hear you nothing?"

"A footstep, cappin; I think a foot coming down the steps."

And, even as he said, they both distinctly heard, the next moment, the tread of a foot cautiously set down, moving toward the back entrance of the house. Barsfield immediately sprang to the window of the apartment, and beheld, in the dim light just then bringing out the trees of the ground and garden into soft and shadowy relief, a slender figure stealing away toward the garden, carefully keeping as much as practicable in the shelter of the huge water-oaks that obscured the alley. A mingled feeling of exultation and anger spoke in his tone, as he exclaimed:—

"I have him now—the doe shall bring him to the hunter—he shall not escape me now! Hark you, Blonay, wait me here! I will get my sabre, and be with you instantly. It will be hard if we can not manage him between us. But there must be no stir—no noise; what we do must be done by stratagem and our own force. Get yourself ready, therefore; your knife will answer, for your rifle will be of little use in the thick shrubbery of that garden. We must sneak, sir; no dove-hunting without sneaking."

With these words, Barsfield left the apartment of the half-breed and proceeded to his own. The feelings of the former, however, scarcely responded to the sanguinary words of the latter. When alone, his soliloquy, brief and harsh, was yet new, seemingly, to his character. Hated and harried as he had been by all before, he had for the first time in his life been touched with the influence of a gentler power; and, muttering to himself during the absence of the tory, he disclosed a better feeling than any that we have been accustomed to behold in him.

"If the gal loves him, and he loves her, I won't spoil the sport atween 'em. She's a good gal, and had me to come to supper at the same table, when the cappin spoke agin it. She didn't laugh at me, nor stare at my eyes, as if I was a wild varmint; and she spoke to me jist as she spoke to other people. Adrat it! he may cut his enemy's throat for himself, I sha'n't; but then I needn't tell him so, neither;" and, as he spoke, he twirled the little purse of guineas in his pocket with a feeling of immense satisfaction. In a moment after Barsfield returned, and led the way cautiously by a circuitous track toward the garden.

Let us now retrace briefly the steps we have taken, and observe the progress of some other of the persons in our narrative.

CHAPTER XIV.

THUMBSCREW IN PRACTICE.

WE have seen, pending the pursuit, that Mellichampe had coolly kept his way through the garden until he reached the forest that lay immediately behind it. Here he paused—he felt secure from any night search by such a force as that under Barsfield. A huge gum, that *forked* within a few feet of its base, diverging then into distinct columns, afforded him a tolerable forest seat, into which, with a readiness that seemed to denote an old familiarity with its uses, the fugitive leaped with little difficulty. The undergrowth about him was luxuriant, and almost completely shut in the place of his concealment from any glance, however far-darting, of that bright moon which was now rising silently above the trees.

But a sharper eye than hers had been upon the youth from the first moment of his flight from the garden. The trusty Thumbscrew was behind him, and a watcher, like himself. He had hurried from the conference with Humphries; and, heedful of his friend, for whose safety he felt all a parent's anxiety, he had pressed forward to the plantation of Mr. Berkeley, and to those portions of it in particular which, as they had been frequently traversed by both of them before, he well knew would be the resort of Mellichampe now. Still, though resolute to serve the youth, and having no more selfish object, he did not dare to offend him by exposing his person to his sight. He arrived at a convenient place of watch just as the pursuit of Barsfield was at its hottest. He saw the flight of the fugitive from the garden, and, himself concealed, beheld him take his old position in the crotch of the gum. His first impulse was to advance and show himself; but, knowing the nature of his companion well, he felt assured he should only give offence, and do no service. His cooler decision was to lie snugly where he was, and await the progress of events.

At length the torches disappeared from the garden, and it was not long after when the lights seemed extinguished in the house — all but one. A candle, a pale and trembling light, was still to be seen in one window of the dwelling, and to this the eyes of Mellichampe were turned with as fond a glance as ever Chaldean shepherd sent in worship to the star with which he held his fate to be connected. The light came from the chamber of Janet Berkeley. It was the light of love to Mellichampe, and it brought a sweet promise and a pleasant hope to his warm and active fancy.

Not long could he remain in his quiet perch after beholding it. He leaped down, glided around the garden-paling, and took his way to the park in front, keeping on the opposite side of the fence which divided the ground immediately about the dwelling from the forest and the fields. The fence, as is common to most fences of like description in the luxuriant regions of the south, was thickly girdled with brush, serving admirably the purpose of concealment. Pursuing it with this object, in all its windings, he at length approached the park where the British troops were encamped. Well and closely did he scan their position; and, with the eye of a partisan, he saw with how much ease a force of but half the number, properly guided, might effect their discomfiture. He did not linger, however, in idle regrets of his inability; but, moving around the chain of sentries, he ascertained that their position had undergone no alteration, and felt assured that he could now penetrate the garden safely. This done, he made his way back to the place of his concealment.

In the examination which he had just taken, he had been closely watched and followed by the faithful Thumbscrew. The movements of the youth regulated duly those of his attendant. When the former halted, the latter fell back behind the brush, advancing when he advanced, and checking his own progress whenever the dusky shadow of Mellichampe appeared to linger even for an instant in the moonlight. He escaped detection. He played the scout with a dexterity and ease that seemed an instinct, and hovered thus around the footsteps of his daring friend throughout his whole progress, to and fro, in the adventures of that night.

From the outside to the inside of the garden was but a step, and in a trice Mellichampe went over the fence. Watching heedfully until the youth was out of sight, and hidden within its intricacies, Thumbscrew followed his example, and was soon wending after him, close along its shady alleys. A dense and double line of box, which, from having been long untrimmed, had grown up into so many trees, afforded an admirable cover; and, pausing at every turning, he looked forth only sufficiently often to keep the course of the lover for ever in his sight.

In the meantime, Mellichampe made his way to the garden entrance. Here he stopped with an unwonted degree of prudence, for which Thumbscrew gave him due credit; he forbore to press forward, as the latter feared he might do — seeking to cross the court, which, though interspersed with trees, was yet not sufficiently well covered to afford the necessary concealment. Keeping within the garden, therefore, he gave the signal, the first sounds of which chilled and warmed with contradictory emotions the bosom of the sweet maiden to whose ears it was addressed. The breath almost left her as she heard it, and she gasped with her apprehensions.

"Too — too rash, Ernest!" she exclaimed in a low tone, as it reached her ears, and her hands were involuntarily clasped together. "Too rash — too daring — too heedless, for me as for thyself. Ah! dearly indeed am I taught how much you love me, when you make these reckless visits, when you wantonly brave these dangers! But I must go!" she exclaimed, hurriedly, as she heard the signal impatiently repeated; "I must go — I must meet him, or he will seek me here. He will rush into yet greater dangers; he will not heed these soldiers; and his old hatred to Barsfield, should he have distinguished him to-night, will prompt him, I fear me much, to seek him out even where his enemies are thickest."

Thus soliloquizing, she approached the couch where Rose Duncan was sleeping.

"Rose—Rose!" She called to her without receiving any answer. Assured that she slept, Janet did not seek to disturb her; but, after a hurried prayer, which she uttered while kneeling by the bedside, she rose with new courage, and, without further hesitation, unclosed the door, passed into the corridor, and descended to meet her daring lover. Little did she dream that the eyes of hate and jealousy were upon her; that a malignant foe was no less watchful than a fervent lover; that one stood in waiting, seeking her love, and, at the same time, no less earnestly desirous of the heart's blood of her lover!

She emerged into the court, which she hurried over incautiously, and was received by Mellichampe at the entrance of the garden. He took her to his arms—he led her away to the shelter of the great magnolias that towered in a frowning group from its centre; and the joy of their meeting, in that season and country of peril, almost took away the sting and the sorrow which had followed their separation, and now necessarily came with their present dangers. The happiness of Mellichampe was a tumult that could only speak in broken exclamations of delight; that of Janet was a subdued pleasure —a sort of bright, spiritual, moonlight gleam, that came stealing through clouds, mingled with falling drops, that were only not oppressive as they seemed to fall from heaven.

"Dear, dearest Janet—my own Janet—my only!—I have you at last; your hand is in mine—your eyes look into my own. I can not doubt that you are with me now. I believe it—I know it, by this new-born joy which is beating in my heart. Ah, dearest, but for that tory reptile, this rapture would have been mine before. But you are here at last, and, while you are with me, I will not think of him. I will think of nothing to vex; I will know but one thought, but one feeling—the long-cherished, dearest of all, Janet—the feeling of adoration, of devoted love, which my bosom bears for you."

The youth, as he spoke, had clasped her hands both in his, and his eyes looked for hers, which were cast down upon the grass below them. When she looked up, and they met his glance, he saw that they were glistening with tears.

"You weep — you weep, Janet. I vex you with my love — you are unhappy. Speak — say to me, dearest, what new affliction — what new strife and sorrow? What do these tears mean? Say out! I am used to hear of evil; it will not disturb me now. Is there any new stroke in store for me? Do not fear to name it; anything, only, only, Janet, if I am to suffer, let it not be your hand which is to deal it."

"There is none; none that I have to deal; none that I know of——"

"Then there is none; none that should trouble me; none that should make you weep. No tears, Janet, I pray you. We meet so seldom, that there should be no cloud over our meeting. See, love, how clear, how beautiful is this night! There were several clouds hanging about the moon at her rising, but they are all gone, and now hang like so much silver canopy above her head: she is almost full and round; and there is something of promise in her smile for us — so, dearest, it appears to me. Smile with me, smile with her, my beloved, and forget your griefs, and dismiss your tears."

"Alas, Ernest! how can I smile, when all things alarm me for you? The pursuit to-night — your vindictive enemy, Barsfield, — oh, Ernest, why will you be so headstrong — so rash?"

"There is no danger. I fear him not, Janet; but he shall learn to fear me: he does fear me, and hence it is that he hates and pursues me. But the fugitive will turn upon his pursuer yet. The time is coming, and, by the God of heaven——"

She put her hand upon his arm, and looked appealingly into his eyes, but spoke not.

"Well, well, say nothing: forgive me, dearest; I will speak no more of him; I will not vex you with his name — you are now sufficiently vexed with his presence. But the time will come, Janet, and, by Heaven — if I mistake not greatly Heaven's justice — it can not be far off, when he shall render me a fearful account of all his doings to me and mine. He has now the power — the men, the arms, but there will be some lucky hour which shall find him unprovided, when——"

She again appealed to the youth, whose impetuosity was again becoming conspicuous.

"You promised me, Ernest."

"Forgive me, dearest — I did promise you, and I will forbear to speak of the reptile; but my blood boils when I but hear his name, and I forget myself for the moment."

"Ah, Ernest, you are but too prone to forgetting."

"Perhaps so, Janet: your charge is true; but you I never forget; my love for you goes along with every thought, and forms a part of the predominant mood, whatever that may be. Thus, even when I think of this man, whose name inflames my blood until I pant for the shedding of his, one of the influences which stimulates my anger is the thought of you. He comes between us; he fills your father's mind with hostility to me, and he seeks you, Janet, he seeks you for his own."

"Nay, Ernest, why should you think so? He has made no avowal; and I am sure the regard of my father for you has undergone no change."

"It is so, nevertheless; and your father is too weak and too timid, whatever may be his affections, to venture to maintain opinions in hostility to those who command him when they please. He has denounced me to your father, that I know; he seeks you, I believe; and much I fear me, Janet, your father will yield to his suggestions in all cases, and both of us will become the victims."

As the youth thus addressed her, the tears departed from her eyes, and the expression which followed upon her face was calm and pleasantly composed. There was no rigidity in its muscles; each feature seemed to maintain its natural place; and her words were slow, and uttered in the gentlest tones.

"Have no fear of this, Ernest, I pray you. Should this man, should my father, should all, so far mistake me, as to entertain a thought that I could yield to a union with Barsfield, do not you mistake me. I will not vow to you, Ernest; I have no protestations to make, I know not how to make them; but you will understand, and you will believe me in the assurance which I now give you, that I can not hold my senses, and consent to any connection with the person you speak of."

"Bless you, dear Janet, but I needed no such assurance. I only feared that you might be driven by circumstances, by trick, by contrivances, to make a sacrifice of yourself for the good of another."

"Alas! Ernest, I now know what you would say. You would tell me that my father, at the mercy of this man, as he is, may require me as the offering by which he is to be saved. God help me! it is a strait I have not thought upon. I will not, I dare not, think upon it! Let us speak no more of this."

Gloomily and sternly the youth replied:—

"But you will think upon it, Janet; it may be required of you ere long. Think upon it, and provide your strength."

"God forbid, Ernest; God forbid! Let me die first! Let me perish before it becomes a question with me, whether to sacrifice peace, hope, the proper delicacy of my sex, and all that I live for, and all that I would love, to the safety of an only parent. Oh, how false I should be to promise love to a being whom I could only hate or despise! What a daughter could I be, to resist the prayers of a father requiring me to do so! Alas, Ernest, you bring me every form of trial. You make me most unhappy. You come rashly into the clutches of your deadly foe, and I tremble hourly, however I may rejoice when I hear that you are coming. I dread to see you perish before my eyes, under the weapons of these men; and, when you come, what is it that I am compelled to hear! what fears are before me! what horrors! Ah, if love be a treasure, if it be a joy to love and to be loved, it is so much the harder to think hourly of its loss, and of its so unguarded condition. Better not to feel, better to be hollow-hearted and insensible, than thus continually to dread, and as continually to desire— to fear with every hope, and to weep even where you would smile the most."

She buried her face in his bosom as she spoke, and her sobs were audible. His arm gently supported while enclasping her, and her afflictions greatly tended to subdue the impetuous character of his previous mood. He replied to her fondly, in those low tones which only the rich sensibility can understand, and the generous, warm spirit, employ understandingly.

"And yet, dearest, those very sorrows have a sweetness. Privation, pain, denial, even the lost love, Janet, are nothing to the choice spirit which has faith along with its sympathy. What consoles me? What has consoled me in the perils and the pains, the losses and the sorrows, which I have undergone in this warfare, and within the last two years? My confidence in you; my perfect faith that, however desolate, poor, denied, and desperate, however parted by enemies or distance, I was still secure of your love; I still knew that nothing, no, not even death, my Janet, could deprive me of that. If you have that confidence in me, my beloved, these sorrows, these trials, are only so many strengtheners. You will then find that the sorrows of love, borne well and without despondence, are the sweetest triumphs of the true affection. They are the honors which time can never tarnish; they are the spoils which last us for ever after. Janet, if, like you, I doubted, if I did not feel assured of your unperishing truth, I should rush this night, madly, and with but one hope of death, upon the swords of these tory-troopers. I should freely perish under your eyes, with but one prayer, that you might be able to behold me to the last."

"Speak not thus!" she exclaimed, with a shudder, looking around her as she spoke; "and do not think, Ernest, from what I have said, that I have not the same perfect faith in you that you feel in me; but I despair of all our hope. I am truly a timid maiden, and I am always fancying a thousand woes and sorrows. I can not dare to believe otherwise than that our loves are unblessed; I can not hope that we shall realize them: and oh, Ernest, your rashness, more than all things beside, tends to confirm in me these apprehensions. Why will you come to me when your enemies are abroad? Promise me, dear Ernest, to fly from this neighborhood until the danger has gone over. There is no dishonor—none."

"Ay, but there is, Janet; but of this we need say nothing. I could tell you much of friends, and good service to be done, but may not. Let us speak of more pleasant matters: of our hopes, not of our fears; of our joys, not of our sorrows; of the future, too, in exclusion of the present."

And thus, loving and well beloved, the two discoursed together; she sadly and despondingly, but with a true devotedness of heart throughout; and he, warm in all things, impetuously urging his love, his hope, his hatred to his enemies, his promises of vengeance, and his fixed determination to pursue the war in the neighborhood, in spite even of her solicitations that he should fly to a region of greater security.

Thumbscrew, meanwhile, had been anything but remiss in his guard. He had cautiously pursued his youthful associate, keeping close upon his heels, yet narrowly watching to avoid discovery. Though a bold and daring man, he yet esteemed the feelings and desires of Mellichampe with a sentiment of respect little short of awe; the natural sentiment of one brought up as he had been, to regard the family of his wealthy neighbor as superior beings in many respects. Apart from this, the quick, impetuous spirit of the youth exacted its own observance; and, as his commands had been positive to his comrade not to attend him, and urged in a manner sufficiently emphatic to enforce respect, the more humble companion felt the necessity of seeming submissive at least. We have seen that his regard trampled over his obedience, and it was well perhaps that it did so. It was not long that Thumbscrew had maintained his watch, before his quick ear detected the approach of footsteps. He ventured to peep out from his bush, and he was able to see the distinct outline of the intruder's person. He saw him approach the long alley in which he himself was sheltered, and within a few paces of the lovers; and he immediately changed his own position. Barsfield — for it was he — came on, passed the spot which sheltered the scout, and, stealing heedfully around a clump of orange, made his way to the rear of the thick bower in which Janet and Mellichampe were seated. The scout tracked him with no less caution and much more adroitness. He placed himself in cover, and coolly awaited the progress of events. The impatient spirit of Barsfield did not suffer him to wait long. The tory, it is probable, heard something of the dialogue between the two, and his movement seemed prompted at the particular moment when it took place by some remark of Mellichampe, which, from the exclamation of Barsfield as he rushed upon the youth, had touched the eavesdropper nearly. Leaping forward from behind one of the magnolias where he had been screened, with drawn sword, and a movement sufficiently hurried to pass the ground which separated them in the course of a few seconds, he cried to his rival in a bitter but suppressed tone of voice—

"You shall pay dearly for that lie, Mellichampe!"

In the next moment, a buffet from an unseen hand, that might have felled an ox, saluted his ear, and he stumbled unharmingly forward at the feet of the man whom he had sought to slay.

"Save me—oh, Ernest, save me! Fly, fly!—away, Ernest—it is Barsfield!"

Screaming thus, at the first alarm, the maiden clung to the youth, and trembled with affright. He, on the instant, had drawn his dirk, and putting her aside almost sternly, threw himself upon the half-stunned person of the tory: but his hand was seized by the watchful attendant. "Let me fix him, Airnest, boy; I knows how to manage the varmint."

"You here, Witherspoon?" demanded the youth.

"As you see him, Airnest—but take care of the gal, and send her safe home and quietly to bed. Ax pardon, Miss Janet, for scaring you, but 'twas the only way to manage the critter; but you had better run now, while I put what I calls my screwbolt upon the tory's jaw. Airnest, boy, let me have your handkerchief, since I may want another. There!"

With his knee upon the bosom of the tory, he busied himself meanwhile in bandaging his mouth. The intruder did not submit quietly, but began to show some few signs of dissatisfaction. His movement provoked an additional pressure of the knee of his assailant upon his breast, while the huge handkerchief which was employed upon his mouth, as he endeavored to cry out, was thrust incontinently into it. He was a child in the hands of his captor.

"Easy, now, Mr. Barsfield—be quiet and onconsarned, and no harm shall come to you; but, if you're at all opstropolous,

I shall be bound to take up a stitch or two in your jaw here, that'll be mighty disagreeable to both of us. Airnest, now, boy, don't stop for last words, but let's be off, or we'll have all the cubs looking after the great bear. I'll hold the lad quiet till you see the gal safe to the gate, but don't go farther."

He kept his word and his good-nature, in spite of all the struggles of his prisoner. Once, and once only, he seemed to become angry, as the tory gave him something more than the customary annoyance; but a judicious obtrusion of a monstrous knife, which was made to flash in the moonlight before the eyes of the captive, was thought sufficient by the scout in the way of exhortation.

"It's a nasty fine piece of steel, now, captain, and if you gives me much more trouble I shall let you have a small taste of its qualities; so you had better lay still till I lets you off, which won't be long, for you're of no more use to me here than a dead 'possum in a hollow thirty miles off. If I had you in the swamp, now, I could drive a little trade in your skin. I could swap you for some better man than yourself; but I'm your friend here, for, to say the gospel truth to you, captain, if I didn't stand between you and Airnest Mellichampe, you wouldn't see what hurt you: he'd be through you like a ground-mole, though in much shorter time; and there wouldn't be an inch of your heart that his dirk wouldn't bite into. But you're safe, you see, as you're my prisoner—the captive, as they used to say in old times, of my bow and spear—though, to be sure, it was only my fist that did your business."

It was thus that, like a good companion as he was, Thumb-screw regaled the ears of his prisoner with a commentary upon the particulars of his situation. In the meantime, Mellichampe conducted, or rather supported, the maiden to the garden entrance. When there she recovered her strength, as she perceived that he designed attending her to the dwelling. This she resisted.

"No, Ernest, no!—risk no more! I will not see—I will not suffer it. Let us part now—in danger still, as we have ever been. In sorrow let us separate—alas! I fear, in sorrow to meet again, if again we ever meet."

"Speak not thus," he replied, hoarsely. "Why these sad misgivings? is our love so much a sorrow, my Janet?"

"Sorrow or pleasure, Ernest, it is still our love—a love that I shall die in, and fear not to die for. But do not linger, I pray you: remember that Witherspoon is waiting for your return before he can release that man."

"Release him!" was the stern exclamation, and a fierce but suppressed laugh of bitterness fell from the lips of Mellichampe with the words.

"Ay, release him, Ernest. What mean you by those words —that laugh? Surely, surely, Ernest, you do not mean him harm?"

"Would he not harm us? has he not harmed me already? Janet, you must remember—I had a father once."

"I do—I do; but oh, Ernest, dismiss your thoughts, which I see are fearful now. Promise me, Ernest, that you will do this man no harm."

Her hand earnestly pressed his arm as she entreated him. He was silent.

"Ernest," she exclaimed, solemnly—"Ernest, remember! the hand of Janet Berkeley can never be won by crime."

He released her hand, which till this moment he had held. There was a strife going on within his bosom. She gazed on him suspiciously, and with terror.

"I leave you, Ernest," she whispered, "I leave you; but do that man no harm."

There was a solemnity in her tones that rebuked his thoughts. She was leaving him, but turned back with a gentler tone—

"I doubt you not, dear Ernest; I doubt you not now. Forgive me that I did so for an instant; and oh, Ernest, come not again into this neighborhood till these men are gone. Promise me—promise me, dear Ernest."

What would not love promise at such a moment? Mellichampe promised—he knew not what. His thoughts were elsewhere; and he felt not, that, in kissing her cheek as they parted, his lips had borne away her tears.

CHAPTER XV.

A FRIENDLY HITCH.

During the momentary absence of Mellichampe, his trusty associate had been equally busy with himself. He had completely gagged his prisoner with a handkerchief of no common dimensions, and not remarkable for the delicacy of its texture. He had finished this labor with a facility that was marvellous, and seemed to speak loudly for his frequent practice in such matters. This done, he took his seat composedly enough upon the body of the tory, and in this manner awaited the return of Mellichampe.

Barsfield, meanwhile, though at first a little uneasy and opstreperous, soon found it necessary to muster all his philosophy in the endurance of an evil that seemed unavoidable for the present. The huge, keen knife of the woodman glared threateningly in his eyes, and he saw that his efforts to escape, in more than one instance already, had provoked an expression of anger from his captor, who at other moments seemed good-natured and indulgent enough. The tory consoled himself, however, with the thought that Blonay could not be far off; and that, having made the circuit of the garden, as it had been appointed to him to do, he would soon come to his assistance and release. With this reflection, though burning for vengeance all the while, he was content to keep as quiet as was consistent with a position so very uneasy and unusual.

The fierce mood of Mellichampe was in action on his return: there was a terrible strife going on within his heart. A sanguinary thirst was striving there for mastery, opposed strongly, it is true, but not efficiently, by a just sense of human feeling not less than of propriety. But there was no calm deliberation, and his passions triumphed. All his more violent and vexing impulses were active in dictation. His eye was full of desperate intention: his hand grasped his bare dagger, and his movement was hurried toward the prisoner, whose eye turned appealingly to that of Witherspoon. The latter had his own apprehensions, but he had his decision also. He saw the manner of Mellichampe's approach; he understood directly the dreadful language which was uttered from his eye, though sleeping upon his lips; and he prepared himself accordingly to encounter and resist the movement which the glance of his comrade evidently meditated.

He was scarcely quick enough for this. A sudden and fierce bound, like that which the catamount makes from his tree upon the shoulders of his approaching victim, carried the form of Mellichampe full upon the breast of the tory, who strove, but vainly, to shrink away from beneath. The impetuous movement half displaced the woodman. In another moment the weapon must have been in the throat of the tory, but for the ready effort and athletic arms of Witherspoon. He grasped the youth from behind. His embrace encircled completely, while securing him from the commission of the deed.

"Release me, Witherspoon," cried Mellichampe to his companion, while the thick foam gathered about his lips and half choked his utterance.

"I'll be G—d derned if I do, Airnest," was the decisive reply. The youth insisted—the woodman was inflexible.

"You will repent it, Witherspoon."

"Can't be helped, Airnest, but I can't think to let you go to do murder. 'Taint right, Airnest; and dang my buttons if any man that I calls my friend shall do wrong when I'm standing by, if so be I can keep his hands off."

"Shall this wretch always cross my path, John Witherspoon?—shall he always go unpunished? Does he not even now seek my life—his hands not yet clean from the blood of my father? Release me, Witherspoon—it will be worse if you do not."

"That's my look-out, Airnest, I know; it's the risk I runs always, and it's no new thing. But, Airnest, I can't let you go, onless you promise not to use your knife. The fellow desarves the knife, I reckon; but, you see he's a prisoner, and can't do nothing for himself. It ain't the business of a sodger and a decent man to hurt a critter that can't fend off."

"A reptile—a viper, who will sting your heel the moment you take it from his head!"

"Maybe; but he's *my* prisoner, Airnest."

"Why, what can you do with him?—you can't carry him with you?"

"No, Airnest; but that's no reason that I should kill him."

"What will you do with him?" inquired the youth.

"Leave him here—jist where he is, on the flat of his back, and mighty oncomfortable."

"Indeed!—to pursue us, and by his cries, direct his hounds upon our heels? Let him rise, rather—give him his sword, and let him fight it out with me in the neighboring wood."

"Not so fast, Airnest—that'll be a scheme that would only hobble both of us, and I'm not going to risk any such contrivance. I have a much better notion than that, if you'll only hear to reason; and all I axes of you is, jist to keep your knife ready at the chap's throat, but not to use it onless he moves and gits obstropolous. Say you'll do that now, while I takes a turn or two upon my shadow, and I'll let you loose."

The youth hesitated. The woodman went on—

"You mought as well, Airnest, I'm not guine to loose you onless you says you won't hurt the critter. Say so, Airnest, and I'll fix him so he can't follow us or make any fuss."

Finding that his companion was inflexible, and most probably somewhat subdued by this time, and conscious of the crime he had striven to commit, Mellichampe consented, though still reluctantly, and the moment after he was released. The woodman rose and began to make some farther preparations for the securing of his prisoner. Meanwhile, with his knee firmly fastened upon the breast of the tory, and his dagger uplifted and in readiness, the eyes of the youth were fastened with all the demon glare of hatred and revenge upon those of the man below him. The feelings of Barsfield under such circumstances were anything but enviable. Accustomed to judge of men by his own nature, he saw no reason to feel satisfied that Mellichampe would keep the promise of forbearance which he had made to his companion; and yet he dreaded to exhibit emotion or anxiety, for fear of giving him sufficient excuse for not doing so. His emotions may well be inferred from the natural apprehensions of such a situation; and his base soul sunk into yet deeper shame, as he lay trembling beneath his enemy, dreading the death which was above him, and which he well knew he so richly deserved.

But Thumbscrew was considerate, and did not long keep the tory in suspense. In the few moments in which he had withdrawn himself from the person of the prisoner, he had made sundry arrangements for better securing him; and, with a cord of moderate length, which he had drawn from a capacious pocket, he constructed a running noose, or slip-knot, with which he now approached the prisoner; speaking in a low tone of soliloquy all the while, as much, seemingly, for Barsfield's edification as for his own.

"I will jist make bold, Cappin Barsfield, to give you a hitch or two in the way of friendship. You shall have as fast binding a title to this little bit of a bed as time and present sarcumstances will permit. It's only for your safe keeping and our safe running, you see, that I does it. I'll hitch up your legs—there, don't be scared, they shall go together—to this same bench here; and that, you see, will keep them from coming too close after ours. And as for the little bandage over your arms, why, you'll have to wear it a little longer, though it's too good a rag for me to leave behind. There—don't jerk or jump now, for it will soon be done. I'm mighty quick fixing such matters as these, and it takes me no time to hitch up a full-blooded tory when once I gits my thumb and forefinger upon him. There."

Thus muttering, he lashed the legs of the prisoner to one of the rude seats under the magnolias; and, freeing his companion from the further restraints of his watch, the two prepared to start—Witherspoon, unseen by Mellichampe, having first possessed himself of the sword of the tory, which he appropriated with all the composure of a veteran scout. They soon found their way out of the garden, through the darkest of its alleys, and they could not have gone far into the forest when Blonay, who seemed to have timed his movements with admirable accuracy, approached the spot where Barsfield lay struggling. The tory was completely in toils—his feet and hands tied securely, and his mouth so bandaged that but a slight moaning was suffered at intervals to escape him in his efforts at speech. With well-acted zeal and a highly becoming indignation, Blonay, as soon as he discerned the situation of his employer, busied himself at his release. Enraged at the humiliation to which he had been subjected, and at the escape of his enemy, Barsfield demanded why he had not come sooner. But to this the other had his answer. He had followed the tory's directions, and had kept the lower fence of the garden winding into the woods, and had crossed it at a point which had been designated for him; by which it had been Barsfield's hope, that, flying from him, the fugitive must be encountered by his coadjutor.

"You went too far round," said the commander, sullenly; "and yet they are but a few moments gone. You say you have not seen them?"

The answer was negative.

"It is strange: but, by G—d, it shall not always be thus. Come with me, sir; I will talk with you in my chamber."

And they retired to confer upon the scheme which the tory had proposed to Blonay just before the adventure of the garden.

We will now leave them and return to the fugitives, who were already far away upon their flight to the spot where their horses had been hidden. The first words of Mellichampe to his companion were those of reproach—

"Why did you follow me when I forbade it, John Witherspoon?"

"Well, now, Airnest, I think that's no sort of a question, seeing the good that's come of my following."

"True, you have served me, and perhaps saved me; but what will Janet think of me when she recovers from her fright? She will think I brought you there, and that you overheard what passed between us."

"Well, she'll think wrong, Airnest, if she does. It's true, I did hear a good deal, but that was owing to the necessity of being close upon the haunches of that other chap. As a true man, Airnest, I never wanted to hear, and I did not get close enough to hear, till that skunk come out from behind the pear-tree, and I saw him sneaking round to the magnolias. Then it was I came out too, and only then it was I heard the talk between you."

"It matters not now, Witherspoon; my fear is that it may pain Janet to suppose that my friends are brought to overhear that language which a young lady should only think to herself, and can only utter to one; and no motive of regard for my safety, though so far warranted by circumstances as upon the present occasion, should have prompted you to do so."

"But I had another reason, Airnest, that is a good reason, I know. Just after.I left you came one of Marion's road-riders, Humphries, you know, calling in the scouts; and you're wanted, and I'm wanted, and we're all of us wanted, for there's to be a power of the tories gathering in two days at Sinkler's Meadow, and the 'fox' is mighty hungry to git at 'em. I have the marks and the signals, and we must push on directly. It'll take us three good hours more to work our way into the swamp."

"Ah! then we have little time to waste," was the prompt reply; and, scouring down the road, they came to the broken branch which lay across the path, and indicated by its own the position of its fellow. Following the directions given by Humphries, they were soon met by the line of sentinels, and the path grew cheery after a while, when the occasional challenge, and the distant hum and stir of an encampment, announced the proximity of Marion in his wild swamp dwelling.

CHAPTER XVI.

THE TORY CAPTAIN AND THE LADY.

The reflections of Barsfield were by no means consolatory or grateful on his return to the mansion. A few moments were devoted to Blonay, of whom the tory felt perfectly secure, and the two then separated for the night, seeking their several chambers. In the morning the latter was up betimes, and, descending to the breakfast-room, the first person who encountered his glance was the fair Janet Berkeley.

She was alone. A slight flush overspread her cheek as he entered the apartment; but he was not the person exactly who could greatly disturb her equanimity. Her eye was cold and unshrinking, and her courtesy as easy, unconstrained, and distant as ever. The case was widely different with him. He started as he beheld her—turned away without the usual salutation—then, suddenly conscious of his rudeness, he wheeled round, as if about to charge an enemy, confronted her valiantly enough, and bowed stiffly, and with evident effort. For a few moments no word passed between the two, and this time was employed by Barsfield in pacing to and fro along the apartment. At length, muttering something to himself, the sounds of which were only just audible to the maiden, he walked into the corridor, looked hastily around, and then quickly, as if he wished to anticipate intrusion, re-entered the room, and at once approached the maiden.

"Miss Berkeley," he said, "it is unnecessary that I should remind you of last evening's adventure. The circumstances can not have been forgotten, though the singular composure of your countenance this morning would seem to imply a strange lack of memory on your part, or a far stranger indifference to its intimations."

He paused, as if in expectation of some reply, and she did not suffer him long to wait. Her response was instantaneous, and her equable expression of countenance unbroken.

"There is nothing strange, sir, I believe, if you will consider well the subject of which you speak. I know of no circumstances so strong in my memory which should disturb my composure, however some of them may affect yours. Are you not suffering from some mistake, sir?"

"Scarcely, scarcely, Miss Berkeley," he exclaimed, hurriedly; "though, I must confess, your reply astounds me not less now than your composure at our first meeting. Will you pretend, Miss Berkeley, that you were not in the garden at a late hour of last night?"

"I saw, sir, that you must labor under some mistake, and such is certainly the case when you presume to examine me thus. But I will relieve the curiosity which seems to have superseded all your notions of propriety, and at once say that I was in the garden last night."

"'Tis well—and there you saw another."

"True, sir. I then and there saw another."

"A rebel—a lurking rebel, Miss Berkeley."

"A brave man, a gentleman, an honest citizen, sir. My friend—my father's friend—"

"Say not so, for your father's sake, Miss Berkeley, I pray you. It would greatly endanger the safety of your father, were it known in the councils of Cornwallis that the son of the notorious Max Mellichampe was his friend; and still more, were it known that they were in intimate communion."

"I said not *that*, Captain Barsfield, I said not *that*," was the hasty reply of Janet, in tones and with a manner that showed how much she apprehended the consequences which might arise from such an interpretation of her remark. Barsfield smiled when he saw this, as he felt the consciousness of that power which her words had given him over her. She continued: "Do not, I pray you, think for a moment that my father knows anything of the visits of Mr. Mellichampe. He came only to see me——"

The tory interrupted her with a sarcastic smile and speech:

"And I am to understand that the dutiful Miss Berkeley consents to receive the visits of a gentleman without the concurrence, and against the will, of her father? A dilemma, is it not, Miss Berkeley?"

"I will not submit to be questioned, sir," was her prompt reply; and her eye glanced a haughty fire, before which that of the lowly-bred tory quailed utterly. "You again mistake me, sir, and do injustice to my father, when you venture such an inquisition into my habits. I am free, sir, to act as my own sense and discretion shall counsel. My father is not unwilling that I should obey my own tastes and desires in the selection of my associates, and to him alone am I willing to account."

She turned away as she spoke, and busied herself, or seemed to busy herself, with some of the affairs of the household, with the object, evidently, of arresting all farther conversation. But with the pause of a few moments, in which he seemed to be adjusting in his own mind the doubt and difficulty, Barsfield put on an air of decision, and readvanced to the maiden.

"Hear me but a few moments, Miss Berkeley, and be not impatient; and, should any of my words be productive of annoyance, I pray you to overlook them, in consideration of the difficulties which, as you will see, may soon lie before you."

"Difficulties!—but go on, sir."

"I need not say that I was a witness to your conference with this young man last night."

"You need not, sir," was her reply, with a manner that gave life to the few words she uttered. A scowl went over the tory's face, obscuring it for a moment, but he recovered instantly.

"I heard you both, and I felt sorry that you should have risked your affections so unprofitably."

The maiden smiled her acknowledgments, and he proceeded.

"Fortunately, however, for you at least, such ties as these, particularly where the parties are so young as in the present instance, are of no great strength, and are seldom durable. They can be broken, and usually are, with little detriment to either party."

"I purpose on my part, sir, nothing of the kind," was her cool reply, interrupting him, as he was about to continue in a speech of so much effrontery, and which was so little gratifying to his auditor; "I purpose not to try the strength or durability of any of the ties which I have made, Captain Barsfield."

"But you will, Miss Berkeley — you must, as soon as you discover that such ties are unprofitable, and beyond any hope of realization. The man with whom your pledge is exchanged is a doomed man!"

"How, sir? — speak!"

"He fights with a halter about his neck, and his appearance last night in the neighborhood of my troop is of itself sufficient for his condemnation, as it leads to his conviction as a spy!"

"I can share his doom, Captain Barsfield, though I believe not that such is within your power. I can not think that Lord Cornwallis has conferred upon you any such authority."

"This parchment, this commission, and these more expressive orders, Miss Berkeley, would tell you even more — would tell you that your own father is at my mercy at this very moment, as one, under your own avowal, privy to the presence of a rebel as a spy upon my command. My power gives me jurisdiction even over his life, as you might here read for yourself, were not my words sufficient."

"They are not — they are not," she exclaimed hastily, and trembling all over. "I will not believe it; let me see the paper."

"Pardon me, Miss Berkeley, but I may not now. It is sufficient for me that I know the extent of my power and its limits. It is not necessary that I should unfold it."

"I will not believe it, then — I will not trust a word that you have said. I can not think that the British general can have thought a thing so barbarous — so dishonorable."

"It is so, nevertheless, Miss Berkeley; but there will be

little or no danger to the father, if the daughter will listen to reason. Will you hear me?"

" Can I do less, Captain Barsfield?—go on, sir."

" I accept the permission, however ungraciously given. Hear me, then. These vows—the ties of childhood, and restraining none but children—can hardly be considered, when circumstances so bear against them. I have a perfect knowledge of all the circumstances between yourself and this rebel Mellichampe."

" You have not said, sir, and I marvel at the omission, with what wonderful ingenuity your knowledge was obtained."

" Your sarcasm is pointless, Miss Berkeley, when we know that a time like the present not only sanctions, but calls for and commands, all those little arts by which intelligence of one's enemies is to be obtained. Is it my offence or my good fortune, to have heard more than concerned the cause for which I contend? Certainly not my offence; it is for you to say how far it may be for my good fortune."

"To the point—to the point, Captain Barsfield, if you please."

" It is quite as well," he responded, with a sullen air of determination, as the impatient manner of Janet showed how unwillingly she listened: "'tis quite as well that I should— and all I ask from you now, Miss Berkeley, is simply that you should heed and deliberate upon what I unfold, and make no rash nor ill-considered decision upon it. First, then, let me say, that your father is in my power—but in mine alone. I am willing to be his friend henceforward, as I have been heretofore. I am able and desirous to protect him, as well against the rebels as from the injustice of such loyalists as might presume upon his weakness to do him wrong; but I am not sufficiently his friend or my own enemy, to do all this without some equivalent. There must be a consideration."

He paused; and, as the maiden perceived it, she spoke, while a smile of the most provoking indifference, suddenly, though for a moment only, curled the otherwise calm and dignified folds of her lips—

" I can almost conjecture what you would say, Captain

Barsfield; but speak on, sir, I pray you. Let there be an end of this."

"I can scruple little to say out what you assume to have conjectured so readily, Miss Berkeley; and I speak my equivalent the more readily, as you seem so well prepared to hear it. You, then, are the equivalent for this good service, Miss Berkeley. Your hand will be my sufficient reward, and my good services shall ever after be with your father for his protection and assistance."

"Think of something else, Captain Barsfield," she replied, with the utmost gravity; "something better worthy of the service — something better suited to you. I am not ambitious, sir, of the distinction you would confer upon me. My hopes are humble, my desires few; and my father — but here he comes. I will speak of this affair no further."

And she turned away with the words, just as the old man, entering, met the baffled tory with some usual inquiry as to the manner in which he had slept, and if his bed had been pleasant; and all with that provoking simplicity that was only the more annoying to Barsfield, as it brought the commonest matters of daily life into contrast and collision with those more important and interesting ones, in the discussion and urging of which he had but a few moments before been so earnest. He replied as well as he could to the old gentleman, who complained bitterly of his own restlessness during the night, and of strange noises that had beset his ears, and so forth — a long string of details, that silenced all around, without the usual advantage which such narrations possess, toward nightfall, of setting everybody to sleep. But the signal was now given for breakfast, and the lively Rose Duncan made her appearance, bright and smiling as ever; then came Lieutenant Clayton; and lastly, our old acquaintance Blonay. Breakfast was soon despatched, and was scarcely over when Barsfield, who had given orders for his troops to move, took Mr. Berkeley aside. Their conversation was long and earnest, though upon what subject remained, for a season at least, entirely unknown to the household, Janet, however, could not but remark that a deeper shadow rested upon the visage of her father; and even Rose Duncan, playful and thoughtless as she ever was, complained that during the whole day her uncle had never once asked her for a song, or challenged her to a game at draughts.

"Something wrong, Janet," she exclaimed to her companion, after freely remarking upon the condition of things; "something wrong, I'm certain. This tory lover of yours is at the bottom of it."

And, without pausing for reply, she whirled away in all the evolutions of the Meschianza, humming, like some errant bird, a wild song, that did not materially disagree with the capricious movement. Janet only answered with a sigh as she ascended to her chamber.

CHAPTER XVII.

THE HALF-BREED TRAILS HIS ENEMY.

BARSFIELD ordered a guard of ten men, and prepared to ride over to the "Kaddipah" plantation—the reward of his good services in the tory warfare. The distance between the two places was but five miles; and, in the present prostrate condition of Carolina affairs, ten men were deemed quite adequate for his protection. They might not have been, had the "swamp fox" been warned of his riding soon enough to have prepared a reception. Clayton was left in charge of the troop; and in no very pleasant humor did the tory proceed to leave the mansion of Mr. Berkeley. He had not, of late years, been much accustomed to contradictions of any sort; and his recent elevation, as an officer of the British army, tended still more to make him restiff under restraint or opposition. He was disappointed in the effect which he had promised himself to produce upon the mind of Janet Berkeley, from a display of the power of which he was possessed, and still more annoyed at the cool, sarcastic temper which she had shown during their conference. Her frank avowal of the interest which she felt in Mellichampe—the calm indifference with which she listened to his remarks upon the nocturnal interview with her lover—and the consequences of that interview to himself—these were all matters calculated to vex and imbitter his mood, as he rode forth from the spot in which they had taken place. His manner was stern, accordingly, to his lieutenant, Clayton, while giving him his orders, and haughty, in the last degree, to the men under him. Not so, however, was his treatment of Blonay, whom he heard calling familiarly to his dog, and who now stood ready, about to mount his tacky, as if going forth with himself.

"You go with me, Mr. Blonay?" was his question to the half-breed, uttered in the mildest language.

"Well, cappin, I reckon it's best that I should go 'long with you 'tell I can hear something of Marion's men. When I hears where to look for 'em I reckon I'll leave you, seeing it's no use for me to go scouting with a dozen.'

"You are right," was the response; "but fall behind till I send the men forward; I would have some talk with you."

Blonay curbed his pony, called in his dog, and patiently waited until, sending his men forward under a sergeant, Barsfield motioned him to follow with himself.

"You were sadly at fault last night, Mr. Blonay," was the first remark which he made to the half-breed, as they entered upon the avenue; "it is to be hoped that you will soon do better."

"'Tworn't my fault, cappin—I did as you tell'd me," was the quiet answer.

"Well, perhaps so; you are right, I believe. I did send you too far round. That confounded garden holds several acres."

"Five, I reckon," said the other. Barsfield did not heed the remark, but abruptly addressed him on the subject which was most active in his thoughts.

"You hold your mind, Mr. Blonay, I presume, for this adventure? You will undertake the business which I gave you in hand? You have no fears—no scruples?"

"Well, I reckon it's a bargin, cappin. I'll do your business if so be I kin, and if so be it doesn't take me from my own. I puts my own first, cappin, you see, for 'twould be agin natur if I didn't."

"You are perfectly right to do so; but I am in hope, and I believe, that you will soon find our business to lie together. If the enemy you seek be one of Marion's men, so is my enemy: should you find one, you will most probably get some clew to the other; and the one object, in this way, may help you to both."

"And you think, cappin, that Marion's men is in these parts?"

"Think!—I know it. The appearance of this youth Mellichampe, with his cursed inseparable Witherspoon, as good as proves it to me. Not that they are strong, or in any force; on the contrary, my letters tell me that the rebels have, in a great many instances, deserted their leader, and gone into North Carolina. Indeed, they say he himself has gone; but this I believe not: he still lurks, I am convinced, in the swamp, with a small force, which we shall quickly ferret out when we have got our whole force together. To-morrow we go to meet our volunteer loyalists at 'Sinkler's Meadow,' where they assemble, and where I am to provide them with arms."

"There's a-many of them to be there, cappin?" was the inquiry of Blonay.

"Two hundred or more. The wagons which you saw carry their supplies."

The tory captain, in this way, civilly enough responded to other questions of the half-breed, the object of which he did not see; and in this manner they conversed together until the guard had emerged from the avenue into the main road, and was now fully out of sight. Interested in giving to his companion as precise a description as possible of the person, the habits, and character of Mellichampe, which he did at intervals throughout the dialogue, Barsfield had moved on slowly, and had become rather regardless of the movement of his men, until, reaching the entrance of the avenue, he grew conscious of the distance between them, and immediately increased his pace. But Blonay did otherwise; he drew up his pony at this point, and seemed indisposed to go forward.

"Why do you stop?" cried the tory, looking back over his shoulder. The answer of Blonay satisfied him.

"I forgot something, cappin—the knife and the pass. I must go back, but I'll be after you mighty quick."

Without waiting for the assent of his employer, he started off on his return, pricking the sides of his pony with a degree of earnestness to which the little animal was not accustomed, and which he acknowledged by setting off at a rate which seemed infinitely beyond his capacities. Barsfield was satisfied to call to him to follow soon; and, putting the rowel to his own steed, he hurried forward to resume his place at the head of his men.

But it was not the intention of Blonay to go back to the dwelling which he had so lately left. He was practising a very simple *ruse* upon his companion. He had forgotten nothing — neither knife nor passport; and his object was merely to be relieved from observation, and to pursue his farther journey alone. He had a good motive for this; and had resolved, with certain efficient reasons, which had come to him at the moment of leaving the avenue, to pursue a different route from that of the tory.

After riding a little way up the avenue, he came to a halt; and, giving the tory leader full time, not only to reach his men, but to get out of sight and hearing with them, he coolly turned himself round and proceeded to the spot where they had separated. Here he alighted, and his keen eyes examined the road, and carefully inspected those tracks upon it, a casual glance at which, as he rode out with Barsfield, had determined him upon the course which he had taken. He looked at all the horse-tracks, and one freshly made in particular. The identical outline of shoe, which he had so closely noticed on the battle-ground of Dorchester, was obviously before him; and, remounting his horse, he followed it slowly and with certainty. Barsfield more than once looked round for his ally, but he looked in vain; and each step taken by both parties made the space greater between them. The half-breed kept his way, or rather that of his enemy, whom he followed with a spirit duly enlivened by a consciousness that he was now upon the direct track.

In this pursuit the route of Blonay was circuitous in the extreme. He had proceeded but a mile or so along the main road, when the marks which guided him turned off into an old field, and led him to the very spot where we discovered Mellichampe and Witherspoon the day before. The keen eye of the half-breed soon discovered traces of a human haunt, but nothing calculated to arrest his progress, as the marks of the flying horseman were still onward. Obliquely from this point, still farther to the right, he entered a dense forest. Here he made his way with difficulty, only now and then catching the indent of the shoe. He soon emerged from the thick wood, and the path was then open. Here, too, he discovered that there had been an assemblage of persons, as the ground, in a little spot, was much beaten by hoofs, and still prominent among them was that which he sought in chief. This encouraged him; and, as the whole body assembled at the spot seemed to have kept together, he had no little difficulty in continuing the search. At length the road grew somewhat miry and sloppy. Little bays at intervals crossed his path, through which the horsemen before him seemed to have gone without hesitation. The forests were now broken into hammocks, which were indented by small bodies of water. Here the cypress began to send up its pyramidal shapes; and groves of the tallest cane shot up in dense masses around it. The cressets lay green upon the surface of the dark pond, and the yellow and purple mosses of the festering banks presented themselves to his eyes in sufficient quantity to announce his proximity to the swamp.

But to Blonay, thoroughly taught in all the intricacies of the "cypress," its presence offered no discouragement whatsoever to the pursuit. At length, reaching an extensive pond, he lost all trace of the horses. He saw at once that they had entered the water; but where had they emerged? The opposite banks were crowded close to the water's edge with the thickest undergrowth mingled with large trees, whose quiet seemed never to have been disturbed with the axe of the woodman or the horn of the hunter. The wild vine and the clustering brier, the slender but numerous canes, the gum-shoots, cypress knees or knobs, and the bay, seemed to have been welded together into a solid wall, defying the footsteps of any invader more bulky than the elastic black-snake, or less vigorous and well-coated than the lusty bear.

Blonay saw the impervious nature of the copse; but he also felt assured that the pursuit must lead him into and through it. He saw that through it the men must have gone whose footsteps he had followed, and he accordingly soon completed his resolves as to what he should himself do. He slowly led his horse back to a spot of land the highest in the neighborhood. Having done this, he fastened him to a shrub; then sought out one of the loftiest trees, which he ascended with habitual and long-tried dexterity.

His elevation gave him a full and fine view of the expansive swamp before him. He looked down upon the pale, ghostly tops of the old cypresses, sprinkled with the green cedar, and here and there, where the sand was high enough to yield a bed sufficiently spacious for so comprehensive a body, the huge and high shaft of the colossal pine. These all lay before him— their tops flat, gently waving under his eye beneath the slight wind passing over them, making a prospect not less novel than imposing.

But Blonay had no eye for the scene, and but little taste for the picturesque. He had sought his giddy perch for another purpose; and he was satisfied with the result of his labor when, at the distance of six or eight hundred yards from the entrance of the swamp, he detected a slight wreath of smoke curling up from among the trees, and spreading around like some giant tree itself, as if in protection over them. He noticed well in what direction the smoke arose, and quietly descended from his place of elevation.

Keeping this direction constantly in mind, he now saw that the persons he pursued must have gone into the pond, and kept in it for some distance afterward, emerging at a point not at that moment within the scope of his vision. He doubted not that, following the same course, he should arrive once more upon their traces at some point of outlet and entrance.

To conjecture thus, was, with him, to determine. He touched his pony smartly with his whip, and, whistling his dog to follow, plunged fearlessly into the pathless space, and his saddle-skirts were soon dipping in the yellow water. He kept forward, however, through the centre of the pond, and was soon gratified to find some appearances of an opening before him. On his right hand the pond swept round a point of land, making into the copse, and forming a way which was imperceptible at the place whence he had originally started. He did not scruple to pursue it; and, passing through a narrow defile of water, over which the vines ran and clambered, thrusting their sharp points continually in his face, and making his progress necessarily slow, he at length ascended a little bank, and once more found the tracks which he had followed so far. Giving his little pony a few moments of rest, he again set forward; and, after an arduous progress of an hour, he began to hear sounds which imposed upon him the necessity of greater caution in his progress. The hum of collected men — their voices — the occasional neigh of the horse — the stroke of the axe — and now and then a shout — announced his proximity to the camp.

He was now within a few hundred yards of one of the famous retreats of "the swamp-fox;" and, dismounting from his nag, which he carefully fastened in a secure place of concealment, he went forward on foot, only followed by his dog; moving slowly, and scrutinizing, as he did so, every tree and bush that might afford shelter to an enemy. He still advanced until he came to a small creek, which wound sinuously along before him, and which now formed the only barrier between himself and the retreat of the partisans. He saw their steeds in groups, fastened to the overhanging branches of the trees; he saw the troopers lying at length in similar places of shelter — some busied in the duties of the camp and of preparation — some taking their late breakfast, and others moving around as sentinels, one of whom paced to and fro within thirty yards of the little copse from which he surveyed the scene in safety.

It was while gazing intently on the personages constituting these several groups, that Blonay discovered his dog in rapid passage across a tree that lay partly over the creek which separated him from the encampment. Attracted, most probably, by the good savor and rich steams that arose from a huge fire, over which our old acquaintance Tom was providing the creature-comforts of the day, the dog made his way without looking behind him, and Blonay was quite too nigh the sentinels to venture to call him back by either word or whistle. Cursing the cur in muttered tones to himself, he drew back to a safer distance, still keeping in sight, however, of the entire circuit occupied by the partisans.

Here he watched a goodly hour, taking care that no single movement escaped his eye; for, as he had now found out one of the secret paths leading directly to the haunt of an enemy so much dreaded as "the swamp-fox," he determined that his knowledge of all its localities should be complete, the better to enhance the value, and necessarily increase the reward, which he hoped to realize from its discovery to some one or other of the British leaders. Let us now penetrate the encampment itself.

CHAPTER XVIII.

THE HALF-BREED IS WINDED.

The hiding-place of Marion was admirably chosen in all respects, whether as regards convenience or security. It was a high ridge of land, well timbered, narrow, and long, and running almost centrally into the swamp. Two or three outlets, known only to the partisans, and these, as we have seen, in the one instance already described, intricate and difficult of access even to the initiated, were all that it possessed; and here, secure from danger, yet not remote from its encounter, if circumstances or his own desires so willed it, "the swamp-fox" lay with his followers during brief intervals of that long strife in which he contended for his country.

His force was feeble at this period. It consisted only of the small bands of natives, gathered under local officers chiefly from the lower country, none of whom had ever seen what was called regular service. He had been deserted by all the continentals with the exception of two, whom he had rescued from their British captors soon after the battle of Camden; but, though thus few in number, and feeble in resource, the partisans, catching the full spirit of their leader, were never inactive.

In the camp, while Blonay looked out on all hands for his particular victim, the stir of preparation was heard by the overlooking spy. Hurried orders were given, horses were put in preparation, swords were brandished, and rifles charged home. Amid all the bustle, there was still room for jest and merriment. Like boys just let loose from school, the men playfully gambolled about among the forest avenues. Here, you saw a little party engaged in leaping; there were others, hurling the bar; others, again, less vigorously limbed or winded, held solemn conclave, in deeper thickets, busy in all the intricacies of "*old sledge*" (or "*seven up*"), which, in that unsophisticated period, had not given place to *brag* and *poker*.

Of all the groups and persons visible in the partisan camp, there was but a single individual who seemed in no way to participate in the moods and employments of the rest — whose thoughts were certainly foreign to all amusements. This melancholy exception was no other than our philosophic epicure, Lieutenant Porgy. You behold him, where he sits upon a fallen tree, his belt undone, his sword across his lap, his elbows on his knees, his great chin within his palms, his eyes looking out vacantly and sadly, without seeming to perceive the groups or the sports around him. He sits in silence, for a wonder; he has no soliloquies; and when he seems to be growing thoughtful, it is with such a disconsolate expression, that one apprehends some very serious misfortunes impending. Why should Porgy be sad? Perhaps he has gone without his supper. The new swamps have probably failed in the treasures of terrapin which endeared those of the Ashley to his affections.

But Tom appears — the cook *par excellence* — and we look to him for explanation. There is no falling off of flesh in the case of Tom, or his master; and there is an unctuous — shall we call it greasy — appearance, about the mouth and cheeks of the negro, that will not permit us to think that he, at least, has suffered any recent diminution of his creature comforts. Now, we can not suppose that, where Tom can find fuel for himself, his master will be permitted to sit without a fire. If Tom can procure hoe-cake and bacon for his own feeding, it is very sure that Porgy will not go without his supper. His cause of trouble lies in some other quarter than the stomach. But Tom is about to clear his voice for speech, as his master looks up, inquiringly, at his approach.

"He's berry bad, maussa!"

"Worse?"

"He's berry bad, sah."

"Worse, I say?"

"Hah! who kin say but he 'se'f? De hoss hab de wuss 'flictions dis time, I ebber see!"

"Will he die, Tom?"

"Ef he no git better, maussa, I 'spec' de buzzard hab fine chance for put up meat to-night."

"You are yourself a buzzard, you rascal; to speak in this way of the condition of the beast."

"Ki! maussa, whey's de ha'm? [harm] Hoss hab for dead jis like white man and nigger. You no bury hoss, like you bury man, and de buzzard *hab* for git 'em!"

"Tom, when you die, there shall be no weight of earth put upon you. You shall be laid out bare, just where the horse is laid—should you suffer him to die! and I shall have a trumpeter to sound a notice to all the buzzards, for fifty miles round, to attend your funeral."

"Come, come, maussa; 'twunt do for talk sich ting! Tom nebber for bury when he dead? None but buzzard for ax to he fun'rel? and jis 'kaise you hoss gwine for dead, and nobody for help 'em! wha' Tom kin do? He a'n't hoss-doctor. 'Speck, maussa, you better try Doctor Oakenburg. 'Speck he hab someting to gee de hoss. He can't cure de *man*, when he sick; may-be, he kin cure de *hoss!* Better ax 'em, maussa."

"What! are you such an enemy of the poor beast, Tom, that you want to subject him to new miseries? What pleasure can you find in seeing such a beast as Oakenburg torturing such a beast as Nabob? and you have fed and groomed Nabob for five years! Have you no affection for an animal that you have been intimate with for so long a time? You have ridden him a thousand times. He has borne you as tenderly as your own mother. Have you no gratitude, you rascal, that you wish to thrust one of Oakenburg's decoctions into his stomach?"

"Oh! go 'long maussa; you too foolish! How I want for gee de hoss misery? I wants for care 'em! Da's it! I 'speck de physic, wha' de doctor mek', will mek' de hoss well—"

"What! though it kills the man! Tom, I sometimes think you are half a fool at best. No, Tom; Nabob must get well without help from Oakenburg, or he's a dead beast. His stomach has always been a good one till now. It shall never be defiled by any of Oakenburg's decoctions. But you, Tom, as a cook, and a good cook, ought to know what's good even for the stomach of a horse. Medicine, itself, is only the proper sort of food for a morbid condition. Is there nothing now that you can think of, Tom, that the poor beast can make out to eat. Think, old fellow; think."

"I see dem gib hoss-drench, mek' wid whiskey, and soot, and salt; but whay you guine git salt here for hoss, and you no hab none for sodger?"

"Where, indeed? The prospect is a sad one enough:—and you say, Tom, that all the salt is gone that came up last week from Georgetown?"

"Ebbry scrap ob 'em, maussa—no hab 'nough to throw on bird tail ef you want to catch 'em. Dis a bad country, Mass Porgy—no like de old cypress, whay you can lap up 'nough salt from de swamp to cure you meat for de year round, and season you hom'ny by looking at 'em only tree minutes by the sun."

"And you know nothing, Tom, that will ease the animal?"

"No, maussa, I see de buckrah gib drench heap time, but I nebber ax how he been mek."

"Has Humphries come in yet, Tom?"

"Long time, sir: he gone ober to Wolf island wid de major bout two hours 'go, and muss be coming back directly; and, jist I speak, look at 'em, coming yonder, by de big gum!"

"I see! I see! I must consult Humphries. You may go now, Tom, and see after your own dinner. I feel hungry, myself, in anticipation of a march that I feel that we shall be called upon to make hurriedly. Yet how to march if Nabob dies, it is difficult to conceive. Tom, unless you have some peculiar delicacy, you need prepare no dinner for me. That beast's misery won't suffer me to eat. Go and see to him, Tom, and report to me how he gets on now."

Tom disappeared, and our fat friend rose from his sitting posture with the air of a man who had no longer any uses in the world. He was sufficiently sad to be thought melancholy, and half suspected it himself.

"D—n the poor beast," he muttered as he went; "I can't

bear to look at him. I can't bear to look at the sufferings I can't help. If by a fierce wrestle now, a hand-to-hand fight with an enemy, or even a match-race on foot with an Indian runner, I could do the creature a service, I could go to work cheerfully. Any physical or mental exertion now — no matter of what sort — that would do him good, I would undertake with a sort of satisfaction. But only to look on, and do nothing, sickens me; it may be because I raised the rascally beast myself!"

Thus muttering to himself as he went, our epicurean moved slowly along by the several groups, taking the route toward Humphries, who was seen approaching on the edge of the island. The philosopher was too sad to enjoy the sports of others at this moment. But his boon companions, who knew his usual humors, and seldom witnessed his exceptional turns, were not disposed to permit his unnoticed progress. A dozen voices challenged his attention from all sides, all anxious to secure the company of a good companion.

"I say, Lieutenant — Lieutenant Porgy. This way."

"And this way," cried another and another.

In all these cries, Porgy fancied there was something of an official tone, and he answered one for all.

"How now, you unfeeling brutes? What are you howling about, at such a rate? Have you no sensibility? Must the dying agonies of the poor beast be disturbed by such horrible sounds as issue from such monstrous throats? or do you suppose me deaf? Say what you want. From whom come you? Speak out, and do not think me so deaf as indifferent. I would not hearken, but that you compel me to hear, and will hardly heed unless you speak in more subdued accents. You will crack the drum of my ear by such howlings!"

"Ho! ho! ho!—Ha! ha! ha!"

"What a damnable chorus!" muttered the philosopher. "And this disrespect is the fruit of my good nature. ·Familiarity breeds contempt. He who sleeps with a puppy is sure of fleas. Now, all because of my taking these rascals into my mess, and treating them like gentlemen, do they presume to howl, and shout, and yell in my ears, as if they were so many bedfellows?

Well, Mr. Mason, what is it *you* would say? Speak out and have done with it. A short horse is soon curried."

Dick Mason growled sulkily at the reflection upon his dwarfish size. He was the monster in little of the camp, being but four feet eight.

"Why, lieutenant," said he, "you're mighty cross to-day."

"Cross!—And well I maybe, since here's Nabob, my nag, as fine an animal as man would wish to cross, racked with all the spasms of an infernal colic! Tell me what I can do for *him;* if not, hold your peace, and go to the devil without bothering me with your sense of what is due to your master."

"Your horse!—what, Nabob?" with interest.

"Yes! my horse! Nabob!" pertinently.

"Give him red pepper tea!" said one.

"Soot and salt!" cried another.

"Gunpowder and rum!" a third.

"Turpentine and castor oil!" a fourth.

"A feed of pine burrs is the very best remedy, lieutenant," said a fifth.

Other suggestions followed, half in jest, half in earnest, until the angry lieutenant, seizing one of the party by the hair of his head with one hand, and snatching up a cudgel with the other, was preparing to make a signal example of the one offender, for the benefit of the now dispersing group, when Humphries seized him from behind, and drew, for a brief moment, the fury of the epicure upon himself.

"Who dares?" he demanded, wheeling about.

"Why, you're as full of fight as a spring terrapin of eggs."

"The comparison saves you a cudgeling, Bill Humphries, though you half deserve it for saving these rascals. They've been jeering me, the heartless blackguards, about the condition of my horse, who's dying of colic!"

"Colic!—do you say? Is he bad off."

"He's no horse if he isn't. Bad as he can be! So bad, that even Tom prescribes Oakenburg."

"Oakenburg will kill him, if he undertakes the cure. But there's a Santee jockey here, that's famous as a horse doctor.

So ho! Here! Tom Jennings," calling to a lanksided sandlapper, "be off quickly, and hunt up Zeke Turpin, and send him here. Tell him that Lieutenant Porgy's horse has colic from eating his master's dinner by mistake."

"Ah! villain, you take advantage of my grief," said Porgy, with an effort to smile.

"He'll cure it if anybody can! So give yourself no concern. Only, you must put yourself in readiness as soon as possible. That's the order now."

"What's to be done, Humphries?"

"Work! Fight's the word!"

"Fight! With whom now?"

"The tories!"

"The tories! Whereabouts do they gather?"

"At Sinkler's meadow, where there's to be a mighty gathering. They are promised arms and ammunition from the city. We are to have warm work, they tell us, for there's to be a smart chance of the rascals together; but devil take the odds. The job will pay for itself, Porgy, since they're to have a barbecue and plenty of rum."

"Ah, ha! That's encouraging as a prospect, Humphries; and now the question is, whether we shall let them feed before we fight them, or fight them before they feed."

"I don't see why that should be a question. We've got to fight them as soon as we can get a chance at them, and whether before or after the barbecue don't matter very much."

"An opinion that argues great simplicity on the part of Lieutenant Humphries," was the reply of Porgy. "The difference is vastly material to our interests, and ought to govern our policy. If we let them feed before we fight them, we shall find them easier customers, since every third man will be surely drunk, and no second man sober."

"Well, there's something in that, certainly," said Humphries.

"Ay, true; but look at the other side. If we fight them before we suffer them to feed, we shall have the greater spoil, since barbecued beef and Jamaica, which have been already consumed by a hundred or two starving tories, is so much clear loss to our commissariat. Now, Bill, I'm for the tougher job of the two—the harder fighting and the greater saving. The wretches! only to think that they are to have a barbecue, while we are compelled to eat—Tom, what are we compelled to eat?—what have you got for dinner, to-day, old fellow?"

Tom reappeared in season to answer.

"Wha' for dinner! Huh! Hab some tripe, sah, and hom'ny, and bile acorns."

"Tripe, hommony, and boiled acorns! And they to have a barbecue! Roast beef—a whole ox—stall-fed, no doubt!—and a puncheon of Jamaica! Ah! Humphries, it is a problem which none of us can solve. There seems to be something unreasonable in this partial distribution of the gifts of Providence. Has a tory a better stomach than a patriot? Is his taste more refined and intellectual? Does he need more fuel for his furnace? Are his nervous energies more exhausting! Are his virtues higher? Has he the right of the political argument? In other words, ought we to prefer George the Third to the Continental Congress, for that is the question that naturally occurs to us when we find the tories better supplied with the creature-comforts than ourselves."

"Well, Porgy, that's certainly a new view of the case."

"Truly; but I see how it's to be answered, without a sacrifice of principle. The rascals have the good things, Bill; but shall they be allowed to keep 'em? That's the question. On the contrary, they are but so many agents of Providence, in gathering and getting ready the feast for us. We shall spoil the Egyptians, Bill; we shall be able to come upon them—shall we not?—before they shall have touched the meat. I like vastly to take a first cut at a barbecue. The nice gravy is then delicious. After a dozen slashes have been made in it, it imbibes a smoky flavor which I do not relish. We must come upon them, Bill, when everything's ready, but before they have made the first cut."

"Right! but I'm afraid *you'll* not be in time for the cut, lieutenant," said Humphries gravely.

"And why not, pray?"

"Your horse!"

"Ah, that I should have forgotten the poor beast, thinking of the barbecue. Tom, how's Nabob now?"

Tom shook his head deplorably.

"Ah! well, I suppose I shall have to lose him. I must leave him with your Santee jockey, Bill, and see what he can do for him. But to that barbecue I'll go! Flat! I'll borrow the nag of that old German that's sick — old ——"

"Feutbaer! Well, he'll carry you safe enough; it will be for the tories to say if he will bring you back. But what's this? — ha!"

Humphries started as the two approached the little hollow in which Tom carried on his preparations for the humble meal of the squad for which he provided. The trooper seized a rifle that stood against a tree beside him, and lifted it instantaneously to his eye. The muzzle of it rested upon the strange dog that burrowed amid the offal strewn about the place, unnoticed by the busy cook who purveyed for him. Porgy was about to declare his wonderment at the sudden ferocity of mood exhibited by his companion, when, motioning him to be silent, the trooper lowered the weapon, and called to John Davis, who was approaching at a little distance.

"Davis," said he, as the other came near, "do you know that dog?"

"I think I do; but where I've seen him I can't say. I'm sure I know him."

"Is it possible?" exclaimed Humphries, somewhat impatiently, "that you should any of you fail to remember the brute? What do you say, Tom? Don't you know the dog?"

This was addressed to the negro in tones that startled him.

"He face is berry familiar to me, Massa Bill," returned Tom after a pause, in which he seemed to study the matter with grave severity; "he face is berry familiar to me, 'cept he a'n't bin wash 'em much. But I loss de recollection ob de name for ebber."

"But why the devil," quoth Porgy, "should that dirty-looking beast so much interest you? Positively, you are all in a stew and sweat."

"And well I may be if all's true that I suspect. I'm a marked man!"

"A marked man! you're dreaming! What do you mean?"

"I can not be mistaken, Porgy. That is the cur of Mother Blonay — Goggle's mother — and the blear-eyed rascal must be, even now, in this very neighborhood."

"Do you think so, Bill?" demanded Davis.

"Think so? I know it; if I know the dog. If that be the same brute, Blonay's here — at hand — in this very swamp; and we are hunted! *I* am hunted! The rascal's on my trail. He seeks my life."

This was a serious suggestion, the importance of which was instantly felt by all the group. If such a scout as Blonay were really on the trail of Humphries, there was not a moment in which his life was secure. There was no path which he could pursue in safety; every bush might give forth the bullet, every tree-top, or hollow, or gulley, or bay, or swamp-border, send forth its sudden messenger of death. The assassin in the scout, and on trail, presents to the imagination of the woodman as complete an idea of danger and terror as it belongs to the human mind to conceive. But Humphries, though rendered very serious by his conjectures, was not appalled, or deprived by his apprehensions of the first attributes of manhood — thought and decision.

"We are hunted," he continued, after closely scrutinizing the dog, "I am now sure of it. Goggle's in this very place, and the bead of his rifle, no doubt ranging, some hundred yards off, upon some one of this party. But don't look up or around," said he quickly, seeing that his companions were about to let their eyes and gestures betray their curiosity. "Do not look, or start, or seem curious. If he be here, as I believe, we must not suffer him to suppose that his presence is suspected. We must play a scout-game with the rascal; while we are all here together, he will scarcely trouble one of us. He will watch his opportunity to find me alone, for I am sure that I am the one he seeks."

"But," said Porgy, "even if this be the rascal's dog, and it has a sufficiently rascally look to be so, why should that prove the master to be present? The brute may have strayed."

"No! such a creature never strays. He can't do without his master. He is a part of him. But let us see, now, if the animal can be made to seek his master. "Tom!"—to the negro.

Tom had been listening curiously. He answered promptly. The dog meanwhile, with his nose about the fires, had been picking up bones and scraps—the remnants of the feast.

"Tom, hit the dog a smart stroke suddenly with your stick— a blow not to hurt him much, but to scare him, and make him run. Do you, Davis, move to the edge of the creek, and watch him well as he runs. If he lacks a master, he will dodge about the island. If he has left him anywhere about, he will make off in that direction. Then we shall see what route to take, and, with half-a-dozen of us on his track, we may make out to cross his path, and cut him off from escape. Keep your eyes about you, Davis."

Davis proceeded in one direction. Two other persons were despatched quietly to place themselves in watch upon other parts of the island overlooking the swamp. Humphries himself prepared to dash forward in a third direction, equidistant from these. Tom, in the meanwhile, with a stick concealed behind him, was sidling forward to a nearer acquaintance with the dog, who, unsuspicious of the designs upon him and greedy for food, was still busy, with nose prying into pots, pans, and kettles. All the parties were prepared, and Humphries gave a sign to Tom to proceed, as soon as possible, to his part of the performance. The negro watched his opportunity, and, soon after, with right good will, he laid the flail over the back of the obtrusive animal. At the smart and unexpected salutation, the dog, with a yell, darted back howling into the swamp; taking, as Humphries had calculated, the very route over which he came, and toward the spot where he had left his master. Humphries, and the companions whom he had selected, at once dashed off in pursuit.

But Blonay was not to be caught napping. He had one chief merit of a scout—indeed, it was his only merit—he never trusted himself within smell and sound of an enemy's camp, without keeping his wits well about him. He had marked well the party on the island; had seen the movement of Humphries toward the dog; beheld his rifle uplifted, and pointed for a moment at the head of the animal; and readily divined the motives which induced his enemy to forbear shooting him, and which finally led to the movement which had been subsequently conceived and acted upon. The great secret in stratagem is to give your enemy credit for an ingenuity and enterprise which are at least equal to your own. Blonay had readily conceived the plan which he himself would pursue in a situation such as that of Humphries. He acted accordingly, felt his own danger, and at once proceeded to a change of ground.

Leaving the advanced position from which he had watched the camp, and running in a straight line about fifty yards above, he then turned suddenly about and kept a forward course in the direction of the spot at which he had first entered the swamp. But he did not take these precautions without some doubts of their adequacy to his concealment. He muttered, to himself, his apprehensions of the keen scent of the dog, which he feared would too quickly find out his track, and lead his pursuers upon it; and, though he doubted not that he should be able to get out of the swamp before any of those after him, he was yet fully aware of the utter impossibility of escaping them on the high road, should any of them mount in pursuit.

Though a hardy and fast animal, his pony was quite too small to overcome space very rapidly; and the determination of Blonay was soon made, if he could mislead the dog, to seek a hiding-place in the swamp, which, from its great extent and impervious density in many places, he knew would conceal him, for a time, from any force which the partisans might send. He hurried on, therefore, taking the water at every opportunity, and leaving as infrequent a track as possible behind him. But he fled in vain from the sagacious and true scent of his dog. From place to place, true in every change, the cur kept on after him, giving forth, as he fled, an occasional yelp of dissatisfaction or chagrin, as much probably on account of the beating he had received as from not finding his master.

"Adrat the pup—there's no losing him. Now, if I had my hand on him, I should knife him, and that's the only way. He'll bring 'em on me, at last, ef I don't."

The half-breed thus muttered, as the bark of the dog on the new trail which he had made, attested the success with which he pursued him. Blonay rose upon a stump, and distinctly beheld the head of Humphries, rising above a fallen log; the proprietor of it, led and excited by the cries of the dog, pressing forward with surprising energy, though still at a considerable distance behind. Blonay murmured to himself, as he watched his enemy :—

"I can hit him now—it's not two hundred yards, and I've hit a smaller mark than that so fur, before now."

And, as he spoke, he lifted his rifle, cocked it, and raised it to his eye, where it rested for a few seconds; but Humphries was now covered by a tree. The dog came on, and Blonay distinguished the voices of the pursuers, and that of Humphries in particular, urging the chase with words of encouragement. Unseen himself, he now took a certain aim at the head of the lieutenant; another moment and he must have fired; but, just then, he beheld the figure of Davis pressing through the brush, at a point higher up than the rest, and seemingly bent on making a circuit, which would enable him to get between their present position and the fugitive's only outlet.

To merely kill his victim, and to run the risk of perishing himself, was not the desire of the half-breed. His Indian blood took its vengeance on safer terms. He slowly uncocked the rifle, let it fall from his shoulder, and once more set off in flight, taking now a course parallel with that which he beheld John Davis pursuing. His object was to reach the same point; and he could only do so, in good time to escape, by keeping the direct route upon which he now found himself.

At this moment his dog came up with him. He was about to plunge into a puddle of mixed mire and water. The faithful animal, unconscious of the danger in which he had involved his master, now leaped fondly upon him; testifying his joy at finding him by wantonly yelping at the highest pitch of his voice, and assailing him with the most uncouth caresses, which added to his annoyance by impeding his flight. His clamors also guided the pursuers upon the true path of the fugitive, and would continue to guide them. The moment was full of peril, and everything depended upon his decision. The savage and ready mood of the half-breed did not long delay in a moment of such necessity. Muttering to himself, in few words, his chagrin, he grasped the dog firmly by the back of his neck, and, as the skin was tightly drawn upon the throat, with a quick movement of his hand he passed the keen blade of his knife but once over it, and thrust the body from him in the ooze.

With a single cry and a brief struggle, the animal lay dead in the path of the pursuers. Hurriedly sending the knife back into its sheath, the savage resumed the rifle which, while he slew the dog, he had leaned against a cypress; and, seemingly without compunction, he again set forward.

His flight was now far less desperate, since his pursuers had no longer the keen faculties of the dog to scent for them the path, and his clamorous yelp to guide them upon it; and, with a more perfect steadiness, Blonay pushed onward until he gained a small, though impenetrable cane-brake. This he soon rounded, and it now lay between him and his enemies. Taking to the water whenever it came in his way, he left but few traces of his route behind him; and to find these, at intervals, necessarily impeded the pursuers. When, at length, they reached the pond in which he had slain his dog, and beheld the body of their guide before them, they saw that the pursuit was almost hopeless.

"Look here!" exclaimed Humphries to the rest, as they severally came up to the spot. "Look here! the skunk, you see, has been mighty hard pushed, and can't be far off; but there's no great chance of finding him now. It's like hunting after a needle in a haystack. So long as we had the dog there was something to go by, for the beast would find his master through thick and thin, and we should have got up with him some time or other. Goggle knew that; and he's done the only thing that could have saved him. He's a scout among a thousand — that same Goggle; and no money, if we had it, ought to be stinted to get him on our side. But he knows the difference between guineas and continental paper; and, so long as Proctor pays him well with the one, he'd be a mighty fool, being what he is, to bother himself about the other."

At that moment the shrill sounds of the trumpet came to them from the camp, and put an end to the pursuit, as it commanded their presence for other duties.

"There's the trumpet, boys; we must put back. We can't stop to bother any longer with a single man; and so little chance, too, of our catching him. We've got other work. The general, you must know, is getting ready for a brush with the tories; and we have permission to lick them well to-morrow at Sinkler's Meadow. If we do we shall all get rich; for Barsfield, they say, is to meet them there with a grand supply of shoes and blankets, muskets and swords, and a thousand other matters besides, which they've got and we want. We must get back at once; and yet, boys, it goes against me to leave this scoundrel in the swamp."

But there they were compelled to leave him in perfect security. The half-breed reached his pony, which he mounted at once and proceeded on his return. He had no reason to be dissatisfied with events. He had tracked his enemy, though his vengeance was still unsatisfied; he had found out the secret pass to the rebel camp, and he estimated highly the value of the discovery.

CHAPTER XIX.

THE GAME AFOOT.

The stirring tones of the trumpet, a long and lively peal, resounded through the swamp. Its summons was never unheeded by the men of Marion. They gathered on all hands, and from every quarter of its comprehensive recesses. From the hammock where they slept, from the lakelet where they fished, from the green where they leaped the frog, hurled the bar, or wrestled in emulous sport, in all the buoyancy of full life and conscious strength. They were soon thick around the person of the partisan, and nothing for some time could be heard but the busy hum, the mingling voices of the crowd, in all the confusion of that sort of preparation and bustle which usually precedes the long march and anticipated conflict.

But the quick, sharp, yet low tones of the "swamp-fox" soon reduced to silence the commotion, and brought to symmetry and order all that was confusion before. His words were powerful, as they were uttered in a voice of unquestionable command, and with that unhesitating decision which, as it compels respect from the foe, is always sure to secure confidence in the follower. Strange that, in domestic life, and in moments of irresponsible and unexciting calm, usually distinguished by a halting and ungraceful hesitation of manner, which materially took from the dignity of his deportment, it was far otherwise when he came to command and in the hour of collision. He possessed a wonderful elasticity of character, which was never so apparent as when in the time of danger. At such periods there was a lively play of expression in his countenance, denoting a cool and fearless spirit. His manner now was marked by this elasticity; and, instead of anticipated battle, one might have imagined that he was about to promise to his men the relaxation and the delights of a festival. But the sagacious among them knew better. They had seen him drinking vinegar and water—his favorite beverage—in greater quantities than usual; and they knew, from old experience, that a rapid march and a fierce struggle were at hand.

"Well, gentlemen," said Marion, seeing his officers and favorite men all around him, "if you are as tired of the swamp as I am, you will rejoice at the news I bring you. We are now to leave it."

"Whither now, general?" asked Horry.

"Ah, that indeed is the question. We must leave it first. That, gentlemen, is the requisition of our old friend Captain Barsfield, of his majesty's loyalists, who is now mustering in force around us. He has instructions to set dog upon dog, and hunt us out with our hounds of neighbors—the tories. It is for you to say whether we shall stand and wait their coming, or give them the trouble of hunting the empty swamp after us. I am for leaving them the ground, and looking out for other quarters and a better business."

Cries of "No, no—let us meet them—let us not fly from any tory!" were heard on all hands; and Horry, Singleton, and sundry others of the most favored officers, seriously interposed with suggestions of their strength, and the ability and willingness of the men to fight. The partisan smiled pleasantly as he listened to their suggestions."

"You mistake me somewhat, gentlemen," was his quiet and general reply; "you mistake me much; and I rejoice that you do so, as I am now so much the better satisfied that your views and feelings accord with my own. To leave the swamp does not mean to fly from the enemy. Oh, no! I propose, on the contrary, that we should leave the swamp in order to seek the enemy before he shall be altogether ready for us. Why should we wait until he has brought his men together?—why wait until the tories from Waccamaw come in to swell the number of our own rascals from Williamsburg?—and why, of all things, wait until Captain Barsfield brings his baggage-wagons with supplies to glut these greedy wretches who expect them? I see no reason for this."

"No, no, general," was the response; "we are ready for them — we need not wait."

"Very well, gentlemen, as you say — we need not wait; and, supposing that such would be your determination, I have already completed my arrangements for departure. We shall move off with midnight; and it is expected, gentlemen, that you so speed in your duties as to suffer no delay after that period in your departure. Colonel Horry will have his squad in readiness to move with me upon Sinkler's meadow, where we must take post before the tories. The route and general orders he will find in this paper. Singleton—"

The chief led the young officer aside.

"Singleton, I have special work for you, which calls for all your activity. Take your whole corps of riflemen, and select your horses. Leave to Captain Melton all those of your men who are most cumbrous or may least be relied upon. The duty is too important to be intrusted to clumsy fingers."

Singleton bowed, and Marion continued :—

"Proceed up the river road to Brooks' mills, and secure the detachment which Watson has placed there. Let none of them escape, if you can, to carry news across the river. Let your return be by daylight, and then take the road toward Berkeley's place, where Barsfield has found lodgings. He will move to-morrow, with the sun, on the route to Sinkler's meadow. He must be met and beaten at all hazards. I will despatch Captain Melton with thirty men for this purpose; and, in order to make certain, as soon as you have surprised the guard at Brooks', you will push down toward Berkeley's, Kaddipah, or in whatever quarter Barsfield may go. Melton probably will do the business; but, as it will be in your subsequent route, you may as well prepare to co-operate with him, should you be in season. We must keep Barsfield from joining these tories, upon whom I shall most probably fall by mid-day. You may find this a somewhat difficult matter, as Barsfield fights well, and is something of a soldier. You must surprise him if you can. This done, you will proceed to scour the upper road, with as much rapidity as comports with caution. The scouts bring me word of a corps in that quarter, which can be no other than Tarleton's. This scrawl, too, comes from that dear old granny, Mother Dyson, who lives near Monk's Corner. Hear what the good old creature says:—

"'DARE GIN'RAL: There's a power of red-coats jist guine down by the back lane into your parts, and they do tell that it's arter you they're guine. They're dressed mighty fine, and has a heap of guns and horses, and as much provisions as the wagons can tote. I makes bold to tell you this, gin'ral, that you may smite them, hip and thigh, even as the Israelites smote the bloody Philistines in the blessed book. And so, no more, dare gin'ral, from your sarvant to command,
"'BETSY DYSON.

"'N. B.—Don't you pay the barer, gin'ral, for he's owing me a power of money, and he's agreed with me that what I gives him for guine down to you is to come out of what he owes me. He's a good man enough, and is no tory, but he a'n't quite given to speaking the truth always; and I'm sorry to tell you, gin'ral, that, in spite of all I says to him, he don't mend a bit. "'B. D.'

"Quite a characteristic epistle, Singleton, and from as true a patriot as ever lived—that same old Betsy Dyson. These troops must be Tarleton's, and I doubt not that he moves with the entire legion. He has pledged himself to Cornwallis to force me to a fight, and he comes to redeem his pledge. This we must avoid, and we must therefore hurry to put these tories out of the way before they can co-operate with the legion. I will see to them. When you have done with Barsfield, should Melton not have struck before you reach him, you will take the upper track until you find Tarleton. But you are to risk nothing: we can not hope to fight him, even with our whole present force, and you must risk nothing with your little squad. You must only hang about him, secure intelligence of all his movements, and, where opportunities occur, obstruct his steps, and cut off such of his detachments as come within your reach.

You can worry the advance, and throw them back upon the foot, for their horses will not hold a leg with the meanest of your troop. We want time, and this will give it to us: and none of these risks should be taken unless you encounter the legion before sunset to-morrow. After that, you are simply to watch and report their movements. Should I succeed in the attack at Sinkler's to-morrow, you will find me at the ferry at midnight. Should you not, take it as a proof of my failure, and look for me at Snow's island."

A few other minor suggestions completed Singleton's commission; and Marion proceeded, in like manner, to detail to every officer, intrusted with command, the duties which were before him. With Colonel Horry's squad, he took to himself the task of routing the tories at Sinkler's meadow. Twenty men, under Captain James, he despatched to waylay the road leading from Waccamaw, over which another small body of tories was expected to pass; and, this done, the rest of the day was devoted by all parties to preparations for the movement of the night.

Promptness was one of the first principles in Marion's warfare. With the approach of evening, the several corps prepared for their departure. Saddles were taken from the trees, on whose branches they had hung suspended all around the camp; steeds were brought forward from the little recesses where they browsed upon the luxuriant cane-tops; swords waved in the declining sunset; bugles sounded from each selected station, where it had been the habit for the several squads to congregate; and, as the sun went really down behind the thick forest, the camp was soon clear of all the active life which it possessed before. All who were able were away on their several duties; and but a few, the invalids and supernumeraries alone, remained to take charge of themselves and the furniture of the encampment.

Our fat friend, Lieutenant Porgy, had a narrow chance of being left. Were we to consider his bulk simply, he might have been classed with those whom Marion spoke of as quite too "cumbrous" for movement. But his energy and impulse were more than a match for his bulk. Still, the best will and blood are not proof against the decrees of fate; and while Marion was yet giving his orders, Tom reported to his master the death of the horse Nabob. The epicure was for a moment overcome. He proceeded, however, with commendable promptness, to what was styled, *par courtesie*, the hospital, where Fentbaer, the German, lay sick. From him he proposed to borrow his horse. But, even while negotiating with the sick man, Tom entered with great outcry and much rejoicing, conducting a sergeant, who brought with him a fine horse, and a message from Singleton, begging Porgy to use him until a better steed could be captured from the enemy. The animal brought him was a noble bay, one of a pair, and Porgy was not the man to underrate a generosity so unusual as well as handsome. Of course, he accepted the gift, and was lavish of thanks. But he said to Humphries, with a sigh: "A handsome present, Bill; our major is the man to do handsome things. This is a very fine animal, and just suits me — perhaps even better than Nabob; but Nabob was a sort of half-brother to me, Bill. I raised the ridiculous beast myself."

Humphries thought the use of the word "ridiculous" rather an abuse of language, but it was employed for a purpose — was in fact designed to conceal a sentiment. When, half an hour after, Porgy beheld Tom stretching the skin of poor Nabob in the sun, he felt like cudgelling the negro, whom he called an inhuman beast.

"Why," he asked, furiously, "why did you skin the animal, you savage?"

"Oh! maussa, kaise I lub 'em so! Nabob and me guine to sleep togedder a'ter this, for ebber and for ebbermore."

Tom was even more "an old soldier" than his master. Porgy growled —

"Some day that will be the scoundrel's apology for skinning me!"

But we are not permitted to linger over the mere humors of our partisans. Let us leave them for a space, and look after the half-breed Blonay. Relieved from the hot pursuit which had been urged after him, he relaxed in the rapidity of his movements, and made his way with more composure out of the swamp. He had not slain his enemy, it is true; but he had been quite as successful in discovering the place of his retreat as his most sanguine hopes had predicted. He had not merely seen his particular foe, and found out his hiding-place, but he had discovered the passage to one of those secret haunts of the " swamp-fox," the knowledge of which, he doubted not, would bring him a handsome reward from the British officers, to whom Marion was becoming, daily, more and more an object of hostile consideration. Satisfied, therefore, with the result of his expedition, though lamenting the unavoidable sacrifice which he had made of his dog—his last friend, his only companion—he at once took his way back to " Piney Grove," where he hoped to meet with Barsfield. It was not long before he stood before the tory, who led him away at once into the woods, anxious, from his intense hate to Mellichampe, to learn how far the half-breed had been successful in his search.

" Well, what have you done? what have you seen? Have you found the trail, Blonay? Have you discovered the hiding-place of this reptile—these reptiles ?"

" Well, cappin, there's no saying for certain, when you're upon the trail of a good woodman. He's everywhere, and then agin he's nowhere. Sometimes he's in one place, sometimes in another; and sometimes it a'n't three minutes' difference that he don't have a change. Now the 'swamp-fox' is famous for drawing stakes, and going there's no telling where."

" True, true, I know all that. But it's for a good scout to find him out, and track him through all his changes. Now, what have you done in your search? You have seen your enemy, have you not? Where have you left him? and, above all, have you seen that boy—he whom, of all others, I would have you see? What of Mellichampe ?"

" I seed him, cappin, but mighty far off—I know'd him from what you tell'd me—I can't be mistaken."

" Well !"

" But, cappin, there's a mighty heap of men with Marion—more than a hundred."

" Impossible! you dream!" responded the tory in astonishment.

"It's a gospel truth, sir, and they looked quite sprigh; and the trumpet blowed, and there was a great gathering. They had a fine chance of horses, too — some of the finest I ever laid eyes on."

"Ha, indeed! This will be work for Tarleton, who must now be at hand. From Monk's Corner to Smoot's, thirty miles — then here — he should be here to-morrow noon, and I must hurry with the dawn for Sinkler's — yes — it must be at daylight."

The tory thus muttered to himself, and the half-breed duly treasured up every syllable. The speaker proceeded again, addressing his companion —

"'Tis well — you have managed handsomely, Blonay; but you have not yet said where the gathering took place. Tell me the route you took, and give me a full description of the spot itself, and all particulars of your adventure."

But the half-breed, though exhorted thus, was in no haste to yield any particulars to Barsfield. The casual reference to Tarleton's approach. which had fallen from the tory's lips in his brief soliloquy, had determined Blonay to keep his secret for one who would most probably pay him better; and, though he replied to, he certainly did not answer, the question of his present employer.

"Well, now, cappin, there's no telling how to find the place I went to. There's so many crooks and turns — so many ins and outs — so many ups and downs, that it's all useless to talk about it. It's only nose and eye that can track it out for you; for, besides that I don't know the names of any places in these parts, I could only find it myself by putting my foot along the track, and taking hold of the bushes which I broke myself. I could tell you that you must take the road back to the left, then strike across the old field to the right, then you come to a little bay, and you go round that till you fall into a little path, that leads you into the thick wood; then you keep a little to the left agin, and you go on in this way a full quarter before you come out into a valley; then —"

"Enough, enough — such a direction would baffle the best scout along the Santee. We must even trust to your own eyes and feet when the time comes to hunt these reptiles, and I trust that your memory will not fail you then."

"Never fear, cappin," responded the other, agreeably satisfied to be let off so easily from a more precise description of the route which he had taken. It is probable that, with a greater force than that which he commanded, and which was entirely inadequate to any such enterprise, Barsfield, solicitous of distinction, and seeking after his foe, would have compelled the guidance of Blonay, and gone himself after the "swamp-fox." As matters stood, however, he determined to pursue his old bent, and, seeking his tories at Sinkler's meadow, leave to the fierce Tarleton the honor of hunting out the wily Marion.

CHAPTER XX.

SHARP PASSAGES AT ARMS.

BARSFIELD retired to his slumbers that night with pleasant anticipations. Blonay again sought the woods, and sleeplessly sought, by the doubtful moonlight, his way into the same swamp recesses which he had traversed through the day. His leading passion was revenge, and he spared no pains to secure it. He could sleep standing against a tree; and he seemed not even to need repose at. all. He was gone all night, yet appeared at the mansion of Mr. Berkeley ready for his breakfast, and seemingly as if he had never felt fatigue.

The two maidens the next morning stood conversing in the piazza. Barsfield, with his corps, baggage-wagons and all, had just departed. Blonay, too, had set off, but in a different direction. Piney Grove was once more left to its old, sweet quiet; and a painful restraint and a heavy weight seemed taken from the heart of Janet Berkeley with the absence of her father's guests.

"Well, Janet," exclaimed the livelier Rose Duncan, as they looked down the long avenue, and surveyed its quiet, "I am heartily glad our military visiters are gone. I am sick of big swords, big whiskers, and big feathers, the more particularly indeed, as, with many of this sort of gentry, these endowments seem amply sufficient to atone for and redeem the most outrageous stupidity, mixed with much more monstrous self-esteem. There was not one of these creatures, now, that could fairly persuade a body, even in the most trying country emergency, to remember she had a heart at all. All was stuff and stiffness, buttons and buckram; and when the creatures did make a move, it was a sort of wire and screw exhibition—a dreadful operation in mechanics, as if a clumsy inventor, armed with thumbs rather than fingers, and mortally apprehensive that his work would go to pieces before he could get it safely out of his hands, had wheeled it out, and was wheeling it in, soured and sullen from a consciousness that, in so wheeling it, the rickety thing had not shown to advantage. And these are soldiers! Well, Heaven save us, I pray, as much from their love as from their anger. The latter might bayonet one, it is true; but I should as surely die of the annoyance and ennui that would inevitably come with the other. Look up, my dear cousin, and tell me what you think."

It was thus that the lively Rose Duncan discoursed of the tory troop to her cousin. Janet replied quietly—a pleasant but subdued smile touching her lips, softly and sweet, as a faint blush of sunlight resting upon some drooping flower by the wayside.

"And yet, my dear Rose, you have no reason to complain; you certainly made a conquest of the young lieutenant, Mr. Clayton. His eyes spoke eloquently enough; and his mouth, whenever it was opened, was full of the prettiest compliments. You must not be ungrateful."

"Nor am I. I do not complain of, nor yet will I appropriate, the 'goods the gods provide me.' I take leave to congratulate myself on their leaves-taking—all—not to omit my simpering, sweet, slender Adonis, the gentle lieutenant himself. Pshaw, Janet, how can you suppose that I should endure such a whipt-syllabub sort of creature? You must have pitied me, hearing, with no hope of escape, his rhapsodies about music and poetry—moonlight and bandana handkerchiefs; for he mixed matters up in such inextricable confusion, that I could have laughed in his face, but that it required some effort to overcome the stupid languor with which he possessed me. You needn't smile, Janet—he did—he was a most delicate bore."

"And you really desire me to believe, Rose, that he has made no interest in your heart?" was the response of Janet to all this tirade. The graver maiden of the two seemed disposed to adopt some of the light humor of her companion, and annoy her after her own fashion.

"Interest! heart!—how can you talk such stuff, Janet, and look so serious all the while? You should be pelted with pine-burs, and I will undertake your punishment before the day is well over. By-the-way, talking of pine-burs, I am reminded, though I don't see why, of the strange blear-eyed countryman. What a curious creature, with that stiff, straight black hair—so glossy black—and those eyes that seem popping from his head, and look of all colors; and then the rigid, yet loose fixture of his limbs, that seem like those of a statue, drawn asunder, and left hanging by the merest ligatures. What a queer creature!"

"He seems poor and humble," replied Janet, "and is probably affected mentally. He seems idiotic."

"Not he—not he! His gaze is too concentrative and too fixed, to indicate a wandering intellect: then, why his frequent conversations with that bull-necked lover of yours, Barsfield? Did he not take him into the woods when the countryman came back yesterday evening, and keep him there a full hour? I tell you what, Janet, that fellow's a spy; he's after no good here: and, as I live, here he is, coming back full tilt upon his crooked pony, that's just as queer and ugly as himself."

As she said, Blonay reappeared at this moment, and the dialogue ceased accordingly between the maidens. The halfbreed grinned with an effort at pleasantness as he bowed to them, and, speaking a few words to Mr. Berkeley, as if in explanation of his return, he proceeded to loiter about the grounds. The eyes of Rose watched him narrowly, and with no favorable import; but Blonay did not seem to heed her observation. He now sauntered in the park, and now he leaned against a tree in the pleasant sunshine; and, by his torpid habit of body, seemed to justify Janet to her more lively cousin in the opinion which she had uttered of his idiocy. But the scout was never more actively employed than just when he seemed most sluggish. He was planning the sale of Marion's camp to Tarleton. He was loitering about Piney

Grove, with the double object of being nigh his enemy's hiding-place and of meeting with the legionary.

"He is a spy, Janet. He has been put here as a watch over us and upon Mellichampe. Barsfield knows Mellichampe to be rash, as he has shown himself, and he has put that fellow here to look out for and shoot him."

Janet shuddered, and her eyes involuntarily turned to the spot where, at a little distance, the half-breed stood leaning against a tree. How imploring was the expression of her eye! Could he have seen it, if such were his purpose, he must have relented. Such was the thought of Rose—such the hope of Janet. The scout had seen that look—he had felt its expression.

"But where is he now, Janet?" was the question of Rose a few moments after. He was gone, and so stealthily, they had not suspected his movement. The half-breed was again upon the track of his enemy.

Barsfield, meanwhile, though dispensing with the attendance of Blonay, did not fail to avail himself, in one respect, of the information which the latter had given him. The proximity of Marion in the swamp, with a hundred men or more, aroused the tory to increased exertion, and counselled the utmost prudence in his march, as it showed the neighborhood of so superior an enemy. The arms, baggage, clothing, and ammunition, intended to supply a large body of tories, and which were intrusted to his charge, were of far more importance to his present purposes than of real intrinsic value. Not to deliver them safely into the hands of those who were to employ them, and whom he was to employ, would be to suffer dreadfully in the estimation of his British superiors, and in his own personal interests. To have them fall into the hands of the rebels, were to accumulate evil upon evil, as no acquisition which the latter could make at this period could be of greater importance. It was well for him that these suggestions filled the mind of the tory. He was a tolerable soldier on a small scale, and was already well conversant with the partisan warfare. He sent forward a few trusty horsemen to reconnoitre and keep the advance; and, moving cautiously and with watchful eyes, he hoped to make his way without interruption. But he was not fated to do so, as we shall see anon.

Major Singleton, having a more extended line of country to traverse, and a greater variety of duties to perform, started from the swamp at dusk, and some time before the rest. Marion set forth by midnight; and Captain Melton, after attending to some matters of minor importance, led off his little corps an hour later. Our attention will chiefly be given to this latter band, of which Ernest Mellichampe was the first-lieutenant, and Jack Witherspoon the orderly. By the dawn they found themselves at one of the lower crossing-places upon the river, probably that at which it would be the aim of Barsfield to cross; but, as this was uncertain, it was not the policy of Melton to await him there. The position was by no means good, and the ground too much broken for the free use of cavalry.

With the dawn, therefore, Melton moved his troop slowly up the road, intending to place them in ambush behind a thick wood which lay in their route, and which had been already designated for this purpose. The road ran circuitously through this wood, forming a defile, around which a proper disposition of his force must have been successful, and must have resulted in the destruction or capture of the entire force of the tories. The spot was well known to the partisans, and had been determined upon, even before the party left the river, as well adapted, beyond any other along the road, for the contemplated encounter. It lay but seven miles off, and one hour's quick riding would have enabled them to reach and secure it. But Melton pursued a regular, or rather a cautious gait, which, under other circumstances, and at another time, would have been proper enough. But now, when the object was the attainment of a particular station, a forced movement became essential, in most part, to their success; certainly to that plan of surprise which they had in view. Mellichampe more than once suggested this to his superior officer; but the latter was one of those persons who have solemn and inveterate habits, from which they never depart. His horse had but one gait, and to that he was accustomed. His rider had but a single tune, and that was a dead march. The consequences of these peculiarities was a funeral movement on the present occasion, and no argument of Mellichampe could induce Melton to urge the advance more briskly. He cursed the monotonous drone in his heart; and, biting his lips until the blood started from them, he predicted to himself that the party would be too late.

And so indeed it happened. Barsfield, whom the intelligence brought by Blonay had prompted to renewed speed in his movements, had set forth, as we have seen, by the dawn of day, and was upon the road quite as soon as Melton, who had been travelling half the night. Had the counsel of Mellichampe been taken, the desired position would have been gained easily by the partisans; for, as it lay a little nearer to "Piney Grove" than to the swamps, and as Barsfield, though urging his course forward with all due rapidity, was unavoidably compelled to move slowly, burdened as he was with his baggage-wagons, nothing could have been more easy than to have attained it with a proper effort.

But Melton was not the man to make an effort—he had no mind for an occasion; and the force of habit, with him, was far more controlling than any impulse from necessity. Such a man is no genius. He stopped his troop here and there, to scour this or that suspicious-looking growth of underwood—sent out his scouts of observation, as if he had been engaged in the vague and various duties of the forager, instead of pushing forward with the single object—the performance of the task which he had in hand. The consequence of this blundering was foreseen, and partially foretold, by the indignant Mellichampe, who could scarcely restrain his anger within terms of courtesy. Bitterly aroused, he was ready almost for revolt; and, but for the presence of the danger, and the necessity of turning his wrath in the more legitimate direction of his enemies, it was apparent to all, that, from the harsh tones and stern looks interchanged by the two officers, an outbreak must soon have followed.

But the thoughts of all were turned to other objects, as, suddenly, one of their troopers rode up, informing Melton of the approach of Barsfield, close at hand. He had only time to marshal his men on the side of a little copse and bay that lay between himself and the foe, when the heavy tramp of the cavalry and the creaking wheels of the baggage-wagons were heard at a little distance. A timely resolution, even then, though comparatively unprepared, might yet have retrieved the error which the commander of the troop had committed; but his looks were now indecisive, his movements uncertain, and he gave his orders for a change of position, imagining that a better stand presented itself a little distance back.

"This must not be, Captain Melton!" cried Mellichampe, indignantly. "It is quite too late, sir, to think of any such change. A retrograde movement full in the face of an advancing enemy, will have the effect of a retreat upon our troop, and give the enemy all the advantage of our panic and confusion, together with the courage and confidence which our seeming flight must inspire in them. We can not change now, and we must make the best of our position. Had my advice been minded—"

He was interrupted as the close sounds of the advancing tories met his ears. Melton saw the impossibility of any change now, and the discovery, on his part, produced in his mind all the feelings of surprise and discomfiture which he had planned for the reception of his foe. He gave his orders, it is true; but he did not look the officer to his men, and they did not feel with him. Not so with Mellichampe: the few words which had passed in the hearing of the troop between him and his commander—the air of fierce decision which his features wore—the conscious superiority which they indicated—were all so many powerful spells of valor, which made the brave fellows turn their eyes upon him as upon their true leader.

And so he was. The imbecility of Melton became more conspicuous as the moment of trial approached. He halted, hung back, as the enemy entered upon the little defile in which only it could be attacked; and thus exposed his men, when the attack was made, to all the disadvantages arising from a suffered surprise. It was then that the impatient blood of Mellichampe, disdaining all the restraints of discipline, urged him forward in the assault with a fierce shout to his men, and a scornful jeer almost in the ears of his commander, as, driving his good steed before him, he advanced to the charge, which he made with so much force and impetuosity as at once to stagger the progress of the tories.

Barsfield was, just then, emerging from the pass—a little cornfield, with its worm-fence enclosure, lay on one hand, and, on the other, the woods were open and free from undergrowth. It was here that Melton's men had been posted, not so advantageously as they would have been had they reached the spot which Marion had designated for them; but sufficiently well to have rendered the attack successful under a spirited charge such as that made by Mellichampe. But the information which Barsfield had received from Blonay had made him extremely cautious, as we have already seen, and he had properly prepared himself against, and was on the look-out for, assaults like the present. With the first appearance of the enemy, his men were ordered to display themselves in open order; the wagons were suffered to fall behind, and were carried back under the escort of a single dragoon to the spot from which they had started in the morning. To this effect the instructions of Barsfield had been already given. Free and unencumbered, the tory met his enemy boldly, and received him with a discharge of pistols. The steed of Mellichampe was at this moment careering within a few paces of him. The sabre of the youth waving above his head, and, with a bitter smile, rising in his stirrups, he cried out, as he prepared to cross weapons with his enemy —

"Dog of a tory, we have a clear field now! There are none to come between us. Strike, villain, and strike well; for, by my father's blood, I will give you no quarter!"

Barsfield calmly seemed to await his approach, and exhibited no lack of courage: yet his sabre was unlifted—his bridle lay slackened in his hand; and, but for his erect posture and firm seat, it might be supposed that he was a mere looker-on in the affray. He replied to the furious language of his youthful opponent in tones and language as fierce.

"You may swear by your own blood soon, boy, or I much mistake your chances."

The sabre of the youth glared in his face at this reply, and the movement of the tory was made in another instant with all the rapidity of thought. His horse, under the quick impulse of a heavy bit, was brought round in a moment: in another, a huge pistol was drawn from his holsters, and the careering steed of Mellichampe received the bullet meant for his master in his own breast. He fell forward upon his knees, made an imperfect effort to rise, and the next moment plunged desperately and struggled almost under the feet of Barsfield's horse. A few seconds sufficed for Mellichampe's extrication; and he was barely in time by throwing up his sabre, to arrest the stroke of his enemy's. On foot he now pressed forward upon Barsfield, and sought to close so nearly in with him as to make it difficult for him to employ his sabre, unless by shortening it too greatly to permit of his using it with any advantage. But the tory saw his design, and immediately backed his steed. Mellichampe pursued him with his accustomed rashness, and must certainly have been slain by the tory, who had now drawn another pistol from his holster, when Witherspoon, who had been hotly engaged, but had seen with anxiety the contest between the two enemies, now rushed between; and, setting the huge and splendid horse which he rode directly in the teeth of that of Barsfield, the shock of their meeting threw the latter completely upon his haunches, and nearly unseated his rider.

The sabres of Barsfield and Witherspoon then clashed hurriedly, and, though chafed to be robbed of his prey even by his friend, Mellichampe was compelled to forbear his particular game, and turn his attention entirely to his own safety. A horse plunged by him riderless, which he was fortunate enough to seize; and he was mounted opportunely just as a fresh charge of the tories separated Witherspoon from his opponent, whom he had pressed back into the defile. This charge drove the sergeant, in his turn, down upon the original position of the attacking party. The impulse was for a few moments irresistible, and two or three of the men fairly turned their horses and fled from before it. Captain Melton seeing this, gave the order to retreat, and the trumpet sounded the quick and mortifying signal. But the voice of the youthful Mellichampe sounded even above the shrill alarum of the instrument, as, with a desperate blow with his sabre, he struck the recreant trumpeter to the earth.

"Shame to you, men of Marion!—shame!—do you fly from the tories of Waccamaw? Do you give back before the Winyah mud-eaters? Follow me!"

The cry of Witherspoon was yet more characteristic, and, perhaps, far more potential.

"You forget, boys, sartainly, that the tories find it nateral to be licked; and if they was to lick you now, that's licked them so often, they wouldn't know what to do for joy. Turn to, and let's lick 'em ag'in!"

The call was not made in vain. True valor is quite as contagious as fear, since it is always quite as earnest. The partisans heard the words of their leaders—they saw the headlong rush of their steeds; and they rushed forward also with as generous an emotion. They were received with a front quite as firm, and a spirit not less forward than their own. The tories, too, had been inspirited by their success in the first shock, and, with loud cheers, they prepared for the second. The encounter, as it was made just at the mouth of the defile, a circumscribed position, where each man found his opponent, had something of the character of the mixed fight of the middle ages.

The rush was tremendous; the strife, for a few moments, terrible. But all in vain did the eye of Mellichampe distinguish, and his spirit burn once more to contend with his deadly enemy. They were kept asunder by the tide of battle. The ranks were broken; the fight became pell-mell; and, on a sudden, while each man was contending with his enemy, a fierce cry of triumph and of vengeance burst from the lips of Barsfield himself. Mellichampe, though closely engaged with a stout dragoon, suffered his eye to seek the spot whence the sound arose, and once beheld its occasion. Barsfield had been contending with a slender, but fine-looking youth, whom he had disarmed. The hand of his conqueror had torn him from his horse with all the strength of a giant. The youth lay at his feet, resting upon one hand, looking partly upon his foe and partly round, as if imploring succor from his friends. Mellichampe distinguished the features instantly, though smeared with blood. They were those of Gabriel Marion, the nephew of the general, a youth of nineteen only.

"He shall not die, by Heaven!" cried Mellichampe aloud; in the same moment, with a daring effort, drawing his horse back from the encounter with the enemy with whom he was engaged, as if in flight — a movement which, encouraging the other to press forward, disordered his guard, and placed him at disadvantage. Meeting his stroke, Mellichampe set it readily aside; then, striking in turn at the head of his opponent, he put spurs to his horse, without looking to see what had been the effect of his blow, and, passing quickly beyond him, rushed forward to meet with Barsfield. But, as he approached, he saw that nothing could be done for the youth, whose hand was uplifted — a frail defence — in opposition to his conqueror's weapon.

"Stay, Barsfield — strike him not, scoundrel, or look for the vengeance —"

But, ere the speech was finished, the youth leaped once more to his feet, and the weapon meant for his head passed over it. Young Marion then grasped the sword-arm of his enemy; but, drawing his remaining pistol in the same moment, Barsfield shot him through the breast.

The cry of grief on the one hand, and of triumph on the other, contributed greatly to discourage the partisans. That moment was fatal to several more in their ranks, and the disparity of force was now in favor of the tories. They were soon conscious of the fact, and pressed upon their enemies. Stung with shame, Mellichampe made a desperate effort, and, nobly seconded by a few, threw himself in the path of the enemy, and bravely disputed every inch of ground, yielding it only under the pressure of numbers.

"I can not fly, Witherspoon — speak not of it, I tell you. I know that the odds are against us, but we must only strike the oftener."

"Well, Airnest, jist as you say. You know best, if you like it; and so, knock away's the word."

Two or three brief sentences between the friends conveyed the difficulties and dangers of the scene and the spirit of the combatants. The partisans fought well, but they grew weaker in numbers and individual strength with every movement of the protracted battle. They had not well calculated the difference of personal capacity for strife and endurance of fatigue between drilled men and volunteers; and, though the spirit of the latter for a time, is more than a match for the hardening practice of the former, yet it very seldom endures so well.

"I will perish on this field—I will not leave it, and show my back to that scoundrel! Come on, men!—come on, Witherspoon!—let us pluck up spirit for another—a last—a desperate charge. I must meet with Barsfield, now; there are too few on either side to keep us long apart."

A brief pause in the combat, as if by tacit consent, enabled Mellichampe, in the breathing time which it afforded, to convey this suggestion and resolve to the few fierce spirits still gathering around him—driven back, but not yet defeated—dispirited, perhaps, but far from subdued. They freely pledged themselves to the resolution, and, with a cheer, as if they had been going to a banquet, they drove the rowels into their jaded steeds, and joined once more in the struggle. But the weapons had scarcely crossed, and the close strife had not yet begun when the shrill notes of a bugle rang through the wood to the left of the combatants.

"It is Singleton's trumpet," cried Mellichampe aloud to his men; and a cheer of encouragement involuntarily went up from their lips as they listened to the grateful music. In the next moment, at full gallop, the reinforcement of Singleton came plunging forward to the rescue from the woods on every side, while the full-toned voice of their gallant leader shouted to the fainting combatants to strike on without faltering. Barsfield, so lately confident of his triumph over his enemy, and of his vengeance upon the one foe, in particular, about to be realized, was compelled to forego the prey almost within his grasp.

"Now, may the hell have him that fights for him!" cried the disappointed tory, as, with the first appearance of Singleton's troop, he ordered his own bugles to sound the retreat. Clearing, with terrible blows, the few enemies that were yet clinging around him, Barsfield wheeled furiously in his flight, while, close at his heels, pursuing to the very gates of Piney Grove, but not fast enough to overtake him, Singleton urged forward his wearied animals in the fond hope of annihilating a foe so insolent, and who promised to become so troublesome.

CHAPTER XXI.

THE MAIDEN'S GIFT.

BARSFIELD had neither ridden so far, nor in such haste, as the partisans that morning. This alone saved him. His horses were inferior; and, but for the fatigue which his enemies had undergone, he must have been overtaken. The judicious disposition which the tory had made of his baggage-wagons, in sending them back to Piney Grove at the first appearance of danger, also contributed greatly to the facility of his movements; and, unimpeded by the necessity of guarding them, and not much breathed by the stirring encounter through which they had passed, the stout horses his men bestrode, though not so swift as those of the Americans, was yet better able to make headway in the flight. The pursuit was hotly urged, though unsuccessful. The horses of Singleton were too much jaded with the hard ride of twenty odd miles which they had taken, and could not be made to keep up even with the fagged animals of Mellichampe's little troop. Barsfield escaped them, and safely passed through the avenue of Piney Grove before the pursuing party came in sight.

The baggage-wagons of the tory had just arrived, and, with a sagacious disposition of his force, which indicated ability worthy of a better cause, he proceeded to make effective arrangements for the reception of Singleton's troop, which was quite too large to suffer him to think that so enterprising a partisan would draw them off without a farther attempt upon him. Dismounting his men rapidly, therefore, he threw open the doors of the basement story of the mansion; and, without leave asked or given—the exigency was too pressing for mere courtesies—he made his dragoons stable their steeds in the spacious apartments. Emptying the baggage-wagons of their contents, he armed his men with the muskets, of which there was sufficient provision; and, having secured the residue of their stores within the walls of the dwelling-house, he proceeded, to the great disquiet of Mr. Berkeley, and the terror of the young ladies, to close the doors and make a fortress of the family mansion. The upper rooms were barricaded with chairs and tables; and, watchful at all the windows, the troopers stood ready with their muskets peering forth conspicuously and warningly in all directions from the building.

This was scarcely done, when the partisans came down the avenue. It was with no little vexation that Singleton surveyed this prospect. His eye at a moment beheld the difficulties of his situation, and the danger of any assault upon a foe so well prepared. To rush on brick walls, and be met by musket-bullets, without being able to obtain sight of the defenders, was not the part of a discreet valor; and yet, to leave an enemy so enfeebled as Barsfield was, without further efforts to overcome or destroy him, was still more irksome to a brave spirit like that of the officer in command. The rash and headlong Mellichampe, however, thinking only of his personal hostility to Barsfield, could hardly be restrained. He was for immediately charging, and trying the weight of an axe upon the doors of the dwelling.

"Ay, ay; but how to get there?" cried the more sagacious Singleton. "No, no, Mellichampe, we must try some better plan—some safer enterprise. To cross the yard in the teeth of those muskets would be certain death to nearly every man who makes the effort, and we are but too poorly provided with soldiers to be thus profligate. We must think of something else; and, in order to have time for it, let us send a message to the tory. Let us see what fair words will do, and the promise of good quarter. Besides, we must make some arrangements for getting the family out of the house before making any assault."

The truth of these suggestions was unquestionable; and Mellichampe volunteered to bear the despatches, but Singleton refused him.

"No, no; the risk will be great to you; and the tory hates you too well to stop at trifles. He might be tempted to some desperate act if you are to be the messenger. I prefer Witherspoon."

"Jist as you say, major; I'm ready, as the alligator said to the duck. I'm ready; though I a'n't a great speaker, yet I can tell Barsfield what he's to reckon on if he don't come to tarms. If so be all I've got to say is to tell him he'll be licked if he don't give up and surrender, I can do that easy enough," was the prompt speech of the scout.

"You know there's danger, Witherspoon," said Singleton. "This fellow Barsfield may not think it becoming to treat with a rebel; and he may send a bullet through the head of a courier, and think no sin of it."

"Well, he'd be a mean skunk to do sich a thing, major; that's agin all the civilities of war. I knows there's danger, but I can't help it. 'Man that is born of woman,' says the Scripture—I don't rightly call to mind the other part—but it means that we've all got to die some time or other, and 'ta'n't the part of a brave man to be always dodging from danger. I must take my chance, major, so git your paper ready."

Singleton pencilled brief but honorable proposals to the tory, pledging the enlargement of himself and party on parole if they would surrender; and denouncing otherwise the well-known horrors of a storm. A permission, in the event of his refusal to surrender, was extended to Mr. Berkeley and his family, but no other person, to leave the beleaguered dwelling. Witherspoon received the paper, and prepared to depart.

"Mayn't I carry my rifle, major?—I don't feel altogether natural when I don't have it, partic'larly when I'm to go seek my enemy."

"No arms, Witherspoon; nothing but the flag."

He handed the weapon to Mellichampe with no small reluctance.

"Take care of her, Airnest; she's a sweet critter, and makes a crack that's born music, and I loves her."

With no more words, and with a single glance toward the youth, that spoke volumes of affection warmly and truly felt, the scout, without any hesitation, turned away from the park where this conference was carried on; and, waving his handkerchief aloft—the substitute for a flag—he proceeded on his way of peril to the dwelling.

"I see a rebel with a flag!" said one of the tories, who first discerned the despatch, to his commander. "Shall I shoot him, sir?"

The hesitation of Barsfield to reply was almost a permission, and the man had his gun lifted and ready; but the tory captain thought it more proper or more prudent to forbear.

"No; let him come: and you, Clayton, receive him at the entrance. But see that no other approaches. Fire at the first man who appears within reach of your muskets."

In an inner room, in the presence of the family, Barsfield received the messenger. His reply to the message was one of scornful disdain.

"Well, now, cappin," said Thumbscrew, coolly, "you'd better not send any sich word to the major, for he's old hell with his grinders, and it'll be pretty bad for you if he once gits them into your flesh. They'll meet, now, I tell you, if he does."

"You are answered," was the temperate reply of the tory, who then turned to Mr. Berkeley.

"The rebel graciously accords you permission, with your family, to leave the dwelling, Mr. Berkeley. You are at perfect liberty to do so, if you please; but, if you will rely on my defences, there is no danger: the place is perfectly tenable."

"No, no, dear father—let us go—let us fly. There is danger; and, even if there be none, it is no place for us."

"But where shall we go, my daughter?" said the old man, utterly bewildered.

"To the overseer's house, father. It is out of the reach of all danger, and there is room enough for us all."

They came forth with Witherspoon, who led them at once into the park, where Mellichampe received and escorted them to the dwelling-house of the overseer, a rude but spacious building, that stood in a field running along at a little distance to the west of the avenue, within sight and hearing of the mansion-house, but beyond reach of fire-arms from that quarter. It was a moment of sweet sorrow, that which Mellichampe and Janet enjoyed in the brief interview which the necessities of the time permitted them. The cheerful and stimulating sounds of the trumpet recalled him to his duties, and, with a word of encouragement and hope, which was answered by her tears, he hurried away to the field of strife, and the presence of the energetic Singleton.

"Lieutenant Mellichampe, take your men, throw down yonder panels, and cross into the garden; keep them under cover where the shelter is sufficient to conceal your movement, and have your horses then fastened at the foot of the hill rising on the right. A couple of sentries will guard them there. This done, return to the post assigned you in the garden, covering the dwelling on the rear with your rifles."

Mellichampe moved promptly, in obedience to his orders, and soon succeeded in securing possession of the garden. Dividing his command in such a manner as to place a similar body of men in watch over each quarter of the building, Singleton proceeded to try the effect of his rifles upon such of the defenders as were more than necessarily exposed. His men were dismounted for this purpose, their horses secured in safety, and each man was put in possession of his tree.

To the rifles of Singleton the muskets of Barsfield's party readily responded, and, for a few moments, the din and uproar were continued with no little spirit. The musketry soon ceased, however. Barsfield discovered that it was not his policy to risk his men, two of whom had fallen in this overture, in any such unequal conflict. The certainty of the rifle, in such hands as those of the partisans, was too great a danger to be wantonly opposed by musket-men. There was no necessity for any such exposure on the part of the besieged: all that they were required to do was to keep watch upon the area below, and prevent the nearer approach of the beleaguering party. After a few rounds, therefore, had shown what results must follow such a combat, Barsfield forbade the firing from the house, and commanded that his men should lie close, only watching for an occasional exposure of the persons of their enemies within certain reach of their muskets.

The bugle of Singleton called up his officers. They assembled, as at a central and safe point, at the overseer's dwelling, to which the family of Mr. Berkeley had retired. A small room was assigned the partisans, and there they carried on their hurried deliberations.

"This is child's play, gentlemen," said Singleton; "can we find no better mode of dislodging these rascals? Our shot do little good now. There is no object to aim at. Barsfield has discovered the difference between rifled and smooth bore, and keeps too snug to suffer any harm at our hands. We must think of something, gentlemen; and it must be done quickly, or not at all, for Tarleton's on the road, and we must beat Barsfield by noon, or leave him. What do you say? I should be pleased, gentlemen, to have your suggestions."

"Many men, many minds." It would be needless to say, that there must be various counsels when there are many counsellors. Each had his notion and his plan, but to all there were objections. Humphries, at length, proposed to fire the dwelling. All agreed that this was the wisest suggestion—the effective plan, if it could only be made available. But who was to carry the fire to the fortress—who was to cross the yard, in the teeth of thirty muskets, and "bell the cat"? and what would be the chances of his life, or of his success, in the endeavor? This was the question, to which there was no ready answer. It was obvious enough that any one approaching the building with such a purpose, or with any purpose, as an enemy, must be shot down by its defenders. A silence of several minutes followed the utterance of these views by Singleton. The silence was broken by one—a slender, pale, and trembling youth, who emerged from behind the commander. His lips quivered as he spoke, but it was not with fear. His eye kindled with light, even while its long dark lashes seemed suffused with the dews of a tender heart.

"I will go, major," were his quickly-uttered words.

"You, Lance?—why, boy, you will be shot down instantly. Impossible!—you must not think of it!" was the imperative reply.

"But, sir, I can run fast: I can first get to the fallen tree, and so quickly, I don't think they can hit me in that time; and then the next push is for the piazza. Once I get under the piazza, I will be safe:" and the lad trembled with his own earnestness.

"Perhaps you might, Lance, but it would be impossible to preserve your fire in such a race, and the risk is too great to be undertaken with such a prospect."

Singleton was imperative, but the youth continued to urge his plan. At that moment a servant, entering the apartment, beckoned Mellichampe away. He was sent for by Janet, who received him in the adjoining room.

"I have heard," said she, "some of your deliberations without intending it: but your voices are loud, and these are thin partitions. The youth must not be suffered to go to certain death. I understand your difficulty, and think it may be overcome. I have a plan for you."

"You!" exclaimed Mellichampe, with a smile.

"Yes: look at this bow and these arrows," pointing to a noble shaft, which leaned in the corner of the room; "they were the gift of a Catawba warrior to my father when I was but a child. They are as good as new. They will convey combustibles to the roof—they will do what you desire."

"But your old home—your family dwelling, Janet—sacred to you as your birthplace, and as the birthplace of your mother—" was the suggestion of her lover.

"Sacred as my home, as my own and my mother's birthplace, it is yet doubly sacred as my country's. Place your combustibles upon these arrows, and send them to the aged roof of that family mansion; and I shall not joy the less to see it burn because it is my father's, and should be mine, when I know that in its ruin the people and the cause I love must triumph. God forbid and keep me from the mean thought that I shall lose by that which to my country must be so great a gain."

The wondering and delighted Mellichampe could only look his admiration. She stood before him, with her dark eye flashing, but suffused, and her lip trembling with the awful patriotism and warm feeling in her soul, as the very imbodiment of liberty itself—that divine imbodiment whose substance is truth, whose light is life, whose aim is a perfect humanity.

"Dearest Janet—worthy of adoration as of love—your self-sacrificing spirit is a rebuke to my own heart. I would have saved that mansion for your sake, though even my enemy—my deadly enemy—should escape his just punishment thereby."

"Go, Ernest," she responded, "go!—you have no time to lose. Let not that noble youth expose himself to certain death. Take the arrows, and do not let the hand tremble and the eye turn aside when you direct them to that sacred roof; it is now devoted to our country."

He seized the bow and arrows, carried her hand to his lips, and rushed back to the place of conference. Singleton was overjoyed when the primitive weapon was put into his hands.

"Happy chance!—and who has given you these, Mellichampe?"

"A woman!"

"What, Miss Berkeley?"

"Yes."

"And with a knowledge of their probable use?"

"With the avowed purpose of destroying by them her father's dwelling and her own."

"Noble creature!" was the only exclamation of Singleton. The thoughts of his mind wandering away, at that instant, without his power to control them; and, in his mind's eye, he surveyed the form of another self-sacrificing maiden—how different from Janet Berkeley in form and character, but, oh! how very like in soul.

CHAPTER XXII.

CAPRICES OF THE CONFLICT.

With the overruling judgment of a master-spirit, Singleton immediately proceeded to make his arrangements. To Mellichampe he gave orders to remount his men, and, leading them around the park, once more gain possession of the avenue. Here he was to await the result of the experiment, and to intercept the flight of the tories when they should be driven out from their fortress by the progress of the flames. Humphries was commanded to scatter his riflemen around the mansion, keeping close watch upon every movement of the garrison within: while two or three of the men, more experienced in such matters, were occupied in preparing the combustibles which were to be fastened to the lighted arrows. Singleton himself took charge of the bow; and, laying aside his sword and every weapon which was calculated to encumber his movement, himself prepared to discharge the more arduous part of the proposed experiment. His commands were nearly all instantly and simultaneously executed. A lively blast of the bugle, from various quarters of the grounds, gave token of concerted preparation. Arming himself with the prepared arrows, the partisan advanced.

"Lie close, men! lie close!" he cried, as he saw several of them emerging from shelter; "Lie close and watch the windows. Go back, Lance, and have your rifle in readiness."

With these words he advanced quickly but stealthily, and with a heedful movement, from one tree to another, until, reaching the inner limit of the park, he looked down upon the yard immediately around the dwelling, and saw that from that part he could certainly send his arrows to the roof.

Coolly preparing himself, therefore, while all behind him were breathlessly watching, now their commander and now the dwelling. Singleton fell back for an instant, and closely observed the probable distance and height of the roof; then advancing to the tree, and planting his right foot firmly behind him, he drew the long arrow to the head, until the missiles which were attached to it grazed against the bended back of the elastic yew. In another instant, and the meteor-like shaft went whizzing and kindling through the air, darting on with a true aim and unvarying flight, until, to the delight of the watching partisans, it buried itself, blazing all the while, in the very bosom of the shingled roof. A long redoubled shout of applause followed the achievement, and but a few moments had elapsed when Barsfield became conscious of the new danger which awaited him.

"'Ha!' he cried, as he beheld the position which Singleton had taken behind the tree, which, however, only in part concealed him. "Send me a score of bullets at the rebel, or he will smoke us out like so many rats. Shoot, men! take good aim, and stop him before it be too late."

A dozen muskets poured forth their contents in the direction of the daring partisan. The bullets flew all around him where he stood, but he stood unhurt. The moment after their fire was favorable to another effort; and, cool and thoughtful, Singleton was soon ready with a second shaft. Once more the whizzing arrow went blazing as fiercely and furiously as the first, and aimed with equal judgment at a different portion of the roof. Another and another followed in quick succession, in spite of the successive volleys of musketry which poured around him from the dwelling. In a little while the success of the experiment was no longer questionable.

"It burns! it burns!" was the cry from the surrounding partisans, and the surface of the roof was now sprinkled with jets of flame, that flickered along the dry shingles, gathering new bulk with every instant, and spreading themselves away in thin layers of light, until the air, agitated into currents by the progress of the fire, contributed to send it in huge volumes, rolling on and upward into the sky. Shout upon shout from the lips of the partisans attested their joy, and congratulated their successful captain, through whose fearless and skilful agency the design had been effected. Their cheering cries, more than anything besides, announced to the tories the new dangers of their situation, and the desperate position in which they stood. Singleton well conceived what might be their course, and gave his orders accordingly.

"Riflemen! stand by to watch the scuttle. Look out for the roof! Mark the scuttle, and shoot closely!"

Ascending to the garret, by the aid of a little ladder which always stood there for such a purpose, Barsfield himself proceeded to throw open the scuttle, when he was warned of the watchfulness of the besiegers by the sharp crack of the rifle, and the instantaneous passage of the bullet through the scuttle-door, and just above his head.

"Too quick, Lance! too quick by half!" cried Singleton to the precipitate youth, who had fired before the tory's head had made its appearance. The boy sank back abashed and mortified. Barsfield, meanwhile, descended with much greater rapidity than satisfaction, and the dense smoke rushed down the aperture after him, filling the chambers with its suffocating and increasing masses.

"It burns like tinder, and we have no water," said Clayton.

"And if we had," cried Barsfield fiercely, "who in the devil's name would apply it under the fire from those rifles?"

"And what are we to do?" cried one of the subordinates, emboldened by the near approach of a common danger; "Shall we stay here to be smoked alive, like so many wild beasts in a hole?"

"Should we not now surrender, Captain Barsfield, if we can get fair terms of quarter?" was the suggestion of Clayton.

"What! beg terms of that youngster? Never!" fiercely responded the tory. "I will perish first!"

"Ay, but we shall all perish with you, and I see no good reason for that, Captain Barsfield," was the calmer speech of Clayton. "We should apply for quarters to any youngster, rather than be smoked alive."

"And, if you did apply, would they hear us, think you?

Would they grant us the terms which we have already refused with insult and disdain? No, no, Lieutenant Clayton; they would cry 'Tarleton's quarters' in your ears in answer to all your applications, and taunt you, while your limbs dangled upon yonder oak, with our own good doings of the same sort."

"What then? Are we to stay here and perish by a death so horrid? Shall we not rather sally forth and fight?"

"Yes, fight them to the last, of course," was the response of Barsfield. "There is a mode, and but one that I can see, of getting out from these difficulties. I've escaped a worse chance than this; and, with a good sword and stout heart, I fear not to escape from this."

"Speak, Barsfield — how?" cried Clayton, impatiently.

"Mount our horses and cut our way through the rebels. They have dismounted and put their horses out of ready reach; and, if we cut our way through them, we shall get start enough to keep ahead of them before they can mount."

"Ay, ay — a good enough plan, were we mounted; but the first step that carries us beyond these walls puts us in the eye of their rifles. How shall we get to our horses, unless by first exposing ourselves in the piazza?"

"You are but young as a soldier, Lieutenant Clayton," was the sarcastic response of the tory captain, "and have much to learn in the way of war and its escapes. I will show you how we shall reach the horses without exposing ourselves, until we rush forth, armed and upon their backs, prepared for fight as well as our enemies. Every man will then be required to rely upon himself; and for the hindmost, God help him! for we may not. Where's Fender?" he concluded, looking round among the men, whose faces the crowding smoke was already beginning to obscure.

"Here, sir," cried the man, coming forward.

"Unsling your axe and throw off your jacket," cried the tory, coolly: "shut your mouth, if you please, sir; you can do nothing so long as you keep it thus ajar. Is your axe ready?"

"It is, sir," was the reply; and, under the direction of Barsfield, the soldier proceeded to tear away the washboard which fastened down the edges of the floor, and then to rip up two or three boards of the floor itself — a duty soon performed by the vigorous axeman. By this time, however, the smoke had become dense and almost insupportable; and the moment the aperture was made in the floor, admitting them to the lower or basement story, where the horses had been stabled, with a rapidity that defied all the efforts of their cooler commander, the tories, huddled upon one another, hurried and tumbled through, glad to escape from their late predicament, even with the chances before them of a hopeless and desperate struggle, such as Barsfield had painted to their eyes.

The stern calmness of their leader, during all this proceeding, was creditable in the highest degree. He exhibited no hurry, no apprehension — none of that precipitate haste which defeats execution, while it exhibits deficient character. When he got below, he himself saw that each man had mounted his proper steed and stood in readiness, before he took the bridle of his own. He then asked if all were ready: he placed himself in the advance, gave orders to one of the men to turn the latch, but not to unclose the door — a duty which he reserved to himself — and then addressed them in terms of the most encouraging composure.

"Have no fear, men; but each man, as he passes through the door, will at once strike for the entrance of the avenue. The brick foundations of the piazza and the smoke will conceal you for a few moments. I will go first from this hole, but I will be the last to move. Lieutenant Clayton will follow me out, but he will lead the way to the avenue. Follow him; keep cool — keep straight forward, and only turn when you turn to strike a foe. Are all ready?"

"Ay, sir, all ready?" was the reply. With the words, with his own steed behind him, Barsfield, on foot, led him forth, and was the first to emerge into the light. He was not instantly perceived by the assailants, such was the cloud of smoke between them and the dwelling; but when, one after another, with a fearful rush, each trooper bounded forth, driving forward with relentless spur to the avenue in front, then did Singleton, becoming conscious of their flight, give his orders for pursuit.

"Double quick step, riflemen; hurry on with you, and skirt the fence. Your rifles will then cover them as they fly, and Mellichampe will answer for the rest. Quick step, men, or you lose the fire."

The partisans were prompt enough in obeying these orders, but there had been some miscalculation in the distance, or the speed of fear had not been taken into the estimate of those advantages, possessed by the enemy, for which Singleton believed himself prepared. The tories were already in the avenue before the riflemen reached the skirts of the park. Barsfield, bringing up the rear, his huge form erect, his hand waving defiance, was the only individual at whom a shot was obtained. At him several bullets were sped; but there is a something in the daring indifference of boldness which not unfrequently deranges the truest aim of an enemy. The tory was unhurt; yet some of the rifles pointed at his back were held by the best marksmen of the lower country.

But a new enemy sprang up in the pathway of the tory, and the sabre of the impetuous Mellichampe once more clashed with that of his enemy.

"Ha, ha!" cried Mellichampe, "you were long in coming, but I have you now. You are mine at last!"

There was a demoniac delight in the expression of the youth's countenance, as, with these words, he confronted his foe.

"Stand aside, boy!" was the hoarse reply of the tory, as, wheeling his horse to the opposite hand of the avenue, he seemed rather disposed to pass than to encounter the youth. Mellichampe regarded no other enemy, and the troop of Barsfield mingled pell-mell in the strife with the partisans, who were scattered before them up the avenue.

With the sidling movement of Barsfield, the steed of Mellichampe, under the impetuous direction of his rider, was wheeled directly across his path, and the tory saw at a glance that the encounter could not be avoided. Preparing for it, therefore, with all his energies, he threw aside the weapon of his enemy, and the swords recoiled from each other in the fierce collision, as if with an instinct of their own. Again they bounded and buckled together; and then there was a momentary pause in the combat, as the weapons crossed in air, in which the eyes of the inveterate foes glared upon each other with the thirstful expression of demoniac hate. Like lightning then, for a few moments, the opposing blades darted around each combatant's head; then came the deadly thrust and the heavy blow — the ready guard, and the swift stroke in return.

Though brave enough in common parlance, there was yet that in the face of Mellichampe from which the tory seemed to shrink. The youth had been roused by repeated wrongs, and maddened by continued disappointments, which defeated his promised hope of vengeance. The accumulated venom of a fierce and injured spirit shot forth from his eye, and gave a dreadful earnestness to every effort of his arm, so that the inequality of physical strength between himself and his enemy did not at first seem so evident.

The consciousness of having wronged the youth, and the moral inferiority which, in all respects, he felt to him, neutralized in some degree the natural advantage which the tory possessed of greater muscle, and the acquired advantage of greater skill and experience. How else, indeed, could one so slender as Mellichampe — his bones not yet hardened to manhood, and he yet in the gristle of youth — contend so long and so equally with a frame so huge as that of Barsfield? How else, if the heart were not conscious of right in the one and of wrong in the other, could the former put aside the weighty blow of his enemy with so much ease, and respond to it with so much power? Thrice, in the deadliest stroke, had he foiled the tory, and now he pressed on him in return.

"It is now for me, villain," cried the youth, as he struck the rowel into his steed, and rose upon his stirrups a moment after, to give point with a downward stroke at the breast of his enemy, whose steed had sunk, under the sudden press of his rider's curb, backward upon his haunches —

"It is now my turn, villain, and my father's blood clamors for that of his murderer. Have at your heart. Ha!"

The stroke was descending, and was with difficulty parried by the sabre of the tory. It was put aside, however, at the utmost stretch of Barsfield's arm — his body being writhed round into an unnatural position for that purpose. The danger was only delayed. In another moment he felt assured that the stroke of Mellichampe — a backward stroke — must be repeated, and that he could not recover his seat in time to ward it aside; but, ere the youth could effect his object — to which he had addressed his entire energies, conscious that he now had the tory at complete advantage — the forefeet of his horse struck upon the carcass of a slain soldier, which slipped from under him, yet carrying him forward, till he stumbled irrecoverably and came to his knees.

The moment was lost; and, in the next, Barsfield had recovered his seat, from which the force of Mellichampe's assaults, and the efforts necessary for his own defence, had half uplifted him. It was his turn now to press upon his foe. Wheeling his horse suddenly round, he dealt him a heavy blow upon the shoulder of his sword-arm, which precipitated the youth to the earth, while wounding him severely. The tory would have paused to render his victory more complete; but, as he looked upon the avenue before him, he saw that he was isolated. Cutting their way, without pausing for any particular encounter such as had controlled the flight of their leader, his men had sped onward; and, though fighting with the partisans at every step, had yet succeeded in carrying the fight forward to the entrance.

The tory captain saw that he had no time for delay. Witherspoon, who had been busily engaged, was now pressing toward him, closely followed by another; and, though casting a wistful look upon his prostrate enemy, as if he longed to make certain his victory, the safety of his own life depended upon his haste, and was infinitely more important to him than even the death of so deadly an enemy as Mellichampe. Even now it was doubtful what success would attend his endeavor to pass the scattered partisans who lay in his path; and he felt that all his energies were required to meet the shock of Witherspoon, who was fast approaching.

While thus he prepared himself, the shrill clamor of a fresh trumpet broke suddenly upon his sense, and brought him relief. It announced the coming of a new force, and the probability was that it was British. Of this Barsfield, in another moment, had no doubt, as he saw Witherspoon, no longer seeking the conflict, rush past him in the direction of the burning mansion. The woodman had beheld the steel caps and the blue uniforms of the approaching force, and at once recognised the formidable corps, two hundred strong, of the legionary Tarleton. Barsfield rode on to meet his superior, and explain the situation of affairs before him. Witherspoon, meanwhile, leaping from his horse, which he let go free, rushed to the spot where Mellichampe had fallen.

"Airnest! Airnest, boy!" he cried, as he stooped down to the insensible body? "Speak to me, Airnest—speak to me, it's me, Jack—it's Thumbscrew, Airnest. Only say something—only a word—I don't care what you says, Airnest; but say something. God ha' mercy! He don't hear!—he can't talk. Airnest! Airnest!"

A groan met his ears and half relieved him.

"Thank God, it 'taint so bad. He's got life in him yet; and, if I can only carry him out of the way of the horses, and let Miss Janet know where to find him—"

Thus speaking, he raised the insensible body in his arms, and hurried with him toward the ditch, over which he sought to pass. His aim was to carry the youth into the thick copse beyond, where he could place him out of sight of the approaching enemy. But he had overtasked his own strength, after the severe fatigue and fighting which he had undergone, and the labor called for more time than the circumstances of the field would allow. The advance of Tarleton was too rapid to permit of his performing the affectionate service which he contemplated for his friend; and, before he reached the ditch, the swords of the legion were flashing before his eyes, as the troop wheeled round a bend in the avenue which hitherto had concealed him from their sight.

"Gimini! I must leave him, I must put you down, Airnest! I cant't help it, boy! I did the best!"

He spoke to the insensible youth as if he could hear;

and, with a groan that seemed to come from the bottom of his soul, he laid the body down in the ditch, where it was partially concealed from sight in the hollow and by the tufts and bushes which grew along its margin. Then, with a grim look of despair cast behind him as he fled, he leaped across the ditch, passed hurriedly through the copse and bordering foliage, and soon gained the station at the bottom of the hill, which had been assigned by Singleton at the commencement of the fray as the place of general rendezvous.

CHAPTER XXIII.

THE THREATENED SACRIFICE.

CHAFED with the excitement of battle, and mortified with the humiliation of defeat, Barsfield dashed forward to meet with Tarleton, to whom he conveyed the particulars of the affray. It needed but few words to do this at such a moment — the scene was in progress even then before the eyes of the legionary. The wild shouts of the partisans, scattered along the fields, and flying from the greater force approaching them — the occasional sounds of the rifle — the lurid glare of the flames, ascending in gigantic columns from the burning mansion, sufficiently informed the ready senses of a leader so intelligent and sagacious as the practised Tarleton. He was a man of deeds rather than of words, and a few brief, quick questions drew from Barsfield all that he sought to know.

"What number of rifles, Captain Barsfield, has Major Singleton?"

"Some thirty, sir, or more."

"What other force?"

"Ten or twenty horse, which we had first broken through, sir, on your approach."

"And from which our approach saved you?"

Barsfield bowed. Tarleton waved his hand, and gave his troop their orders with coolness and decision. In the next moment he led them forward with a fleet pace down the avenue, toward the burning dwelling and the park. He thought to find his enemy scattered and unprepared, as he now and then beheld in the distance, by the light of the flames, an occasional figure darting by, seemingly in flight, and the shouts of the partisans rose here and there from opposite quarters of the area.

THE THREATENED SACRIFICE.   209

The sight of these figures and the insulting shouts stimulated his advance, and aroused his natural appetite for strife. With habitual impetuosity, he hurried forward in a quick trot, making for the point which most immediately promised him an encounter with his foe.

He found them much sooner than he had expected. His enemy was prepared for him. Singleton was apprized of the approach of Tarleton quite as soon as Barsfield in the avenue, and he now prepared to execute the orders of Marion, for which the present condition of things gave him a favorable opportunity. He threw his men without the park. The fences lay between the two parties. One half of his force he immediately sent down the hill to prepare the horses, putting them in readiness for instant flight. His riflemen, who had been too late to check the retreat of Barsfield, were nevertheless just in time on the outer edge of the park, and skirting one side of the avenue, with its thick copse interposing sufficiently to protect them from a charge of cavalry, to gall the advance of Tarleton. They received their orders, and stood prepared to execute them. Covered by the trees, each man stood in silence, prepared to single out his enemy, and immediately after scud off along the fences, and join his comrades at the foot of the hill. Cool and watchful, Singleton remained at hand to watch the progress of both parties. He himself had prepared to do a like duty with his men. He had thrown aside the sabre, and a favorite rifle in his hands was quite as deadly a weapon as in that of any other of his troop. The legion came bounding forward, and the signal for their hostile reception came from the rifle of the partisan commander. It had its echoes—each an echo of death—and the advancing column of Tarleton in that narrow avenue, reeled and recoiled under the fatal discharge. A dozen troopers fell from their saddles with the fire, stiffening in the fast embrace of death, and scarce conscious of their wounds. But in another instant the fierce voice of Tarleton, clamorous and shrill, rose like that of a trumpet above all other sounds—

"Scoundrels, forward! Wherefore do ye pause? Through the bush to the right—charge, rascals, ere I cleave ye down to the earth! Charge the d——d rebels—charge—and give no quarter!"

The ditch was cleared—the obedient troopers, accustomed hitherto only to victory under the lead of Tarleton, went over the bank and scrambled through the copse with more daring than success. The overhanging branches were hewn away in an instant—a path was cleared for the advance through the close foliage, and, like bold cavaliers, a score of the troopers made their way through the obstruction. But where was the enemy? Where were they whose fatal rifles had dealt them so much loss? They had melted away like so many shadows—they were gone. Fiercely the dragoons dealt idle blows upon the surrounding bushes, which might have been supposed to shelter a lurking rifleman, but their sabres clashed together and found no foe. The partisans had vanished from their sight, but they had not yet gone. While yet the dragoons gazed bewildered and in wonderment, the repeated shot from the same select and deadly marksmen singled them out, one by one, from another sheltered clump of wood, not more than fifty yards in advance; and the remaining few who had passed into the open ground and were still exposed, could hear the distinct commands of Singleton—

"Another round, men—one more. Each his man."

The partisan had managed admirably, but he was now compelled to fly. The advantage of ground was no longer with him. Tarleton, with his entire force, had now passed through the avenue, and had appeared in the open court in front. The necessity of rapid flight now became apparent to Singleton, and the wild lively notes of his trumpet were accordingly heard stirring the air at not more than rifle distance from the gathering troop of Tarleton. Bitterly aroused by this seeming audacity—an audacity to which Tarleton, waging a war hitherto of continual successes, had never been accustomed, his ire grew into fury—

"What, men! shall these rebels carry it so?" he cried aloud. "Advance, Captain Barsfield—advance to the right of the fence with twenty men, and stop not to mark your steps. Advance, sir, and charge forward. You should know the ground by this time. Away!"

To another he cried — striking the neck of his steed impatiently with the broad side of his sabre —

"Captain Kearney, to yon wood! Sweep it, sir, with your sabres; and meet me in the rear of the garden!"

The officers thus commanded moved to the execution of their charges with sufficient celerity. The commands and movements of Major Singleton were much more cool and not less prompt. He hurried along by his scattered men, as they lay here and there, covered by this or that bush or tree.

"Carry off no bullets that you can spare them, men — fire as soon as they reach the garden, and, when your pieces are clear, take down the hill and mount."

Three minutes did not elapse before the rifles had each poured forth its treasured death; and, without pausing to behold the effects of their discharge, each partisan, duly obedient, was on his way, leaping off from cover to cover through the thick woods to the hollow where their horses had been fastened.

The furious Tarleton meanwhile led the way through the garden, the palings of which were torn away to give his cavalry free passage. With a soldier's rage, and the impatience of one not often baffled, he hurried forward the pursuit, in a line tolerably direct, after the flying partisans. But Singleton was too good a soldier, and too familiar with the ground, to keep his men in mass in a wild flight through woods becoming denser at every step. When they had reached a knoll at some little distance beyond the place where his horses had been fastened, he addressed his troop as follows:—

"We must break here, my men. Each man will take his own path, and we will all scatter as far apart as possible. Make your way, all of you, for the swamp, however; where, in a couple of hours, you may all be safe. Lance Frampton, you will ride with me."

Each trooper knew the country, and, accustomed to individual enterprise and the duties of the scout, there was no hardship to the men of Marion in such a separation. On all hands they glided off, and at a far freer pace than when they rode together in a body. A thousand tracks they found in the woods about them, in pursuing which there was now no obstruction—no justling of brother horsemen pressing upon the same route. Singleton and his youthful companion darted away at an easy pace into the woods, in which they had scarcely shrouded themselves before they heard the rushing and fierce cries of Tarleton's dragoons.

"Do you remember, Lance," said Singleton to the boy—"do you remember, the chase we had from the Oaks, when Proctor pursued us?"

"Yes, sir—and a narrow chance it was when your horse tumbled. I thought they would have caught and killed you then, sir; but I didn't know anything of fighting in the woods then."

"Keep cool, and there's little danger anywhere," responded Singleton. "Men in a hurry are always in danger. To be safe, be steady. But—ha! do you not hear them now? Some of them have got upon our track."

"I do hear a noise, sir—there was a dry bush that cracked then."

"And a voice—that was a shout. Let us stop for a moment and reload. A shot may be wanted."

Coolly dismounting, Singleton proceeded to charge his rifle, which had been slung across his shoulder. His companion did the same. While loading, the former felt a slight pain and stiffness in his left arm.

"I am hurt, Lance, I do believe. Look here at my shoulder."

"There's blood, sir—and the coat's cut with a bullet. The bullet's in your arm, sir."

"No—not now. It has been there, I believe, though the wound is slight. There, now—mount—we have no time to see it now."

"That's true, sir, for I hear the horses; and, look now, major, there's two of the dragoons coming through the bush, and straight toward us."

"Two only?" said Singleton, again unslinging his rifle.

The boy readily understood the movement, and proceeded to do likewise, but he was too late. The shot of Singleton was immediate, and the foremost trooper fell forward from his horse. His companion fled.

"Don't 'light, Lance—keep on. There's only one now, and he won't trouble us. The other—poor devil! his horse was too fleet for his master's safety. Away, sir."

It was time to speed. The report of the shot and the fall of the dragoon gave a direction to the whole force of the pursuers, whose shouts and cries might now be heard ringing in all directions of the forest behind them.

"They can't reach us, Lance. We shall round that bay in a few seconds, and they will be sure to boggle into it. On, boy, and waste no eyesight in looking behind you. We are safe. I only hope that all our boys are as much so. But I fear that we have lost some fine fellows. Poor Mellichampe! but it is too late now. Push on—the bay is before us."

Thus speaking, guiding and encouraging the boy, the fearless partisan kept on. In a few minutes they had rounded the thick bay, and were deeply sheltered in a dense wood, well known at that period by a romantic title, which doubtless had its story.

"My Lady's Fancy. We are safe now, Lance, and a little rest will do no harm."

The partisan, as he spoke, drew up his horse, threw himself from his back, fastened him to a hanging branch, and, passing down to a hollow where a little brooklet ran trickling along with a gentle murmur, drank deeply of its sweet and quiet waters, which he scooped up with a calabash that hung on a bough, waving in the breeze above. Then throwing himself down under the shadow of the tree, he lay as quietly as if there had been no danger tracking his footsteps, and no deadly enemy still prowling in the neighborhood and hungering for his blood.

The chase was given over, and the lively tones of the bugle recalled the pursuers. The legionary colonel stood upon a hillock, awaiting the return of the men, who came in slowly and half exhausted from the profitless pursuit. He wiped the dust and sweat from his brow, but a rigid and deep blue vein lay like a cord across his forehead. A gloomy cloud hung about his eyes, and yet his lips, pale, and seemingly passionless, were parted with a smile. They quivered slightly, and the tips of his white teeth rested upon the lower lip for a moment, as if to control his speech, when he beheld the person of the tory captain among those approaching him.

"And now, what of this affair, Captain Barsfield? We have time now to speak of it," was the salutation of Tarleton; and he alighted from his steed as he spoke, and the point of his sabre was made to revolve quickly, while he listened upon the up-curling peak of his thick military boot. Barsfield briefly narrated the events which we have witnessed, and, saving some little natural exaggeration of the numbers on the side of the partisans, with tolerable correctness. The narrative, as he listened, did not seem to diminish the disquiet of his hearer.

"But fifty men, you say? the entire force of the rebels but fifty men! and your force, if I err not, thirty at the least. But fifty men!"

"There may have been; indeed, sir, there must have been —more; and—"

"A bad business, sir; a very bad business, Captain Barsfield," said the other interrupting him. "The affair has not been rightly managed, though where the defect lay may not now be said. What force was it you encountered in the morning?"

"A squad of thirty, sir, and more. I had defeated them, and they would have been cut to pieces, but for the sudden appearance of the troop of Major Singleton, which you have just dispersed."

"No more, sir; no more. Take your men, and examine the ground and the avenue. See to the wounded prisoners, Captain Barsfield; have them well secured, and ascertain the extent of your own loss. There must be an inquiry into this business quickly. Move, sir—we have no time to lose."

The blood mounted into the tory's cheek as he listened to these orders; the fire of intense satisfaction glared and gathered in his eye, and, fearful that his feeling would be seen by the piercing glance of Tarleton, he turned away instantly in the execution of his orders. A fierce hope of vengeance, yet to be satisfied, was at his heart. He had not forgotten that his mortal enemy lay wounded on that field. He knew that, although wounded, Mellichampe was yet alive. The command to scour the scene of conflict was precisely the command which he most desired; affording him, as it did, an opportunity of making certain the stroke which even in the hurry of battle, he had considered incomplete. A fierce emotion of delight, under which he trembled, seized upon his frame as he heard the command; and, bowing with ill-concealed satisfaction to his superior, he hurried away with all the rapidity of a newly-stimulated passion, not merely to the execution of his orders, but to the final consummation of his own bloody scheme of vengeance — the death of that hated rival, in the pursuit of which he had been so often baffled when most sanguine of success. The knife was now in his hand, however, and the devoted victim lay before him.

CHAPTER XXIV.

SKETCHES OF THE STRIFE.

Let us retrace our steps; let us go back in our narrative, and review the feelings and the fortunes of other parties to our story, not less important in its details, and quite as dear in our regards. Let us seek the temporary dwelling of the Berkeley family, and contemplate the condition and the employment of its inmates during the progress of the severe strife of which we have given a partial history. Its terrors were not less imposing to them than they were to those who had been actors in the conflict. To the young maidens, indeed, it certainly was far more terrible than to the brave men, warmed with the provocation and reckless from the impulses of strife. And yet, how differently did the events of the day affect the two maidens—how forcibly did they bring out and illustrate their very different characters! To the casual observer, there was very little change in the demeanor of Janet Berkeley. She seemed the same subdued, sad, yet enduring and uncomplaining creature, looking for affliction because she had been so often subjected to its pressure; yet, from that very cause, looking for it without apprehension, and in all the strength of religious resignation.

Not so with her more volatile companion. The terrors of the fight, so near at hand, so novel in its forms, and so fearful to one who never, till now, had associated it in her thought with any other features than those of old romance—where the gorgeousness and the glitter, the cheering music and the proud array, were contrived to conceal the danger, if not to salve the hurts—brought to her other and more paralyzing sensations. All her levity departed with the approach and presence of the reality, of which, hitherto, she had but dreamed, and the images of which, seen through the medium of her imagination and not her heart, had until now presented her with no other forms than those of loveliness or power. The first dread sounds of battle, the first crash and commotion of the conflict, taught her other feelings; and, with each reiterated shout or groan, her emotion increased to a passion of fear that became painful even to her companion — herself full of the warmest apprehensions for her lover's safety, and laboring under a true sense of the growing and gathering miseries around her. But it is at such a moment that the true nature of the mind — the true strength of the heart — the spirit, and the soul, and the affections, rise into impressive and controlling action. It was then that the majesty of a devoted woman, conscious of all the danger, yet not unprepared to meet it with him to whom her heart was given, shone forth in the bearing of Janet Berkeley.

The light, thoughtless heart of Rose Duncan, untutored and unimpressed as yet by any of the vicissitudes of life, had few moods but what were hurrying and of a transient nature. She was unprepared for any but passing impressions. Her fancy had been active always, and her heart, in consequence, had grown subordinate. Affliction, the subduer, the modifier — she who checks passion in its tumults, and tempers to sedateness the warm feelings which would sometimes mount into madness — had brought her no sober counsels. Small but accumulating cares, which benefit by their frequent warnings, had never taught her to meditate much or often upon the various sorrows and the many changes, as frequent in the moral atmosphere as in the natural, which belong to life. That grave tale-bearer Time, whose legends are never wanting in their moral to those who read, had taken no heed of her education. That stern strengthener and impelling mistress, Necessity, had never, in order to bring out its resources, subjected each feeling of her heart to bondage, putting a curb upon the capricious emotion and the buoyant fancy. She heard of care from books, which seldom describe it in its true features, but it was only to regard it as a something which is to give a zest to pleasure by sometimes changing its aspect; as in conserves we employ a slight bitter, in order to relieve pleasantly the cloying insipidity of their sweet. She had never yet seen in Sorrow the twin-sister of Humanity, born with it at its birth, keeping due pace with it, though perhaps unseen, in its progress through the flowery places as well as through the tangled wilderness; clinging to it, inseparably, through all its fortunes; clouding, at times, its most pleasant sunshine with a look of reproof; chiding its sweetest anticipations with the language of homily; and pressing it downward, at last, to the embrace of their common mother Earth, until even Hope takes its flight, yielding the struggle for the present, and possibly withholding its assurance from the future.

Thus, utterly uneducated by the heart's best tutors, the novel terrors now before her eyes left her entirely without support in reflection. She was convulsed with apprehension; the fierce oaths of the hurrying troops grated with a new form of danger upon her fancy; every wild shout smote painfully upon her senses; and the sharp shot, directed, as she now knew it to be, against the bosom of a feeling and a living man while teaching her properly to realize the truth, totally unnerved and left her powerless. She shrank upon the floor in her terrors, as the dreadful din came to her ears, and crawled to the window, where her cousin sat in speechless apprehension. There, like a frightened child, she sat clinging to the drapery of Janet, while continued sobs and momentary exclamations betrayed her new consciousness of danger, and her own inadequacy of strength to contend with it.

How different was the deportment of Janet! How subdued her grief—how unobtrusive her emotions—how sustained her spirit—how governing her reason! She shrunk not from the contemplation of that danger whose terrors her mind had long since been taught to contemplate at a distance. Drawing her chair beside a little window, which looked forth directly upon the scene of battle, and scarcely in perfect security from its random shot, she gazed upon the progress of events, and exhibited in comparison with Rose, who sat upon the floor and saw nothing, but little consciousness, and certainly no fears, of its awful terrors. Yet her emotions were not less active, her feelings not less susceptible and warm, than those of her companion. It was, indeed, because her consciousness was so deep, her love so abiding, her fears so thick and overflowing, that she had no audible emotions. The waters of her heart were too far down for display; it is only in the shallows that the breakers leap up, and chafe, and murmur. They speak not for themselves, but for the overfull and heaving ocean that gathers and settles, gloomily and great, in the distance. The clamor of her cousin's fear had spoken for hers; and yet how full of voice, how touching the language of silence, when we know that the full heart is running over. How thrilling is the brief, gasping, sudden exclamation, which utters all, because we feel that it has uttered nothing!

She sat with her hands clasped; her soul sad and sick, but strong; her eyes intently gazing, as if they would burst from their sockets, upon the wild scene of confusion going on around her. And when the strife began warmly in the first stage, and before the house was fired—when she knew nothing of the progress of events, and heard nothing but the sharp and frequent shot, without knowing what had been its effect; when the shriek of agony reached her ears faintly from afar, and there came no word to her to say that the wounded victim was not the one, of all in that controversy, to whom her thought and her prayer were most entirely given—it was then that she felt the agony which yet she did not speak. In her mind she strove to think a prayer for his success and for his safety, and sometimes the words of aspiration were muttered brokenly from her lips; but the prayer died away in her heart, and the dreadful incidents of earth going on around her kept back her thoughts from God.

A terrible cry of satisfaction was uttered by the partisans, as in the conflict they beheld one of the defenders of the house distinctly fall back from the window at which he had exposed himself. The rifle had been too quick and fatal for his escape. The sound smote upon the senses of Janet with a new fear; and Rose, in her childish terror, nearly dragged her from the seat.

"Father of mercies, spare him! spare them all! Soften their hearts—let them not spill blood!" was the involuntary prayer of Janet. "Rose, do not go on so; do not fear; you are not in danger, dear Rose: but keep on the floor; the shot can not reach you there."

"But you, Janet—you are in danger at the window: come down, dear Janet, and sit with me. The bullets will be sure to hit you. Come down. I'm so afraid."

"Pull me not down, Rose; there is no danger here, for the shot do not fly in this direction. They fly all toward the garden, where our people are, under the trees."

"Where? do you see them, Janet?" cried Rose, half rising.

"Yes; hush—there!" But a cry and a shot at that moment frightened the other to her place upon the floor, and she sank down with renewed trepidation.

"I see them now, all of them: some stand behind the water-oaks; and I see two crawling along under the bushes. God preserve them! Should Barsfield know they are there, he could kill them, for there are no trees between them and the house—nothing but the bushes. Oh God!"

The exclamation startled Rose with a new terror.

"What, Janet?"

"I see him! Rash Mellichampe! I see him, and he is mounted. The tories must see him too. Why! oh, why will he expose himself! why does he not keep behind the trees! He stands—he does not move. Barsfield must soon see him now. Fly, fly, Ernest!" and, her emotion assuming the ascendency, she arose from her chair, and motioned with her hand, and cried with her voice, now feeble and husky from affright, as if he to whom it was addressed could hear it at such a distance.

"He hears me—he moves away. Oh, dear Ernest! he is now behind the trees. Thank God, he is safe!" and she sank again into her seat, and fondly believed, at that moment, that he had heard her warnings and complied with her entreaties. There was a pause in the conflict. Neither shot nor shout came to their senses.

"Is it over, Janet?" cried Rose. "Have they done fighting? I hear nothing. There is no danger now."

"Would it were over, Rose; but I fear it is not. I see the men watching behind the trees. Some are riding away, and some are creeping still around the fence. It blinds me to look; it maddens me to think, Rose, that he is there, exposed to the murderous aim of those merciless tories, in the danger which I may not keep him from, which I do not share with him. Pray, Rose—pray, dearest, for the safety of our men. Pray, for I can not. I can only look."

"Nor I. But how can you look? The very thought of it is too horrible."

"The thought of it to me is more dreadful than the sight," was the answer of Janet. "Months have gone by, Rose, since I first began to think of battle and of Mellichampe's hourly danger; and when I thought of it then, it was far more terrible than now, when I look upon it before me. But oh, dearest Rose, how awful is that silence! There is no shouting; there are no cries of blood and death, and yet they are planning death. They are meditating how best to succeed in slaughtering their fellow-creatures."

"Do you see them now, Janet?"

"Yes, there, behind the trees. Look now, Rose. There is now no danger, I think."

The more timid girl rose to survey the distant array, which she did with all the eager curiosity of childhood. The bugle sounded.

"Ah, Rose, they are in council. See them under the great oak, yonder, to the left—there, close by the stunted cedar?"

"I see, I see. How their swords glitter, Janet. How beautiful, how strange! And that trumpet, how shrilly sweet, how strong and wild its notes, seeming like the cry of some mighty bird as it rushes through the storm. Oh, Janet, what a beautiful thing is war!"

"So is death, sometimes. Beautiful, but terrible. Alas that man should seek to make crime lovely! Alas that woman should so admire power and courage as to forget the cruelties in their frequent employ. God keep us! they are going to fight again."

With a scream Rose sank again to the floor, grasping the

dress of her companion, and clinging to it with all the trepidation of childhood.

"Ah! they lift their rifles. I see three of them that kneel behind the trees, and they have their aim upon something, but what I can not see. What is it they would shoot? They are pointed to the house, too. I see now: two of the tories are at one window. God help them, why do they not hide themselves?"

"Are they gone now, Janet?" asked Rose in the momentary silence of her companion.

"I know not; I can not look again. Ha! the shot! the shot! the rifles! They are slain!"

The sharp, sudden sound of the rifles followed almost instantly the inquiry of Rose Duncan, and the eyes of Janet instantly turned, as under some fascination, toward the window. The troopers were no longer to be seen. Shuddering as with convulsion, she turned from the window and sank down beside her more timid companion. But her heart was too full of anxiety to suffer her to remain long where she had fallen. The sounds again ceased, and she ventured to rise once more and look forth upon the prospect. She now saw the scene more distinctly. The partisans had somewhat changed their position, and were now nearer the cottage. Singleton stood beneath a tree, with several of his officers about him. The quick eye of Janet readily distinguished her lover among them. He stood erect, graceful, and firm as ever, and she forgot her fears, her sorrows: he was unhurt. While she looked, they moved away from the spot, and she now beheld them making a circuit round the park so as to avoid unnecessary exposure to the tory bullets, and approaching the little cottage in which the family found shelter.

"Heavens! Rose, they are coming here—the officers. What can they want? There may be some one hurt. Yet no, it does not look so."

"Then the fighting is over, Janet."

"No, no, I fear not, for I see the riflemen all around the house, and watching it closely from beneath the trees. But here they come, the officers, and he is among them. Go, Rose, dearest, and send my father to meet them. I can not. I will rather sit here and wait until they are gone."

The partisans sought the house the better to carry on their deliberations. They obtained some refreshments from Mr. Berkeley, and then proceeded to confer on the subject of the leaguer. We have seen the result of their deliberations, in the gift which Janet had made to her lover of the bow and arrows. It will not need that we dwell longer upon the event. Let us proceed to others, in which she also had a share.

CHAPTER XXV.

THE COURAGE OF LOVE.

THROUGHOUT the conflict, a close and deeply interested observer, Janet Berkeley had never once departed from her post of watch. She had felt all the sickness—the dreadful sickness—of suspense. She suffered all the terrors of one anxious in the last degree about the result of the battle, yet perfectly conscious of its thousand uncertainties. The wild and various cries of the warriors—now of triumph and now of defeat, or physical agony—went chillingly to her heart; yet, the sentinel of love, jealous of her watch, and solicitous of the safety of that over which it was held, she kept her place, in spite of all the solicitations of Rose and of her equally apprehensive father. She did not seem conscious of her own danger while she continued to think of that of Mellichampe; and, so long as the battle lasted, could she think of anything else? She did not.

We have seen the patriotic resolution with which she devoted the family mansion to destruction. She had beheld the application of the torch—she had seen the arrow winged with flame smiting the sacred roof which had sheltered so many generations, and with that glorious spirit which so elevated the maidens of Carolina during the long struggle of the revolution—making them rather objects of national than of social contemplation—she had felt a triumphant glow of self-gratulation that it had been with her to contribute to a cause doubly sacred, as it involved the life of her country not less than that of her lover. With hands clasped and tearful eyes, she had prayed as fervently for the conflagration of the dwelling as, at another time and other more favorable auspices, she would have prayed and labored for its preservation and safety.

With an intensity of feeling not surpassed by that of any one of the brave men commingling in the strife, she had beheld the progress of the flame. How her heart beat when, more remote from the smoky cloud which hung all around the dwelling, she had seen, sooner than the partisans, the impetuous rush — mounted all, and with blazing weapons — of Barsfield and his party! But when she heard the clash of sabres in front of the dwelling, and in the narrow avenue which led to it, when she listened to the sounds of that conflict which she could no longer see, it was then that her spirit sickened most. Imagination — the feverish fancy — grew active and impatient. Crowding fears came gathering about her heart, which grew cold under their influence. Her head swam dizzily, until at length, in utter exhaustion, she sank from the seat at the window, and strove feebly, on bended knees, by the side of the trembling Rose, once more to pray. But she could not: the words refused to come to her lips; the thoughts of her mind were too wild, too foreign, and not to be coerced; they were in the field of battle — striving in its strife — in the cruel strife of man with man. How could she bring her mind, thus employed, and at such a moment, with all its horrid and unholy associations of crime and terror, even for the purposes of supplication, into the presence of her God? She dared not.

She started from her knees as she heard the tread of hurrying feet around the dwelling. She reached the window in time to see that four of the partisans were employed in bearing one in their arms, who seemed dead or fatally wounded. They laid him down under the shelter of some trees behind the house, and the moment after she saw them hurrying back to the avenue. She tried to call to them, she sought to know who was the wounded man; but the words died away in inarticulate sounds. She could not speak; and, in an instant, they were out of sight. Her agony became insupportable. Who was the victim? Her fears, her imagination, answered. She watched her time, during the momentary inattention of her father, and, without declaring her intention to Rose, she stole out of the apartment. She hurried from the house unseen. She reached the tree under which the dead body had been laid. It was covered with a cloak, which was stained with blood, apparently still flowing from the bosom of the wounded man. She dared not lift the garment. Her hand was extended, but trembled feebly above it. But she heard approaching voices, and was nerved for the occasion. She hastily threw the cloak from the face, and once more she breathed freely: the features were unknown—happily unknown. There was none to feel the loss while bending over him; and she rejoiced, with a sad pleasure, that the loss was not hers.

She hurried back with a new life to the apartment, and had scarcely reached it when she heard the sound of a trumpet borne upon the winds from a direction opposite, and beyond, that in which the combatants had been engaged. A new enemy was at hand. The shrill and inspiring notes approached rapidly, swelling more and more loudly until the avenue was gained, and then there was a pause—a dreadful silence—among those who had lately been so fearfully at strife. In a few moments after, and she saw Major Singleton rush toward her, followed by several of his men. She heard his orders distinctly, and they brought a new terror to her soul.

"Forward, John Davis, with a dozen rifles, and bring off Mellichampe: that bugle is Tarleton's, and the whole of the mounted men of the legion are upon him. Give the advance a close fire, and that will relieve him; then fall back behind those bays—reload, and renew your fire. That done, take to the branch, and stand prepared to mount. Away!"

They obeyed him promptly, stole up behind the copse, and received the advance of Tarleton with a fire as of one man. We have seen the result: the enemy leaped the ditch, broke through the copse, and found no foe. But the purposed relief of Mellichampe came too late to bring off the brave youth for whose succor it had been intended. The personal effort of Witherspoon had failed also. That faithful attendant had barely crossed the ditch when the riflemen came forward. Having no rifle, he could not contribute to their strength; and, with a word, pointing out to them a proper cover, he hurried forward with all despatch to the place of rendezvous. But, though he strove to avoid being seen by any of the household while passing, as he was compelled to do, the little cottage in which the Berkeley family were collected, he could not escape the quick, apprehensive eye of Janet. She saw him approaching, she saw that he was seeking safety in flight, and, what was of more appalling concern to her, knowing his attachment to Mellichampe, she saw that he fled alone. How quick, how far-darting, is the eye of apprehension! She could read the expression of his countenance as he approached, even as a book. She saw the question answered in his face which her lips had yet not asked. How slowly did he approach: she rose—her hand was lifted and waved to him; but, when he looked toward her, he increased his speed. She cried aloud to him in her desperation:—

"Come to me, John Witherspoon—come to me, if you have pity—but for one moment!"

Did he hear her? He did not answer; but, as if he guessed her meaning from her action, he flung up his arms in air, as if to say, "Despair, despair!—all's lost!"—for so her heart interpreted his action—and in another instant he was out of sight. The riflemen followed soon behind him, stealing from cover to cover in the neighboring foliage, and had scarcely been hidden from her gaze before the fierce troopers of Tarleton came bounding after them. Vainly did her eyes strain in the examination of the forms of those who fled; she saw not the one of all—he whom alone she sought for; and the fear of his fate grew into absolute certainty when the blue uniforms of the terrible legion came out on every hand before her. She saw them hurrying fast and far after the flying partisans, and every blast of the trumpet, as it died away in the distance, brought a new pang into her mind, until the agony became insupportable. She determined to suffer no longer under the gnawing suspense which clamored at her heart.

"I will know the worst: I cannot bear this agony, and live!"

Thus murmuring, she started from her place by the window,

and turned to the feeble Rose, who still lay upon the floor at her feet, in a degree of mental and physical prostration full as great, even now, as at the first moment in which the battle joined.

"Rose, dear Rose, will you go with me?"

"Where, go where, Janet? You frighten me!"

"There is no danger now. Go with me, Rose, dear cousin, let me not go alone."

"But tell me where, dearest Janet? Where would you go? and you look so strange and wild; put up your hair, Janet."

"No—no—no matter. It is no time. I must go, I must seek him, Rose, and I would not go alone. Come with me, dearest, my sister, come with me. Believe me, there can be no danger — only to the avenue."

"What, where they've been fighting, and in all that horrid blood?" cried the other, in a voice that was a shriek.

"Even there—where there is blood—where—oh, God be with me! where there must be death. I go to seek for it, Rose, though, I would not find it if I could," solemnly, and with clasped and uplifted hands, responded the devoted maiden.

"Never, never," cried the other.

"Rose, dear Rose, will you let me go alone? I beg you, Rose, on my knees, there is no danger now."

"There is danger, Janet, and they will murder us. I heard them crying and shouting only a minute ago; and, there, there is that dreadful trumpet now, whose sounds go like a sword-stab to my heart. I can not, Janet — I dare not: there is danger."

"None: on my life, Rose, there is no danger now. Our people have retreated, and the dragoons have all gone off in pursuit. They are now a great way off, and we can get back to the house long before they return. Do not fear, Rose, but go with me, only for a little while."

"I can not, I will not go among the dead bodies. You would not have me go there, Janet; you surely will not go yourself?"

"Ay, there, Rose, even there, among the dying and the dead, if it must be so. I may serve the one, I have no cause to fear the other. It may be — it must be — dreadful to look upon, but my heart holds it to be a duty that I should go there now, and, if not a duty, it is a desire that I can not control. I must go, Rose, and I would not go alone."

"I will not; forgive me, Janet, but I should go mad to see the blood and the dead bodies. I can not go."

"God be with me! I must go alone:" and, as she replied thus, giving her solemn determination, her eyes were uplifted in a holy appeal to the Almighty Being, whose presence, in the absence of all others, she had invoked for her adventure.

"Hold me not, Rose, I am resolved. I must go, though I go alone. Yet, I should not, Rose, if you would but reflect. There are no noises now, there are no alarms; the troops have gone; there is no sort of danger."

She looked appealingly to her companion while she spoke, but her eye met no answering sympathies in that of Rose Duncan. The terrors of the latter were unabated. There was a vital difference of character between the two. The elastic spirit of the more lively maiden was one merely of the physical and external world. She was the summer-bird, a thing of glitter and of sunshine. She could not live in the stormy weather; she could not bide the turbulence of strife. It was at such a time that the spirit of Janet Berkeley came forth in strength, if not in buoyance; even as the eagle, who takes that season to soar forth from his mountain dwelling, when the black masses of the tempest growl and gather most gloomily around it.

"You will not, Rose?"

"No, do not ask me, Janet."

The firm and determined maiden, without another word, simply raised her finger, and pointed to the adjoining apartment, where her father was. The uplifted finger then pressed her lips for a moment, and in the next she was gone from sight. Rose did not believe that she would go forth after her refusal to accompany her, and she now earnestly called her back. But she was already out of hearing: she had gone forth to the field of blood and battle; and, strong in love, and fearless in absorbing and concentrative affections, she had gone alone.

CHAPTER XXVI.

THE WOUNDED LOVER.

Love is the vital principle of religion—it is religion. It is the devotion that fears not death—which is not won by life—which can not be seduced from duty—which is patient and uncomplaining amid privation. Its existence becomes merged in that of the object which it worships, and its first gift is the sacrifice of—self. There is no love if the heart will not make this sacrifice, and the heart never truly loves until this sacrifice be made. Self is that life which we surrender when we gain the happiness of the blessed. Seldom made in this life, it is yet the only condition upon which we are secure of the future. Ah! happy the spirit which is soonest ready for the sacrifice. To such a spirit, Heaven and Immortality are one!

The destiny of such a creature as Janet Berkeley might even now be written. She is secure. There can be no change in such a character. Time, and fortune, sickness, the defeat of hope, and the consciousness of approaching death, could never alter one lofty mood, one self-devoting impulse of her soul. Surely, though she seeks the field of terror unaccompanied by human form, she will not necessarily be alone. The God whose worship calls only for love, will not be heedless of the safety of her who toils for the beloved one. He is with her.

Resolute as she was to seek the field of strife, and fearless as her conduct approved her spirit, she was yet sufficiently maiden in her reserve, to desire as much as possible, to conceal from stranger eyes the object of her adventure. With a cautious footstep, therefore, she stole from cover to cover, until she reached the artificial bank, clustering and crowded with shrubs and vines, which supported the trees on one side of the spacious avenue. With a trembling hand she parted the shrubbery before her, and her eyes took in for an instant the field of battle, and then, immediately after, shutting out its objects, closed, as if with a moral comprehension of their own. She could not be mistaken in the dreadful objects in her sight. The awful testimonies of the desperate fight were strewed around her. Her uplifted foot, in the very first step which she had been about to take from the bank, hung suspended over the lifeless body of one of its victims. She turned suddenly and sickeningly away. She strove, but she could not pass into the avenue at that point, and she receded through the thicket, and made her way round to another quarter, in which she hoped to find an unobstructed passage. There was but little time for delay, and with this thought a new resolution brought strength to her frame. Again her hand parted the copse, making a passage for her person. This time she dared not look. She did not again permit herself either to think or to look, but resolutely leaping across the ditch, she stood for a moment, awed and trembling, but still firm, in the presence of the dead.

She was motionless for several seconds; but her mind neutralized, in its noble strength of purpose, the otherwise truly feminine feebleness of her person. She was about to move forward in her determined task; but when she strove to lift her foot, it seemed half-fastened to the ground. She looked down, and her shoe was covered with clotted blood. She stood in a fast-freezing puddle of what, but an hour before, had been warm life and feeling. But she did not now give heed to the obstruction; she was unconscious of this thought. Her mind was elsewhere, and her eyes sought for another object. The anxiety of her heart was too intense to make her heedful of those minor influences, which at another time would have shocked the sensibilities and overthrown all the strength of her sex. She hurried forward, and her eyes were busy all around her. The whole length of the avenue seemed marked by the suffering victims, or those who had ceased to suffer. Death had been busy in this quarter, and tory and rebel had equally paid tribute to the destroyer. A deep moaning, feebly uttered but full of pain, came to her ears. It guided her steps. She followed the one sound only. A wounded man lay half in the ditch, to which he had crawled as if to be out of the way of the horses. His head and shoulders were on the bank, the rest of his body was concealed. A frightful gash disfigured his face, and the blood-smeared features were yet pale with the sickness of death. He stretched out a feeble arm as she approached. He muttered a single word —

"Water."

At another time, she would have run with the speed of charity to bring him the blessed draught for which he prayed; but now she gave him no heed. There was nothing in his face which spoke to her heart; and that moaning sound yet reached her ears at intervals. She hurried onward, and the pleading wretch sank back and perished, even as he prayed. She heard his last gasping groan, but it had no effect upon her feeling. Her mind was sensible only of the one sound which had so far guided her footsteps. It seemed, through the medium of some strange instinct, at once to convey itself to her soul. She reached the bend in the avenue whence it came. On the edge of the ditch, half-buried in the water and the long grass, lay the wounded man. A single glance informed her. She could not mistake the uniform.

"Mellichampe!" she cried, in a thrilling voice of terror, as with one desperate bound she rushed forward to the spot, and, heedless of the thick blood which had dyed the grass all around where he lay, sank on her knees beside him, while her enfolding arms were wrapped about his bosom.

"Ernest — dear Ernest! speak to me; tell me that you live; say that you are mine still — that I do not lose you. Look at me, Ernest — speak to me — speak to me only once."

He was in her arms — he breathed — he felt; but he spoke not, and did not seem conscious. Her heart was strong, though suffering; and her feeble strength of person, under its promptings, was employed with an energy of which she had never before conjectured one half the possession, to drag him forth from the vines and brambles which lay thick around his face — the concealing cover in which he had been studiously placed by the trusty Witherspoon the moment before his own flight. From this cover she now strove to lift the form of her lover; and, though wounding her delicate fingers at every effort with the thorns, the devoted Janet felt nothing of their injuries as she labored with this object. With great effort she succeeded in drawing him upon the bank, and his head now rested upon her arms. A writhing of his person, a choking, half-suppressed groan, attested the returning consciousness, with the increased pain following this movement, and mixed moans and menaces fell incoherently from his lips. Even these signs, though signs of pain to him, and holding forth no encouragement of hope to her, were yet more grateful than the unconsciousness in which he lay before. She spoke to him — the words bursting forth in an intensity of natural eloquence from her tongue, which could scarce have failed to arouse him, even from the stupor of overcoming death itself.

"Speak to me, Mellichampe: dear Ernest, speak to me. tell me that you live — that you are not hurt to death. It is Janet, your own Janet, that calls upon you. Look up and see; look up and hear me. It is my arms, dear Ernest, that hold you now; the bloody men are all gone."

And his dim eyes did unclose, and they did look up with a sweet mournfulness of expression, vacant and wild, that grew into a smile, almost of pleasure, when they met the earnest, commiserating glance of hers. They closed again almost instantly, however; but he murmured her name at the moment.

"Janet — you?"

"Your own, in life and death, Ernest — ever your own."

And she clung to him with a tenacious hold, at that instant, as if determined that death should take no separate victim. He was again conscious, and spoke, though feebly: —

"I fear me it is death, Janet. I feel it; this pain can not long be endured, and my limbs are useless."

"Speak not thus, Ernest; I know it is not so. Stay — move not. I will lift you to the house — I will —"

"You!" and he smiled feebly and fondly, as he arrested the idle speech.

"God of heaven! have mercy! what shall I do? I may not help him:" and the exclamation burst spontaneously from her lips, as she found, after repeated efforts, that her feeble arms were inadequate to the task even of lifting him from his present painful position to a drier spot upon the bank. In her bewilderment and anguish, she could only call his name in a bitter fondness. He heard her complaints, and seemed to comprehend their occasion. His lips parted, and, though with pain and a sensible effort, he strove to speak to her. The words were faint and inaudible. She bent down her ears, and at length distinguished what he said. He but named to her the faithful negro who had once before stood so opportunely between him and his enemy, and had nearly suffered a dreadful and ignominious death in consequence of his fidelity.

"Scip — Scipio — he will come — Scip."

His eyes closed with the effort, but her face brightened as she listened to the words, She immediately laid his head tenderly upon the bank, pressed the pale, unconscious forehead with her lips, and, bounding away through the thicket, hurried with all the fleetness of a zealous and devoted spirit to the completion of her task.

CHAPTER XXVII.

LOVE'S BARRIER.

She was not long in finding the faithful Scipio. He sprang with all the alacrity of a genuine zeal in obedience to her commands. When he heard from her faltering lips the melancholy occasion which called for his attendance, his own emotion was unrestrainable, though he affected to doubt the certainty of her information.

"Who — who da hurt, Missis? You no say da Mass Arnest? I no blieb it. Mass Arnest, he too strong, and he too quick for let dem dam tory hurt a bone in he body. He somebody else, missis. You no 'casion for scare; he somebody else hab knock on he head: no Mass Arnest, I berry sartin. But I go long wid you all de same, dough I no guine tink da Mass Arnest git hurt. He hab much hurt, I turn soger mysef. I run way from ole maussa, and take de bush after dem tory. I sway to God nothing guine 'top me I once in de woods. But, come, young missis, show me de place whay de person hurt, dough I know berry well taint Mass Arnest."

Denying her assertion, yet fearing at every step that he took — and, indeed, only denying that he might the more readily impose upon himself with the unbelief which he expressed, but with which he was yet not satisfied — the sturdy Scipio followed his young mistress toward the avenue. They had not reached the little copse, however, by which it was girdled, before they heard the rush of horses, and the shrill blast of the bugle.

"'Top in dis bush, young missis; squat down here under dis persimmon, whay day can't see you."

"No, Scipio, let us go forward. I think we can get to the avenue before they come up, and I would have you lift him into the bushes out of the way of the horsemen, before they have passed by. Do not fear, Scipio; we shall have time, but you must go forward quickly."

The black looked into her face with astonishment, as well he might. Her words were unbroken, and her tones quick and unaffected, equable, even musical; while his own, accustomed as he had been all his life to utter and complete subordination, were tremulous with timidity and fear.

"Gor-a-mity, Miss Janet, you no scare? You no frighten, and you only young gal? Scip member when you been only so high, and here you tall—you 'tan up traight—you look all round—you no trouble, dough you hear de horn blow and de sogers coming. Wha' for you no scare like Scipio?"

She could not smile at that moment, as at another she could scarcely have refrained from doing; but her eye was turned upon the half-unnerved negro, and her taper finger rested on his sable wrist, as she said in tones which strengthened him, as he felt they came from one who was herself supernaturally strengthened—

"Fear nothing, but come on quickly. I need all your strength, Scipio; and, if you will mind what I say to you, there will be no danger. Come on."

He opposed nothing farther to her progress, but followed in silence. They had reached an outer fence, the rails of which had been let down in order to the free passage of the cavalry before, when the increasing clamor of the approaching detachment under Barsfield again impelled Scipio to other suggestions of caution to his youthful mistress. But she heeded him not, and continued her progress. Nor did he shrink. He could perish for her as readily as for Mellichampe; and, to do the faithful slave all justice, his exhortations were prompted not so much by his own danger or hers, as by a natural sense of the delicacy of that position in which she might involve herself, under that strong and passionate fervor of devoted love which blinded her to all feeling of danger, and placed her infintely beyond the fear of death. Other fears she had not. Her maiden innocence had never yet dreamed of a wrong to that purity of soul and person, of which her whole life might well have been considered the embodied representative.

But the forbearance of the negro, and his ready compliance hitherto, all disappeared when, on reaching the copse, he beheld the bright sabres flashing in his eyes immediately in the courtyard, as, rounding the yet blazing fabric, the troopers of Barsfield were even then making with all speed toward the avenue. He caught the wrist of his mistress, and pointed out the advancing enemy. She saw at a glance that, in another moment, they would make their appearance in the avenue quite as soon as herself. But a few paces divided her from Mellichampe; and, as she hesitated whether to pause or proceed, she trembled now, for the first time in her movement. In that moment of doubt, the more ready physical energy of the negro obtained the ascendency. With something like fear he drew her to a part of the copse which was thicker than the rest, and here she partially crouched from sight, he taking a place humbly enough immediately behind her. What were her feelings then, in that position — what her fears! She bore them not long. The anxiety and the suspense were infinitely beyond all estimation of the danger in her mind; and, with fearless hands, after a few moments of dreadful pause and apprehension, she divided the crowding bushes from before her, and looked down into the ditch which separated her from the avenue.

At that moment, leading his squad and moving rapidly at their head, Barsfield rode into the enclosure. Instinctively, as she beheld his huge form and fiercely-excited, harsh features, her hands sunk down at her side, and the slender branches which she had opened in the copse before her, with their crowding foliage, resumed in part their old position, and would most completely have concealed her; but when, in the next instant, she beheld the fierce tory ride directly to the spot where Mellichampe lay, when she saw him rein up his steed and leap with onward haste to the ground, when her eye scanned the intense malignity and mingled exultation and hatred of his glance, and she saw that his bloody sabre was even then uplifted—she had no further fears—she had no further thoughts of herself. She tore the branches away from before her, and, in defiance of all the efforts of the faithful Scipio to restrain her, she leaped forward directly into the path of the tory, and in the face of his uplifted weapon.

Her appearance was in the last degree opportune. Another moment might have ended all her cares for her lover. Barsfield was standing above him, and Mellichampe had exhibited just life enough to give the tory an excuse sufficient to drive the sword which he held into the bosom of that enemy whom, of all the world, he was most desirous to destroy. The meditated blow was almost descending, and the feeble youth, stimulated by the presence of his foe, was vainly struggling to rise from the earth, which was all discolored with his blood. His dim eyes were opening in momentary flashes, while his sinewless arm was feebly striving to lift the sabre, which he had still retained tenaciously in his grasp, in opposition to that of Barsfield. The instinct rather than the reason of love prevailed. Indeed, the instinct of love is woman's best reason. With a shriek that rose more shrilly upon the air than the bugle of the enemy, she threw herself under the weapon—she lay prostrate upon the extended and fainting form of her lover—she clasped his head with her arms, and her bosom formed the sweet and all-powerful barrier which, in that perilous moment, protected his. The weapon of the tory was arrested. He had heard her cry—he had seen the movement—and he did not, he could not then, strike.

"Save him, spare him, Barsfield!—he is dying—you have already slain him! Strike no other blow; have mercy, I pray you—if not upon him, have mercy upon me. I have never wronged you—I will not—let us go free. Why will you hate us so—why—why?"

"Fear not, Miss Berkeley—you mistake my purpose: I mean not to destroy him. Leave him now—let one of my men attend you to the house; and Mr. Mellichampe shall be taken care of."

"I will not leave him," she exclaimed; "I dare not trust you, Barsfield—I can take care of him myself."

The fierce brow of the tory blackened as this reproachful speech met his ears.

"What! not trust me, Miss Berkeley?"

"Why should I? Did I not behold you, even now, about to strike his unguarded bosom?"

"He strove to fight — he offered resistance," was the somewhat hasty reply of the tory.

"He strove to fight! — he offered resistance! — oh, shame, Captain Barsfield — shame to manhood — that you should speak such language! What resistance could he offer? how could he fight, and the blood that could only have given him strength for such a conflict soaking up the earth about him? If that blood were now in his heart, Mr. Barsfield, you would not now speak thus, nor would I have occasion, sir, to plead for his life at any hands, and, least of all, at yours."

She had raised herself from the body, over which she still continued to bend, under the indignation of her spirit at the unmanly speech of the tory. Her eyes flashed forth a fire as she spoke, 'neath which his own grew humbled and ashamed. His muscles quivered with rage and vexation, and his only resort for relief was to that natural suggestion of the lowly mind which seeks to conceal or fortify one base action by the commission of another.

"Take her away, Beacham," he said to one of the troopers; "carry her to the house — tenderly, Beacham — tenderly; hurt her not. Be careful, as you value my favor."

"Touch me not," she cried aloud, "touch me not: put no hand upon me. This is my home, Captain Barsfield — I am here of right, while you are but the guest of our hospitality. Do not suffer these men to lay hands upon me."

"But you are here in danger, Miss Berkeley."

"Only from you, sir — only from you and yours. I am in no danger, sir, from him — none — none. I will cling to him for safety to the last, though he hear me not — though he never hear me again. He is mine, sir and I am his; but you knew this before. He is mine — you shall not tear me from my husband."

"Husband!" cried Barsfield, in unmitigated surprise and unconcealed vexation.

"Yes, husband, before God, if not in the eye of man! Living or dead, Ernest, I am still yours—yours only. I swear it by this unconscious form—I swear it by all that is good and holy—all that can hallow an innocent love, and make sacred and strong so solemn and so dear a pledge! You can not now separate us—you dare not!"

"You know not, Miss Berkeley, how much I can dare in the performance of my duty."

"This is no duty of yours—I need none of your guardianship."

"Ay, Miss Berkeley, *you* do not, perhaps, but *he* does. He is my prisoner, under charge of a heavy crime—of treason to his sovereign, and of being a spy upon my camp."

"What! he—Mellichampe! Oh, false, false—foolish and false!" was her almost fierce exclamation.

"True as gospel, Miss Berkeley, as I shall prove to his conviction, if not yours. But this is trifling, surely. Beacham, remove the lady; treat her tenderly, but remove her from the body of the prisoner: we must secure him at all hazards—living or dead."

The rugged soldier, in obedience to these commands, approached the maiden, who now clung more firmly than ever to the half conscious form of her lover. Her arms were wound about his neck, and, with convulsive shrieks at intervals, she spoke alternately to Barsfield and her lover. In the meantime, beholding the approach of the soldier who had been instructed to bear her away, the faithful Scipio, though entirely unarmed, did not hesitate at once to leap forward to her assistance. He made his way between her and the soldier Beacham, and, though his arms hung without movement at his side, there was yet enough in his manner to show to the tory that he meditated all the resistance of which, under the circumstances, he could be considered capable. His teeth were set firmly; his eyes sought those of the soldier, and were there fixed; and his head rested upon one shoulder with an air of dogged determination which, even before he spoke, conveyed all the eloquence of his subsequent words.

"Say de wud, missis—only say de wud, and I hammer dis poor buckrah till he hab noting leff but de white ob de eye. He hab sword for stick, and Scip only hab he hand and teet'; but I no 'fraid ob um; only you say de wud—dat's all!"

But poor Scipio, as was natural enough at such a moment, in the presence of his mistress, and his blood mounting high at seeing the condition of Ernest Mellichampe, had grievously miscalculated his own strength. He had scarcely spoken when a stroke from the back of a sabre across the head brought him to the ground, like a stunned ox, and taught Janet how little commiseration she was to expect from the fierce man who stood before her, wielding, at that instant, her entire destiny. The soldier advanced, though with some evident reluctance, and he laid his hand upon her. She started, on the instant, and rose immediately to her feet.

"If you are resolved upon violence toward me, Captain Barsfield, I will spare myself, as much as possible, the pain of suffering it. You have, sir, all the shame of having commanded it. I know that you have the strength to tear me away from him; you are wise, perhaps, as you seem only to employ it when the difference is so manifest. But I will not be separated from him, though you declare him your prisoner: I will be a prisoner also; I will cling to him wherever you may decree that he shall be carried; for know, sir, that I trust you not. The man who will employ violence to a woman would murder his sleeping enemy!"

"Remove her to the house, Beacham," was all that the tory said; but his words were uttered with teeth closely clinched together, and his whole frame seemed to quiver with indignation. At that moment the sound of Tarleton's returning bugle smote suddenly upon the ears of all; and the quick sense of Janet immediately saw, in the features of Barsfield, that the intelligence was not pleasing to his mind. He hurried his commands for the removal of Mellichampe's body, and was now doubly anxious to convey her to the house. Without a definite motive for refusing now to do that to which, but a moment before, she had consented, she sprang again to the person of her lover, again threw her arms about him, and refused to be separated. While thus situated, the tones of another voice were heard immediately behind the group. The deep, subdued, but stern accents of Tarleton himself were not to be mistaken; and Barsfield started in obvious agitation, as he heard the question which first announced to him the presence of his superior.

CHAPTER XXVIII.

TARLETON IN TIME.

The group, at that moment in the avenue, formed a striking picture. The voice of Tarleton seemed to have the effect of paralyzing and fixing to his place each of the parties. Janet, on bended knee, with her person half stretched over the insensible body of her lover, her face turned and her hand uplifted to the legionary colonel, looked, at the same moment, relieved and apprehensive. She felt that the presence of Tarleton was a restraint upon the vindictive personal hostility of Barsfield; but did she not also know that the name of the legionary was synonymous in Carolina with everything that was bloody and revengeful? She hoped and trembled, yet she was better pleased that the destinies of her lover should rest with the latter than the former. Tarleton could have no individual hatred to Mellichampe; she well conceived the viperous and unforgiving hate which rankled against him in the bosom of the tory.

The quiet inquiry, the even and subdued tones, of Tarleton, had the effect of a like paralysis upon the limbs of Barsfield. His mood was rebuked — his violent proceedings at once arrested, as he heard them; yet they were words of simple inquiry.

"What does all this mean, Captain Barsfield? why is this lady here?"

The tory explained, or sought to explain, but he performed the task imperfectly.

"A wounded enemy — a prisoner, sir. I would have conveyed him where he could procure tendence, but Miss Berkeley resisted."

The maiden rose. She approached Tarleton, and said to him, in low, but still audible tones,

"Because I would not trust him. He would have killed him — he would have murdered him with his bloody sword, if I had not come between."

"But who is he, young lady, what is the youth in whom you take such interest?"

Her lips quivered, and a faint flush spread itself over her cheeks, but she did not reply.

"Who is the prisoner, Captain Barsfield?"

"A rebel, sir — one Mellichampe."

"Son of Max Mellichampe?" demanded Tarleton, interrupting him.

"The same, sir; as malignant a rebel as his father; and one not only liable to be dealt with as such, but one whom I would secure for trial as a spy."

At these words she spoke. The accusation against her lover aroused her. Her eye flashed indignant fires upon the tory as she spoke fearlessly in reply.

"It is false, sir — a wilful falsehood, believe me. Ernest Mellichampe was no spy; he could not be. This man conceives his enemy's character from his own. Mellichampe is incapable, sir, of so base an employment; and Captain Barsfield knows him sufficiently well to know it. Ernest did but come to the house to see us, as he was accustomed to come; and it so happened that Captain Barsfield, with his troop, came that very day also. My father always extended to Ernest Mellichampe the same hospitality which he extended to Captain Barsfield; and so, sir, you see that Ernest was our visiter, our guest, like Captain Barsfield, and one of them could no more be a spy than the other. Captain Barsfield knows all this; and, if he did not hate Ernest, I should not have to tell it you. But I tell you the truth, sir, as I am a woman: Ernest was no spy, and the charge against him is false and sinful."

She paused, breathless and agitated. Tarleton smiled faintly as he heard her through, and his eyes rested with a gentle and most unwonted expression upon the glowing face of the fair pleader. Her eye shrunk from, while her whole frame trembled beneath, his gaze.

"But why is he here, my good young lady? why, if he is our friend, why is he here?" inquired Tarleton, in the gentlest language.

"I said not that, sir; I said not that he was a loyalist; Ernest Mellichampe, sir, is one of Marion's men."

"Ha!" was the quick exclamation of Tarleton, and his brow was furrowed with a heavy frown as he uttered it.

"But not a spy—oh no, sir, not a spy!—an open, avowed, honorable enemy, but no spy. He fought against this man, sir—this man Barsfield—who hates him, sir, and came here only just now, sir—I saw it myself—and would have killed Ernest with his sword, sir, and he senseless, if I had not come between him and the weapon."

"Is this so, Captain Barsfield?" inquired Tarleton, gravely.

"The rebel's weapon was uplifted, Colonel Tarleton, and he opposed me when I sought to make him my prisoner."

"Oh! false—false, sir—and foolish as it is false!" was her reply; "for how could he fight, sir, when he was so hurt, and lying almost senseless on the grass?"

"He could offer but little resistance, indeed, Captain Barsfield!" remarked Tarleton, sternly and coolly; "and this reminds me that he will the more speedily need the assistance of our surgeon. Here, Decker—Wilson—Broome—go one of you and request Mr. Haddows to prepare himself for a wounded man—sabre-cut, head and shoulder—away!—and you—a score of you, lift the body and bear it to the house. Tenderly, men—tenderly: if you move so roughly again, Corporal Wilson, I'll cleave you to the chine with my sabre. Ha! he shows his teeth again!—a fierce rebel, doubtless, young lady, and a troublesome one, too, though you speak so earnestly in his behalf."

The latter remark of Tarleton was elicited by the feverish resistance which the partly-aroused Mellichampe now offered to his own removal. The soldiers had sought to wrest his sabre from his grasp, and this again, with the pain of the movement, had provoked his consciousness. He struggled desperately for an instant, gnashed his teeth, threw his eyes upon the group with an air of defiance even in their vacancy, then closed them again, as he fainted away in a deathlike sickness in the arms which now uplifted him.

Janet would have clung still to her lover as they bore him toward the dwelling, but Tarleton interposed. He approached her with a smile of gentleness, which was always beautiful and imposing when it made its appearance upon his habitually sombre features.

"Come, Miss Berkeley, let us go forward together. You will not fear to take the arm of one whom you doubtless consider in the character of an enemy — one, probably, of the very worst sort. Your rebel there, in whom you have taken such a sweet interest, has no doubt taught you to believe me so: and you have readily believed all that he has taught you. I see how matters stand between you, nay, blush not, you have nothing to blush for. You have only done your duty — the duty of a woman, always a more delicate, often a more holy, and sometimes a far more arduous duty than any of those which are particularly the performance of man. I admire you for what you have done, and you will regard me as a friend hereafter, though I am at war now with some of those whom you love most dearly. This matters nothing with me: nor am I always the stern monster which I appear to so many. I am, they say, fond of blood-spilling, and I fear me that much of what they say is true; But Bannister Tarleton was not always what he now appears. Some of his boy feelings have worked in your favor; and, so long as they last — and Heaven grant that they may last for ever — I will admire your virtues, and freely die to preserve and promote them. Go now and attend upon this youth: and, hear me, young lady, persuade him back to his true allegiance. You will do him as good a service by doing that, as you have done him now. He will be well attended by my own surgeon, and shall want for nothing; but he must remain a prisoner. The charges of Captain Barsfield must be examined into, but he shall have justice."

"Oh, sir, do not believe those charges — do not believe that man. He is a bad man, who personally hates Ernest, and will do all he can to destroy him, as he destroyed his father."

"His father! Yes, yes, I remember. Max Mellichampe, His plantation was called—"

"Kaddipah."

"I see—I see," responded Tarleton, musingly, and his eyes were on the ground; while the sabre which he had carried in his hand, still in its sheath, came heavily to the earth with a clatter that made the maiden start. A few moments' pause ensued, when Tarleton proceeded:—

"Fear nothing for the safety of the youth. He shall be tried impartially and treated honorably, though we must now keep him a prisoner, and Barsfield must have his keeping."

"Oh, sir, not Barsfield—anybody else."

"It can not be," was the response; "but there is no danger, I shall say but a few words to Barsfield, and Mr. Mellichampe will be much safer in his custody than in that of any other. Take my word that it will be so. You have some prejudices, I perceive, against Barsfield, which do him injustice. You will discover, in the end, that you have wronged him."

"Never, sir, never. You know him not, Colonel Tarleton, you know him not."

"Perhaps not, my dear young lady; but I know that Mr. Mellichampe will be safer after I have given my orders. All I request of you is to be patient, Encourage the prisoner; tell him to fear nothing; and fear nothing yourself."

She hesitated: she would have urged something further in objecting to Barsfield as the keeper of her lover; but a sudden change came over the countenance of the legionary, even as an unlooked-for cloud enlarges from a scarce perceptible speck, and obscures the hitherto untroubled heavens. His figure suddenly grew erect, and his air was coldly polite, as he checked her in the half-uttered suggestion.

"No more, Miss Berkeley, I have determined. The arrangements most proper for all parties shall be made, and all justice shall be done the prisoner. Have no doubts; rely on me, I pray you, and be calm; be confident in the assurances I give you. For once, believe that Bannister Tarleton can be humane; that tenderness and justice may both be found at his hands. Go now to your dwelling. You have duties there; and oblige me, if you please, by saying to your father that, if agreeable to him, I will take dinner with him to-day."

He kissed her hand as he was about to leave her, with a grave, manly gallantry, that seemed to take the privilege as a matter of course; and she did not resist him. Murmuring her acknowledgments, she hurried away to the dwelling, and was soon out of sight. Tarleton stood for a few moments watching her progress, with a painful sort of pleasure evident upon his pale countenance, as if some old and sacred memories, suddenly aroused from a long slumber, were busy stirring at his heart.

CHAPTER XXIX.

THE HALF-BREED AND THE TORY.

TARLETON, however, whatever may have been his feelings or his thoughts, gave but little time to their present indulgence. As soon as Janet Berkeley was out of sight, he again sought out Barsfield, whom he found in no very excellent humor. The tory was mortified on many accounts. He was irritated at the escape of Mellichampe, a second time, from the fate which he had prepared for him, and which at one moment he had considered certain. He was annoyed at the sudden appearance of his superior, and that superior Tarleton, just when his controversies with a woman placed him in an attitude so humiliating to a man and a soldier. His brow was clouded, therefore, as these thoughts filled his mind, and the scowl had not left his features when Tarleton again made his appearance. The fierce legionary was a man of promptitude, quick decision, and few words:—

"So, Captain Barsfield, this prisoner of yours is the son of Max Mellichampe!"

"The same, sir; a malignant I had thought quite too notorious to have escaped your recollection."

"It had not; though, at the moment when I first heard it, I was confounding one name with another in my memory."

"I thought it strange, sir."

"You must have done so," was the cool reply of Tarleton; "for the fine estate and former possessions of Mellichampe, now yours through our sovereign's favor, are too closely at hand not to have kept the old proprietor in recollection. But our speech is now of the son: what of him, Captain Barsfield?"

There was a good deal in this speech to annoy the tory;

but he strove successfully to preserve his composure as he replied to the latter part of it.

"He, sir, is not less malignant, not less hostile to our cause and sovereign, than his father. He is an exceedingly active officer among the men of Marion; and, like his father, endowed with many of the qualities which would make him troublesome as an enemy. He is brave, and possessed of considerable skill; quite too much not to render it highly advantageous to us to have him a prisoner, and liable to certain penalties as a criminal. It was my surprise, Colonel Tarleton—" and a little hesitation here, in the words and manner of the tory, seemed to denote his own apprehensions of encroaching upon delicate ground quite too far—"it was my surprise, sir, that, knowing his name and character, you should have proceeded toward him with so much tenderness."

The legionary did not seem to feel the force of the rebuke which this language conveyed. His thoughts were elsewhere, evidently, as he replied, with an inquiring exclamation:—

"Eh?"

"You knew him, sir—a rebel—a spy; for such I asserted and can prove him to be; yet you spared him."

"I did," said Tarleton; "you wonder that I did so. Does your surprise come from the belief that I did him or myself injustice? To what do you ascribe my forbearance? or would you rather have had me truss him up to a tree, because he merited such a doom, or sabre him upon the ground, in order to preserve my consistency?"

The tory looked astounded, as well he might. There was a strange tone of irony in the language of Tarleton, and the words themselves had a signification quite foreign to the wonted habit of the latter. He knew not how to construe the object or the precise nature of the question. The whole temper of the fierce legionary seemed to have undergo a change, and was now a mystery to Barsfield, as it had been a wonder to the men around them. There was a sarcastic smile on the lips of the speaker, accompanying his words, which warned the tory to be heedful of the sort of reply to which he should give utterance. He paused, therefore, for a few moments, in order so to digest his answer as to guard it from every objectionable expression; yet he spoke with sufficient promptitude to avoid the appearance of premeditating what he said.

"Surely, Colonel Tarleton, the rebel who resists should die in his resistance—"

"But when wounded, Barsfield—when wounded and at your feet"—was the abrupt interruption of Tarleton, who certainly did not diminish the surprise of Barsfield while thus making a suggestion of mercy to the conqueror. The tory could not forbear a sarcasm: with a smile, therefore, he proceeded:—

"And yet, Colonel Tarleton, it has seldom been the case that you have left to his majesty's enemies, even when you have overthrown them, a second opportunity of lifting arms against him."

The bitter smile passed from the lips of the legionary, and his eye rested sternly upon the face of the tory. The sarcasm was evidently felt, and, for a few moments, there was in Tarleton's bosom something of that fierce fire which at one period would have replied to the sharp word with the sharper sword, and to the idle sneer with a busy weapon. But the sternness of his brow, a moment after, became subdued to mere seriousness, as he replied:—

"It is true, Captain Barsfield, my sabre has perhaps been sufficiently unsparing. I have been a man of blood; and heretofore, I have thought, with sufficient propriety. I have deemed it my duty to leave my king as few enemies as possible, and I have not often paused to consider of the mode by which to get rid of them; but—"

He did not conclude the sentence. His face was turned away from the listener. Thought seemed to gather, like a cloud, upon his mind; and a gloomy and dark hue obscured his otherwise pale features. The tory regarded him with increased surprise as he again addressed him; he could no longer conceal his astonishment at the change in the mood and habits of the speaker.

"May I ask," he continued, "what has wrought the alteration which I can not but see now in your deportment, Colonel Tarleton?"

"Is it not enough," was the quick response of the legionary, "that Cornwallis has grown merciful of late?"

"It has been of late that he has become so," said Barsfield with a smile; "only since the battle of Gum Swamp, may we reckon?"

"He, at least, requires that I shall be so," said Tarleton, calmly, "though the indulgence of a different temper he still appears to keep in reserve for himself. He would monopolize the pleasure of the punishment, and perhaps the odium of it also. That, at least, I do not envy him."

"And in that respect your own mood seems to have undergone a change which could not have been produced by any command of his?"

Barsfield was venturing upon dangerous ground in this remark; but he presumed thus freely as he listened to the tacit censure which Tarleton had expressed in reference to the conduct of his superior.

"It has, Captain Barsfield, and the proof of it is to be found in the proceedings of this day. Under your representations I should at another time, with the full sanction of Cornwallis, have strung up this rebel Mellichampe to the nearest tree, though but a few moments of life were left him by the doubtful mercies of your sabre or mine. I have not done so; and my own mood is accountable for the change, rather than the orders of my superior. The truth is, I am sick of blood after the strife is over; and I relieve myself of the duties of the executioner by the alteration of my feelings in this respect. Mellichampe will perhaps complain of my mercy. He must remain your prisoner, to be carefully kept by you, for trial in Charleston, as soon as his wounds will permit of his removal to the city. An execution is wanted there, for example, in that unruly city; and this youth, coming of good family, and an active insurgent, is well chosen as the proper victim. I am instructed to secure another for this purpose, and my pursuit now is partly for this object. Two such subjects as Walton and Mellichampe carted to an ignominious death through the streets of Charleston, will have the proper effect upon these insolent citizens, who growl where they dare not bite, and sneer at the authority which yet tramples them into the dust. You must keep this youth safely for this purpose, Captain Barsfield; I shall look to you that he escape not, and that every attendance and all care be given him, so that he may as soon as possible prepare for his formal trial, and, as I think, for his final execution. My own surgeon shall remain with him, the better to facilitate these ends, which, as you value your own loyalty, you will do your utmost to promote."

"Am I to remain here, then, Colonel Tarleton? Shall I not proceed to Sinkler's Meadow, agreeably to the original plan, and afterward establish myself in post at Kaddipah?"

"No! you must establish yourself here. The position is safer and better suited to our purposes than Kaddipah. Surround yourself with stockades, and summon the surrounding inhabitants. The probability is, that you are too late for the gathering at Sinkler's Meadow. I fear me that Marion is there now. You should have crossed the river yesterday; the delay is perhaps as fatal in its consequences as it was unadvised and injudicious. But it is too late now to think upon. To-morrow I will move to Sinkler's Meadow, if I do not first find Marion in the Swamp."

The conference was interrupted at this moment by the approach of Blonay. His features suddenly caught the eye of the legionary, who called him forward. The half-breed with his ancient habit, stood leaning against a neighboring tree, seeming not to observe anything, yet observing all things; and, with a skill which might not readily be augured from his dull, inexpressive eye and visage, searching closely into the bosoms of those whom he surveyed, through the medium of those occasional expressions of countenance, which usually run along with feeling and indicate its presence.

"Ah! you are the scout," said Tarleton. "Come forward: I would speak with you."

The half-breed stood before him.

"And you promise that you can guide me directly to the camp of the rebel Marion?"

"Yes, colonel, I can."

"You have seen it yourself?"

"I have, colonel."

"Unseen by any of the rebel force?"

"Yes, colonel."

"Can you guide us there, too, undiscovered?"

"Adrat it—yes—if the scouts a'n't out. When I went the scouts were all in, since there was no alarm, and Marion was guine upon an expedition."

"What expedition?"

"Well, I don't know, colonel—somewhere to the north, I reckon—down about Waccamaw."

"And suppose his scouts are out now—will they see us—can we not make our way undiscovered?"

"'Taint so easy, colonel; there's no better scouts in natur than the 'swamp fox' keeps. They will dodge all day long in one thicket from the best ten men of the legion."

"Is there no way of misleading the scouts?"

"None, colonel, that I knows. If you could send out a strong party of the horse in a different direction, as if you was trying to get round them, you might trick the old fox into believing it; but that's not so easy to do. He's mighty shy, and a'n't to be caught with chaff."

"Nor will I try any such experiment. Hark'ee, fellow; if I find that you deceive me, I shall not stop a moment to give your throat the surety of a strong cord. Your counsels to break my force, to be cut up when apart, are those of one who is drawing both right and left, and argues but little respect for my common sense. But I will trust you so far as you promise. You shall guide me to the hole of the fox, and I will do the rest. Guide me faithfully, and stick close to your promise, and I will reward you; betray me, deceive me, or even look doubtfully in our progress, and, so sure as I value the great trust in my hands, your doom is written. Away now, and be ready with the dawn."

The scout bowed and retired. The moment that his back had been turned upon the speaker, Tarleton motioned two soldiers, who stood at a little distance, and who kept their eyes ever watchfully upon Blonay. They turned away at the signal, and followed the scout at a respectful distance, but one not too great to render the escape of the suspected person at all easy. Every precaution was taken to prevent the scout from noticing this surveillance; but the half-oblique eye which he cast over his shoulder at intervals upon the two, must have taught any one at all familiar with the character of the half-breed, that he was not unconscious of the close attention thus bestowed upon him. He walked away unconcernedly, however, and it was not long before, upon the edge of the forest, he had gained a favorite tree, against the sunny side of which he leaned himself quietly, as if all the cares and even the consciousness of existence had long since departed from his mind.

It was in this spot, an hour after, that he was sought out by Barsfield. The tory captain had some cause of displeasure with the scout, who had evaded his expressed wish to gain the clew to the retreat of Marion. He had other causes of displeasure, which the dialogue between them subsequently unfolded.

"Where did you meet with Colonel Tarleton to-day, Mr. Blonay? You had no knowledge of his approach?"

"None, cappin—I heard his trumpet a little way off, when I was making a roundabout for the swamp thicket, and he came upon me with a few dragoons afore I seed him."

"It is strange, Mr. Blonay, that a good scout, such as you are, should be so easily found when not desiring it. Are you sure that you tried to keep out of his way?"

"No, cappin—there was no reason for me to try, for I saw first that they were friends and not rebels: and so I didn't push to hide, as I might have done, easy enough."

"And by what means did Colonel Tarleton discover that you could lead him to the camp of Marion, unless you studiously furnished him with your intelligence?"

"I did tell him, cappin, when he axed me. He axed me if I knowed, and I said I did, jist the same as I said to you; and he then axed me to show him, and I said I could."

"But why, when I asked you, did you deny your ability to show me the way? Was it because you looked for better pay at the hands of Tarleton?"

"No, cappin: but you didn't ax me to show you—you only

axed me to describe it, and that I couldn't do. I can go over the ground, cappin, jist like a dog; but I can't tell the name of the tree that I goes by, or this bush, or that branch, and I ha'n't any name for the thicket I creeps through. I knows them all when I sees them, and I can't miss them any more than the good hound when he's once upon trail; but, if you was to hang me, I couldn't say it to you in talking, so that you could find it out for yourself."

Blonay was right in a portion of his statement, but his correctness was only partial. He could not, indeed, have described his course; but he had been really averse to unfolding it to Barsfield, and he had, with the view to a greater reward, thrown himself in the way of Tarleton, of whose approach he had been apprized. He was true in all respects, to the simple and selfish principle upon which his education had been grounded by his miserable mother. Barsfield had no farther objection to urge on the subject. He was entirely deceived by the manner of the scout. But there was yet another topic of interest between them, and to this he called his attention.

"You have not yet been successful with this boy?—he lives yet—"

"Yes, but you have him now, and he can't help himself. He is under your knife."

"Ay!" exclaimed the tory, with an expression of countenance the most awfully stern, and with a tone of concentrated bitterness, "ay! but I am as far off, farther off, indeed, than ever. My hands are tied; he is intrusted to my charge in particular, and my own fidelity is interested in preserving him."

"Eh?" was the simple and interrogative monosyllable with which the scout replied to what was too nice a subtilty in morals to be easily resolvable by a mind so unconventional as his own. Barsfield saw the difficulty, and tried to explain.

"I can not violate a trust which is confided to me. I must preserve and protect, and even fight against his enemies, so long as he remains in my custody."

"He is your enemy?" said Blonay, still wholly uninfluenced by the remark of Barsfield.

"Yes, he is still my enemy."

"And you his?"

"Yes."

"He is aneath your knife?"

"Yes, entirely."

The savage simply replied by taking his knife from its sheath and drawing its back across his own neck, while his countenance expressed all the fierce emotions of one engaged in the commission of a murder. The face of Barsfield took no small portion of the same fierce expression: catching the hand of the speaker firmly in his own, he replied—

"Ay, and no stroke would give me more pleasure than that. It would be life to me—his death—and why may it not be done? It may be done! Blonay, we will speak again of this; but be silent now, keep close, and tell me where I may look for you to-night?"

"There!" and he pointed to a little swamp or bay, in which he had slept before. It lay at the distance of a mile, more or less, from the camp, which had been already formed in the park, and near the yet consuming mansion.

"There—I keep in the bay at night; for, though it taint got no cypresses, sich as I used to love down upon the Ashley, and about Dorchester, yet it's a close place, and the tupolas and gums is mighty thick. You'll find me there any time afore cockcrow. You have only to blow in your hands three times—so—" producing a singular and shrill whistle at the same time, by an application of his mouth to an aperture left between his otherwise closed palms, "only blow so three times, and I'll be with you."

The tory captain tried to produce the desired sounds, in the suggested manner, which he at length succeeded in doing. Satisfied, therefore, with the arrangement, he left his accomplice to the contemplation of his own loneliness, and hurried away to his duties in the camp.

CHAPTER XXX.

THE WOLF IN NEW COLORS.

MEANWHILE the hurts of Mellichampe had all been carefully attended to. Tarleton, so far, had kept his pledged word to the maiden. He was removed to a chamber in the house which gave temporary shelter to the family, and the surgeon of the legionary colonel had himself attended to his injuries. They were found to be rather exhausting than dangerous. A slight sabre-stroke upon his head had stunned him for the time, but afforded no matter for very serious consideration. The severest wound was the cut over the left shoulder, which had bled profusely; but even this required little more than close attendance and occasional dressing. A good nurse was more important than a skilful surgeon, and no idle and feeble scruples of the inferior mind stood in the way to prevent Janet Berkeley from devoting herself to the performance of this duty to her betrothed.

The intelligence of Mellichampe's true situation was conveyed by Tarleton himself to Mr. Berkeley, in the presence of his daughter. It seemed intended to, and did, reassure the maiden, whose warm interest in the captive was sufficiently obvious to all; as her tearful and deep apprehensions on his account, and for his safety, had been entirely beyond her power of concealment.

Tarleton dined that day with the Berkeley family. His manners were grave, but gentle — somewhat reserved, perhaps, but always easy, and sometimes elegant. He spoke but little, yet what he said contributed, in no small degree, to elevate him in the respect of all around. His air was subdued, when he spoke, to a woman-mildness; and his words were usually uttered in a low, soft tone, little above a common whisper, yet sufficiently measured and slow in their utterance to be heard without difficulty by those to whom they were addressed. What a difference was there between the same man sitting at the hospitable board, and, when leading forward his army but a few hours before, he rushed headlong, with kindled and raging spirit, upon the tracks of his flying foe! There was nothing now in his look or language which could indicate the savage soldier. Was he, indeed, the same bloodthirsty warrior, whose renown, by no means an enviable one, had been acquired by the most wanton butcheries in the fields of Carolina? This was the inquiry in the minds of all those who now looked upon him. Certainly a most remarkable alteration seemed, in the eyes of all who before had known him, in a little time to have come over the spirit of the fierce warrior; and it is somewhat singular and worthy of remark, that he gained no distinction, and won no successes of any moment, after this period. His achievements were few and unimportant; and two repulses which he received at the hands of Sumter, followed up, as they were, by the terrible defeat which he sustained at the Cowpens, finished his career as a favorite of fortune in the partisan warfare of the South. His name lost its terrors soon after this among those with whom it had previously been so potent; and, though his valor was at all periods above suspicion, yet, in his reverses, it became the fashion to disparage his soldierly skill, even among those whom he commanded. It was then discovered that he had only contended, hitherto, with raw militiamen, whom it required but little merit, beyond that of mere brute courage, to overthrow; and that his successes entirely ceased from the moment when that same militia, taught by severe and repeated experience of defeat, had acquired, in time, some little of the address of regular and practised warfare. There was, no doubt, much that was sound in this opinion.

But — the dinner was fairly over, and Tarleton withdrew, after a few moments devoted to pleasant conversation with the now composed Rose Duncan, from whose mind all the terrors of the previous combat, in which she had shared so much, seemed entirely to have gone. She was only a creature of passing impressions. To Janet he said but little; but his eyes sometimes rested upon her with an air of melancholy abstraction, which gave to his otherwise pale features an expression of feeling and nice sensibilities, which his profession might seem to belie. But, before he took his departure, he led her aside to a window in the cottage, and thus addressed her, in the style of one sufficiently her friend and senior to speak firmly and directly, even on a topic the most difficult and delicate in the estimation of a maiden.

"I have given Captain Barsfield his orders touching our prisoner, Miss Berkeley; perhaps it would not be unpleasing to you to know what those orders are?"

She looked down, and her desire to hear was sufficiently shown in her unwillingness to speak. He proceeded, after a brief pause. in the course of which his lips put on the same sweet smile of graciousness which had won the heart of the maiden before; while, at the same time, it commanded a something more in the way of return than a mere corresponding deference of manner. So foreign to his lips was that expression, so adverse to his general character was that smile of gentleness, that even while it gratified her to behold it, she looked up to the wearer of it with a feeling little short of awe.

"Mr. Mellichampe is in no danger—no present danger—as my surgeon informs me; but he must be kept quiet and without interruption until well, as he appears feverish, and his mind seems disposed to wander. The better to effect this object, I have ordered, that except my surgeon and his assistant, none but your father and yourself shall be admitted to his chamber. I have made this exception in your favor, Miss Berkeley, as my surgeon at the same time informs me that he will need the offices of a careful nurse—"

"Oh, sir—" was the involuntary exclamation of Janet, as she heard this language; but Tarleton did not allow her to proceed.

"No idle objections, my dear young lady, no false notions of propriety and a misplaced delicacy at this moment. I know sufficiently your secret; which is no secret now to any in our troop. Your duty commands that you attend this young man, and none but the feeble mind will find any fault with you for its performance. In matters of this sort, your own heart is the best judge, and to that I leave it, whether you will avail yourself of the privilege which I have granted you or not. The youth is in no danger, says my surgeon, but he may be if he is not carefully nursed. Pardon me for so long detaining you, I shall do so no longer. My orders are given to secure you at all times admission to the chamber of Mr. Mellichampe, should you desire it."

"But, oh! sir, what of Captain Barsfield? These charges—"

"Are slight, no doubt, but must be inquired into. Mr. Mellichampe is the prisoner of Captain Barsfield, and must await his trial. I can do nothing further, unless it be to promise that all justice shall be done him."

"But may he not be put in other hands, Colonel Tarleton, than those of Captain Barsfield? Oh! sir—I dread that man. He will do Mellichampe some harm."

"Fear not, Captain Barsfield dare not harm him, he has quite too much at venture. It is for this very reason, with the view to the perfect security of the prisoner, that I have made Barsfield his keeper. His fidelity is pledged for the security of his charge, and I have dwelt upon the responsibility to him in such language as will make him doubly careful. But you do Captain Barsfield wrong; he has no such design as that you speak of; his hostility to Mr. Mellichampe is simply that of the soldier toward his enemy. Unless in fair fight, I am sure he would never do him harm."

Janet shook her head doubtfully, as she replied, "I know him better, sir, I know that he hates Mellichampe for many reasons, but I may not doubt the propriety of your arrangements. I will, sir, take advantage of the permission made in my favor, and will myself become the nurse of Mr. Mellichampe. Why should I be afraid or ashamed, sir? Am I not his betrothed—his wife in the sight of Heaven! I will be his nurse—why should I be ashamed?"

"Ay; why should you, Miss Berkeley? Truth and virtue

may well be fearless, at all times, of human opinion; and they cease to be truth and virtue when the fear of what men may think, or say, induces a disregard of that which they conceive to be their duty. With me you lose nothing by the declaration you have just made. It is one I looked for from you. The confidence of virtue is never unworthy of the source from which it springs, and it doubly confirms and strengthens virtue itself, when it shows the possessor to be resolute after right, without regard to human arrangements, or the petty and passing circumstances of society. It is the child's love that is driven from its ground by the dread of social scandal. The only love that man esteems valuable is that which can dare all things, but wrong, in behalf of the valued object. This is your love now, and you have my prayer — if the prayer of a rough soldier like myself be not a wrong to so pure a spirit — that it be always hallowed in the sight of Heaven, and successful beyond the control of earth."

He took a respectful parting, and on leaving her to rejoin the party, his manner changed to that of the proud man he commonly appeared. An inflexible sternness sat upon his pale and stonelike countenance — the lips were set rigidly — the eye was shrouded by the overhanging brow, that gathered above it like some heavy cloud over some flaming and malignant planet. He spoke but few words to the rest of the family. A cold word of acknowledgment to Mr. Berkeley, a courteous bow and farewell to Rose Duncan, whose confidence was now half restored, the din of battle being over, and a single look and partial smile to Janet, preceded his immediate departure to the edge of the forest, where, during the dinner repast, his temporary camp had been formed. From this point he threw out his sentinels and sent forth his scouting parties. These latter traversed the neighboring hummocks, and ransacked every contiguous cover, in which a lurking squad of rebels might have taken up a hiding-place, in waiting for the moment when a fancied security on the part of the foe should invite to the work of annoyance or assault. Such was the nature of the Indian warfare which the " swamp fox," with so much general success, had adopted as his own. Tarleton knew too well the danger of surprise, with a foe so wary in his neighborhood, and accordingly spared none of those precautions to which, in ordinary cases, hitherto, he had been rather indifferent. He cited Blonay before him on reaching his camp, examined him closely as to the route they were next day to pursue, and concluded by warning him to be in readiness with the dawn of day.

"You shall be well rewarded if we succeed," were his concluding words to the scout, " well rewarded if you are faithful, even though we do not succeed; but if you fail me, sirrah, if I catch you playing false, the first tree and a short cord are your certain doom."

The half-breed touched his cap, and, without showing any emotion at this language, retired from the presence of the legionary.

CHAPTER XXXI

SCOUTING.

THAT night, as soon as he deemed it prudent, Barsfield, punctual to his engagement with the half-breed, left the camp, and, without observation, proceeded to the place of meeting which had been determined upon between them. He was not long in finding the person he sought. Blonay was no less punctual than his employer, and the shrill whistle of the latter, thrice repeated through his folded hands, soon brought him from his cover. The half-breed answered the signal readily, and in a few moments after emerged from the hummock in which, with a taste of his own, he had taken up his abode. A dim light was shining from the sky, only sufficient to enable the tory to recognise the outline, but not the several features, of his companion's person. Blonay freely extended his hand, and the fleshless, bony fingers took in their grasp those of Barsfield, who did not hesitate to follow his guidance, though he somewhat loathed the gripe of his conductor.

"Why go further—why not remain and talk here?" was his demand.

"There's no telling, cappin, who's a listening. Singleton's men's watching me now; and Colonel Tarleton, he doesn't trust me, and there's two of the dragoons that's kept close on my heels ever since I seed him last. It's true I dodged 'em when the sun went down, but they're on the look-out yet, I reckon."

"And why did you dodge them—you didn't mean to run?" demanded the other.

"No, but I'd rather a man shoot me than peep over my

shoulder; it's like a log round the neck, to be always looked after."

"And why do you think that Singleton's men are also looking out for you?"

"'Cause one of them knows I'm in these parts, and he knows I'm dangerous."

"But can he find you?"

"He's a born swamp-sucker like myself, and he's dangerous too. He knows I'm hereabouts, and I reckon he can't sleep easy till he finds me — or I find him."

Barsfield no longer objected, and together they penetrated the covert until they reached a dry spot, where, with a fancy as natural as it was peculiar, the half-breed had chosen his temporary dwelling, in preference to that of the camp or plantation. A few brands of the resinous pine, in which commodity the country around was abundantly supplied, were huddled together and in a blaze, which, though bright enough to illumine all objects around them, was imperceptible on the outer edge of the hummock, from the exceeding density of its foliage. A huge gum-tree, that stood upon the bank, sent up bulgingly above the surface a monstrous series of roots, which, covered with fresh moss, had made the pillow of the inhabitant. A thick coat of clustering oak-leaves, the tribute of a tree that had made such a deposite probably for a hundred winters, composed the sylvan couch of the outlier, while the folding and thickly-leaved branches overhead afforded him quite as gracious a cover from the unfriendly dews as it was in the nature of a form so callous to need or to desire. But the place seemed cheerless to Barsfield, in spite of the genial temperature of the season, and the bright flame burning before him.

"And you sleep here, Mr. Blonay?" was his involuntary question.

"Yes, cappin, here or further in the bush. If I hear strange noises that I don't like, I slips down further into the bay, and then I'm sure to be safe, for it's a mighty troublesome way to take, and very few people like to hunt in such bottoms; it's all sloppy, and full of holes, and the water's as black as pitch."

"What noise is that?" said Barsfield.

"Oh, that? that's only my big alligator: I can tell his voice from all the rest, for it sounds hoarse, as if he had cotched a cold from coming out too soon last May. He's a mighty big fellow, and keeps in a deep, dirty pond, jist to the back of you. I shouldn't be supprised to see him crawling out this way directly; he sometimes does when I'm lying here in the daytime."

Barsfield started and looked round him, as an evident rustling in the rear seemed to confirm the promise of Blonay. The latter smiled as he proceeded:—

"Don't be scared, cappin, for if a body aint scared he can't do no harm with 'em. When he comes out and looks at me, I jist laughs at him, and claps my hands, and he takes to his heels directly. They won't trouble you much only when they're mighty hungry, and aint seed hog-meat for a long time, and then they won't trouble you if you make a great noise and splash the water at 'em."

"Why don't you shoot him?"

"Adrat it! I didn't load for him; it's no use: if I had been to shoot alligators, I needn't have come up from Goose creek. I could have had my pick there, at any time, of a dozen, jist as big and not so hoarse as this fellow: I picked my bullet for quite another sort of varmint."

"And what of *him*? Have you seen *him*?"

"Yes," was the single and almost stern reply.

"Within rifle shot?"

"Not twenty yards off," was the immediate answer.

"And why did you spare him?"

"Other people was with him: I would have shot him by himself."

"I see; you had no wish to be cut up immediately after. Your hatred to your enemy, Blonay, does not blind you to the wisdom of escaping after you have murdered him."

The half-breed did not seem to understand what Barsfield said; but his own meaning was so obvious to himself, that he did not appear to think it necessary to repeat his words, or undertake more effectually to explain them. His, indeed, was the true Indian warfare, as, in great part, his was the

Indian blood and temper. To win every advantage, to secure success and triumph without risk and with impunity, are the principles of the savage nature always; and to obtain revenge without corresponding disadvantage, makes the virtue of such an achievement. These, indeed, may be held the principles of every people conscious of inferiority to those whom they oppose and hate.

So far the dialogue between Barsfield and his comrade had been carried on without any reference to the particular subject of interest which filled the bosom of the former. He seemed reluctant to speak further upon this topic; and, when he did speak, his reluctance, still preserved, produced a halting and partial utterance only of his feelings and desires, as if he somewhat repented of the degree of confidence which he had already reposed in the person to whom he spoke. But the desire to avail himself of the services of this man, and the consciousness of having already gone so far as to make any future risk of this sort comparatively unimportant, at length impelled him to a full expression of his desire to get Mellichampe out of his way, and, with this object, to hear from Blonay, and to suggest himself, sundry plans for this purpose. The great difficulty consisted in the position of Barsfield himself in relation to the prisoner so particularly intrusted to his charge by Tarleton, and with orders so imperative and especial. This was the grand difficulty, which it required all the ingenuity of Barsfield to surmount. Had Mellichampe been the prisoner of Tarleton, or of any other person than Barsfield himself, the murder of the youth would most probably have been effected that very night, such was the unscrupulous hatred of the tory, if not of Blonay. For the present, we may say that the half-breed might not so readily have fallen into any plan of Barsfield which would have made him the agent in the commission of the deed.

"You go with Tarleton to-morrow: you will not keep with him, for he goes down to Sinkler's Meadow. When do you return?"

"Well, now, there's no telling, cappin, seeing as how the colonel may want me to go 'long with him."

"He will not, when you have shown him to the camp of Marion."

"Well, if so be he don't, I'll be back mighty soon after I leaves him. I don't want to go with him, 'cause I knows there's no finding a man's enemy in pertic'lar, when there's a big company 'long."

"It is well. You will be back, then, by to-morrow night, and I will then put you upon a plan which will enable you to get this boy out of the way for me."

"Well, but, cappin, ha'n't you got him now? It's mighty easy now, as I tell'd you before, to do for him yourself."

"You do not seem to understand, Blonay. I am prevented from doing anything, as Tarleton has made me directly responsible for the appearance of the prisoner."

"Adrat it, who's to know when the colonel's gone? The chap's hurt and sick. Reckon he can die by natur."

Barsfield understood him, and replied —

"Yes, and nature might be helped in his case, but that Tarleton's own surgeon and assistants remain, and none but the Berkeley family are to be admitted to the prisoner. If I could report at my pleasure on his condition, it might easily be done; but I can not. It must be done by another, if done at all, and in such a way as will show that I could have had no hand in it. I have a plan in my mind for this purpose, which you shall execute on your return, by which means I shall avoid these difficulties. You are willing?"

"Well, yes, I reckon. It don't take much to finish a chap that's half dead already; but—I say, cappin—does you really think now that that 'ere gal has a notion for him?"

The question seemed to Barsfield exceedingly impertinent, and he replied with a manner sufficiently haughty:—

"What matters it to you, sirrah, whether she has such a notion or not? How does it concern you? and what should you know of love?"

"No harm, cappin—I doesn't mean any harm; it don't consarn me, that's true. But, adrat it, cappin, she's a mighty fine gal: and she does look so sweet and so sorry all the time, jist as if she wouldn't hurt a mean crawling black spider that was agin the wall."

Barsfield looked with some surprise at the speaker, as he heard him utter a language so like that of genuine feeling, and in tones that seemed to say that he felt it; and he was about to make some remark when Blonay, who had stood during this dialogue leaning with his shoulder against a tree, and his head down in a listless manner upon his bosom, now started into an attitude and expression of the most watchful consciousness. A pause of a few moments ensued, when, hearing nothing, Barsfield was about to go on with the speech which the manner of his companion had interrupted, when the half-breed again stopped him with a whisper, while his finger rested upon the arm of the tory in cautious warning.

"Hist; I hear them—there are no less than three feet in that swamp—don't you hear them walking in the water? There, now. You hear when the flat of the foot comes down upon the water."

"I hear nothing," said Barsfield.

Without a word, the half-breed stooped to the single brand that was now blazing near them, and gathering a double handful of dirt from the hillock, he threw it upon the flame and extinguished it in an instant. The next moment they heard the distant crackling of dry sticks and a rustling among the leaves.

"It may be your great alligator," said Barsfield.

"No—it's men—Marion's men, I reckon—and there's three of them, at least. They are spying on the camp. Lie close."

Barsfield did not immediately stoop, and the half-breed did not scruple to grasp his arm with an urgency and force which brought the tory captain forward. He trod heavily as he did so upon a cluster of the dried leaves which had formed the couch of Blonay, and a slight whistle reached their ears a moment after, and then all was silence. The tory and his companion crouched together behind the huge gum under which the latter had been accustomed to sleep, and thus they remained without a word for several minutes. No sound in all that time came to their senses; and Barsfield, rather more adventurous than Blonay, or less taught in the subtleties of swamp warfare, tired of his position, arose slowly from the ground and thrust his head from behind the tree, endeavoring, in the dim light that occasionally stole from the heavens into those deep recesses, to gather what he could of the noises which had disturbed them. The hand of the half breed, grasping the skirts of his coat, had scarcely drawn him back into the shelter of the tree, when the whizzing of the bullet through the leaves, and the sharp crack of the rifle, warned him of his own narrow escape, and of the close proximity of danger.

"I knows where they are now," said Blonay, in a whisper, changing his position; "we are safe enough if you can stick close to me, cappin."

"Lead on—I'll follow," was the reply, in the same low whisper which conveyed the words of Blonay. The half-breed instantly hurled a huge half-burnt chunk of wood through the bushes before him, the noise of which he necessarily knew would call the eyes of the scouts in that direction; then, in the next instant, bounding to the opposite side, he took his way between two clumps of bays which grew in the miry places along the edge of the tussock on which they had been standing. Barsfield followed closely and without hesitation, though far from escaping so well the assaults of the briers and bushes upon his cheeks. His guide, with a sort of instinct, escaped all these smaller assailants, and, though he heard the footsteps behind of his pursuers, he did not now apprehend any danger, either for himself or his companion, having thrown the thick growth of bays between them.

The party which so nearly effected the surprise of the two conspirators came out of their lurking-place an instant after their flight. The conjecture of the half-breed had been correct. They were the men of Marion.

"You fired too soon, Lance," were the words of Humphries, "and the skunk is off. Had you waited but a little longer we should have had him safe enough. Now there's no getting him, for he has too greatly the start of us."

"I couldn't help it, Mr. Humphries. I saw the shiny buttons, and I thought I had dead aim upon him."

"But how comes he with shiny buttons, John Davis?" said Humphries, quickly. "When you saw him to-day he had on a blue homespun, did he not?"

"Yes—I seed him plain enough," said Davis, "and I could swear to the homespun—but didn't you hear as if two was walking together?"

"No."

"Well, I did; and 't was reasonable I should hear before you, seeing I was ahead. I heard them clear enough, first one and then t'other, and one walked in the water while t'other was on the brush."

"D—n the skunk, that I should lose him; it's all your fault, Lance. You're too quick and hot-headed, now-a-days; and it'll be a long time before you can be a good swamp-fox, unless you go more slowly, and learn to love less the sound of your rifle. But it's useless to stay here now, and we've got other work to do. Our sport's spoiled for this time, and all we can do is to take off as quick as we can; for it won't be long before the scouts of Tarleton will be poking here after us. That shot must bring them in this direction, so we'll push round to the opposite side of the bay, where the rest of the red-coats are in camp."

"But, Mr. Humphries, can't I go now and pick off that sentry we passed by the avenue?" demanded Lance Frampton, with much earnestness.

"No, d—n the sentry; if you had picked off this skunk of a half-breed, it would have been something now I should have thanked you for; that's what I mostly come after. As for the other, there's too much risk now. We must take a cross-track, and get round to the river by the gun-flats. Come, push—away."

They had scarcely moved off when a stir and hum in the direction of Tarleton's camp announced to them that the alarm had been given, and hurried the preparations of Humphries for their departure. The scouts of Barsfield, led by the tory himself and guided by Blonay, after a while scoured narrowly the recesses of the bay: but the men of Marion had melted away like spectres in the distant woods; and, chafed and chagrined, the tory went back to his quarters, fatigued with the unprofitable pursuit, and irritated into sleeplessness, as he found himself in the close neighborhood of a foe so wary and so venturesome.

CHAPTER XXXII.

THE BIRD FLOWN.

At day-dawn the next morning, the trumpet of the legion sounded shrilly over the grounds where Tarleton, during the night, had made his encampment. With the signal each trooper was at his post. Tarleton himself was already dressed, and about to buckle the heavy sabre at his side which his arm had ever been so proverbially ready to wield. The fire, the stern enthusiasm, which grew out of his impatience for the strife, already glowed balefully and bright upon his countenance. He was joined at this moment by another — an officer; a man something his senior, and, like him, accustomed seemingly to command.

"Your trumpets sound unseasonably, Tarleton, and destroyed as pleasant a vision as ever came from the land of dreams. I fancied the wars were over — that I was once again in old England, with all the little ones and their sweet dam about me; and your heartless trumpet took them all from my embrace — all at one fell swoop."

Tarleton smiled, but smiled in such a sort that the speaker almost blushed to have made his confession of domestic tenderness to such uncongenial ears. He continued: —

"But you care nothing for these scenes, and scruple not to break into such pleasures to destroy. You have no such sweet cares troubling you at home."

"None, Moncrieff — none, or few. Perhaps I might please no less than surprise you, were I to say that I wish I had; but I will not yield you so much sympathy; particularly, indeed, as there is no time for these matters or such talk when we are on the eve of grappling with an enemy."

"Enemy? what enemy?" demanded the other.

"Our old enemy, the 'swamp-fox,'" responded Tarleton, coolly.

"What, Marion! why, where is he?"

"But a few miles off. I hope to have late breakfast with him—time serving, God willing, and our appetite for fight as good as that for breakfast."

"But know you where he is, and how? Will he stand for your coming? Will he not fly, as usual—double himself round a cypress while you are piercing your way through its bowels?"

"Ay, doubtless if he can; we must try to prevent that, and I have hopes that we can do it. His scouts have been around us, like so many vultures, all night; and Barsfield reports that one has had the audacity to fire upon a sentinel. This shows him to be at hand, and in sufficient force to warrant the belief that he will stand a brush."

"But how find him, Tarleton? His own men can not easily do that, and you have never yet been allowed to see his feathers."

"I shall now, however, I think; for I perceive our guide stands in readiness. Look at him, Moncrieff: did you ever see such a creature? Look at his eyes; do they not give you pain, positive pain, to survey them? They seem only to be kept in his head by desperate effort; and yet, behold his form. He does not appear capable of effort—scarcely, indeed, of movement. His limbs seem hung on hinges, and one leg, as you perceive, appears always, as now, to have thrown the whole weight of the body upon the other."

"A strange monster, indeed: and is that the creature to serve you? Can he put you on the trail?"

"He pledges himself to do so. He has seen the 'swamp-fox' and his men, all at ease, in their camp, and promises that I shall see them too, under his guidance."

"And you will trust him?"

"I will."

"What security have you that he does not carry you into trap?"

"His own neck; for, as sure as he makes a false move, he swings from the nearest sapling. He shall be watched."

"If this be the case, Tarleton, how can you go forward? Will it not be for me then to execute my mission?"

"Not till I fail. If I can drub Marion, and either put him to death or make a prisoner of him, your mission will be null. There will be no use in buying one whom we can beat. But if he now escapes me, I give it up. He would escape the devil. You may then seek him out with your most pacific aspect; offer him his pension and command among us, as our sagacious commander-in-chief has already devised, and make the best use afterward of his skill in baffling Green, as he so long has baffled us. If he does half so well for his majesty as for his continental prog-princes, he will be worth quite as much as you offer for him, and something more."

"True; but, Tarleton, this chance may never offer again. We may never get a guide who will be able to pilot me through these d—d impervious and pestilential morasses—certainly few to show me where to find him out."

"We must risk that, Moncrieff. I will not give up my present chance of striking him, though you never have the opportunity you seek. He has baffled me too long already, and my pride is something interested to punish him. The prospect is a good one, and I will not lose it. Hark you, fellow!"

The last words were addressed to Blonay, who, in sight of the speaker all the while, now approached at the order. The stern, stony eye of the fierce legionary rested upon him searchingly, with a penetrating glance scarcely to be withstood by any gaze, and certainly not by that of the half-breed, who never looked any one in the face. Some seconds elapsed before Tarleton spoke; and when he did, his words were cold, slow, brief, and to the purpose.

"You are ready, sir?"

The reply was affirmative.

"You hold to your assertion that you can lead me to where Marion camps?"

"I can lead you, sir, to his camp, but I can't say for his

being in it. He may get wind of you, if his scouts happen to be out."

"I know, I know, you said this before, and proposed, if I remember rightly, that I should divide my force in order to mislead. But I know better than to do that. I risk nothing now when I know nothing of his force, and I am not so sure, sir, that you are altogether the man to be relied on. I shall watch you, sirrah; and remember, it is easier, fellow, to hang you up to a bough than to threaten it. Go—prepare. Ho! there, Hodgson, put half a dozen of your best dragoons in charge of this guide, and keep him safe, as you value your bones."

"I will not run, sir," said Blonay, looking up for the first time into the face of Tarleton.

"I know that, sir—you shall not," responded the other coolly.

The signal to move was given in a few moments after, and Barsfield saw the departure of Tarleton in pursuit of Marion with a singular feeling of satisfaction and relief.

It is not our present purpose, however, to pursue the route taken by Colonel Tarleton in search of his famous adversary. Such a course does not fall within the purpose of our present narrative. It may be well, however, as it must be sufficient, to say, that, under the guidance of Blonay, he penetrated the spacious swamp of the Santee, and was led faithfully into and through its intricacies—but he penetrated them in vain. Step by step, as the dense body pressed its way through brake, bog, and brier, did they hear the mysterious signals of the watchful partisans, duly communicating to one another the approach of the impending danger.

Vainly did Tarleton press forward his advance in the hope of arriving at the camp before these signals could possibly reach it; but such a pathway to his heavily-mounted men was very different in its facilities to those who were accustomed daily to glide through it; and the scouts of Marion hung about Tarleton's advance in front, sometimes venturing in sight, and continually within hearing, to the utter defiance of the infuriated legionary, who saw that nothing could be done to diminish the distance between them. At length they reached the island where the "swamp-fox" made his home, but the bird had flown.

The couch of rushes where Marion slept was still warm—the fragments of the half-eaten breakfast lay around the logs which formed their rude boards of repast, but not an enemy was to be seen.

Stimulating his men by promises and threats, Tarleton still pursued, in the hope to overtake the flying partisans before they could reach the Santee; but in vain were all his efforts; and, though moving with unexampled celerity, he arrived on the banks of the rapid river only in time to behold the last of the boats of the "swamp-fox" mingling with the luxurious swamp foliage on the opposite side. The last twenty-four hours had been busily and profitably employed by Marion. He had utterly annihilated the tories who had gathered at Sinkler's Meadow. Never, says the history, had surprise been more complete. He came upon the wretches while they played at cards, and dearly did they pay for their temerity and heedlessness. They were shot down in the midst of dice and drink, foul oaths and exultation upon their lips, and with those bitter thoughts of hatred to their countrymen within their hearts which almost justified the utmost severities of that retribution to which the furious partisans subjected them.

CHAPTER XXXIII.

LOVERS' DOUBTS AND DREAMS.

LET us now return to Janet Berkeley and the wounded Mellichampe. Tarleton had not deceived the maiden. The hurts of her lover, though serious and painful, were yet not dangerous, unless neglected; and as the privilege was accorded her —the sweetest of all privileges to one who loves truly—of being with and tending upon the beloved one, there was no longer reason to apprehend for his safety, from the injuries already received. The apprehensions of Janet Berkeley were, naturally enough, all addressed to the future. She knew the enemy in whose custody he lay; and, though half consoled by the positive assurances of Tarleton, and compelled, from the necessity of the case, to be satisfied, she was yet far from contented with the situation of her lover.

His first moment of perfect consciousness, after his wounds had been dressed, found her, a sweet minister waiting at his side. Her hand bathed his head and smoothed his pillow— her eye, dewy and bright, hung like a sweet star of promise above his form—her watchful care brought him the soothing medicine—her voice of love cheered him into hope with the music of a heaven-born affection. Every whisper from her lips was as so much melody upon his ear, and brought with it a feeling of peace and quiet to his mind, which had not often been a dweller there before. Ah, surely, love is the heart's best medicine! It is the dream of a perfect spirit—the solace of the otherwise denied—the first, the last hope of all not utterly turned away from the higher promptings and better purposes of a divine humanity.

How sweet became his hurts to Mellichampe under such attendance! The pain of his wounds and bruises grew into a positive pleasure, as it brought her nigh to him — and so nigh? — as it disclosed to his imagination such a long train of enjoyments in the future, coming from the constant association with her. Love no longer wore her garb of holyday, but, in the rustic and unostentatious dress of home, she looked more lovely to his sight, as she seemed more natural. Hitherto, he had sought her only for sweet smiles and blessing words; now she gave him those cares of the true affection which manifested its sincerity, which met the demand for them unshrinkingly and with pleasure, and which bore their many tests, not only without complaint or change, but with a positive delight. It was thus that her heart proved its disinterestedness and devotion; and though Mellichampe had never doubted her readiness to bestow so much, he yet never before had imagined the extent of her possession, and of the sweet liberality which kept full pace with her affluence. Until now, he had never realized, in his most reaching thought, how completely he should become a dependant upon her regards for those sweet sympathies, without which life is a barren waste, having the doom of Adam — that of a stern labor — without yielding him any of the flowers of Eden, and certainly withholding all, if denying that most cherished of all its flowers which he brought with him from its garden — the flower of unselfish love.

To be able to confide is to be happy in all conditions, however severe; and this present feeling in his heart — the perfect reliance upon her affection — assured and strengthened the warm passion in his own, until every doubt and fear, selfishness and suspicion, were discarded from that region, leaving nothing in their place but that devotedness to the one worthy object which, as it is holy in the sight of Heaven, must be the dearest of all human possessions in the contemplation of man.

With returning consciousness, when he discovered how she had been employed, he carried her hand to his lips and kissed it fervently. He felt too much for several minutes to speak to her. When he did, his words were little else than exclamations.

"Ah, Janet — my own — my all! — ever nigh to me, as you

are ever dear, how can I repay, how respond to such sweet love? I now feel how very poor, how very dependent, how very destitute I am!"

These were almost the first words which he uttered after awakening from a long, deep, and refreshing sleep, into which he had been thrown by an opiate judiciously administered for that object. She had no reply, but, bending down to his pillow, her lips were pressed upon his forehead lightly, while her uplifted finger warned him into silence. He felt a tear, but a single tear, upon his cheek, while her head hung above him; and so far from being destitute, as he had avowed himself before, he now felt how truly rich he was in the possession of such dear regards.

"Heaven bless you, my angel," he continued, "but I must talk to you, unless you will to me. Speak to me, tell me all, let me know what has passed. What of Major Singleton and our men?"

"They are gone—safe."

"Ah! this is good. But Witherspoon—what of him? he was fighting, when I saw him last, with two: they were pressing him hard, and I—I could give him no aid. What of him; is he safe? Tell me; but do not say that harm has befallen him."

"He, too, is safe, dear Ernest; I saw him as he fled."

"Ha! did he leave me, then; and where? I looked not for that from him. Perhaps, it is so, he brought me to you, did he not?"

"He did not, but then he could not, dearest. He was compelled to fly in haste. I saw him while he fled, and the dragoons came fast after him."

He would have put a thousand other questions, and vainly she exhorted him to silence. She was compelled to narrate all she knew, in order to do that which her entreaties, in the great anxiety and impatience of his mind failed to effect. She told him of the continued fight in the avenue, of the approach of Tarleton, and how, when the enemy had gone in pursuit of the flying partisans, she had sought and found him. Of these events he had no recollection. She suppressed, however, all of those matters which related to the second attempt of Barsfield upon his life while he lay prostrate, and of her own interposition, which had saved him; and took especial care to avoid every topic which could stimulate his anger or increase his anxiety. Of the conduct of Tarleton, so unusual and generous, she gave a full account; an account which gave the hearer quite as much astonishment as pleasure. It certainly presented to his mind's eye a new and much more agreeable feature in the character of that famous, or rather infamous, soldier.

So sweet was it thus for him to hear, and so grateful to her to have such a pleased auditor, that the hours flew by imperceptibly, and their mutual dream of love would not soon have been disturbed but for the sounds of Barsfield's voice, which came from the passage-way, while he spoke in harsh dictation to the sentinels who watched the chamber of the wounded Mellichampe.

The youth started as the well-known and hated accents met his ears. His brow gathered into a cloud, and he half raised himself from his pillow, while his eye flashed the fire of battle, and his fingers almost violently grasped the wrist of the maiden, under the convulsive spasm of fury which seized upon and shook his enfeebled frame.

"That voice is Barsfield's. Said you not, Janet, that I was Colonel Tarleton's prisoner?"

She answered him quickly, and with an air of timid apprehension—

"I did, dear Ernest; but Colonel Tarleton has gone in pursuit of General Marion."

"And I am here at the mercy of this bloody wretch, this scoundrel without soul or character; at his mercy, without strength, unable to lift arm or weapon, and the victim of his will. Ha! this is to be weak, this is to be a prisoner, indeed!"

Bitterly and fiercely did he exclaim, as he felt the true destitution of his present condition.

"Not at his will, not at his mercy, dear Ernest. Colonel Tarleton has promised me that you shall be safe, that he dare not harm you."

She spoke rapidly in striving to reassure her lover. Her

arm encircled his neck, her tears flowed freely upon his cheeks, while her voice, even while it uttered clearly the very words of assurance which Tarleton had expressed, trembled as much with the force of her own secret fears as at the open expression of his. But her lover remained unsatisfied. He did not know the nature of those securities which Barsfield tacitly placed in the hands of his superior.

"Alas, Janet, I know this monster but too well not to apprehend the worst at his hands. He is capable of the vilest and the darkest wrongs where he hates and fears. But why should I fear? The power of the base and the tyrannical, thank Heaven! has its limits, and he can but—"

"Say not, Ernest, say not. He dare not, he will not. I believe in Colonel Tarleton."

"So do not I; but I fear not, my beloved. I have dared death too often already; I have seen him in too many shapes, to tremble at him now. I fear him not: but to die like a caged rat, cooped in a narrow dungeon, and only preparing myself for the knife of the murderer, is to die doubly; and this, most probably, is the doom reserved for me."

"Think not so, think not so, Ernest, I pray you, think not so. God keep me from the horrible thought! It can not be that Tarleton will suffer it; it can not be that God will suffer it. I would not that you should speak so, Ernest; and I can not think that this bad man, bad enough, though I believe him to be, for anything, will yet dare so far to incur the danger of offending his superior as to abuse his trust and gratify his malignity in the present instance. Oh, no! he greatly fears Colonel Tarleton; and, could you but have seen the look that Tarleton gave him, as he ordered him to take all care of you, had you but heard his words to me and to him both, you would not feel so apprehensive; and then, you know, Colonel Tarleton's own surgeon is left with you, and none are to be permitted to see you but myself and such persons as he thinks proper.

"I fear nothing, Janet, but distrust everything that belongs to this man Barsfield. Colonel Tarleton, I doubt not, has taken every precaution in my favor, though why he should do so I am at a loss to determine; but all precautions will be unavailing where a man like Barsfield is bent upon crime, and where, in addition to his criminal propensity, he has the habitual cunning of a man accustomed to its indulgence. He will contrive some means to shift the responsibility of the charge, in some moment or other, to other shoulders, and will avail himself of that moment to rid himself of me, if he possibly can. We must only be heedful of all change of circumstances, and seek to apprise Witherspoon of my situation. He will not be far off, I well know; for he must be miserable in my absence."

"Oh, trust me, Ernest, I shall watch you more closely than those sentinels. Love, surely, can watch as well as hate."

"Better—better, my Janet. May I deserve your care—your love. May I always do *you* justice, living or dying."

Her cheek rested upon his, and she wept freely to hear his words. He continued—

"I know that you will watch over me, and I chafe not more at my own weakness than at the charge and care that this dreary watch must impose upon you."

"A sweet care—a dear, not a dreary, watch. Oh! Ernest—it is the sweetest of all cares to watch for the good of those we love."

"I feel it sweet to be thus watched, dearest; so sweet that, under other circumstances, I feel that I should not be willing to relieve you of the duty. But you have little strength—little ability, in corresponding even with your will to serve me. This villain will elude your vigilance—he will practise in some way upon you; and oh, my Janet, what if he succeed in his murderous wish—what if—"

"With a convulsive sob, that spoke the fullness of her heart and its perfect devotion, she threw herself upon his bosom, and her lips responded to his gloomy anticipations while interrupting them.

"I am not strong enough to save you, Ernest, and to contend with your murderer, if such he should become; but there is one thing that I am strong enough for."

"What is that, dearest?"

"To die for you at any moment."

And, for an hour after, a tearful silence, broken only by an occasional word, which spoke, like a long gathering tear, the overcrowding emotions to which it brought relief, was all the language of those two loving hearts, thus mingling sweetly together amid the strife and the storm — the present evil, the impending danger, and the ever-threatening dread. The strife and the hate without brought neither strife nor hate to them; and, like twin forms, mutually devoted to the last, amid the raging seas and on a single spar, they clung to each other, satisfied, though the tempest raged and the waves threatened, to perish, if they might perish together. They were not, in those sad moments, less confident and conscious of the sweets of a mutual love, though filled with anticipations of evil, and though they well knew that a malignant and unforgiving Hate stood watching at the door. And the affection was not less sweet and sacred that it was followed by the thousand doubts and apprehensions which at no moment utterly leave the truly devoted, and which, in the present instance, came crowding upon them with a thousand auxiliar terrors to exaggerate the form of the danger, and to multiply the accumulating stings of fear.

CHAPTER XXXIV.

LOVE PASSAGES.

"How sweet the days of Thalaba went by!" Mellichampe, under such attendance, soon grew insensible to all his sufferings. The bruises quickly disappeared—the wounds were healing rapidly. The care of the nurse surpassed in its happy effects the anticipations of the physicians, and the youth was getting well. The spirits of the two became strong and confident with the improvement of the patient: and their hearts grew happier, and their hopes more buoyant, with each day's continued association. The world around them was gradually excluded from their contemplation; and, blessed with the presence of each other, the chamber of Mellichampe—his prison, as it was—closely watched by hostile eyes and guarded by deadly weapons—was large enough for the desires of one, at least, of the two within it. The relation existing between Janet Berkeley and Ernest Mellichampe appeared now to be understood by all parties. Her father had nothing to oppose —the maiden herself in the perilous moment, as it was thought, to the safety of her lover, had fearlessly and proudly proclaimed the ties existing between them; and, if the prude Decorum could suggest nothing against the frequent and unobstructed meeting of the two, Virtue herself had no reason to apprehend; for, surely, never yet did young hearts so closely and fervently cling to one another—yet so completely maintain the purity and the ascendency of their souls. Love, built upon esteem, is always secure from abasement—it is that passion, falsely named love which grows out of a warm imagination and wild blood only, which may not be trusted by others, as it is seldom entirely able to trust or to control itself.

Rose Duncan complained, however, as she suffered much by the devotion of Janet Berkeley to her lover. This young girl was one of those, thousands of whom are to be met with hourly, who derive all their characteristics from the color of events and things around them. She had little of that quality, or combination of qualities rather, which we call character. She was of a flexible and susceptible temperament. The hues of her mind came from the passing zephyr, or the overhanging cloud. She lacked those sterner possessions of intrinsic thought which usually make their proprietor independent of circumstances, and immovable under the operation of illegitimate influences. Unlike her graver companion, she had no sorrows, simply because she had little earnestness of character. She was usually lively and elastic in the extreme; and he who only casually observed might have imagined that a spirit so cheerful as hers usually appeared would not readily be operated upon or kept down by the occurrence of untoward events. But, if she lacked all of those features of sadness which mellowed and made the loveliness of Janet's character, and softened the quicker emotions of her soul, she was, at the same time, entirely wanting in that concentration of moral object which enables the possessor to address himself firmly and without scruple to the contest of those evils, whether in prospect or in presence, which, nevertheless, even when overcome, make the eye to weep and the soul to tremble. Rose Duncan would laugh at the prediction of evil, simply because she could never concentrate her thoughts sufficiently upon its consideration; and thus, when it came upon her, she would be utterly unprepared to encounter it. Not so with Janet Berkeley. Her heart, gentle and earnest in all its emotions, necessarily inclined her understanding and imagination to think upon and to estimate all those sources of evil, not less than of good, which belong to, and make up, the entire whole of human life. Its sorrows she had prepared herself to endure from the earliest hours of thought; and it was thus that, when sorrow came to her in reality, it was the foregone conclusion to which her reflections had made her familiar, and for which her nerves were already prepared. The tale of suffering brought forth no less grief than the actual experience of it, and far less of that active spirit of resistance and that tenacious soul of endurance with which she was at all times prepared to contend with its positive inflictions. It was thus that she was enabled, when her more volatile companion lay unnerved and terrified at her feet, to go forth fearlessly amid all the danger and the dread, traverse the field of strife unshaken by its horrors, and, from among the dying and the dead, seek out the one object to whom, when she had once pledged her heart, she had also pledged the performance, even of a duty so trying and so sad; and, though she had sickened at the loathsome aspect of war around her, she had felt far less of terror in that one scene of real horrors than she had a thousand times before in the dreams begotten by an active imagination, and a soul earnest, devoted, and susceptible in the extreme.

Often did Rose Duncan chide the maiden for her exclusive devotion to her lover, as she herself suffered privation from her devotedness.

"There is quite too much of it, Janet; he will be sick to death of you before you are married, if, indeed, you ever are married to him, which ought to be another subject of consideration with you. It would be very awkward if, after all these attentions on your part—this perfect devotion, I may call it—he should never marry you. I should never trust any man so far."

"Not to trust is not to love. When I confide less in Mellichampe, I shall love him less, Rose, and I would not willingly think of such a possibility. In loving him I give up all selfish thoughts: I must love entirely, or not at all."

"Ah, but how much do you risk by this?"

"It is woman's risk always, Rose, and I would not desire one privilege which does not properly belong to my sex. I have no qualifications in my regard for Mellichampe. To my mind, his honor is as lofty as, to my heart, his affections are dear. I should weep—I should suffer dreadfully—if I thought, for an instant, that he believed me touched with a single doubt of his fidelity."

"Very right, perhaps, Janet, and you are only the better

girl for thinking as you do; but marriage and love are lotteries, they say, and it is no wisdom to stake one's all in a lottery. A little venture may do well enough, but prudent people will be well-minded, and keep something in reserve. I like that Scotchman's advice of all things —

> "'Aye free aff han' your story tell
> When wi' a bosom crony,
> But still keep something to *yoursel*,
> You seldom tell to ony.

> "'Conceal yourself, as well's ye can,
> Fra' critical dissection,
> But keek through every other man
> Wi' sharpened sly inspection.'"

"And I think it detestable doctrine, Rose Duncan," Janet responded, with something like indignation overspreading her beautiful, sad countenance for the instant, as a flash of parting sunlight sent through the deep forests in the last moment of his setting —

"I think it detestable doctrine, only becoming in a narrow-minded wretch, who, knavish himself, suspects all mankind of a similar character. Such doctrines are calculated to make monsters of one half of the world and victims of the other. This one verse I regard as the blot in a performance otherwise of great beauty, and wisely true in all other respects. No, no, Rose — I may be wrong — I may be weak — I may give my heart fondly and foolishly — I may train my affections unprofitably — but, oh, let me confide still, though I suffer for it! Let me never distrust where I love — where I have set my heart — where I have staked all that I live for."

Rose was rebuked, and here, for a few moments, the conversation ended. But there was something still in the bosom of Janet which needed, and at length forced, its utterance :—

"And yet, Rose, there is one thing which you have said which pains me greatly. It may be true, that though, in seeking Mellichampe day by day, and hour by hour, I only feel myself more truly devoted to him; it may be that such will not be the feeling with him; it may be that he will, as you say, grow tired of that which he sees so frequently; it may be that he will turn away from me, and weary of my regards. I have heard before this, Rose, that the easy won was but little valued of men—that the seeker was still unsought—and that, when the heart of woman was secured, she failed to enchain that of her captor. Oh, Rose, it is death to think so. Did I dream that Mellichampe would slight me—did I think that he could turn from me with a weary spirit and an indifferent eye, I should pray to perish now—even now, when he speaks to and smiles upon me in such sort as never man spoke to and smiled upon woman whom he could deceive, or whom he did not love."

And her head sank upon the shoulder of her companion, and she sobbed with the fullness of her emotion, as if her heart were indeed breaking.

It was long that day—long in her estimate, not less than in that of Mellichampe—before she paid her usual visit to the chamber of her lover. She was then compelled to listen to those reproaches from his lips which her own heart told her were justly uttered. Influenced more than she was willing to admit, even to herself, by the suggestions of Rose Duncan, she had purposely kept away until hour after hour had passed (how drearily to both!) before she took courage to reject the idle restraints of conventional arrangement, which never yet had proper concern with the business of unsophisticated affection. Gently he chid her with that neglect for which she could offer no sort of excuse; but she hid her head in his bosom, and murmured forth the true cause of her delay, as she whispered, in scarce audible accents:—

"Ah, Ernest, you will tire of me at last; you will only see too much of me; and I am always so same, so like myself, and have so few changes by which to amuse you, that you will weary of the presence of your poor Janet."

"Foolish fears—foolish fears, Janet, and too unjust to me, and too injurious to us both, to permit me to suffer them longer. It is because you are always the same, always so like yourself, that I love you so well. I am secure, in this proof, against your change. I am secure of your stability, and feel happy to believe that, though all things alter besides, you at least will be inflexible in your continued love for me."

"Ah, be sure of that, Ernest; it is too sweet to love, and too dear to be loved by you, for me to change, lest I should find you change also. I can not change, I feel, until my very heart shall decay. The seeds of love which have been sown within it were sown by your hands, and they acknowledge you only as the proper owner. Their blight can only follow the blight of the soil in which they are planted, or only perish through —"

She paused, and the tears flowed too freely to permit her to conclude the sentence.

"Through what, Janet?" he demanded, In a murmuring and low tone she replied, instantly: —

"Only through the neglect of him who planted them."

He folded her to his heart, and she believed the deep, fond asseveration in which he assured her that no fear was more idle than that which she had just expressed.

The shrill tones of the trumpet startled the lovers from their momentary bliss.

"That sound," he said — "it makes my wound shoot with pain, as if the blood clamored there for escape. How I hate to hear its notes — sweet as they are to me when I am on horseback — here in this dungeon, and denied to move!"

An involuntary sigh escaped the maiden as she listened to this language, and it came to her lips to say, though she spoke not: —

"But you are here with me, in this dungeon, Ernest, and with you I am never conscious of restraint or regret. Alas for me! since I must feel that, while I have no other thought of pleasure but that which comes with your presence, Ernest, your pulse bounds and beats with the desire of a wider world, and of other conquests, even when I, whom you so profess to love beyond all other objects, am here sitting by your side!"

The sigh reached the ears of Mellichampe, and his quick sense and conscious thought readily divined the cause of her emotion.

"Wonder not, my Janet," he exclaimed. as he caught her

to his bosom—" wonder not that I chafe at this restraint, even though blessed with your sympathy and presence. Here, I am not less conscious of the tenure by which I hold your presence and my own life, than of the thousand pleasures which your presence brings me. I love not the less because I pine to love in security; and feel not the less happy by your side because I long for the moment to arrive when no power can separate us. Now, are we not at the mercy of a wretch, whom we know to possess no scruples of conscience, and who feels few, if any, of the restraints of power? In his mood, at his caprice, we may be torn asunder, and—but let us speak of other things."

And the conversation turned upon brighter topics. The uttered hopes and the wishes of Mellichampe cheered the heart of the maiden, until, even while the tears of a delicious sensibility were streaming from her eyes, she forgot that hope had its sorrows; she forgot that love—triumphant and imperial love—has still been ever known as the born victim of vicissitudes.

CHAPTER XXXV.

GUILTY SCHEMES.

Three days elapsed from the departure of Blonay with Colonel Tarleton before he returned to Piney Grove. Barsfield grew impatient. He had matured his plan in his mind; he had devised the various processes for the accomplishment of his purpose, and he was feverish and restless until he could confer with his chief agent in the business. He came at last, and first brought intelligence to the tory of the failure of the legionary colonel to surprise the wary Marion.

"And where now is Colonel Tarleton?" demanded Barsfield.

"Gone up after the 'game cock.'"*

"I'm glad of it," said the tory, involuntarily. "He might have been in our way. When did you separate from him?"

"Day before yesterday: he went up the river. I went back into the swamp."

"And why? Had not the rebels left it? Did you not say that they crossed the river on the approach of Tarleton?"

"Yes—but, adrat it! they crossed back mighty soon after Tarleton had gone out of sight."

"And they are even now in the swamp again?"

"Jist as they was at first."

"The devil! And you have seen them there since the departure of Tarleton?"

"Reckon I has."

"They are audacious, but we shall rout them soon. My loyalists are coming in rapidly, and I shall soon be able, I

---

* Colonel Sumter—so styled by Tarleton himself. This was no less the *nomme de guerre* of Sumter than was "the swamp-fox" that of Marion. Both names are singularly characteristic.

trust, to employ you again, and I hope with more success, in ferreting them out. But why did you delay so long to return? Have you seen your enemy?"

"Adrat it, yes," replied the other, coldly, though with some show of mortification.

"Where—in the swamp?"

"No; on the road here, jist afore dark last night; a leetle more than long rifle shot from the front of the avenue."

"Well?"

"'Tworn't well. I tracked him over half a mile afore I could git a shot—"

The half-breed paused.

"What then?" demanded Barsfield, impatiently.

"Adrat it! jist as I was guine to pull trigger, a pain, something just like a hammer-strike, went into my elbow, and the bullet—'twas a chawed one, too—must have gone fur enough from the skull 'twas aimed fur."

"You missed him?" inquired Barsfield.

"Reckon I did. He stuck to his critter jist as if nothing had happened strange to him, and rode off in a mighty hurry."

"And how came you to miss him? You hold yourself a good shot."

"'Tain't often I miss; but I felt all over, afore I pulled upon him, that I was guine to miss. Something seemed to tell me so. I was quite too quick, you see, and didn't take time to think where I should lay my bullet."

"Yet you may have hit him. These men of Marion sometimes stick on for hours after they get the death wound—long enough, certainly, to get away into some d—d swamp or other, where there's no getting at the carcass."

"Adrat it—I'm fear'd I hain't troubled him much. I felt as if I shouldn't hit him. I was so consarned to hit him, you see, that my eye trimbled. But there's no helping it now. There's more chances yet."

"You seek him every day?" inquired Barsfield, curious to learn the habits of a wretch so peculiar in his nature.

"And night, a'most every day and night, when I reckon there's a chance to find him."

"But how do you calculate these chances?"

"I've got amost all his tracks. He's a master of the scouts, and as I knows pretty much where they all keeps, I follows him when he goes the rounds."

"Why, then, have you not succeeded better before? Have you not frequently seen him before last night?—did you never get a shot till then?"

"Yes, three times; but then he had other sodgers with him, good shots, too, and rall swamp-suckers, sich as John Davis, who's from Goose Creek, and can track a swamp-sucker jist as keen as myself. A single shot must be a sure shot, or 'taint a safe one. So we always says at Dorchester, and its reason, too. It wouldn't be no use to shoot one, and be shot by two jist after. There wouldn't be no sense in that."

"No, but little; and yet I shall probably have to take some risk of that sort with my enemy. Do you know Blonay, that I'm thinking to let Mellichampe run?"

"You ain't, sartin now, cappin! Don't you hate him?"

"Yes! as bitterly as ever. You wonder that I should so determine toward my enemy. He is still such, and I am his, not less now than ever. But I have been thinking differently of the matter. I will meet him only like a man, and a man of honor. His life is in my hands; I could have him murdered in his bed, but I will not. More than this, my word, as you know, will convict him as a spy upon my camp, and this would hang him upon a public gallows in the streets of Charleston. I will even save him from this doom. I will save him, that we may meet when neither shall have any advantage other than that which his own skill, strength, and courage, shall impart. You shall help me, or rather help him, in this."

"How?" was the very natural response of the half-breed.

"Assist him to escape. Hear me, if he does not escape before the week is out, I am commanded to conduct him to Charleston, to stand his trial as a spy, under charges which I myself must bring forward. He must be convicted, and must perish as I have said, unless he escapes from my custody before. He is too young, and, I may add, too noble, to die in so disgraceful a manner. Besides, that will be robbing me of my own revenge, which I now desire to take with my own hands."

The last suggestion was better understood by the Indian spirit of Blonay than all the rest. The tory captain proceeded —

"There are yet other reasons which prompt me to desire his escape, reasons which, though stronger than any of those given, it is not necessary, nor, indeed, would it be advisable, for me to disclose now. It is enough that I save him from a fate no less certain than degrading. You can not object to give your co-operation in saving the life which you were employed to take."

The half-breed did not refuse the new employment thus offered to his hands; but his words were so reluctantly brought forth as clearly to imply a doubt as to whether the one service would be equally grateful with the other.

"How?" exclaimed Barsfield; "would you rather destroy than save?"

"Adrat it, cappin, it's easier to shoot a man than take a journey."

The tory captain paused for a moment, and surveyed closely the features of the savage. His own glance denoted no less of the fierce spirit which had dictated the answer of the latter, and gladly, at that moment, would he have sent the assassin forward to the chamber of his enemy, in order to the immediate fulfilment of the contemplated crime. But a more prudent, if not a better thought, determined him otherwise. He subdued, as well as he could, the rising emotion. He strove to speak calmly, and we may add, benevolently, and a less close observer of bad passions and bad men than Blonay might have been deceived by the assumed and hypocritical demeanor of Barsfield.

"No, no, Mr. Blonay, it must not be. He is my enemy, but he is honorably such; and as an honorable enemy, I am bound to meet him. I must take no advantage of circumstances. He must have fair play, and I must trust then to good limbs, and what little skill I may have in my weapon, to revenge me in my wrongs upon him. You, perhaps, do not comprehend this sort of generosity. Your way is to kill your enemy when you can, and in the most ready manner; and, perhaps, if the mere feeling of hostility were alone to be considered, yours would be as proper a mode as any other. But men who rank high in society must be regulated by its notions. To gratify a feeling is not so important as to gratify it after a particular fashion. We kill an enemy for our own satisfaction; but our seconds have a taste to be consulted, and they provide the weapons, and say when and how we shall strike, and stand by to share the sport."

"Adrat it, but there's no need of them. A dark wood, close on the edge of the swamp, where you can roll the carrion in the bog, and that's all one wants for his enemy after the bullet's once gone through his head."

"So you think, and so, perhaps, you may think rightly; but I move in a different world from you, and am compelled to think differently. I can not revenge myself after your fashion. I must give my enemy a chance for a fair fight. I must devise a plan for his escape from the guards, and in that, Blonay, I require your assistance."

"Adrat it, cappin, if so be all you want is to let the fellow off, why don't you let him run without any fuss. You don't want my help for that. He'll promise to meet you, I reckon, in any old field, and then you can settle your concern without more trouble."

"What! and be trussed up by Cornwallis or Tarleton a moment after, as a traitor, upon the highest tree! You seem to forget, Mr. Blonay, that, in doing as you now advise, I must be guilty of a breach of trust, and a disobedience of orders, which are remarkably positive and strict. Your counsel is scarcely agreeable, Blonay, and anything but wise."

"Adrat it, cappin, won't it be a breach of trust, any how, supposing the chap gits off from prison by my help?"

"Not if I can show to my superior that I maintained a proper guard over him, and used every effort for his recapture."

"But how can he git off if you does that?" inquired the seemingly dull Blonay.

"I will not do so. I will not maintain a proper guard. I will give you certain opportunities, which shall be known only to yourself, and, at the same time, I shall keep up an appearance of the utmost watchfulness; so that whatever blame may attach to the proceeding, will fall full, not upon my head, but the sentinel's."

"Adrat it, cappin, I suppose it's all right, as you say. I can't say myself. I don't see, but should like to hear, cappin, what all's to be done."

"Hear me: the prisoner must be taught that you are his friend, willing, for certain reasons, and for good rewards, to extricate him from his predicament."

"Yes, but how is he to know that? You wouldn't let anybody to see him, nobody but the doctor and the young lady."

"True; but it is through the young lady herself that the matter is to be executed—"

"I won't do nothin' to hurt the gal, cappin," exclaimed Blonay, quickly and decisively.

"Fool! I ask no service from you which can possibly do her harm. Be not so hasty in your opinions, but hear me out. It is through her that you are to act on him. She has distinguished you with some indulgences—she sent you your breakfast this morning—"

"She's a mighty good gal!" said the other, meditatively, and interrupting the now deeply-excited and powerfully-interested Barsfield.

"She is," said the tory, in a tone artfully conciliatory; "she is, and it will both serve and please her to extricate this youth from the difficulties which surround him. He is an object of no small importance in her sight."

"The gal loves him," still meditatively said the other.

"Yes, and you now have an excellent opportunity to offer her your service without being suspected of any wrong. You are to seek her, and tell her what you have heard respecting the prisoner. Say that he is to be sent to town to stand his trial; that there is no doubt that he will be convicted if he goes, and that his execution will follow as certainly as soon. You can then pledge yourself to save him—to get him out of the camp—to place him safely in the neighboring woods, beyond my reach and my pursuit. She will, no doubt, close with your offer and by this act you will serve me quite as much as the prisoner and herself."

To this plan Blonay started sundry little objections, for all of which the tory had duly provided himself with overruling answers. The half-breed, simply enough, demanded why Barsfield, proposing, as he did, to render so great a service to the prisoner, should scruple to say to him and to the young lady who watched—both sufficiently interested to keep his secret—what he now so freely said to him? This was soon answered.

"They will suspect me of a design to involve the prisoner in some new difficulty, as they have no reason to suppose me desirous of serving either. I have no motive to befriend him —none. But, on the contrary, they know me as his enemy, and believe the worst of me accordingly. *You* only know why I propose this scheme."

The half-breed was silenced, though not convinced. Suspicious by nature and education, he began to conjecture other purposes as prevailing in the mind of his employer; but, for the time, he promised to prepare himself, and to comply with his various requisitions. It was not until he reached the woods, and resumed his position against his tree, that the true policy of the tory captain came out before his mind.

CHAPTER XXXVI.

THE SUBTLETY OF THE TORY.

What were the designs of the tory? "What bloody scene had Roscius now to act?" Could it be that Barsfield was really prompted by a new emotion of generous hostility? Had his feelings undergone a change, and did he really feel an honorable desire, and meditate to save his rival Mellichampe from an ignominious death, only for the self-satisfying vengeance which he promised to himself from the employment of his own weapon? No: these were not the thoughts, not the purposes, of the malignant tory.

The half-breed was not deceived by the gracious and strange shows of new-born benevolence which appeared to prompt him. Had the death of Mellichampe been certain, as the result of his threatened trial, Barsfield would have been content to have obeyed his orders, and to carry the victim to Charleston for trial and execution. But that fate was not certain. He felt assured, too, that it was not even probable. Cornwallis and Tarleton, both, had shed more blood wantonly already than they could well account or atone for to public indignation. The British house of commons already began to declaim upon the wanton and brutal excesses which popular indignation had ascribed to the British commanders in America; and the officers of the southern invading armies now half repented of the crimes which, in the moment of exasperation, they had been tempted to commit upon those who, as they were familiarly styled rebels, seemed consequently to have been excluded hitherto from the consideration due to men. There was a pause in that sanguinary mood which had heretofore stimulated Cornwallis, Rawdon, Tarleton, Balfour, and a dozen other petty tyrants of the time and country, to the most atrocious offences against justice and humanity. They began to feel, if not the salutary rebukings of conscience, the more obvious suggestions of fear; for, exasperated to madness by the reckless want of consideration shown to their brethren-in-arms when becoming captives to the foe, the officers of the southern American forces, banded and scattered, pledged themselves solemnly in writing to retaliate in like manner, man for man, upon such British officers as should fall into their hands; thus voluntarily offering themselves to a liability, the heavy responsibilities of which sufficiently guarantied their sincerity. To the adoption of this course they also required a like pledge from the commander-in-chief; and General Greene was compelled to acquiesce in their requisition. The earnest character of these proceedings, known as they were to the enemy, had its effect; and the rebukes of conscience were more respected when coupled with the suggestions of fear.

Barsfield knew that the present temper of his superiors was not favorable to the execution of Mellichampe. He also felt that his own testimony against the youth must be unsatisfactory, if met by that of Mr. Berkeley and his daughter. He dreaded that Mellichampe should reach Charleston, though as a prisoner, and become known in person to any of the existing powers, as he well knew the uncertain tenure by which the possessions were secured which had been allotted to him, in a moment of especial favor, by the capricious generosity of the British commander. Guilt, in this way, for ever anticipates and fears the thousand influences which it raises up against itself; and never ceases to labor in providing against events, which for a long time it may baffle, but which, in the moment of greatest security, must concentrate themselves against all its feeble barriers, and overthrow them with a breath.

Barsfield had also his personal hostility to gratify, and of this he might be deprived if his prisoner reached the city in safety. His present design was deeply laid, therefore, in order that he might not be defrauded. Janet Berkeley was to be the instrument by which Mellichampe was to be taught to apprehend for his life, as a convicted spy under a military sentence. The ignominious nature of such a doom would, he was well aware, prompt the youth to seize upon any and every chance to escape from custody. This opportunity was to be given him, in part. The guards were to be so placed as, at the given moment, to leave the passage from his chamber free. The road was to be cleared for him at a designated point, and this road, under the guidance of Blonay, the youth was to pursue.

But it was no part of Barsfield's design to suffer his escape. An ambush was to be laid for the reception of the fugitive, and here the escaping prisoner was to be shot down without a question: and, as he was an escaping prisoner, such a fate, Barsfield well knew, might be inflicted with the most perfect impunity. The cruel scheme was closely treasured in his mind, and only such portions of his plan as might seem noble without the rest were permitted to appear to the obtuse sense of the half-breed, who was destined to perish at the same moment with the prisoner he was employed to set free.

Long and closely did the two debate together on the particular steps to be taken for carrying the scheme of the tory into execution; and it was arranged that, while he, Barsfield, should, in the progress of the same day, apprise Janet of the contemplated removal of Mellichampe to the city for his trial, Blonay should mature his plan for approaching the maiden on a subject in which, to succeed at all, it was necessary that the utmost delicacy of address should be observed. The half-breed was to assume a new character. He was to appear before her with an avowal of sympathy which seemed rather a mockery, coming from one so incapable and low. He was to make a profession of regard for her, and for him whom she regarded, and thus obtain her confidence, without which he could do nothing. Barsfield did not believe it possible for such a creature to feel, and his only fear was that the task would be too novel and too difficult for him to perform decently and with success. But the tory was mistaken in his man. He did not sufficiently dive into the nature of the seemingly obdurate wretch before him; and he had not the most distant idea of the occult and mysterious causes of sympathy for the maiden which were at work in the breast of the savage, whom he loathed even while employing, and for whom he meditated the same doom of death, at the same time, which his hands were preparing for Mellichampe.

But Blonay saw through his intentions; and, confident that the plan was designed for the murder of Mellichampe, he suspected, at the same time, the design upon himself.

"He won't want me after that," he muttered to himself, as soon as he got into the woods; and he chuckled strangely and bitterly as he thought over the affair. In the woods he could think freely, and he soon conceived the entire plan of his employer. He determined accordingly. He was a tactician, and knew how much was to be made out of the opinion entertained by Barsfield of his stolidity. He was an adept at that art which governs men by sometimes adopting, seemingly, their own standards of judgment.

He went instantly back to the tory, and, drawing from his purse the sum of five guineas which the other had given while engaging him, he spoke thus, while returning it:—

"I reckon, cappin, you'd better git somebody else to do your business for you in this 'ere matter. I can't.

"Can't! why?" responded Barsfield, in astonishment.

"Well, you see, cappin—I've been thinking over the business, and, you see, I can't see it to the bottom. I don't understand it."

"And what then? Why should you understand it? You have only to do what is told you. I understand it, and that's enough, I imagine."

"I reckon not, cappin—axing your pardon. I never meddles with business I don't understand. If so be you says, 'Go to the chap's room, and put your knife in him,' I'll do that for the money; but I can't think of the other business. I don't see to the bottom—it's all up and down, and quite a confusion to me."

The proposal to murder Mellichampe off-hand for the five guineas would have been accepted instantly, were it the policy of Barsfield to have it done after that fashion; but he dared not close with the tempting offer. The willingness of Blonay, however, to commit the act, had the effect upon Barsfield's mind which the half-breed desired. It induced a degree of confidence in him which the tory was previously disposed to withhold. He now sought to test his agent a little more closely.

"And you will go now to his room and put him to death for the same money?"

"Say the word, cappin," was the ready response, uttered with the composure of one whose mind is made up to the performance of the deed. The tory paused—he dared not comply.

"And why not help in getting him clear? Where's the difference?"

"'Cause I can't see what you want to clear him for, when you want to kill him, and when you knows he's guine to be hung. I can't see."

"Never mind: it is my desire—is not that enough? I choose it—it is my notion. I will pay you for my notion. Do what I have said—here are five guineas more. Go to Miss Berkeley, and tell her what I have taught you."

The half-breed hesitated, or seemed to hesitate. The bright gold glittered in his eye, and he was not accustomed to withstand temptation. His habit almost overcame his reflection, and the determined conviction of his mind; but he resisted the suggestion and adhered to his resolve.

"I'd rather not, cappin; I reckon I can't. If you says now that you wants to kill him, I'll help you, 'cause then I understands you; but to git him out, and let him run free, jist when there's no need for it, and when you hates him all over, is too strange to me—I can't see to the bottom."

"And you will not do as you have said?" demanded the other, with some vexation in his tone and countenance.

"Well, now, cappin, why not speak out the plain thing as it is," said the half-breed, boldly; "don't I see how 'tis? When you gits him out, you'll put it to him—that's what I understands. If it's so, say so, and I'll go the death for you; but I a'n't guine to sarve a man that won't let me know the business I'm guine upon. Let me see your hand, and I'll say if I back you."

This was bringing the matter home, and Barsfield at once saw that there was no hope for the aid of the half-breed but in full confidence. He made a merit of necessity.

"I have only sought to try you. I wished to know how far you were willing and sagacious enough to serve me. I am satisfied. You are right. The boy shall not escape me, though I let him run. You hear me — can I now depend on you?"

"It's a bargain, cappin," and the savage received the guineas, which were soon put out of sight, "it's a bargain: say how, when, and where, and there's no more fuss."

They closed hands upon the contract, and Barsfield now unfolded his designs with more confidence. It was arranged that Blonay should carry out the original plan, so far as to communicating with Janet. Her acquiescence following, Mellichampe was to be led, at a particular hour, on a specified night, through a path in which the myrmidons of the tory were to stand prepared; and nothing now remained — so Barsfield thought — in the way of his successful effort at revenge, but to obtain the ministry of the devoted maiden in promoting the scheme which was to terminate in the murder of her lover.

Barsfield, in the part prosecution of his design, that very evening sought a private conference with Janet Berkeley which was not denied him.

"What!" exclaimed Rose Duncan, as she heard of the application and of her cousin's compliance, "what! you consent — you will see him alone? Surely, Janet, you will not?"

"Why not, Rose?" was the quiet answer.

"Why not!— and you hate him so, Janet?"

"You mistake me, Rose. I fear Mr. Barsfield — I dread what he may do; but, believe me, I do not hate him. I should not fear him even, did I not know that he hates those whom I love."

"But, whether you hate or fear, why should you see him? What can he seek you for but to make his sickening protestations and professions over and over again? and I don't see that civility requires that you should hear him over and over again, upon such a subject, whenever he takes it into his head to address you."

"It will be time enough to declare my aversion, Rose, when I know that such is his subject. To anticipate now would be not only premature, but in very doubtful propriety, and surely in a taste somewhat indelicate. Such, indeed, can scarcely be the subject on which he would speak with me, for I have already answered him so decisively that he must know it to be idle."

"Ah, but these men never take an answer: they are pertinacious to the last degree; and they all assume, with a monstrous self-complaisance, that a woman does not mean 'no' when she says it. Be assured Barsfield will have little else to say. His speech will be all about hearts and darts, and hopes and fears, and all such silly stuff as your sentimentalists deal in. He will tell you about Kaddipah, and promise to make you its queen, and you will tire to death of the struggles of the great bear in an element so foreign to his nature as that of love."

And, while she spoke, the lively girl put herself in posture, and adopted the grin and the grimace, the desperate action and affected enthusiasm, which might be supposed to belong to the address of Barsfield in the part of a lover. Janet smiled sorrowfully as she replied—

"Ah, Rose, I would the matter upon which Barsfield seeks me were not more serious than your thoughts assume it to be. But I can not think with you. I am troubled with a presentiment of evil; I fear me that some new mischief is designed."

"Oh, you are always anticipating evil; you are always on the look-out for clouds and storm."

"I do not shrink from them, Rose, when they come," said the other, gently.

"No, no! you are brave enough: would I were half so valiant, sweet cousin of mine! But, Janet, if you dread that Barsfield has some new mischief afoot, that is another reason why you should not see him. Be advised, dear Janet, and do not go."

"I must, Rose, and I will, for that very reason, I will look the danger in the face; I will not blind myself to its coming. No! let the bolt be shot—let the wo come—let the worst happen, rather than that I should for ever dream, and for ever dread, the worst. Suffering is one part of life—it may be the greatest part of mine. I must not shrink from what I was designed to meet; and God give me strength to meet it as I should, and cheer me to bear up against it with a calm fortitude. I feel that this man is the bringer of evil tidings: I am impressed with a fear which almost persuades me to refuse him this meeting. But, as I know this feeling to be a fear, and at variance with my duty to myself not less than to Mellichampe, I will not refuse him, I will go; I will hear what he would say."

And here I must remain, stuck up like a painted image, to listen to Lieutenant Clayton's rose-water compliments. The man is so bandboxy, so excruciatingly tidy and trim in everything he says, so measured and musical, and laughs with such continual desperation, that he sickens me to death to entertain him."

"Yet you do entertain him, Rose."

"How can I help it? You will not; and the man looks as if he came for an entertainment."

"And you never disappoint him, Rose."

"'Twould be too cruel, that, Janet; for you neither look nor say anything toward it. You might as well be the old Dutch Venus, stuck up in the corner, whose fat cheeks and small eyes used to give your grandfather such an extensive subject for eulogy. You leave all the task of keeping up the racket, and should not wonder if I seek, as well as in me lies, to maintain your guests in good humor with themselves, at least."

"And with you. You certainly succeed, Rose, in both objects. Task or not, you are not displeased with the labor of entertaining Lieutenant Clayton, if I judge not very erroneously of your eyes and features generally. And then your laugh, too, Rose—don't speak of the lieutenant's—your laugh is, of all laughs, the most truly natural when you hearken to his good sayings."

"Janet, you are getting to be quite censorious. I am shocked at you. Really, you ought to know, that to entertain a body, if you set out with that intention, you are not to allow it to be seen that you are making an effort. To please others, the first rule is always to seem pleased yourself."

"True; you not only seem pleased yourself, but, Rose, do you know I really think you are so? You laugh as—"

"Pshaw! Janet—pshaw! I laugh at the man, and not with him."

"I fear me, now I think of it, Rose, that he has discovered that. Methinks he laughs much less of late than ever: he looks very serious at times."

"Do you really think so, Janet?"

"I do, really."

"What can be the cause, I wonder?"

"Perhaps he has been ordered to join Cornwallis. He spoke of some such matter, you remember, but a week ago."

"Yes, I remember; and at the time, if you recollect, Janet, he looked rather grave while stating it, though he laughed afterward; and yet the laugh did not seem altogether so natural: there was something exceedingly constrained and artificial in it."

"It must be so," replied Janet, as it were abstractedly. The momentary humor which had prompted her to annoy her thoughtless companion had passed away, in the sterner consideration which belonged to her own difficulties. She turned away to a neighboring window, and looked forth upon the grove, and a little beyond, where, on the edge of the forest, lay the encampment of Barsfield, a glance at which involuntarily drove her away from the window. When her eyes were again turned upon Rose Duncan, she saw that the usually light-hearted girl was still seated, in unwonted silence, with her face buried in her hands. The whole air of the damsel was full of unusual thought and abstraction, and Janet might have seen that a change had come over the spirit of her dream also, but that her fancy was saddened by the strong and besetting fears which promised her a new form of trial in the meeting with the tory.

CHAPTER XXXVII.

PICTURE OF LYNCH-LAW.

THAT evening, as she had promised, Janet Berkeley indulged Captain Barsfield with the interview which he desired; and while Rose Duncan was left to the task, pleasant or otherwise, of entertaining the sentimental yet laughter-loving lieutenant, the graver maiden, in an adjoining apartment, was held to the severer trial of maintaining the uniform complaisance of the lady and the courteous consideration of the hostess, while listening to one whose every movement she distrusted, and whose whole bearing toward her and hers had been positively injurious, if not always hostile. Barsfield, too, though moved by contradictory feelings, was compelled to subject them all beneath the easy deportment and conciliatory demeanor of a gentleman in the presence of one of the other sex. He rose to meet her upon her entrance, and conducted her to a chair. A few moments elapsed before he spoke, and his words were then brought forth with the difficulty of one who is somewhat at a loss where to begin. At length, as if ashamed of his weakness, he commenced without preliminaries upon the immediate subject which had prompted the desire for the interview.

"My surgeon tells me, Miss Berkeley, that his patient— yours, I should rather say—Mr. Mellichampe, will soon be able to undergo removal."

"Removal, sir!" was the momentary exclamation of Janet, with a show of pain, not less than of surprise, in her ingenuous countenance.

"My orders are to remove him to the city, as soon as the surgeon shall pronounce him in a fit condition to bear with the fatigue. He tells me that such will soon be the case. Mr. Mellichampe now walks his chamber, I understand, and is in every respect, rapidly recovering from his hurts."

"He is certainly better than he was, Captain Barsfield; but he is yet very, very feeble—too feeble quite to bear with the fatigues of such a journey."

"You underrate the strength of the young gentleman, Miss Berkeley. He is a well-knit, hardy soldier for one so youthful, and will suffer less than you imagine. I trust that my surgeon does not report incorrectly, when he states that in all probability it will be quite safe to remove him at the commencement of the ensuing week."

"So soon!" was the unaffected, the almost unconscious exclamation.

"It is painful to me to deprive you, Miss Berkeley, of any pleasure—of one, too, the loss of which, even in anticipation, seems to convey so much anxiety and sorrow; but the duties of the soldier are imperative."

"I would not wish, sir, to interfere with yours, whatever my own wishes may be, Captain Barsfield," replied the maiden, with a degree of dignity which seemed provoked into loftiness by the air of sarcasm pervading the previous speech of the tory.

"It is for you, sir," she continued, "to do your duty, if you so esteem it, without reference to the weaknesses of a woman, and, least of all, of mine."

"You mistake, Miss Berkeley—you mistake your own worth, not less than my feelings and present objects. Your weaknesses, if it so pleases you to call them, are sacred in my sight; and, though my duty as a soldier prompts me to take the course with the prisoner which I have already made known to you, such is my regard to your wishes, and for you, that I am not unwilling, in some particulars, to depart from that course with the desire to oblige you."

The maiden looked up inquiringly.

"How am I to understand this, Captain Barsfield?"

"Oh, Miss Berkeley, there needs no long explanation. If Mellichampe has loved you, you have been no less beloved by me. I can not now deceive myself on the subject of your regards. I am not so self-blinded as to mistake your feelings for him."

"Nor I to deny them, Mr. Barsfield. There was a time, sir, when I should have shrunk, as from death, from such an avowal as this. It is now my pride, my boast — now that he is deserted by friends, and in the hands of enemies —"

"In your hands, Miss Berkeley," he said, interrupting her.

"How, sir ?"

"In no other hands than yours. Let me show you this. He is not in the hands of enemies, only as you so decree it."

"Proceed, sir, proceed," she said, impatiently, seeing that he paused in his utterance.

"A few words from you, Miss Berkeley, and, such is your power over me, such my regard for you, that, though Mellichampe be my deadly enemy — one who has sought my life, and one whose life my own sense of self-preservation prompts me with like perseverance equally to seek, I am yet willing, in the face of my pledges, my interest, my duty, to connive at his release from this most unpleasant custody. I am willing to place the key of his prison-door in your hands, and to give the signal myself when he shall fly in safety."

"You speak fairly, sir, very fairly, very nobly, indeed, if you have spoken all that you design, all that you mean. But is it your regard for me alone that prompts these sentiments — are there no conditions which you deem of value to yourself? Let me hear all — all that you have in reserve, Captain Barsfield, for you will pardon me if, hitherto, I have not esteemed you one to forfeit your pledges, your interests, your duty, to serve, without conditions, a poor maiden like myself."

The cheek of the tory grew to a deep crimson as he spoke, and his words were crowded and uttered chokingly when he replied:—

"I am not now to learn for the first time, that, influenced as she has been by the speech of others, unfriendly and malignant, the opinions of Miss Berkeley have done me at all times less than justice. The words of old Max Mellichampe, the father of this boy, were thus hostile ever: and they have not been poured into unwilling ears, having you for an auditor, Miss Berkeley. And yet I had thought that one so gentle as yourself would have shrunk from the language of hatred and denunciation, and been the last so keenly to treasure up its remembrance."

"Can Captain Barsfield wonder that I should remember the opinions of Colonel Mellichampe with reference to himself, when after-circumstances have so completely confirmed their justice? Is not Captain Barsfield an active and bloody enemy to the people of his own land—fighting against them under the banner of the invader—and proving himself most bloody and hostile to those with whom he once dwelt, and by whose indulgence, as I have heard, his own infancy was nurtured? Can I forget, too, that by his own hands the brave old colonel perished in a most unequal fight?"

"But still a fair one, Miss Berkeley—still a fair fight, and one of his own seeking. But what you have just said, Miss Berkeley, gives me a good occasion to set you right on some matters, and to unfold to you the truth in all. The taking arms under the flag of England, which you style that of the invader, and the death of Colonel Max Mellichampe, form but a single page of the same drama. They are as closely related, Miss Berkeley, as cause and effect, since it was Max Mellichampe that made me—why should I blush to say it?—a tory, in arms against my countrymen: and to that enrolment— fatal enrolment! for even now I curse the day on which it was recorded, and him no less that moved it—he owes, and justly owes, his own defeat and death."

"I believe it not, sir. Colonel Mellichampe move you to become a tory—to lift the sword against your people? Never —never!"

"Hear me out, and you will believe—you can not else. He did not move me—did not argue with me to become a tory, oh, no! He forced me to become one. Would you hear?"

"Speak on."

"When this cruel and unnatural war commenced in South Carolina, I had taken no part on either side. The violence of the whigs around me, Colonel Mellichampe among them, and the most active among them, toward all those not thinking with themselves, revolted my feelings and my pride, if it did not offend my principles. I was indignant that, while insisting upon all the rights of free judgment for themselves, they should at the same time deny a like liberty to others. And yet they raved constantly of liberty. It was, in their mouths, a perpetual word, and with them it signified everything and nothing. It was to give them a free charter for any and every practice, and it was to deprive all others of every right, natural and acquired. I dared to disagree—I dared to think differently, and to speak my opinions aloud, though I lifted no weapon, as yet, to sustain them. Was I then a criminal, Miss Berkeley? Was it toryism to think according to my understanding, and to speak the opinions which I honestly entertained? Do me justice and say, so far I had transgressed no law, either of morals or of the land."

"Do not appeal to me, Captain Barsfield; I am but a poor judge of such matters."

"If you have not judged, Miss Berkeley, you, at least, have sentenced upon the authority of others; and it is your sentence, and their authority, that I seek now to overthrow."

"Go on, sir; I would not do you injustice, and I would rejoice to think that you could relieve yourself from the unfavorable opinions even of one so humble as myself. But I fear me you will fail, sir."

"I hope not, at least, Miss Berkeley; and the fear that you have uttered encourages and strengthens my hope. I now proceed with my narrative. I had, as I have told you, my own opinions, and this was presumption in the eyes of a dictatorial, proud man, like Max Mellichampe. I uttered them, and loudly too, and this was the error of one so weak, so wanting in public influence and wealth as myself. Would you hear how this monstrous error was punished? this part of the story, perhaps, has never reached your ears."

"Punished, sir!" replied the maiden, with some show of astonishment in her countenance, "what punishment? I had not heard of any punishment."

"I thought not, the punishment was too light—too trivial—

too utterly disproportioned to the offence, to make a part of the narrative. But I was punished, Miss Berkeley, and, for a crime so monstrous as that of thinking differently from my neighbor, even you will doubtlessly conceive the penalty a slight one."

He paused; bitter emotions seemed to gather in his bosom, and he turned away hastily, and strode to the opposite end of the room. In another moment he returned.

"You have heard of my offence—you should know how it was dealt with—not by strangers, not by enemies—but by those with whom I had lived—by whose indulgence I had been nurtured. Would you hear, Miss Berkeley?"

"Go on, sir."

"Hear me then. My neighbors came to me at midnight—not as neighbors, but armed, and painted, and howling—at midnight. They broke into my dwelling—a small exercise of their newly-gotten liberty; they tore me from the bed where I was sleeping: they dragged me into the highway, amid a crowd of my brethren—my countrymen—all cheering, and most of them assisting in the work of punishment."

"They surely did not this?" was her exclamation.

"They surely did! but this was not all. An offence so horrible as mine, free thinking in a free country, was yet to have its punishment. What was that punishment, do you think, Miss Berkeley?"

His eyes glared upon her with a ghastly stare as he put this question, from which her own shrank involuntarily as she replied,

"I can not think—I know not."

"They bound me to a tree—fast—immovable. I could only see their proceedings, I could only endure their tortures—I could stir neither hand not foot to resist them—"

He shivered, as with a convulsion, while recalling these memories, though the sympathizing and pitying expression of her face brought, a moment after, a smile into his own. He continued—

"There, bound hand and foot, a victim, at their mercy, and hopeless of any plea, and incapable of any effort to avoid their judgment, I bore its tortures. You will ask, what more?"

He paused, but she spoke not, and he went on almost instantly,

"The lash, the scourge, rods from the neighboring woods were brought, and I suffered until I fainted under their blows."

She clasped her hands, and closed her eyes, as if the horrible spectacle were before her.

"I came to life to suffer new tortures. They poured the seething tar over me —"

"Horrible! horrible!"

"Then, hurrying me to the neighboring river, your own Santee, they plunged me into its bosom, and more than once, more merciful than the waters, which did not ingulf me, they thrust me back into their depths, when with feeble struggles I had gained the banks. I was saved by one, one more tender than the rest, and left at midnight, exhausted, by the river's side, despairing of life and imploring death, which yet came not to my relief."

"Dreadful, dreadful!" exclaimed the maiden, with emotions of uncontrolled horror, while her ghastly cheeks and streaming eyes attested the deep pain which the cruel narrative had imparted to her soul.

Quivering in every limb with the agonizing recollection which his own horrible narrative had awakened in his mind, Barsfield strode the floor to and fro, his hands clinched in his hair, and his eyes almost starting from their sockets.

In another moment Janet, recovering herself, with something of desperation in her manner, hurried and breathless, thus addressed him —

"But the father of Ernest Mellichampe, he was not one of these men? he had no part in this dreadful crime? You have not said that, Mr. Barsfield?"

"No!" was his bitter and almost fierce exclamation.

"Thank God! thank God!" she exclaimed, breathlessly. He rapidly crossed the floor, he approached her, and his finger rested upon her arm —

"Stay!" he exclaimed, "be not too fast. The father of ur — of Ernest Mellichampe, did, indeed, lift no hand — he was not even present on the occasion, but he was not the less guilty, the deed was not the less executed by him."

" How! speak!"

" He was the most guilty. The mere instruments of the crime—the miserable, and howling, and servile wretches, who would have maimed and mangled a creature formed in their own, not less than in the image of God, were not the criminals; but he who set them on, he whose daily language was that of malignant scorn and hostility, he was its author, he was the doer of the deed, and to him I looked for vengeance."

But how know you that he set them on? Did you hear?"

" Oh, Miss Berkeley, I say not that he told them, ' Go, now, and do this deed;' I know not that he did; but had not Max Mellichampe pronounced me deserving of Lynching, had he not said that I was a tory, and that tar and feathers were the proper desert of the tory, had he not approved of those tortures, and of others which degrade humanity, the torture of the rail, the suffocation of the horse-pond, would these wretches, think you, who take their color and their thoughts always from the superior, would they have been prompted, by their own thoughts, to such a crime? No! they were prompted by him. He approved the deed, he smiled upon its atrocities, and he perished in consequence. Hence my hate to him and his, and it is the hatred of justice which pursues even to the third and fourth generations; for crimes and their penalties, like diseases, are entailed to son and to son's son, all guilty, and all doomed, alike. Hence it is, that I am a tory. Hence it is, that I lift the sword, unsparingly to the last, against the wretches who taught me in that night of terror, of blistering agony, of manhood's shame, and a suffering worse infinitely than death, of what nature was that boon of liberty which they promised, and which it was in the power of such monsters to bestow. Can you wonder now, Miss Berkeley, not that I am what I am, but that I am not worse? You can not. I were either more or less than human to be other than I am. Whether these things may excuse my conduct, I do not now ask; all that I may claim from you is, that you will, at least, spare your sarcasms in future upon what you are pleased to call the unnatural warfare which I wage against my countrymen."

CHAPTER XXXVIII.

UNPROFITABLE INTERVIEW.

The maiden was indeed silenced. If she did not sympathize entirely with Barsfield, she at least saw what a natural course had been his, under the dreadful indignities which he had been made to suffer. She now looked on him with a feeling of pain and mortification as he paced the apartment to and fro; and her eyes more than once filled with tears, as she thought how far guilty in this transaction had been the father of her lover. At length the tory captain turned to her once more. His countenance had recovered something of its serenity, though the cheek was yet unusually flushed, and when he spoke there was a convulsive unevenness in his accent, which denoted the yet unsubdued emotions of his heart. Still, with a moral power which he certainly possessed, however erringly applied, he subdued the feverish impulse; and, after the pause of a few moments, which the excited and wounded feelings of Janet did not suffer her to interrupt, he proceeded to a more full development of his purpose and his desire.

"I have said to you, Miss Berkeley, that I am commanded, so soon as the condition of my prisoner will permit, to convey him to the city. Are you aware with what purpose? have you any notion of his probable destiny?".

The manner of the question alarmed the maiden much more than the question itself. It was grave and mysteriously emphatic. His face wore all the expression of one conscious of the possession of a secret, the utterance of which is to produce the most trying emotions in the hearer, and which the possessor, at the same time, however, does not yet dare to withhold. Janet was silent for a few seconds while gazing into the countenance of the speaker, as if seeking to gather from his glance what she yet trembled to demand from his lips; but remembering the solemn decision of her thoughts when she granted the interview, to seek to know the worst that her enemy could inflict, she recovered and controlled her energies. With a firm voice, therefore, unfaltering in a single accent, she requested him to proceed.

"I am not strong—not wise, Captain Barsfield, and I am not able to say what my thoughts are now, or what my feelings may be when I hear what you have to unfold, But God, I trust, will give me strength to endure well, if I may not achieve much. Your looks and manner, more than your words, would seem to imply something which is dangerous to me and mine. Speak it out boldly, Captain Barsfield—better to hear the worst than to imagine error, and find worse in wrong imaginings. I am willing to hear all that you would say, and I beg that you would say it freely, without hesitation."

"I am glad that you are thus strong—thus prepared, Miss Berkeley; for it pains me to think how deeply must be your sorrow and suffering when you learn the truth."

He paused, and with a hypocritical expression of sympathetic wo in his countenance, approached her when he had done speaking. His hand was even extended with a condoling manner, as if to possess itself of hers; but she drew herself up reservedly in her chair, and he halted before her. Her words promptly followed the action—

"I am neither strong to endure much, nor prepared to hear any particular cause of sorrow, as I can think of none in particular. Speak it, however, Captain Barsfield, since, whether strong or prepared, I am at least desirous to know all which may concern my feelings in the matter which you have to communicate."

"You will think me precipitate in my communication when you have heard it; and that you have not thought of it hitherto, leads me to apprehend that you will even feel it more forcibly than I had imagined. I deem it doubly important, then, to bid you prepare for a serious evil."

These preparatory suggestions, as they were designed to do, necessarily stimulated still further the anxieties and apprehensions of the hearer, though she strove nobly, and well succeeded, in mastering her emotions.

"Speak — speak — I pray you, sir," she cried, almost breathless.

"Do you know, then, Miss Berkeley, with what object I am required to convey Mr. Mellichampe to the city?"

"No, sir — object — what object — none in particular. He is your prisoner — you convey him to prison," was the hurried reply.

"I do — I carry him to prison, indeed — but I also carry him to trial."

"To trial!"

"To trial as a spy."

"A spy! — and what then?"

"He will be convicted."

"Impossible! he is no spy — who will dare to utter such a falsehood?"

"I will dare to utter such a truth. I will accuse — I have accused him. I will prove my accusation; and you, Miss Berkeley, can assist me in establishing the proof. I could rest the entire proof upon your testimony."

"Never — never! God help me, what audacity is this! I scorn your assertion — I despise — I fear nothing of your threats. I know better, and am not to be terrified by a tale so idle as this."

"It is no idle tale, Miss Berkeley, and you are terrified, as you must feel conscious of its truth. You know it to be true."

"I know it to be false! — false as — Heaven forgive me, but this insolence also makes me mad. But I have done now, and you too, sir, have done, I trust. I am not to be frightened by such stories as these; for, know, sir, that when this strange tale was uttered by you before, I had the assurance of Colonel Tarleton — your superior, sir — that there was nothing in it, and that I must not suffer myself to be alarmed. Colonel Tarleton's words, sir, I remembered — he would not give them idly, and I believe in him. He will be there to see justice done to Mellichampe, and with his pledge, sir, I defy your malice. I, too, will go to the city — though I tread every step of the way on foot—I will see Colonel Tarleton, and he will protect the man whom you hate—but whom you dare not fairly encounter—from your dishonorable malice."

"That I dare meet him, Miss Berkeley, his present situation attests—it was by my arm that he was stricken down in fair conflict—"

"I believe it not—you dared not. Your myrmidons beset him, while you looked on. It was many to one: but of this I think not. It is enough that I am required to speak with one, and to look upon one, who has sought to destroy him, and me in him. It is enough—I would hear no more. I believe not in this trial—Colonel Tarleton will not suffer it, and I will go to him. He will see justice."

"He will," said Barsfield, coolly, in reply to the passionate and unlooked-for vehemence of the maiden—so unlike her usual calm gravity of deportment.

"Colonel Tarleton will do justice, Miss Berkeley—it is my hope that he will do so. I have his words for it, indeed, and it is from him the orders come which call for the trial of the prisoner."

"The orders—Colonel Tarleton!" were the simple exclamations of the maiden, as she listened to the assertion. Barsfield calmly drew the paper from his pocket, and placed it in her hands. As she read, the letters swam before her eyes; and, when she had finished, the document fell from her nerveless fingers, and she stood like a dumb imbodiment of wo, gazing with utter vacancy upon her companion. They were the orders, plainly and unequivocally written by Tarleton, as Barsfield had said. Not a word wanting—not a sentence doubtful in its import. Tarleton, who had promised her that her lover was secure, or had led her, by his language and general manner, to believe so, had commanded his trial. Recalling all her energies, with eyes that never once were removed from the countenance of Barsfield, she again took the paper from his hands, as he was lifting it from the floor, and once more read it carefully over—counting the words—almost spelling them—in the hope to find some little evasion of the first meaning—some loop-hole for escape—some solitary bough upon which a fond hope might perch and rest itself. But in vain. The letter was a stern and business-like one.

"You must convey the prisoner, Mellichampe," so ran that portion of it which concerned the maiden, "so soon as his wounds will permit, under a strong guard, to the city, where a court of officers will be designated for his trial as a spy upon your encampment. You will spare no effort to secure all the evidence necessary to his conviction, and will yourself attend to the preferment of the charges." And there, after the details of other matters and duties to be attended to and executed, was the signature of the bloody dragoon, which she more than once had seen before--

"B. Tarleton,
"Lt. Col. Legion."

She closed her eyes, gave back the paper, and clasped her hands in prayer to Heaven, as the last reliance of earth seemed to be taken away. She had so confidently rested upon the personal assurances of Tarleton, that she had almost dismissed entirely from her thought the charge in question; and which Barsfield had originally made when the legionary colonel was at "Piney Grove." Now, when she read these orders, she wondered at herself for so implicitly confiding in the assurances of one so habitually distrusted by the Americans, and so notoriously fond of bloodshed. Yet, why had he deemed it necessary to give these assurauces to a poor maiden—one not a party to the war, and to whom he could have no cause of hostility. Why practise thus upon an innocent heart and a young affection? Could he be so wanton—so merciless—so fond of all forms of cruelty? These thoughts, these doubts, all filled the brain of the maiden, confusedly and actively, during the brief moments in which she stood silently in the presence of Barsfield, after having possessed herself of the orders with regard to Mellichampe. Her fears had almost stupefied her, and it was only the voice of the tory which seemed to arouse her to a full consciousness, not less of the predicament in which her lover stood, than of the presence of his enemy. She raised her eyes, and, without a word, listened anew to the suggestions of Barsfield, who—speaking, as he did, ungrateful and unpleasant things—had assumed his most pleasant tones, and put on a deportment the most courteous and respectful.

"You doubt not now, Miss Berkeley?—the facts are unquestionable. These are direct and positive orders, and must be obeyed. In a few days Mr. Mellichampe must be conveyed to the city; his trial must immediately follow, and I need not say how immediately thereupon must follow his conviction and—"

"Say no more—say no more," shrieked, rather than spoke, his auditor.

"And yet, Miss Berkeley—"

"Yet what?" she demanded, hurriedly.

"These dangers may be averted. The youth may be saved."

She looked up doubtingly, and, as she saw the expression in his eyes, she shook her head in despair. She read at a glance the conditions.

"I see you understand me, Miss Berkeley."

"I can not deny that I think I do, sir," was her prompt reply.

"And yet, as you may not, better that I speak my thoughts plainly. I can save Mr. Mellichampe—I am ready to do so; for, though my enemy, I feel that I love another far more than I can possibly hate him. I will save him for that other. Does Miss Berkeley hear? will she heed?"

Barsfield might well ask these questions, for the thoughts of Janet were evidently elsewhere. His finger rested upon her hand, and she started as from a sudden danger. There was a bitter smile upon the lips of the tory, as he noticed the shuddering emotion with which she withdrew her hand. Her attention, however, seeming now secured, he continued his suggestions.

"I will save the life of the prisoner—he shall be free as air, Miss Berkeley, if, in return, you will—"

"Oh, Captain Barsfield, this is all very idle, and not less painful than idle. You know it can not be. You know me not if you can think it for a moment longer. It is impossible, sir, that I can survive Mellichampe; still more impossible that I can survive his love, or give my own to another. Leave me now, sir, I pray you. Leave me now. We can speak no more together. You can have nothing further to say, as you can have nothing worse to communicate."

"But, Miss Berkeley—"

He would have spoken, but she waved her hand impatiently. He saw at a glance how idle would be all further effort, and the murderous nature within him grew active with this conviction. His hate to Mellichampe was now shared equally between him and his betrothed. The parting look which he gave her, as he left the apartment, did not encounter any consciousness in hers, or she might have dreaded, in the next instant, to feel the venomous fang of the serpent. Her strength failed her after his departure. Restrained till then, her emotions grew insupportable the moment she was left alone; and when Rose Duncan, apprised of Barsfield's absence, sought her in the room where the conference had taken place, she found her stretched upon the floor, only not enough insensible to escape from the mental agony which the new situation of things had forced upon her.

CHAPTER XXXIX.

TROUBLES OF THE LOVERS.

"Is he gone?" were the first, shudderingly-expressed words, which the suffering maiden addressed to Rose Duncan, as the latter assisted her in rising from the floor. Her eyes were red and swollen; her glance wild, wandering, and strangely full of light; her lips compressed with a visible effort, as if to restrain the expression of those emotions which were still so powerfully felt and shown. Instead of replying to the question of Janet, Rose could not forbear an exclamation of partial rebuke.

"I warned you—I told you not to see him, Janet. You are now sorry for it."

"No—no! I must have known it, and better as it is—better, better as it is—to know it all; there is no second stroke—no other that can now be felt, except—God of heaven! have mercy, and save me from that!"

She buried her face in the bosom of Rose, and sobbed with convulsive sorrows, as her imagination presented to her eye the probable result of the trial to which her lover was to be subjected.

"He never spares, Rose—he has no mercies! From the place of trial to the place of death, it is but a step! So the malignant Barsfield said it, and so it will be with such judges as Balfour and Tarleton." And, as she spoke, she closed her eyes, as if to shut out the dreadful images of doom and death which were gathering thickly before her. It was only in fitful starts of speech that Rose could gather from her companion the truth of her situation and the cause of her grief. It was only by successive pictures of the dreadful events which she anticipated, as they severally came to her mind, and not by any effort at narration, that she was enabled to convey to that of Rose the cruel nature of the intelligence which Barsfield had conveyed in his interview. The anger of Rose grew violent when she heard it, and that of Janet immediately subsided. She could the better perceive the futility of uttered grief, when she perceived the inadequacy of all words to describe her emotions. Grief, like Rapture, was born dumb.

But if Janet suffered thus much at first hearing of this sad intelligence, she did not suffer less when communicating it that evening to her lover. Could she have suffered for him — could she have felt all the agony of her present thoughts, assured that it lay with her alone to endure all and let him go free, she would not have murmured — she would have had no uttered grief. But the dreadful task was before her of saying to her lover that the hour of their parting and probably their final parting, was at hand. How much less painful to have heard it from his lips to her, than to breathe it from her lips into his ears. She could endure the stroke coming from him, but she thought — and this was the thought of one who love unselfishly — that she shared in the cruelty — that she became a party to the crime, and its immediate instrument, in unfolding the dreadful intelligence to him. "He will hate me — he will regard it as my deed — and oh! how can I look as I tell him this — how can features express such feelings — such a sorrow as is mine!"

Such were the sobbing and broken words with which she sought her lover. She strove, however, to compose her countenance. She even labored — foolish endeavor! to restrain — to subdue her emotions. But when was the heart of woman — properly constituted only for intense feeling, and entire dependence that admits of no qualified love — to be restrained and subjected by a merely human will. There was that at her heart which would not be compelled. The feeling only gathered itself up for a moment the better to expand. The restraint gave it new powers of action, and, though she appeared in the presence of Mellichampe with a countenance in which a smile even strove for place and existence, it was yet evident to herself that the power of self-control was rapidly departing from her. The strife of encountering feelings was going on within—the earthquake toiling below, though sunshine and flowers only were visible without.

It was with a joy so intense as to be tremulous, that Mellichampe received her. His confinement had made him still more a dependent upon her presence and affections. His love for her had duly increased with its daily exercise; and, in the absence of other and exciting influences, it had become a regular, constant, and increasing flame, which concentrated almost all his thoughts, and certainly governed and linked itself with all his emotions. He longed for her coming as the anticipative boy longs for the hour of promised enjoyment—with a feverish thirst no less intense, and an anxious earnestness far more lofty and enduring. When the latch was lifted he ran forward to receive her, caught her extended hand in both of his own, and carried it warmly and passionately to his lips. She could scarce effect her release, and the blush mingled with the laboring smile upon her lips, which it rather tended to strengthen than displace.

"Oh, Janet—my own Janet—what an age of absence! How long you were in coming this evening!—what has kept you, and wherefore? Truly, I began to fear that you were tired of your office."

"No—no, Ernest—I can not tire, since it is so sweet to serve. If I sought for mere pleasure and amusement in love, I might tire of its sameness; but the love of my heart is its devotion, and the better feelings of our nature, like the God from whom they come, are the more dear to us, and the more lovely in his sight, as they are never subject to change."

"Beautiful sentiment!" was the involuntary exclamation of the youth, as he looked in her face and saw, through the gathering tears in her eyes, the high-souled seriousness—the sanctified earnestness of heart, which proved that she felt the truth of the thought which she had uttered. Love was, indeed, the religion of Janet Berkeley. It was in her to love all things in nature, and to gather sweets from all its influences.

Even the subduing grief to which she was more than commonly subject, brought into increased activity the love which she felt for him who stood before her, yet awakened no opposite feeling in her bosom against those who sought to do him wrong.

"Beautiful sentiment!" he exclaimed, passionately, "and worthy of your heart, my Janet. Love is its constant occupation, and I believe, dearest, that you could not help but love on, even if I were to forget your devotedness and my own pledge to you. Would you not, Janet?"

"I know not that, Ernest. I have never thought of that, but I think I could die then;" and the last words were uttered in his folding arms, and came to his ears like the sweet murmur of angel voices in a dream.

"Heaven forbid, my Janet, that I should ever do you wrong, however slight? It would pain me to think that you could imagine the possibility of a wrong at my hands, and through my agency. True love, dearest, is a thing of entire confidence, and nothing seems to me so sweet as the knowledge that you have no emotion, no feeling or thought, which you do not give up to my keeping. It may be, indeed, that the thoughts and feelings of women have little comparative value, so far as the interests of men and of nations are concerned; but, valueless or not, they are thoughts and feelings with her—her all—her only—and, as such, they should be of permanent value with him who loves her. How much that was unimportant—nay, how much that was positive nonsense—did we say to each other last evening—and yet, Janet, to me it was the sweetest nonsense."

And, smiling and folding her in his arms with the respectful fondness of a natural affection, he poured forth as garrulous a tale in her ears as if he had not long and frequently before narrated to her his own experience of heart, and demanded hers in return. But she could not now respond to his garrulity. It was not that she felt not with him—not that the heart had suffered change, and the love had grown inconstant, though, beholding her abstraction, with this he had reproached her; but, reminded as she was of the joys which they had promised themselves together in their frequent and sweet interviews, she was now only the more forcibly taught to feel the violent wrenching away from hope which the cunning of Barsfield, and the bloody tyranny of Balfour and Tarleton, were preparing for them both. She could only throw herself upon his manly bosom, like some heart-stricken and desponding dependant, and sob, as if, with every convulsion, life would render up its sacred responsibility.

It is needless to say how alarmed—how shocked was Mellichampe, as he witnessed emotions so suddenly and strangely violent. Since he had been a prisoner and wounded, with Janet attending upon him, life had been to them both all *couleur de rose.* Insensibly they had both forgotten the restraints and difficulties, if not the dangers, of his situation. They had lived only for love; they had forgotten all privations in its enjoyments; and, as the circumstances attending Mellichampe had made all further concealment unnecessary of the tie which bound them so sweetly and inseparably together, their mutual hearts revelled in the freedom which their release from all the old restraints necessarily brought to them. Next to the joy of contemplating the beloved object, is the pride with which we can challenge it for our own; and that feeling of pride, of itself, grew into a sentiment of pleasure in the hourly and free survey of the object in the eye of others; as the devotee of a new faith, who has long worshipped in secret, avails himself of the first moment of emancipation to build a proud temple to the God of his hidden idolatry. Thus moved toward each other, and free, as it were, to love securely for the first time, the two, so blessed, had forgotten all other considerations. His wound ceased to be a pain, and almost a care, since it was so entirely the care of the maiden; and her tendance made the moments precious of his confinement, and he blessed the evils which placed him in a relationship the most desirable, and far the most delightful, of any he had ever known.

To the maiden, the very assumption of some of the cares of life, in attending upon the object most beloved, was eminently grateful, as it was the first step which she had yet taken toward the performance of some of those duties for which woman is peculiarly formed, and for which her gentle regards and affectionate tendernesses make her particularly fitted. They occupied her mind while they interested her heart the more; and so completely did they absorb thoughts and affections in the brief period of his confinement and sickness, that she no longer heeded the hourly din of the military music around her; and the shrill note of the bugle, which heretofore sent a thrill of dreadful apprehension to her soul whenever its warlike summons smote upon her ear, now failed entirely to remind her of those causes of apprehension to which she had been before always most sensitively alive. From this dream of pleasure, in which every thought and feeling which might have counselled pain or doubt had been merged and lost sight of, she had been too suddenly aroused by the cruel communication of Barsfield. The long train of pleasant sensations, hopes, and joys, departed in that instant; and in their place rose up all the accustomed forms of fierce war and brutal outrage, with the additional horrors of that peculiar danger to which the circumstances connected with her lover's captivity and situation had subjected him. As these successive images of terror rose up before her imagination and crowded upon her mind, the strong resolution with which she had determined upon their mastery quite gave way, and she fell upon the neck of her lover, yielding to all the weakness of her heart, and refusing any longer to contend with her griefs.

Nor could he for some time obtain from her a knowledge of her cause of sorrow. She could only sob, not speak. Once or twice she strove earnestly to articulate, but the words choked her in their utterance, and they terminated in convulsive but unsyllabled sounds. He bore her to a seat, and knelt down beside her, supporting her head upon his shoulder. Earnestly and fondly did he seek to sooth the paroxysm under which she suffered, and vainly, for a long while, did he implore her to be calm and speak forth her griefs. When at length she so far recovered herself as to raise her head from his shoulder and fix her eye upon his face, the glance was instantly averted, as if with horror, and the tears burst forth afresh. With that glance came the thought of the hour when that noble head should be in the grasp of the executioner — that manly, high, pure white brow obscured by his cowling blind — and that polished and lifted neck grasped by the polluting halter.

These were the dreadful thoughts which came crowding to her mind on that instant; and they might have been the thoughts and the apprehensions, at that period, of a far more masculine mind than that of Janet Berkeley; for, what was so common then as the certainty of execution to the accused American? what so sure as the execution of death to one doomed by Balfour, Tarleton, or Cornwallis? In these hands lay the destiny of her lover. A few days would convey him to the place of trial. A few hours travel through all its abridged forms, and the hurried process of examination, misrepresenting justice; and how brief was the sad interval allowed for the final preparation between the doom and its execution. These thoughts, which, to the strong and fearless man, would have been only so many stirring apprehensions, were a full conviction in the gentle heart of the timid and fond Janet. She feared the worst, and, being of no sanguine temper, she saw no hope upon which to lean for succor. Nothing but clouds and storms rose before her sight, and her love, undeviating and growing warmer to the last, was the only star that rayed out in blessing through the thickness and the gloom.

"Oh, what, dearest Janet, is this suffering that wrings you thus? What dream of danger, what wild apprehension, troubles you? Speak to me, say what you know. Let me relieve your sorrows, or, at least, share them with you."

It was thus that the youth pleaded, it was thus that he fondly implored her to pour the griefs of her bosom into his, and make him a partaker of those evils which she evidently was not strong enough to bear alone. She replied by sobs, and it was only at remote intervals that, coupling together the broken parts of her speech, he was enabled to gather from her that he was about to be carried to Charleston as a prisoner. Hearing thus much, the first thought of Mellichampe was one gratifying to his vanity, and grateful in the extreme to his own warm affection. He clasped her fervently to his heart as he replied,

"And you grieve thus at our parting, at the prospect of our separation. Ah, dearest, sweet is this additional evidence of your sole-hearted love. But it will not be long, I will soon return, I only go to be exchanged."

"Oh, no, no, no!—never—never! You will return no more. It is false, Ernest—false! No exchange—no exchange! They carry you to Balfour and to Tarleton, to be tried—to die! to die!"

Incoherently then, but with the utmost rapidity, she explained to him the circumstances which Barsfield had narrated to her. His astonishment far exceeded her own apprehensions, and, after the first feeling of indignant surprise was over, he calmly and confidently enough sought to reassure her mind on the subject.

"Fear nothing, my Janet. They dare do nothing of what you fear; and this charge against me, of being a spy upon their camp, is too ridiculous to need any refutation, and should occasion no concern."

The composure of her lover failed to satisfy her.

"Alas! Ernest, no charge is too ridiculous with them. How many have suffered from charges equally idle in the minds of honest men!"

This was a truth well known to Mellichampe, and fully as strong in his mind as a cause of apprehension as it was in the mind of the maiden; but, with that pride of character and soldierly resolve which were becoming in the man, he did not allow his own fears to strengthen hers. He overruled her reply, and rejected entirely the anticipation of any danger resulting from the prospect of a trial in the city under an allegation which, in his case, be esteemed so idle.

"I can soon disprove the charge, my Janet, I have witnesses enough to show what my motives were in coming to Piney Grove that night. For, Janet, you yourself, dearest, could speak for me—"

"I could, I could, dear Ernest."

"But should not," he replied; "you should not suffer such exposure to the rude soldiers as such a task would call for. No, no, my love, there will be no need of this. The scoundrel

Barsfield only seeks to alarm or to annoy you. Perhaps, too, he has some object in it. This affair is his entirely; Tarleton and Balfour have nothing to do with it, and Cornwallis is far off in North Carolina."

"Not so, Ernest. Barsfield has convinced me that the orders are from Tarleton: for, when I doubted his word, he showed me the letter of Tarleton, written with his own hand."

"Ah! then, there is something in it," was the involuntary exclamation of the youth. Then, as he beheld the immediate effect of his own gloomy look and speech upon the countenance of the maiden, he proceeded in a more cheerful manner.

"But I fear them not, my Janet, they can not, they dare not harm me. I can prove my innocence, even should they proceed to the threatened trial, which I misdoubt they never will do; and, if they do me less than justice, my countrymen will avenge it."

But such an assurance gave no animated hope to Janet. Her tears burst forth afresh, and she clung to his arm and hung upon his shoulder droopingly and despondingly.

"Hear me, Janet, dear love, and have no apprehensions. You know not how strong is our security now against any such crimes in future, as these tyrants have been in the habit of committing upon the brave men who have fallen into their hands. We have required our commander to retaliate unsparingly, and Marion has pledged himself to do so. When his pledge is given it is sacred. We have called upon him to avenge upon a prisoner of equal grade any execution of our officers by the British commanders; and we have freely subscribed our names to the paper, in which we offer our lives freely to sustain him in such a course, and thus afford a solemn proof of our sincerity. The enemy is not unadvised of this, and they have become cautious since that affair at Camden. We hear of no more executions; they know better, my love, than to proceed in this matter to any length. They will pay dearly for every drop which is shed of my blood."

"Alas! Ernest, this consoles me nothing. On the contrary, this very pledge which you have given to Marion, calling for retaliation upon the British, and promising to abide the consequences with your own life, will it not make you only the more obnoxious to them? Will they not be the more disposed to punish you for that; and will it not prompt them to receive the most ridiculous charge with favor, if it promises to secure them a victim in one who has shown so much audacity? I fear me, Ernest, that this very matter has led Tarleton to forget his promise to me, and determines him to make you abide the penalty for which you have pledged yourself. Perhaps, too, it may be, that Marion, in obedience to the pledge given to you, has executed some British officer."

This was a plausible suggestion, and did not tend in the slightest degree to assure Mellichampe of the integrity of his own opinions. It made him thoughtful for a while, and increased the gloomy density of the prospect before him; but he did not suffer himself to forget for an instant that it was his business to prevent the maiden from brooding apprehensively upon a subject so calculated to make her miserable, and which had already so painfully worked upon her feelings. He strove, by alternate defiance and ridicule, to show that the danger was not so great when it was approached — that the British did not dare do what was threatened; and that, however willing and desirous they might be to shed the blood of their enemies, a discreet consideration of their own safety would keep them in future from any wanton execution of their prisoners.

"And should they, in their madness, attempt my life, the vengeance which would follow the deed would be such as would make them repent of the error to the latest moment. Life for life would be the atoning requisition of Marion, and of every officer pledged to retaliation along with myself."

But that which in the shape of revenge, had the power to console in part the audacious soldier, failed utterly to produce a like effect upon the maiden. Her tears came forth afresh at these words, and mournfully she sobbed out the reply which most effectually silenced all further assurances of this nature.

"Alas! Ernest, but this vengeance, which would be taken by your brethren in arms, would be nothing to me. To revenge your fate would not be to restore you; and for all my vengeance I look only to Heaven. Speak not to me of these things, dearest Ernest, they only make the danger seem more real, and it looks more closely at hand when you speak thus."

"Then hear me on another topic, Janet."

She looked up inquiringly, and the tears began to dry upon her cheek as she beheld a bright light and a gathering elasticity of expression in his eyes. Her head was thrown back as she looked up into his face, while his extended hands grasped her arms tenderly.

"I will not risk this trial, Janet, I will escape from this double bondage, yours and the enemy's."

"How!" was the wondering exclamation of the maiden.

"I have a thought, not yet fully matured in my mind, by which I think my escape may be effected. But no more of it now. That is the footstep of the surgeon. Away, dearest, and have no fears. Despond not, I pray you, but be ready with all your strength of mind to give me your assistance, for I greatly depend on you in my design."

With a hurried embrace they separated as the surgeon entered the chamber; and Janet hurried away, with a full heart and troubled mind, to pray for her lover's safety, and to dream of his coming danger.

CHAPTER XL.

THE HALF-BREED BETRAYS THE TORY.

But it was not for the maiden to retire that night to her slumbers without some better assurances for hope than those contained in the parting intimation of her lover. An auxiliary, but little looked for, was at hand; and, as she left the little ante-chamber in which her interview with Mellichampe had taken place, she felt her sleeve plucked by some one from behind. She turned in some trepidation, which was instantly relieved, however, as her eye distinguished the intruder to be Blonay. The distorted features of this man had never offended Janet, as they were apt commonly to offend those of others. She saw nothing in mere physical deformity, at any time, to hate or to despise; and, as pity was always the most ready and spontaneous sentiment of her soul, she had regarded him from the first, as she knew nothing of his moral deformities, with none but sentiments of commiseration and indulgence.

The effect of this treatment, and of these invariable shows of sympathy on her part, was always made visible in his deportment and look whenever he approached her. He strove, on all such occasions, to subdue and keep down those expressions of hate, cunning, and cupidity, which a long practice in the various arts of human warfare had rendered, if not the natural, the habitual features of his face. A ludicrous combination of natural ugliness with smiles, intended for those of complaisance and regard, was the consequence of these efforts; and, however unsuccessful the half-breed may have been in the assumption of an expression so foreign to his own, the attempt, as it conveyed a desire to please and make himself agreeable, was sufficient to commend him to the indulgence of one of so gentle a mood as Janet Berkeley.

Approaching her now, the countenance of Blonay wore its most seductive expression. The grin of good-feeling was of the most extravagant dimensions, expanding the mouth from ear to ear; while the goggle eyes above, from the vastness of the effort below, were contracted to the smallest possible limits. But for this good-natured expression, the mysterious caution of his approach might have alarmed the maiden. A single start, as she recognised him, only testified her surprise, and she paused quietly the moment after, to learn his motive for the interruption.

"Hist, miss! I ax your pardon, but please let me come after you in the room; I want to tell you something."

She did not scruple to bid him follow her, and they entered the apartment in which she had conversed with Barsfield. There she found Rose Duncan awaiting her. Janet signed to Rose to leave them for a while, and the moment they were alone, the half-breed drew nigh, and in a whisper, and with an air of great mystery, commenced as follows:—

"You've hearn from the cappin, miss, about the young man what's a prisoner here?"

He spoke affirmatively, though with an inquiring expression of countenance, and Janet nodded her head assentingly.

"Adrat it, miss, if they ever gits the young man to Charleston city, there's no chance for him; so the cappin says."

He paused. At a loss to determine what could be the motive of the scout in thus addressing her upon this topic, yet fondly believing that he had some plan of service in reserve, by which he hoped to commend himself, she strongly mastered her feelings, which every reference to the painful topic brought into increased and trying activity; and, bowing her head as she spoke, she simply responded:—

"True, sir; yes, I fear it—but what can be done?"

This question, though uttered unconsciously, and entirely unintended, was, however, to the point, and the answer of Blonay was immediate:—

"Ah, that's it, miss—what's to be done? The cappin says

something's to be done, but he can't do it, you see, 'cause they trusts him, and he can't break his trust. It's much as his neck's worth, you see, to do it."

With some surprise, she inquired of whom he spoke.

"Why, you don't know the cappin that's here — Cappin Barsfield? He says as how the young man's to be hung if he gits to Charleston, and how he must get away before; and he tells me I'm to try and git him off, without letting the sogers see."

"Barsfield — Barsfield say this? Barsfield do this, Mr. Blonay? Impossible! You do not know the man."

"It's a round truth, miss — he tell'd me so with his own mouth, and tell'd me — ax pardon, miss, but I must tell you all what he said —"

He paused hesitatingly.

"Speak boldly," she said, encouragingly.

"He said, miss, as how he loved you, though you didn't fancy him no how, and hadn't no thought 'cept for the young fellow that's a prisoner; and how he wanted to help the young man, though he didn't like him no how; and he would do so, if 'twas only to do you pleasure."

"And he told you this?" inquired the maiden, in unmixed astonishment.

"Jist the words, miss."

"Indeed!"

"Yes; and he said as how he couldn't help the young man off, for he had to watch him, but that I must do it; and he gave me this money to do it."

"And did he counsel you to tell me of this?"

"No, miss, he only tell'd me to tell you that I could git the young fellow out of prison, and git you to make him know how he was to do, and all about it; but the cappin told me I wasn't to say nothing about him in the business, for he said you hated him so you would think something wrong if you knew he had a hand in it."

"And I do think there is something wrong in it. Heaven help me! what new plot is he weaving now? What new mischief would he contrive? Is Mellichampe never to escape his toils? Would to Heaven that I had a friend?"

"Adrat it, miss, but aint I willing to be your friend? and I won't ax you for no pay. I'm a poor sort of body enough, and you're a sweet lady; but I'm willing to be your friend, and to pull trigger for you, if needs be and the time comes for it. Jist say now that I shall be your friend, and there's no telling how much I can help you in this here squabble."

"You can help me nothing, I fear me, Mr. Blonay; and as for this plan of Captain Barsfield, I will have nothing to do with it or him. I doubt—I suspect all his plans; and however he may profess of regard for me, I look upon this employment of you, for the purpose of which you speak, as only a new scheme for the entrapment of Mr. Mellichampe."

"That's jist what I was going to tell you, miss; for, you see, it don't stand to reason, that when a man hates another to kill, he's going to help him to git away; and so, when the cappin first spoke to me, I was bewildered like, and said I'd do it; but, soon as I got in the bush and began to think about it, adrat it! the whole contrivance stood clear before me, and so I went back to him."

"For what?"

"Well, you see, to tell him as how I couldn't think to handle the thing, for I didn't see to the bottom of it."

"Well—what then?"

"Why, then he up and tell'd me all the whole truth—all what he kept before: and, sure enough, 'twas jist as I thought, and jist what you think. The cappin only wanted to have a drive himself at the young fellow, and he thought, if he could git me to talk to you, and make fine promises as how I could git him out of prison, why, I should lead him into a trap that he'd set, so that there would be no gitting off."

"You refused?"

"No, reckon not. I worn't a fool, you see. I know'd if I said no, it wouldn't be so safe for me any longer in these parts; and then agin I know'd if he didn't git me he'd git somebody else, so I took the money, and promised to do my best and to try you."

"I thank you, Mr. Blonay—from my heart I thank you. You have done me good service indeed, and you shall be rewarded. Had you not told me all of this business—had you suppressed the connection of Captain Barsfield with the design—I might have accepted your services for Mr. Mellichampe; nay, I must have been driven, by the desperate situation in which he stands, to consent to his flight under your direction. And then—oh, horrible to think upon!—my hand would have been instrumental in his murder. I should have prepared the snare which was to give his victim to this bloody man!"

She preserved her coolness, though trembling with the new emotions which the communication of Blonay had inspired, and drew from him, by a series of questions, the whole dialogue which had taken place between him and the tory. From these developments she was persuaded—not that her lover was likely to escape at the coming trial, and thus defeat the wishes of his enemy—but that the anxious thirst of Barsfield for his revenge in person made him unwilling to lose his prey, even through the hands of the executioner. With this impression her misery was doubly increased. She saw nothing but dangers and difficulties on every hand. Should Mellichampe be carried safely to the city, what but a cruel and bitter death awaited him there? But could he be carried there in safety? This seemed to her impossible. Would he not go under the custody of Barsfield's creatures? No longer guarded by her watchful attendance—no longer safe from the presence and the obtrusion of others, would not his enemy then have those thousand opportunities for working out his vengeance which now were denied him by the excellent arrangements made by Tarleton? And if he fled before that period came, what but the knife or the pistol of the waylaying ruffian could she expect for him in his flight? As these fears and thoughts accumulated in her mind, she found herself scarcely able to maintain a proper firmness in the presence of the savage. She accordingly prepared to dismiss him, and had already put in his hands a small sum of gold, which he did not demur to receive, when she remembered that it might be of advantage, and was certainly only her duty, to disclose these circumstances to Mellichampe before finally rejecting the proposition.

"Seek me to-morrow," she said, hurriedly, "seek me in private, when the troops are on parade. Keep yourself unseen, Mr. Blonay, and we will then speak more on this matter."

At the earliest opportunity on the morning of the next day she sought Mellichampe, and unfolded all the particulars of the interview with Blonay. The speech of her lover, as he listened to her communication, astounded her not a little.

"Admirable!—Excellent!" were the words of exultation with which he received the intelligence. "This will do admirably, dear Janet, and corresponds finely with a plan which I had conceived in part. A good plan, attended with difficulties, however, which, without the aid of Blonay, I could not so easily have overcome. I now see my way through. The scheme of Barsfield will help me somewhat to the execution of my own project, and must greatly facilitate my chances of escape."

"Speak—how—say, dear Ernest," cried the maiden breathlessly.

"Hear me. We will accept of the services of this fellow Blonay—I will take his guidance."

"What! to be murdered!"

"No! to escape."

She shook her head doubtfully.

"Listen!" he proceeded. "Blonay is trusted by Barsfield, and evidently does not trust in return. It is shown sufficiently in the development which he has made to you of all the plans of the tory. We do not see exactly why this should be so, but so it evidently is. The probability is, indeed, that Blonay is conscious that he has no claim upon Barsfield after he shall have served him by my death, and he fears that he himself will be as soon murdered by his employer when he shall have discharged his agency, in order to the better concealment of his own share in my escape. There are no ties among ruffians save those of a common interest, and the policy of Barsfield will be the destruction of one to whom he has been compelled to confide so much. According to Blonay's own showing, the necessity of the case extorted from the tory a confession of his true design, which, before, he was disposed to withhold. Unfaithful to Barsfield, the half-breed will be faithful to me; and, from all that I can see, there must be some secret reason for his desire to serve you, which you will learn in time. Meanwhile we will accept his services—we will make the most of him, and bribe high in order to secure him at all points."

"But may not all this be only another form of deception, dear Ernest?" cried the less sanguine maiden. "Think you we can rely upon one whom money can buy? Alas! Ernest, it seems to me that these dangers grow more terrible and numerous the more we survey them."

"To be sure they do, dear Janet—the thing is a proverb. But we should never look at the fear, but the hope—never at the danger, always at the success. Whether Blonay be honest or not, it matters no great deal to me in the plan which I have formed. To a certain extent we may still rely upon him, and be independent of him in every other respect. We want but little at his hands—little in his thought, and little in that of Barsfield—if it be the design of the latter to entrap me into flight the better to effect my murder. I only desire to secure my escape beyond this dwelling—to escape these sentinels, and once more plant my footstep in the green woods that grow around us. Let him help me but to that degree of freedom, and I ask nothing further. Let the strife come then—let the ambuscade close then its toils about me, and the danger appear. I shall then be free: my arms to strike—my voice to shout aloud—my soul to exult in the fresh air of these old forests, though I perish the very next moment."

"Speak not so, Ernest," she implored.

"I must: for I will then breathe again in freedom, though I breathe in death. I shall complain nothing of the fight."

"This is madness, Ernest. This is only flying from one form of death to another."

"Granted—and that is much. Who would not fly to the knife, or the sudden shot, to escape the cord—the degradation—the high tree—and the howling hate that surrounds it, and mingles in with the last agonies of death. Such escape would be freedom, though it brought death along with it. But I would not die, my Janet; with proper management I should be secure." He spoke with an air of confidence that almost reassured her.

"How?" she cried, anxiously; "tell me all — tell me your hope, Ernest. How will you escape — by what management?"

"By the simplest agency in the world. Hear me: Even now that trusty fellow, Witherspoon, is lurking around my prison. Only last night, just after you left me, I heard his signals close upon, and evidently this side of, the avenue. But for the fear of provoking suspicion I should have answered them. He is about me night and day — he will sooner desert the squad than me. And thus he will remain; if I can convey intelligence to him, I can do anything — I can effect my escape. I can put it out of the power of Barsfield to do me any harm, unless he does it in fair fight."

"But how will you do this; and what can I do toward it?"

"Much, dearest — very much. But hear me further. If I can say to Witherspoon, 'On such a night I fly from my prison — I meet you at such a place — I pursue such a course — I apprehend an ambuscade, and will require that a counter-ambuscade be set'— ha! do you see?"

"Yes — yes — go on."

"He will understand — it will come to him like a light — like a light from Heaven. He will not be able to bring men enough to encounter Barsfield's whole force, which has been growing largely, you tell me, but he will bring enough to tell against the few whom the tory will employ for my murder, and thus — ah! you understand me now."

"Yes, Ernest, but still I fear."

"I hope! — what do you fear?"

"The fighting —"

"And, if I am free, dear Janet, I should still have to fight until the war is over — until the invader has gone from the land."

"Yes, but — oh, Ernest, if there should not be men enough? — if they should not come in time —?"

"These are risks which I must take hourly, my beloved, and of which I may not complain now. Remember the dreadful risk which I incur while remaining. Is there no risk in going under a guard to Charleston, to be tried as a spy — and by such judges as Balfour, Rawdon, and Tarleton?"

She shuddered, but said nothing. He continued —

"No, my love, I must not scruple to avail myself of the help of Blonay, whether he be true or false. Let him but help me beyond this prison — to those woods — I ask from him no more. Let him lead me to the ambuscade. If we can convey intelligence to Witherspoon, we shall provide for it. I shall withhold everything from Blonay that might place us in his power. He shall know nothing of our plans, but be suffered to pursue his own. He shall guide me beyond the prison — that is all that I require; and as it is Barsfield's own plan which we so far follow up, he will doubtless effect all necessary arrangements for speeding me beyond the regular guards in safety. Once let me reach the avenue, and I leave his guidance and take the opposite path, where I propose that Witherspoon shall place his men."

"And you will, then, employ Blonay to convey this matter to Witherspoon?"

"No, no. We must have a trustier friend than Blonay for such a business, and this is another difficulty. Blonay could never find Witherspoon unless provided with certain passwords, which, as they furnish the key to the very dwelling of the 'swamp-fox,' I may not confide wantonly."

"Trust me, then, dear Ernest; I will seek him — I will not betray the trust, though they make even death the instrument for extorting it from my lips."

"True heart — dear love — I thank you for this devotion, but I must seek an humbler agent."

"Who?"

"Scipio. I will trust him, and you shall counsel him, as I am not permitted to see him here, or to go beyond my prison. To you will I give these words — to you will I confide all the requisitions which I make upon Witherspoon for the object in view, and we must then arrange with Blonay to pave the way for my flight from the dwelling, holding him, and, through him, his base employer, to the idea that I fly upon the first suggestion of Blonay, having no hope of aid from without."

And thus, strong in his hope of success, and buoyant with the promise of an escape from the dangers of that mock trial, but real judgment, which had been held up before him, and which he regarded with no less earnestness, though with nothing of the fear of his feminine companion, he detailed to the maiden the entire plan which he had formed of flight, and, whispering in her ear the passwords which led her through every scout and sentry watching around the camp of Marion, he left it to her to pencil the message to Witherspoon, which he calculated would bring sufficient aid for the service upon which he was required. The spirits of Janet rose with the task thus put upon her. To be employed for him she loved, in peril no less than in trouble, was the supremest happiness to a heart so loving and so true as hers. Her quick mind readily conceived the tasks before her, and her devoted heart led her as quickly to their performance.

CHAPTER XLI.

THE TORY EXULTS IN HIS HOPES OF VENGEANCE.

JANET lost no time in the performance of her duties. She immediately sought out the half-breed. He lingered about the dwelling, and was soon called into her presence. It was with no small surprise that he now listened to the determination of the maiden, to avail herself, on behalf of her lover, of the services of the scout in the very equivocal aid which he had been prompted to offer by the tory. His astonishment could not be suppressed.

"It surprises you," she said, "but so Mr. Mellichampe has determined. He thinks it better to risk all other dangers than that of a dishonest trial before bloody judges in the city."

The half-breed shook his head.

"Well, now, it's mighty foolish; for, as sure as a gun, Miss Janet, the cappin's mighty serious about this matter, and there'll be no chance for the young gentleman, no how. He'd better not think of it now, I tell you."

"I thank you, Mr. Blonay—I thank you, I'm sure, for the interest you take in me and him; but, whatever be the danger, Mr. Mellichampe is determined upon it, if you'll only give your assistance."

"Adrat it! he shall have that, fur as I can go for him. Say what I'm to do that's in reason, and I'll do it."

"You must procure him some arms for his defence. If there is danger, you know, he should be provided with some weapons to meet it."

"Arms!—a sword p'rhaps—a knife—reckon he'd like pistols too—"

"Whatever he can get."

"I'll try—but there's no saying. I'll do what I can."

"He desires no more of you. Next, you must find out exactly where Captain Barsfield puts his ambuscade."

"Eh!—that's the trap, you mean?"

"Yes—find out that, get the weapons, and at midnight to-morrow he will be ready to go with you."

"To-morrow night—midnight!—well, now, Miss Janet, that'll be a bad time, seeing that ther'll be a bright moon then."

She paused—hesitated—but a moment after repeated the order.

"It must be then. He wishes it to be so—he has so determined."

"Jist as you say, miss. I'm ready—though it's a mighty tough sort of business, I tell you; and the cappin's got a ground knife for the lad, I reckon. He hates him pretty bad, and won't miss his chance if he can help it."

"Be you true to us, Mr. Blonay; be you true, and I hope for the best. Be you true to us, as you would hope for God's blessing on your life hereafter. Take this purse, Mr. Blonay—the gift is small, I know, but it will prove to you how grateful I am for what you have done for me, and be an earnest of what I shall give you for your continued fidelity."

She put a richly wrought purse of silk into his hands, through the interstices of which the half-breed beheld distinctly the rich yellow of the goodly coin which filled it. It was no part of his morality to refuse money on any terms, and he did not affect any hesitation on the present occasion. It found its way readily into a general reservoir, which was snugly concealed by his dress, and there became kindred with the guineas which Barsfield had bestowed upon him for a very different service.

Though without doubt intending to be faithful to Janet, and distrusting Barsfield on his own account, the gift of the maiden stimulated his fidelity, and he seriously, though in his own rude and broken manner, attempted to dissuade her from the project. Janet heard him patiently, thanked him for his counsel, but reiterated the determination of Mellichampe to abide his chance.

"Well—if that's the how," he exclaimed, conclusively, the butt of his rifle sinking heavily upon the floor as he spoke—"if that's the how and he's bent to take his chance, he must go through with it—though I warn you, Miss Janet, there'll be main hard fighting—"

"Be sure you get the weapons," she said, interrupting him.

"I'll try; for he'll want 'em bad, I tell you. I'll do my best, and if so be I can get him out of the scrape, it won't be the guineas, Miss Janet, that'll make me do it. You're a lady, every inch of you, and I'll work for you jist the same as if you hadn't gi'n me anything; and—" in a half-whisper concluding the sentence—"if it comes to the scratch, you see, adrat it' I won't stop very long to put it to the cappin's own head," and he touched significantly the lock of his rifle. She shuddered slightly, not so much at the action or the words as at the dreadful look which accompanied them.

"To-morrow I shall see you, then?" she said, as he was about to leave her. "You go now, I suppose, to communicate to Captain Barsfield?"

"Yes—off hand. He tell'd me to come to him soon as I'd got your answer."

"Do so, Mr. Blonay—and, remember the hour—remember the arms!"

The scout was gone—the die was cast—and the feelings of the woman grew uppermost with his departure. She sank into a chair, and was relieved by a flood of tears.

The intelligence brought by the half-breed rejoiced the heart of the tory.

"And when does he propose to take advantage of your offer? What time has he appointed for the flight?" he demanded, eagerly. The scout, more cunning than Janet, had his answer:—

"That he leaves to me. I'm to git things ready, you see, cappin, and when I tells him I'm ready to show the track, he'll set out upon it with me."

"'Tis well! You have done excellently, Blonay, and shall fare the better for it. I feared that she might be suspicious of you: but the case is desperate—she thinks so, at least, and that is enough. Tarleton and Balfour are not known as merciful judges, and Mellichampe is prudent to take any other risk."

The tory spoke rather to himself than to his companion. The latter, however, did not suffer him to waste much time in unnecessary musing. He put his inquiries with the freedom of one confident of his importance.

"And now, cappin, which track am I to take? You wants to fix a sort of trap, and—"

"Ay—yes! But you must let me know the hour upon upon which you start, in order that I may prepare beforehand."

"Sartain," was the unhesitating reply. Barsfield proceeded:—

"The mere departure from the house will be easy enough. He must go in safety out of the immediate enclosure. Nothing must be done to harm him in close neighborhood of the dwelling. The sentinel guarding the gallery will be missing from the watch at the hour on which you tell me the prisoner is disposed to start. Determine upon that as soon as possible, in order that I may arrange it. The sentinel at the back-door will also be withdrawn, and you will have no difficulty in getting to the bay in the hollow between the house and the avenue. Lead him by the bay toward the garden-fence; follow that close until you reach the avenue, and by that time you will be relieved of your company, or never!"

The tone of Barsfield's voice rose into fierce emphasis as he uttered the last words, and the triumphant and bitter hope of his malignant heart spoke out no less in the glare of his eyes and the movement of his uplifted arm, than in the language from his lips. He thus continued:—

"Go now and complete your arrangements with the lady. Come to me then, and tell me what is determined upon. Be prompt, Blonay, and 'stick to your words, and you shall be properly rewarded."

The half-breed promised him freely enough, and left him instantly to do as he was directed. The soul of the tory spoke out more freely when he was alone.

"Ay, you shall be rewarded, but with a fate like his. I

should be a poor fool, indeed, to leave such a secret in custody like yours."

He little knew that the keen thought of the stolid-seeming Blonay had seen through his design, and meditated a treachery less foul, as it had its cause and provocation.

"He can not escape me now!" said Barsfield to himself, as he paced to and fro among the trees where he had spoken with Blonay. "Not even Tarleton shall now pluck him from my grasp. His doom is written: and she—she, too, shall not live for another, who scorns to live for me! I punish her when I put my foot on him. This mockery of a trial, which Tarleton has devised to effect his escape, deludes not me. I see through him. He would clear him: he aims at my ruin. I see through the drift of this order. His own testimony would be brought to bear in behalf of my enemy, and I should only be cited to prove that which he would find others to disprove. I shall disappoint his malice. Mellichampe, by his own precipitation, shall disappoint him. His benevolent plan to take my enemy from my grasp shall be defeated, and I shall yet triumph in his heart's best blood. Had he not been my enemy, he would not have troubled himself with such unusual and unbecoming charity. No! he must glut his own passion for revenge and blood whenever his humor prompts him, and deny to all others a like enjoyment. He shall not deny me—not in this! The doom of Mellichampe is written—his hours are numbered—and, unless hell itself conspires against me, he can escape me no longer!"

CHAPTER XLII.

SCIPIO SET ON TRACK.

Blonay soon made his communication to Janet, and bore his intelligence back to Barsfield.

"To-morrow night, then, is resolved upon?"

"Midnight," replied the scout, telling the truth, which he could not otherwise avoid, as the sentinel was to be withdrawn from the gallery only at the time when Mellichampe was prepared to sally forth. Had it been possible to conceal the fact, Blonay would not have exposed it.

"He lives till then!" was the fierce but suppressed exclamation of the tory.

"Where do you go now, Mr. Blonay?" he inquired, seeing the half-breed about to move away.

"Well, cappin, I'm jist guine to give a look after my own man, seeing that I've been working hard enough after your'n."

"You are for the swamp, then?"

"Well, yes."

"Remember not to delay; without your presence the prisoner will hardly venture on a start."

"I'll be mighty quick this time."

"And let me know all that you can about the 'fox.' See to his force, for I shall soon be ready to take a drive after him."

The half-breed promised, and soon set out on his journey, while Barsfield proceeded exultingly to arrange his murderous projects. That night, Janet Berkeley conveyed to Mellichampe the particulars of her further progress.

"Well, dearest, does he give the route we are to take? Have you got that?"—was the first inquiry of the youth.

She repeated the words of Blonay, which detailed the route in the very language of the tory.

"This is most important. As we have that, we now know what to do. We can countermine his projects, I trust. We can prepare an offset for his ambush which will astound him. The villain! Along the bay, by the fence, and toward the mouth of the avenue—his ambush is there: there, then, must the struggle come on. Well, well—it must be so. There is no retreat now, Janet—there is no help else!"

"Oh, Mellichampe! there is retreat—there must be retreat, if you really think the ambush lies in that quarter. You must take another path, or—"

"No, no, Janet—no. Think you, if he designs to murder me, that he will not watch my flight? Every step which I take from these apartments will be with the eyes of his creatures upon me."

"Then go not, since you will only go to death."

"I will go, Janet—I must. It is my hope, and out of his malice I hope to make my security. Hear me, and understand his plan. He will assist me forth from his encampment until I reach its utmost limit, and he will then set upon me. To slay me within its boundary would be to incur the suspicion of foul play on the part of his superiors. He only seeks to avoid that—that is all; and once having me beyond his bounds, and, as it were, beyond his responsibility, he will then have no scruple to slay me, as he will then have his ready reply to any charge of foul practice. What will it be then but the shooting down a prisoner seeking to escape—that prisoner under charges, too, of being a spy, and notoriously hostile to his master and his cause?"

"And yet, dearest Ernest, you will adventure this flight even with this apprehension, and so perfect a consciousness of it in your mind?"

"Even so, Janet, even so. I think he may be foiled. Next to knowing the game of your enemy is the facility of beating him at the play. I think to overmatch him now, if my friends serve me, as I think they will, and if they are still in the neighborhood. We must lay ambush against ambush, we must oppose armed men to armed men, and then, God forget us if we play it not out bravely."

"But suppose, dear Ernest, that Scipio finds not the men, or any of them."

"I can then defer the flight, Janet: but he will find them; they are even now about us, and so bent to serve me is Witherspoon, that I make no doubt they would attempt to rescue me from the clutches of the tory if I were even under strong guard on my way to Charleston. They know my danger, and will look to it. Witherspoon must be in the neighborhood — I am sure of it, and — ha! hear you not, my love — even as I speak, hear you not that whistle? far off, slight, but yet distinct enough. Hear it now again, and again. You will always hear it thrice distinctly, and, if you were nigh, you could distinguish a slight quivering sound, with which it diminishes and terminates. That's one of our signals of encouragement, and to my mind it conveys, as distinctly as any language, the words, 'Friends are nigh — friends are nigh!" We have a song among us to that effect, written by George Dennison, one of our partisans, a fine, high-spirited and smart fellow, which I have hummed over to myself a hundred times since I have been here, it promises so sweetly to one in my condition: —

"'Friends are nigh! despair not,
In the tyrant's chain —
They may fly, but fear not,
They'll return again.

"'Not more true the season
Brings the buds and flowers,
Than, through blight and treason,
Come these friends of ours.'

"I believe the assurance. That song has strengthened me, that single whistle note, and hear, Janet, hear how it comes again, closer and closer, stronger and clearer. That Witherspoon is a daring fellow, and can not be far from the avenue. No doubt he is even now gazing down from some tree upon the unconscious sentinels. If so, I am safe. He has seen all their positions — all their movements — and has an eye and a head that will enable him to note and take advantage of even the smallest circumstance. You will see!"

"Then hurry, dear Ernest, that Scipio may find him even now in the neighborhood. Write — write."

She stood beside him while he pencilled a scrawl for the courier negro, and gave it into her hand.

"One thing, Janet," he exclaimed, as she was about to leave him. She returned. He whispered in her ear,

"Let him bring me weapons, some weapon, any weapon, which may take life, and which he may conceal about him."

She said nothing of her directions to Blonay on this very subject. He mistook her silence, and his words were intended to reassure her.

"I must not be unarmed, my Janet, if possible. I must have something with which to defend myself, or the veriest trumpeter in the troop may destroy me at odds with his own instrument."

The youth wrote briefly his directions to Witherspoon — described his situation — his prospect of escape — the route which he was to take, and the dangers which attended it. This done, Janet immediately sought out Scipio, in whose skill, courage, and fidelity, Mellichampe placed the utmost confidence. Before giving him his instructions, she strove in the most earnest language, to impress upon him the necessity of the utmost caution. Of this there was little need. Scipio was a negro among a thousand; one of those adroit agents who quickly understand and readily meet emergencies; one who never could be thrown from his guard by any surprise, and who, in the practice of the utmost dissimulation, yet wore upon his countenace all the expression of candor and simplicity. Add to this, that he loved his master and his master's daughter with a fondness which would have maintained him faithful, through torture, to his trust, and we have the character of the messenger which the urgencies of his situation had determined Mellichampe to employ.

The difficulties in the way of Scipio were neither few nor inconsiderable. He was first to make his way, without search or interruption, beyond the line of sentinels which Barsfield had thrown around the family enclosure. These sentinels were closely placed, almost within speaking distance from each other, within sight at frequent intervals while going their rounds, and changed frequently. Succeeding in this, the negro was to go forward to the adjoining woods, and make his way on until he happened upon Witherspoon, who was supposed by Mellichampe to be in the neighborhood, or some other of the men of Marion, who could be intrusted to convey safely the paper which he carried, and which, describing Mellichampe's situation and hopes, suggested the plan and agency necessary for his deliverance. The difficulty, and, indeed danger of this latter part of Scipio's performance, was even greater than that of passing the tory sentinels. since it was important that his missives should fall into the right hands. To be so far deceived as to place the passwords of Marion's men and camp in other than the true, would be to sacrifice, in all probability, the hardy but little troop of patriots who found refuge in the swamps around.

Scipio well understood the importance of his trust, and needed no long exhortation from his mistress on the subject. After hearing her patiently for a while, he at length, with some restiffness, interrupted her in the midst of her exhortations :—

"Da's 'nough, missis, I yerry you berry well; you no 'casion say no' mo' 'bout it. Enty I know dem tory? Ef he git any ting out of Scip, he do more dan he fadder and granfadder ebber 'speck for do. He's a mean nigger, Miss Janet, can't trow dus' in the eye of dem poor buckrah, for it's only dem poor buckrah dat ebber tu'n tory. Let um catch Scip bu'ning daylight. Enty my eye open? da's nough. I hab for pass de sentry, I know dat, da's one ting, enty, I hab to do fuss?"

"Yes, that is first to be done, Scipio, and you know how close they are all around us. I know not how you will succeed."

"Nebber you mind, Miss Jennet; I know dem sentry; whay he guine git gumption for double up Scip in he tum and forefinger, I wonder? Da' tory ain't born yet for sich ting, and I ain't fraid 'em. Well' speck I gone through dem sentry, I catch the clean woods, and I can laugh out, wha' den?"

"Why, then you must look out for Mr. Witherspoon."

"Masser Wedderspoon, why you no call um Tumbscrew, like udder people? Well, I hab look for um; 'spose I no fin' 'em, wha' den?".

"You must look out, then, for some other of Marion's men; and this, Scipio, is the difficulty."

"Wha' make him difficulty more dan tudder, I wonder?" responded the confident negro.

"Because, Scipio, if the passwords get into the possession of any of the British or tories — if you happen to mistake and—"

"Gor-a'mighty, Miss Jennet, you only now for mak' 'quaintan' wid Scipio? You tink I fool — blind like ground-mole, and rooting 'long in de ploughed ground widout looking wedder I guine straight or crooked? You 'spose I don't know tory from gempleman? I hab sign and mark for know 'em, jist de same as I know Mass Ernest brand on he cattle from old maussa's."

"Well, Scipio, I trust in your knowledge and your love for me."

"Da's a missis — da's a trute, missis, wha' I say — I 'speck if ebberybody bin lub you like Scip and Mass Mellichampe, you git more lub in dis life dan you can ebber carry wid you to Heabben. He keep you down from Heabben — da's a God's trute, missis — so much lub as you git on dis airt'. But dis is all noting but talk and cabbage. You mus' hab meat and sarbice — I know dat. I guine — I ready whenebber you tell me; but s'pose, when I gone, old maussa call for me. He will call for me, I know dat; he can't do widout me; and he bery bex if you no talk to um and tell um Scip gone upon transactions and degagements, young missis."

"Don't let that trouble you, Scip; I will speak to my father when you are going; but it is not time for you to go yet; something more is to be done, and we must wait until night before you can set forth."

"Berry well; whenebber you say de word, missis, Scip ready."

The faithful negro took readily the instructions given him in their fullest scope. He comprehended, so far as it was thought advisable to trust him with the scheme, the nature of the proposed adventure. He was fully informed on all the part he himself was required to play, and was prepared to communicate freely to the woodman. Advising and imploring to the last, the maiden dismissed him from her presence to put himself in readiness for his nocturnal journey, with a spirit full of trembling, and many an inaudible but fervent prayer, from the bottom of her heart, to Heaven.

CHAPTER XLIII.

SWAMP STRATEGICS.

BLONAY, as we have seen, had proceeded, after leaving the tory captain, upon his old mission as the avenger of blood. Night after night, day after day, he had gone upon the track of his enemy, and, as yet, without success. But this did not lessen his activity and hope; and we find him again, with un diminished industry, treading the old thicket which led to the camp of Marion. Let us also proceed in the same direction, and penetrate the gloomy swamp and dense woodland recess which sheltered the little army of the lurking partisan. The pomp and circumstance of war — the martial music — the gorgeous uniform — the bright armor of a systematic array of military power, were there almost entirely wanting. The movements of the partisan were conducted without beat of drum or bray of trumpet. In the silent goings on of the night his movements were effected. Mysterious shadows paced the woods amid kindred shadows; and, like so many ghosts trooping forth from unhallowed graves, the men of Marion sallied out in the hour of intensest gloom, for the terror of that many-armed tyrant who was overshadowing the land with his legions.

Never was a warfare so completely one of art and stratagem as that which Marion carried on. Quick in the perception of all natural advantages which his native country presented for such a warfare, he was not less prompt in availing himself of their use and application. Hardy and able to endure every privation and all fatigue, he taught his men to dwell in regions where the citizen must have perished, and to move with an alacrity which the slower tactics of European warfare could never have conceived of. In his camp the men soon learned to convert their very necessities into sources of knowledge and of independence. The bitter of the acorn soon ceased to offend their appetites and tastes. The difficulties of their progress through bushes and briers soon taught them a hardiness and capacity to endure, which led them, after no long period of initiation, to delight in all the necessities of their situation, and to rejoice at the sudden whisper which, at midnight, aroused them from their slumbers under the green-wood tree, to sally forth by moonlight to dart upon the new-forming camp of the marauding tory or unsuspecting Briton.

It was the morning of that day on which Blonay had made his communication to Barsfield, announcing the acceptance by Janet Berkeley of his offer to aid in the escape of Mellichampe. The camp of the "swamp-fox" lay in the stillest repose. The spacious amphitheatre was filled up with the forms of slumbering men. The saddle of the trooper formed a pillow, convenient for transfer to the back of the noble steed that stood fastened in the shelter of another tree close behind him, the bridle being above him in the branches. The watchful sentinel paced his round slowly on the edge of the swamp, looking silently and thoughtful in the deep turbid waters of the river. No word, no whisper, broke the general stillness—and the moments were speeding fast on their progress which should usher in the dawn. At length the stillness was broken. The tramp of a steed beat heavily upon the miry ooze which girdled the island, and, soon following, the clear challenge of the sentry arrested the progress of the approaching horseman.

"Who goes there?" was the prompt demand. The answer was given.

"Dorchester!" The scout entered the lines and proceeded on foot to the little clump of trees which had been devoted to Marion. The new-comer made but little noise; yet, accustomed to continual alarms, and sleeping, as it was the boast of Marion's men, with an ear ever open and one foot always in stirrup, the sound was quite sufficient to raise many a head from its pillow, and to persuade many an eye to strain through the gloom and shadow of all objects around, to catch a glimpse of the person, and, if possible, guess the object of his visit.

Here and there a whisper of inquiry assailed him as he passed along; and, half asleep and half awake, but still thoughtful of one leading topic of most interest with him, one well-known voice grumbled forth an inquiry after the provision-wagons, and growled himself to sleep again as he received no reply. A full half-hour, perhaps, had elapsed before the visiter came forth from the presence of Marion to the spot of general encampment. Thence he proceeded to a tree that stood by itself on the verge of the island, where he found a group of three persons huddled up together, and still engaged in a slumber which seemed silent enough with all, though scarcely very deep or perfect with any. One of the three started up as the person approached, and hastily demanded the name of the intruder. The voice of the inquirer was that of Thumbscrew, and his gigantic frame was soon uplifted as the respondent announced himself as Humphries.

"Come with me, Witherspoon—I want you," said the trooper.

"Wait a bit, till I pull up my suspenders, and find my frogsticker, which has somehow tumbled out of the belt," was the reply.

A few moments sufficed to enable him to effect both objects, and the two emerged from the shelter of the tree together. Day was dawning as they gained the skirts of the island where Humphries had fastened his horse, and where they were, in great part, free from the observation of their comrades, who were now starting up from their slumbers on every side. When they had reached this point, Humphries, without further preliminary, unfolded his business to his companion.

"Thumby—old fellow—I'm hunted, and need your help."

"Hunted? how—by whom?"

"By a scoundrel that seeks my life—a fellow from Dorchester, named Blonay."

"Blonay—Blonay—I never heard that name before."

"Goggle, then; that's the nickname he goes by. You've heard John Davis speak of him. I happened to ride over his old mother the time of that brush at Dorchester, when Major

Singleton got Colonel Walton out of the cart, and he's been hunting me ever since."

"The d—l! But how could he find you out? how could he track you so?"

"That's the wonder; but the fellow's got Indian blood in him, and there's no telling where he can't go. He's as keen upon trail as a bloodhound."

"Have you seen him? How do you know he's on trail?"

"I haven't seen him? but I know he's been after me for some time." And Humphries then reminded the inquirer of the pursuit of Blonay from the very skirts of the camp, when, to save himself, the half-breed slew his own dog, which had led to his detection, and so nearly to his capture.

"And why do you think that he's still after you? Don't you think the run that you give him then has pretty nigh cured him of his hunt?"

"No, no! The scoundrel will never give up the hunt till he can see my blood, or I draw his. There's no help for it; he will hunt me until I set seriously to hunt him."

"And you have heard of him lately, Bill?"

"Ay—'heard of him'—felt him! Look here."

And as he spoke, lifting the cap from his head, he showed his comrade the spot through which the passage of the bullet was visible enough. Then, putting aside the hair from his forehead, he placed the finger of Witherspoon upon the skull, along which the ball had made its way. The skin was razed and irritated into a whelk, such as a severe stroke of a whip might occasion upon the skin. An eighth of an inch lower, and the lead would have gone through the brain.

"By the etarnal scratch!" exclaimed Witherspoon, as he felt and saw the singular effect which the shot had produced, "that, I may say, was a most ticklish sort of a trouble. It was mighty close scraping, Bill; and the fellow seems to have been in good airnest when he pulled, though it's a God's marcy he took you to have more head high up than o' one side. Had he put it here now, to the right or to the left, I don't care which, and not so immediately and ambitiously up in the centre, he would have mollified your fixings in mighty short order, and the way you'd have tumbled over would be a warning to tall men like myself."

Humphries winced as much from the remarks of Witherspoon as under the heavy pressure of his finger, which rambled over the wounded spot upon his head with the proverbial callousness of a regular army-surgeon's.

"'Tis just as you say, Thumby," replied the other, with much good-humor—"a mighty close scrape, and ticklishly nigh. But a miss is good as a mile; and though this shot can't be considered a miss exactly, yet, as no harm's done, it may very well be counted such. The matter now is, how to prevent another chance, and this question leads to a difficulty. How did the fellow come to take track upon me so keenly from the jump? and how has he contrived to keep on it so truly until now? These are questions that aint so easy to answer, and we must find out their answer before we can fall on any way to circumvent the varmint. I thought at first that he might have got information from some of Barsfield's tories; but since we've been in the swamp they can't take track upon us, and only he has done it; for the general now knows that it was this same skunk that showed the back track of the swamp to Tarleton, and that he most certainly found out only by following after me. I've been thinking over all these matters for a spell now of more than ten days, and I can make little or nothing out of it; and to say truth, Thumby, it's no little trouble to a man to know there's a hound always hunting after him, go where he will, in swamp or in thicket, on the high-road and everywhere—that never goes aside—thirsting after his blood, and trying all sort of contrivances to git at it."

"It's mighty ugly, sir, that's clear," said his companion, musing.

"Yet, this trouble I've known ever since we chased the fellow along the back track, when he cut the throat of his dog, which only an Indian would do, to put us off his own trail."

"It's an ugly business, that's a truth, Humphries; for, not to know where one's enemy is, is to look for a bullet out of every bush. It can't be that some of our men have been playing double, and have let this fellow on track?"

"No, there's no reason to think it, for none of them have been always able to find me when they wanted to, and we know where to look for them always."

"It's mighty strange and hard—and what are you to do, Bill?"

"You must tell me—I know not what to do," was the desponding answer: "I've no chance for my life at this rate, for, soon or late, the fellow must git his shot. He'll never give up hunting me till he does. It's the nature of the beast, and there's no hope for me until I can put upon his trail, and hunt him just as he hunts me. The best scout will then win the game and clear the stakes."

"It's mighty sartin, Bill, that he's got some string on you in partic'lar: you've kept too much on the same track."

"No—from the moment I found that the fellow was after me in the swamp, I've been changing every day."

"And still he keeps after you?"

"His bullet tells that."

"It's mighty strange. Have you had your nag's hoofs trimmed lately?"

"No, they don't need it—they're shod."

"Shod!"

"Yes, in the forefeet."

"Well, now, it's mighty foolish to shoe a horse that's got to travel only in swamp and sand; but I'd like to look at them shoes."

"Come, then." As they walked, they conversed further on the same subject.

"Where was them shoes put on?" inquired Thumbscrew.

"In Dorchester, about three months ago."

"And where was this Ingen fellow then?"

"I don't know; somewhere about, I reckon."

"Show me the critter: I'm dub'ous all the mischief lies in them shoes."

And, following Humphries, Thumbscrew went forward to the spot where the horse was tethered.

"Lead him off, Bill — there, over that soft track — jist a few paces. That'll do."

The busy eye of Witherspoon soon caught the little ridges left by the crack in the shoe, which had so well conducted the pursuit of Blonay.

"I guessed as much, Bill, and the murder's out, you've given the fellow a sign, and he's kept trail like a turkey. Look here, and here, and here, a better mark would not be wanted by a blind man, since his own finger could feel it, even if his eyes couldn't see. There it is, and what more do you want?"

Humphries was satisfied, no less than his companion. They had indeed discovered the true guide of Blonay in his successful pursuit, so far, of his destined victim. Nothing, indeed, could be more distinct than the impression left upon the sand, an impression not only remarkable as it was so unusual, but remarkable as it occurred upon a small shoe, and seemed intentionally made to divide it, the fissure forming the ridge making a line as clearly distinct upon the shoe, as that made by the shoe itself in its entire outline upon the pliable sand.

"Well," said Thumbscrew, after they had surveyed it for several minutes, "and what are you going to do now?"

"That's what I'm thinking of, Thumby, and it's no easy matter yet to determine upon."

"How! why, what have you to do now but to pull off the shoe, and throw the fellow from your haunches, which you must do the moment you take him off his track."

"No, no," coolly responded the other, "that will be making bad worse, Thumby, since to throw him off one track will be only to make him hunt out for another, which we may not so readily discover. A fellow that really hungers after your blood, as this fellow does after mine, ain't so easily to be thrown off as you think. To throw off this scent would be only to gain a little time, and botch up the business that we had better mend. The shoes must stay on, old fellow; and, as we've found out that they are guides which he follows, why, what hinders that we should make use of them to trap him?"

"How?" said Witherspoon, curiously.

"Easy enough, Thumby, if I've got a friend in the world who's willing to risk a little trouble, and perhaps a scuffle, to help me out of the hound's teeth."

"Gimini! Bill Humphries, you don't mean to say that you ain't been my friend, and that I ain't yours? Say the word, old fellow, and show your hand, and if I ain't your partner in the worst game of old-sledge you ever played, with all trumps agin you, and a hard log to set on, and a bad fire-light to play by, then don't speak of me ever again when your talk happens to run on Christian people. Say the word, old fellow, and I'm ready to help you. How is it to be done? what am I to do?"

"Take my track also, follow the shoe, but take care to give me a good start. I will ride on the very route where I got the bullet."

"What! to get another?"

"No. I will ride in company, and Blonay is quite too cunning to risk a shot, with the chance of having his own head hammered the next minute by my companion, even if he tumbles me."

"I see? I see! He will be on your track, and will follow you, as he has done before, in hope to get another chance. That's it, eh?

"Yes, he will not be easily satisfied. Nothing but his blood or mine will satisfy any such varmint as this half-breed, who takes after the savages, from whom he comes half way. He will be on the old ground which he's travelled so long, and that I've travelled; and he will keep close about me, day by day, and month after month, and year after year, until he gets his chance for a sure shot, and then the game's up, and he'll not rest quietly before. I know it's the nature of the beast, and so I'm sure of my plan if you only follow it up as I show you, and as I know you're able to do easy enough."

"I'm ready, by gum, Bill. You shan't want a true heart and a stiff hand in the play on your side, so long as Thumbscrew can help a friend and hurt an enemy. I'm ready — say the word — the when and the how — and here's your man."

"Thank'ee, Thumby, I knew I shouldn't have to ax twice, and so now listen to me."

"Crack away."

"I set off in two hours for the skirts of Barsfield's camp, where I'm to put a few owls who shall roost above him. After that I take the back track into the swamp, and John Davis and young Lance will keep along with me. I pretty much guess that this fellow Blonay will not let half an hour go by, after I've passed him, before he gets upon trail somewhere or other, and fastens himself up in some bush or hummock, waiting a chance at me when he finds I'm going back. If my calculation be the right one, then all you've got to do is to take the trail after me, keeping a close look-out right and left, for the fresh track of an Indian pony. If you see that little bullet foot of a swamp-tacky freshly put down in the swamp or sand after mine, be sure the skunk's started."

"I see, I see."

"Well, when you've once got his track, we have him. If he finds he's got some one on his skirts, he'll go aside, and you'll lose his trail, to be sure; but you'll know then he's either on one side or 'toder in the woods about you; and all you've got to do is to ride ahead a bit and go into the bush too."

"Good, by gimini!"

"What then? Soon as he finds all things quiet, he'll come out of the bush and take up my trail as he did before; and, if you git a good place to hide in, so as to be concealed and yet to watch the road, you can't help seeing when he goes ahead."

"That's true; but suppose he goes into the bush again, what must I do then?"

"Just what you've done before, the very thing, until he gets to the bayou that opens the door to the swamp. If you can track him that far, you can track him farther; for when he once gets there he'll be sure to go into hiding in some corner or other where he knows I must pass, waiting the chance to crack at me again."

"Yes, yes! And I'm to try and find out his hollow? I see, I see. It ain't so hard, after all, for I'm a very bear in the swamp, and can go through a cane-brake with the best of them. We shall have the skunk, Bill, there's no two ways about it. If he can keep the track of a horseshoe through mud and mire for a month, hunting an enemy, 'twont be very hard for me to keep it too, helping a friend : and though, between us, Bill — I'm mighty conflustered about Airnest, and that d — d tory Barsfield, and what to do to help the lad out of his hobbles, yet I'm not guine to let this matter stand in the way of yours. I'll go neck and shoulders for you, old fellow, and here's a rough fist on it."

A hearty gripe testified the readiness of the one to assist his friend, and the warm acknowledgments of the other. The two then proceeded to make their arrangements for the prosecution of a scheme so truly partisan. In this affair it may be proper that we should attend them.

CHAPTER XLIV.

THE COLD TRAIL.

THE half-breed that morning had taken a stand upon the road side to which he had been long accustomed. The route was one frequently trodden by his enemy. This fact Blonay had ascertained at an early period in his pursuit, and here, day after day, had he watched with a degree of patient quietude only to be comprehended by a reference to the peculiar blood which was in him. The instincts of the Indian character were his instincts. Hardily to endure, stubbornly to resist, perseveringly to prosecute his purpose—that purpose being a revenge of wrong and indignity—all these seem to have been born within him at his birth, and to have acquired a strength corresponding with that of his continued growth and accumulating vigor. Such instincts are scarcely to be controlled even by education—the education which he had received had only made them more active and tenacious.

The half-breed had little hope, on the present occasion, to meet again with his enemy. The attempt which he had recently made on the life of Humphries, and which he thought to have entirely failed, would, he believed, have so alarmed the trooper as to have impelled him to seek another route, or, at least, have prompted him to the precaution of taking companions with him when he again rode forth. It was with a faint hope, therefore, that he now resumed his place. On the ensuing night he was to effect the escape of Mellichampe, the successful prosecution of which attempt would, he doubted not, result in raising for him a new enemy in the person of the tory captain. About the issue of this adventure he had various misgivings. He questioned the practicability of success, as he knew nothing of the design of Mellichampe, and of the despatch which had been sent by Scipio. He was certain that Mellichampe would be slain, but he concurred in the supposed preference which the youth gave to the mode of dying, in the stroke or shot of sudden combat, rather than by the degrading cord. He was pledged to serve the maiden, and to comply with her wishes was the best mode in his estimation.

He had concealed his pony, and covered himself by the thick umbrage around him, in his old retreat, when the sound of approaching horses called for his attention. With a feeling of gratified surprise he saw his enemy. But he was accompanied: John Davis rode on one side of Humphries, and Lance Frampton on the other—all well mounted, and carrying their rifles.

"How easy to shoot him now," thought the half-breed—" I couldn't miss him now—but it's no use:" and his rifle lay unlifted across his arm, and he suffered the three to pass by in safety. To forbear was mortifying enough. The party rode by within twenty yards, seemingly in the greatest glee, laughing and talking. A less cool and wary enemy than Blonay, having a similar pursuit, could not have forborne. The temptation was a trying one to him; but, when he looked about in the woods around him, and saw how easily they might be penetrated by the survivers, even if he shot Humphries, he felt convinced that the death of his enemy would be the immediate signal for his own. His revenge was too much a matter of calculation—too systematic in all its impulses—to permit him to do an act so manifestly disparaging his Indian blood, and his own desire for life, and his habitual caution. The cover in which he stood, though complete enough for his concealment while it remained unsuspected, was otherwise no shelter; and, subduing his desire, he quietly and breathlessly kept his position, till his ears no longer distinguished the tramp of their departing horses.

It was then that the half-breed rose from his place of shelter. Gliding back to the deeper recess where his pony had been hidden, he was soon mounted, and prepared to take the track after his enemy.

"He's gone to place the sentries and send out the scouts. He won't have 'em with him by the time he gits to the swamp, and I'll take the short track at the bend and git there before him. Adrat it, that I should have missed him as I did!"

Thus muttering, he left the woods, and was soon pacing, with the utmost caution, upon the road which had been taken by his enemy.

Marking his time duly, and heedful of every object upon the road, our friend Witherspoon might have been seen, a little while after, going over the same ground with no little solemnity. He had carefully noted the several tracks made by the horse of Humphries, along with those of his companions, and, step by step, had kept on their trail until he reached the spot at which, emerging from the place of his concealment, the waylaying Blonay had set off also in pursuit. The observant eye of Witherspoon, accustomed to note every sign of this description, soon detected the track made by the hoof of the animal which Blonay bestrode. He alighted from his horse, and carefully examined it; then, entering the woods on that side from which the pony had evidently emerged, he traced out the course of the half-breed by the crushed grass and disordered foliage, until he found, not only where the pony had been kept, but the very branch to which he had been tethered. The branch was broken at the end, and the bridle, having been passed over it, by its friction, had chafed a little ring around the bark. From this spot he passed to that in which Blonay himself had been hidden on the roadside when Humphries had ridden by. His exclamation, as he made this discovery, was natural and involuntary—

"Gimini, if Bill had only know'd it, how he could have wound up the animal! Only to think—here he squatted, not twenty steps off, and a single leap of a good nag would ha' put a hoof on each of his shoulders! But it ain't all a clear track for him yet. Push is the word; and, if he don't keep wide awake, he'll larn more in the next two hours than he'll ever understand in a week after. Come, Button, we'll know this place next time in case we have to look after the Indian agen."

He resumed his course, and with something more of rapidity, as he now discovered that the game was fairly afoot. The track was distinctly defined for him; and, wherever the foot of Humphries' horse had been set down, there, with unerring certainty, immediately behind, was that of the pony. Excited by the prospect of the encounter which he now promised himself, he began unconsciously to accelerate the movements of his horse, until he gained rapidly, without knowing it himself, upon the footsteps of the rider he pursued.

Blonay had not, however, laid aside his habitual wariness, and the precipitancy of Witherspoon betrayed his approach to the watchful senses of the half-breed. He had himself gained so much upon Humphries as to hear the sound of his horse's tread, and his quick ear soon detected the corresponding sound from the feet of Witherspoon's horse in the rear. He paused instantly, until assured that his senses had not deceived him, and silently then he slided into the bushes on one side of the road, availing himself of a deep thicket which spread along to the right. Nor, having done this, did he pause in a single spot and simply seek concealment. He took a backward course for a hundred yards or more, and awaited there in shelter, watching a single opening upon the road, which he knew must be darkened by the figure of the approaching person.

Witherspoon rode on, passed the designated spot, and was recognised by the outlier. But, as it was not the policy of Blonay to be discovered now by any, he did not come forth and remind our friend of their former meeting on the highway. The partisan kept on his way until he missed the track of the pony. There was that of Humphries plainly enough; but that of the pony was no longer perceptible. He checked his own steed, and rebuked himself for his want of caution. He saw that he must now change his game; and, and without stopping to make an examination which might startle Blonay into suspicion — for he knew not but that the half-breed was even then looking down upon him from some place of safe concealment — he rode on a short distance farther, and then sank, like Blonay, into the cover of the very same woods, though on the side opposite to that which had given shelter to the latter. Here he dismounted, hid his horse in a recess sufficiently far in the rear to prevent any sounds which he might utter from reaching any ear upon the road, and, advancing to a point sufficiently nigh to command a view of passing objects, sought a place of concealment and watch for himself. This he soon found, and, like a practised scout, he patiently concentrated all his faculties upon the task he had undertaken, and, with all the energies of his mind, not less than of his body, prepared for the leap which he might be required to take, he lay crouching in momentary expectation of his prey.

Here he waited patiently, for the space of half an hour, in the hope of seeing the pursuer go by. But he waited in vain: the road remained undarkened by a solitary shadow — his ears were unassailed by a solitary sound. The half-breed well knew what he was about. Familiar with the course usually taken by Humphries, he did not now care to tread directly upon his footsteps, particularly as such a progress must have placed him upon the same road with that taken by the stranger, whose unlooked-for coming had driven him into shelter. It was enough that he could reach, a mile above, the narrow track which, darting aside from the main road, led obliquely into the swamp. There he knew he should again come upon the track of Humphries, and with that hope he was satisfied. Keeping the woods, therefore, on the side which he had entered, he stole along among the shadows of the silent pines sufficiently far to be both unseen and unheard by those upon the road; and while the scout lay snugly watching for him in the bush, the subtle half-breed had gone ahead of him, and was now somewhat in advance, though still moving slowly between him and Humphries. Witherspoon was soon convinced that this must be the case, and, throwing aside his sluggishness, he prepared to resume his progress.

"The skunk will double round us after all," he muttered to himself, "if I don't keep a better lookout. But he sha'n't. There's only one way. It won't do to go on sich a trail on the back of a nag that puts down his foot like an elephant. Shank's mare is the only nag for this hunt, and you must keep quiet where you are, Button, till I get back. I can do well enough for a while without you, and you must be reasonable, and be quiet, too."

Thus addressing his horse, he tightened the rope which fastened him to the tree, and prepared to continue the pursuit on foot.

"I can walk jist as fast as that 'ere pony can trot, at any time, and the skunk that straddles him is too cunning to go fast now. I can outwalk him, I know; and, if he could hear Button's big foot, it's more than his ears can do to hear mine."

Thus reasoning, the scout left his steed, pressed forward upon the highway, and, with rapid strides, pushed for the recovery of lost ground.

Blonay, meanwhile, had gained a sight of the person he pursued. Humphries had lingered behind with this very object. As soon as the half-breed heard the sounds of feet above him, and so near the swamp, he sank into the deepest cover and began to prepare himself. He first alighted from his pony, which he led as far into the shelter of the woods as seemed advisable. His own concealment was more easily effected while on foot than when mounted, and the proximity of his enemy rendered every precaution necessary. The sudden rush of a fleet steed, like that bestrode by Humphries, would have brought the latter upon him long before he could conceal himself, if he happened to be mounted at the time. On foot he pressed forward until he beheld the three and distinguished their movements. Humphries was in the rear, Davis and Frampton were about to enter the swamp, and, indeed, had already done so.

It was then that Blonay urged the pursuit most rapidly; and, with rifle ready to be lifted to his shoulder the moment the opportunity should offer for its use, he leaped cautiously, in a circuitous route, from cover to cover, and in the greatest silence, in order to secure a position which might command the pond, through which he well knew the partisans must go before entering the swamp. He was the more stimulated in this object, as he thought it not improbable that, as the companions of Humphries were ahead of him, they might go so far forward as to throw the entire length of the pond, and the intervening thicket (which, thrusting itself up from one side of it, and running far out into its centre, almost entirely concealed its opposite termination), between themselves and the enemy he pursued. If this had been the case, his opportunity to shoot down Humphries, and make his escape before the other two could possibly return, would be complete.

All these conjectures and calculations were instantaneous, and the result of his natural instinct. The image of his success rose vividly before him as he pressed forward to secure a fair shot at the figure of which he momently caught glimpses through the foliage; and, but for the heedful thought of Humphries — with whom the present was the life and thought-absorbing affair — the opportunity might have been won by the vindictive pursuer who desired it. The partisan was sufficiently observant, however, of all these chances. He knew not that his enemy was at hand, and, indeed, did not think it; but he omitted no precaution, and clung close to his companions. They moved forward together into the pond; and when Blonay reached the edge of it, they had emerged through its waters, and, gaining the opposite side, were out of his reach and sight, and in safety for the present.

Blonay was a patient enemy — no less patient than persevering. He sank back into cover, and prepared to wait, as he had often done before, for the return of his victim.

"He goes to place his scouts — he will come back alone," were the muttered words of the half-breed; and, unconscious that he himself was an object of as close a watch as that which he maintained on Humphries, he coolly sought his place of rest behind a little clump of cane and a thicket of close brier, which formed much of the undergrowth among the gigantic cypresses spreading around him, and formed no unfitting fringe for the edge of tha swamp.

Meanwhile, Witherspoon had not been idle or unobservant. He had pushed forward after Blonay with precautions similar to those which the latter had practised; and, with a speed accelerated in accordance with the due increase of confidence arising from the absence of his horse, he had contrived to gain a point of observation which commanded the entrance to the swamp quite as soon as Blonay, and just when Humphries and his companions were about to pass into the pond. At first he saw none but the three companions; but, even while he gazed upon them from a place of shelter by the wayside, and at the distance of a few hundred yards, he became conscious, though yet without seeing the object, of the approach of some one on the opposite hand. The three disappeared from his sight, and, as the last sounds reached his ears of the tread of their horses as they plashed through the turbid waters of the creek, he distinctly beheld the person of a man moving hurriedly along its margin. In the next glance he saw that it was the half-breed.

"I have him—here's at you!" he cried to himself, as he raised his rifle. But, before he could pull trigger, his victim had disappeared.

Vexed and mortified, he was compelled to squat down in quiet in order to avoid being seen; and, hiding himself closely behind a bush, he waited and watched for a second opportunity. But this he was not destined to get so readily. While he looked he saw the whole line of canebrake, on the edge of the lagune, slightly agitated and waving at the tops as if under a sudden gust, but he saw no more of the person he pursued. In a little while he heard the feet of the returning horses once more plunging through the pond; and again did he see the cane-tops waving suddenly in front of a grove of huge cypresses, and as suddenly again subsiding into repose. Witherspoon could see no more of the enemy, and, half-bewildered, he awaited the return of Humphries, to unfold to him what he knew and how he had been disappointed.

Blonay, meanwhile, though maintaining a solicitous regard to his own concealment, kept a no less heedful watch upon the progress of his enemy. He looked out from his cover upon the return of Humphries; but, as he continued to be still accompanied by Davis and Frampton, there was evidently no opportunity for prosecuting his purpose. He sank back in silence to his place of shelter among the canes and cypresses.

Witherspoon had again noted the disturbance among the cane-tops, but he failed to see the intruder. It was with no small mortification that he unfolded to Humphries, as he came, the unsuccessful results of his watch.

"He is there, somewhere among the canes; but, d——n the nigger, you might as well look for a needle in a haystack as after him in such a place as that."

"But we will look for him there!" cried Humphries, dashing forward to the designated region. The rest followed him in several directions, completely encircling in their hunt the supposed place of Blonay's concealment.

He looked upon their search in composure and with scornful indifference; but he remained quiet all the while. They hunted him with all the passion of hatred, disappointment, and anxiety. They penetrated through brake and through brier; they tore aside the thickly-wedged masses of cane-twigs and saplings; traversed bog and water; pressed through bushes; and encircled trees — searching narrowly every spot and object, in the locality designated by Witherspoon, which might conceal a man: but they labored in vain. They did not find the fugitive. Yet his traces everywhere met their eyes. His footsteps were plainly perceptible on one or two miry banks; but the whole neighborhood was half-covered with water, and the traces which he made were accordingly soon lost. For more than an hour did they continue the search, until they wandered from the spot entirely. The quest was hopeless; and, vexed at his disappointment, Humphries was compelled to give up the pursuit in the performance of other duties. They had scarcely left the ground, however, before Blonay came forth from his place of concealment — the body of a hollow cypress, divided from the canebrake by a narrow creek, in a portion of which it grew.

"Adrat it! they thought to catch a weasel asleep, did they? I reckon it won't do this time. And now, I s'pose—"

The words were interrupted, and the soliloquy discontinued. The fugitive stooped to the earth as if to listen, then immediately hurried back through the shallow water, and into the tree where he had previously hidden himself.

CHAPTER XLV.

HUMPHRIES TREES THE HALF-BREED.

He had barely attained his place of shelter when Humphries returned. He returned alone. He had dismissed his comrades as no longer essential to his search, and had determined upon stealing back to the neighborhood where the half-breed had been last seen, placing himself in a position to watch him, and lingering till the latest possible moment, in the hope to see him emerge. The thoughts of Humphries were of the most annoying description. He reflected bitterly on the chances now before him, not only of his enemy's escape, but of his own continued danger. The whole labor of pursuit and stratagem was again to be taken over; and with this disadvantage, that, as they had now alarmed the half-breed, who must have been conscious of their recent pursuit and search, it would be necessary to adopt some new plan of action, and contrive some new scheme, before they could possibly hope to entrap him. In the meantime, to what danger was his threatened victim not exposed, since, while effecting nothing toward his own security, the recent adventure must only contribute to the increased wariness of his enemy.

Full of these bitter and distracting thoughts, he took post upon a little hillock, which rose slightly above the miry surface which spread all around him. A huge cypress, rising up from a shallow creek, stood like a forest monarch directly before his eyes. The cane, in which he had pursued so hopeless a search, spread away in a winding line beyond the creek, and upon its slightly-waving surface his eyes were fixed in intense survey.

"It was there—there he must be still," he said to himself,

as he looked upon its dense inclosure. "He will come out directly, when he thinks me quite gone, and when he can hear nothing. I will wait for him, though I wait till sunset."

He had taken a place of watch which gave him a full view of the canebrake and the scattered cypresses before it, while his position was concealed at the same time, by a cluster of bushes, from any one emerging from the region he surveyed. Here, squatting low, he prepared his rifle, having carefully prepared an opening for it through the bushes, whence its muzzle might be projected at a moment's warning; and, with eyes sharpened by a feeling of anxiety little short of desperation, he lay quietly, the agent of a deadly hate and a shuddering fear, watchful for that opportunity which should gratify the one passion, and silence all the apprehensions of the other.

While he watched in quiet, he heard a slight noise immediately at hand. Something reached his ears like the friction of bark. His breathings became suppressed in the intenseness of his anxiety. He felt that his enemy was near him, and his hope grew into a gnawing appetite, which made his whole frame tremble in the nervous desire which it occasioned. The noise was repeated a little more distinctly—distinctly enough, indeed, to indicate the direction from which it came. His glance rested upon the aged cypress which stood immediately before him.

"Could he be there?" was his self-made inquiry. The tree stood in the water. The hollow did not seem large enough above the creek to admit the passage of a human body. "Yet it might be so." He regretted, while he gazed, that they had not examined it; and he regretted this the more as he now saw that the upper edges of the hollow above the creek were still wet, as if they had been splashed by the hurried passage of some large body into the tree. He kept quiet, however, while these thoughts were going through his mind, and determined patiently to wait events.

"He must come out at last," was his muttered thought, "if he is there, and I can wait, I reckon, jist as long as he."

Was it an instinct that prompted him to raise his eyes at this moment, from the hollow at the foot of the cypress to the shaft of the tree, as it stretched away above? He did so; and, in the sudden glance which he gave, the glare of a wide and well-known eye met his own, staring around, from a narrow and natural fissure in the stupendous column some ten feet from its base. With a howl of positive delight he sprang to his feet, and the drop of the deadly instrument fell upon the aperture. But, before he could spring the lock or draw the trigger, the object had disappeared.

The half-breed, for it was he, had sunk down the moment Humphries met his eye, and was no more to be seen. But he was there! That was the consolation of his enemy.

"He is there, I have him!" he cried aloud. No answer reached him from within. Humphries bounded into the water to the hollow at the bottom of the tree, through which the slender form of Blonay had resolutely compressed itself. He thrust his hand into the opening, and endeavored, by grasping the legs of the half-breed, to drag him down to the aperture; but he failed entirely to do so. A bulging excrescence on the tree, a knob or knee, as it is called, within, served the beleaguered man as a place of rest; and upon this, firmly planting his feet, no effort of his enemy could possibly dislodge him. To thrust his rifle up the hollow, and shoot as he stood, was the next thought of Humphries; but the first attempt to do this convinced him of the utter impracticability of the design. The opening, though sufficiently large for the entrance of a body so flexible as that of a man, was yet too short to admit of the passage of a straight, unyielding shaft of the rifle's length, unless by burying the instrument in the water to a depth so great as would bring the lock much below it. The difficulty was a novel one, and for a moment the practised woodman was at fault. What was he to do? His enemy was within his reach, yet beyond his control, and might as well be a thousand miles off. To leave the tree, to go in search of his companions, or to procure an axe to fell it, would only be to afford an opportunity for the egress and escape of his victim. This was not to be thought upon. He seized his knife, and though assured that by its use he could do no more than annoy the half-breed, situated where he was, and could by no possibility inflict a vital injury, he yet proceeded to employ it.

"It may bring him out," he muttered to himself, "it'll vex and bring him out."

He thrust the weapon up the hollow, and struck right and left at the feet and ankles of the inmate. But with the first graze of the weapon upon his legs Blonay drew them up contracting his knees, an effort which the immense size of the tree, the hollow of which might have contained three men with ease, readily enabled him to make. Humphries soon saw the fruitlessness of his effort with the knife, and, seemingly, the fruitlessness of any effort which he could then make. In his rage, exasperated at the vicinity of his foe, yet of his seeming safety, he shouted aloud, in the hope to bring back his departed companions. A fiendish chuckle sounded scornfully from within the tree, and seemed to taunt him with his feebleness and fury. He renewed his efforts, he struck idly with his knife within the hollow, until, burying the blade in one of the projecting knobs, it snapped off short at the handle, and was of no more service. Furious at these repeated failures, and almost exhausted by his efforts, he poured forth curses and denunciations in the utmost profusion upon the unheeding and seemingly indifferent half-breed.

"Come out like a man," he cried to him, in an idle challenge; "come out and meet your enemy, and not, like a snake, crawl into your hollow, and lie in waiting for his heel. Come out, you skunk, and you shall have a fair fight, and nobody shall come between us. You shall have your distance jist as you want it, and it shall be the quickest fire that shall make the difference of chances between us. Come out, you spawn of a nigger, and face me, if you're a man."

Thus did he run on in his ineffectual fury, and impotently challenge an enemy who was quite too wary to give up the vantage-ground which he possessed. The same fiendish chuckle which had enraged the trooper so much before, again responded to his challenge from the tree, again stimulated him to newer efforts, which, like the past, were unavailing. The half-breed condescended no other reply. He gave no response whatsoever to the denunciations of his enemy; but, coolly turning himself occasionally in his spacious sheath, he now and then raised himself slightly upon his perch, and placing his mouth abreast of the upper aperture in the tree, gratified himself by an occasional inhalation of the fresh air — a commodity not so readily afforded by his limited accommodations.

Humphries, meanwhile, almost exhausted by his own fury not less than by its hopeless labors, had thrown himself upon the bank in front of the opening, watching it with the avidity of an eagle. But Blonay gave him no second chance for a shot while he lay in this position. He watched in vain. Even as he lay, however, a new plan suggested itself to his mind, and one so certain of its effect, that he cursed himself for his stupidity that did not suffer him to think of it before. With the thought, he started to his feet. Detached masses of old decaying trees, the remains of many a forest of preceding ages, lay scattered around him. Here and there a lightwood knot, and here and there the yet undecayed branch, the tribute of some still living pine, to the passing hurricane, lay contiguously at hand. He gathered them up with impetuous rapidity. He collected a pile at the foot of the cypress, and prepared himself for the new experiment. Selecting from this pile one of the largest logs, he thrust it through the water, and into the hollow of the tree, seeking to wedge it between the inner knobs on which the feet of Blonay were evidently resting. But the half-breed soon became aware of the new design, which he opposed, as well as he could, with a desperate effort. He saw, and was instantly conscious of, his danger. With his feet he baffled for a long time the efforts of his enemy, until, enraged at length, Humphries seized upon a jagged knot of lightwood, which he thrust against one of the striving legs of the half-breed, and employing another heavy knot as a mallet, he drove the wedge forward unrelentingly against the yielding flesh, which was torn and lacerated dreadfully by the sharp edges of the wood. Under the sudden pain of the wound, the feet were drawn up, and the woodman was suffered to proceed in his design.

The miserable wretch in the tree, thus doomed to be buried alive, was now willing to come to terms with his enemy. His voice hollowly reached the ears of his exulting captor, as he agreed to accept his terms of fight, if he would suffer him to come down. But the reply of Humphries partook somewhat of the savage nature of his victim.

"No, no! you d—d skunk, you shall die in your hole, like a varmint as you are; and the cypress shall be your coffin, as it has been your house."

The voice within muttered something of fight..

"It's too late for that," was the reply. "I gave you the chance once, and you wouldn't take it. It's the worse for you, since you don't get another. Here you shall stay, if hard chunks and solid lightwood can keep you, until your yellow flesh rots away from your cursed bones! Here you stay till the lightning rips open your coffin, or the hurricane in September tumbles you into the swamp."

The voice of Blonay was still heard, though more and more feebly, as the hard wood was driven into the hollow—mass wedging mass—until all sounds from within, whether of pleading or defiance, seemed to die away into a plaintive murmur, that came faintly through the thickening barrier, and was almost unheard by Humphries, as, with the knotty lever which he employed, he sent the heavy wedges, already firm enough, more thoroughly into the bosom of the tree.

His labor was at length completed. The victim was fastened up securely, beyond his own efforts of escape. He was effectually sealed up, and the seal could only be taken off by a strong hand from without. Where, in that deep forest recess, wild and tangled, could succor find him out? What hope that his feeble voice could reach the ears of any passing mortal! There was no hope but in the mercy of his enemy, and of that the captive and doomed man could have no hope, even if he pleaded for his life,—an idea that never once entered into his mind.

His doom was written, and the partisan paused before the tree, and his eye rested on the aperture above. The body of the imprisoned man was heard to writhe about in his cell. Humphries stepped back, the better to survey the aperture. In another moment he beheld the blear eyes of his victim peering forth upon him, and, firm and fearless as he was, he shuddered at their expression. Their natural ugliness was enlarged and exaggerated by the intensity of his despair. Before, they had been but disgusting—they were now frightful to the beholder. As he looked upon him, the first feeling of Humphries was to lift his rifle and shoot him; but, as the weapon was elevated, he saw that the half-breed no longer shrank from the meditated shot. On the contrary, he seemed now rather to invoke his death, as even a mercy in that preferable form, at the hands of his enemy. But his desire was not complied with.

"No, no. Why should I waste the bullet upon you? You took to the hollow like a beast. You shall die like one. It's a fit death for one like you. You've been hunting after my blood quite too long. I won't spill yours, but I'll leave it to dry up in your heart, and you shall feel it freezing and drying up all the time."

He surveyed his victim as he spoke with a malicious joy, which at length grew into a painful sort of delight, it was so intense—so maddening—so strange, since it followed a transition from the extremest sense of appreciation to one of unlooked-for security. His ecstasies at length broke forth into tumultuous and unmitigated laughter.

The deportment of the half-breed was changed. His features seemed to undergo elevation, and the utter hopelessness of his fate, as he now beheld it, even gave dignity to their expression. He spoke to his enemy in language of the most biting asperity. His sarcasm was coarse, but effective, as it accorded with his own nature and the education of his foe. He taunted him with cowardice, with every meanness, and strove to irritate him by reproaches of himself and his connections, aspersions upon his mother and his sister, in language and assertion, which, among the vulgar, is almost always effectual in irritating to the last degree of human violence. The object of Blonay was to provoke Humphries to the use of the more ready weapon, which would have given him death without the prolonged torture consequent upon such a doom as that to which he was now destined. But the partisan readily divined his object, and denied him the desired boon.

"No, no, catch old birds with chaff," he replied, coolly, "You shall die as you are. I'll just take the liberty of putting a plug into that hollow, which will give you less chance to talk out, as you now seem pleased to do. I'll stop out a little more of the sweet air, so that you may enjoy better what I leave you."

Thus saying, he threw together a few chunks at the foot of the tree, and, rising upon them, well provided with a wedge estimated to fit the aperture, he prepared to drive it in, and placed it at the opening for that purpose. The desperate Blonay thrust one hand through the crevice, in the vain hope to exclude the wedge. But a blow from the lightwood knot with which Humphries had provided himself as a sort of mallet, crushed the extended fingers almost into a mass, and the half-breed must have fainted from the pain, as the hand was instantly withdrawn; and when the partisan drove in the wedge, the face of the victim had sunk below the opening, and was no longer to be seen. His task completed, he descended from his perch, threw aside the chunks which had supported him, and set off to find his horse. He was at last secure from the hunter of blood—he had triumphed—and yet he could not keep down the fancy, which continually, as he went, imbodied the supposed cries of the half-breed in little gusts of wind, that seemed to pursue him; and, when he emerged from the wood, a strange chill went through his bones, and he looked back momently, even when the gigantic cypress, which was the sepulchre of his enemy, no longer reared up its solemn spire in his sight. It was no longer behind him. It seemed to move before him faster than his horse; and he spurred the animal furiously forward, seeking to pass the fast-travelling tree, and to escape the moaning sound which ever came after him upon the breeze.

CHAPTER XLVI.

THE SIGNAL.

The deed was done; and Humphries, fatigued by a long and arduous duty on the previous night, and doubly so from the exciting circumstances just narrated, hurried to his place of retreat and repose in the swamp covert of the partisans. He could sleep now. For a long period his sleep had been troubled and unsatisfactory. His apprehensions were now quieted, and sweet must be that first sleep which we feel to be secure from the efforts of a long-sleepless enemy.

His companions, meanwhile, had the duties of the scout to execute, and each had gone upon his several tasks. Witherspoon, with whom our course now lies, true to his friend, proceeded at once to the woods that surrounded the camp of Barsfield. He maintained a close watch upon the premises in which Mellichampe lay a prisoner. How he knew of the youth's predicament may not be said, but certain it is he was informed both as to the nature of his injuries and his condition. He had, probably, lurked in the hollow, or listened from a tree, while an incautious sentinel prattled to his comrade; or, which is not less probable, he had gathered his intelligence from some outlying negro of the plantation, whose address enabled him to steal forth at intervals, in spite of the surrounding sentinels.

Solicitous, to the last degree, for the safety of the youth, of whose safety, while in the custody of Barsfield, he half-despaired, he availed himself of his duties as a scout to lurk about the neighborhood, in the faint hope to communicate with, or in some other way to serve, the prisoner. Night after night, for a week before the period to which we have now come, had he cheered the heart and strengthened the hope of Mellichampe with his well known-wnistle. It may be scarce necessary to say, that the faithful inferior found no less gratification in this sad office than did the youth to whom it taught the unrelaxing, though as yet ineffectual, watchfulness of a friend.

The dexterity of Witherspoon admirably sorted with his fidelity and courage. Fearlessly did he penetrate the nearest points to which he might approach, without certainty of being seen, of the camp of his enemy. The frequent exercise of his faculties as a woodman, a native ease and self-confidence, and a heart too much interested in a single object to feel any scruples or fear any danger, prompted him to a degree of hardihood which, in a less admirable scout, would have been childish audacity; but it was in him the result of a calm conviction of his own readiness of resource, and of his general ability to meet emergencies. He knew himself as well as his enemy, and relied upon his own sense of superiority. This confidence, however, seduced him into no incautiousness. He timed his movements with a just reference to all the circumstances of his situation; chose his route and designed his purpose well before entering upon it; and, this done, dashed forward with the boldness of the tiger, and the light, scarce perceptible footstep of the wild turkey in April.

It was night when, after making a circuit around Barsfield's position, and scanning it carefully on every side, he reached a copse at the head of the avenue, where, on a previous occasion, we found himself and Mellichampe concealed. It was an old haunt, and he threw himself on the grass and mused listlessly, like one who, after long strifes and a heating exercise abroad, comes home to the repose and permitted freedoms of his own fireside and family. The camp-fires were sprinkled about the woods before him, looking dimly enough in contrast with the pale but brighter gleams of the now ascending moon. The house in which Mellichampe was confined stood a little beyond, but as yet undistinguishable. The scout lay and mused upon the fate and probable fortunes of his friend, and his thoughts, breaking through the bounds of his own restraining consciousness, were framed into words upon his lips. without his own volition.

"I could swear he answered me last night. There's no mistake. Three times it come upon the wind; first, quick and shrill, to ketch the ear — then slow and sad — and then quick and shrill agin. 'Twas a great distance to hear a whistle, but the wind come up jist then, and I'm sure I heard it; and it was sich a blessed sort of music, coming from Airnest, that, by gracious! — I can't help it — I'll go closer agin, and see if I can't git some more of it. It's a sign he's doing better if he's able to whistle, and it's a clear sign he hears me, when he's able to answer. I'll try it agin soon as I see that big fire kindled that burns upon the left, for then I know they'll be busy at the supper. He shall hear me agin, by gimini! He shall know I ain't forgotten him — though, to be sure, there's but little can be done for him yet. Them d—d blasted tories are too thick about Barsfield, and the 'fox' must wait and watch a little longer before he can make a break. Gimini! it's hard enough, but there's no way to help it."

He soliloquized thus upon a variety of matters, all bearing upon this subject; and, had a scout of the enemy been crouching among the branches of the tree above him, he might have picked up for Barsfield many a valuable little secret touching the condition and the force of Marion. The faithful Witherspoon was one of those ingenuous persons who do not hesitate to speak their thoughts out freely, and who, thinking to himself, is yet quite as likely to be confiding and communicative, as if he was really engaged in delivering a message to his superior. You could have heard from his lips on this occasion, without much striving to hear, what were the general objects of the partisan — how he was busy gathering his men in the swamp for the co-operation, in future strife, with the newly-forming army of Greene — of designs upon the rapidly-rushing, and perhaps too self-confident, career of Bannister Tarleton; and, to come more immediately to the interest before us, he might have learned now, for the first time, as we do, of the organization of an especial corps, to be commanded by Major Singleton, having for its object the rescue of the youthful Mellichampe, whenever it should be ascertained that he was to be removed to Charleston. This was a primary consideration with the partisan. The tender mercies of a Charleston commandant, and of a board of British officers for inquiry, were well known; and the sacrifice of the youth was a fear with all his friends, should he not be rescued from the clutches of his foe before his transfer to the scene of trial. Too hazardous an enterprise to aim at this rescue while the youth lay in Barsfield's well-defended encampment, the partisan simply prepared himself to be in readiness at the moment when a signal from his scouts should apprise him of the movement of any guard of the enemy in the direction of the city. An ambush on the wayside was the frequent resort of warriors who were only too few, too poorly armed and provided, to risk a more daring sort of warfare.

The camp of Barsfield was soon illuminated by the additional fire of which Witherspoon had spoken. As soon as he beheld it he proceeded, cautiously but fearlessly, to pass the intervening road; then, keeping close alongside of the left or upward bank of the avenue leading to the settlement, he stole along from tree to tree, until he heard the measured tread of the more advanced sentinels. A necessity for greater precaution induced a pause. He stole, a moment after, to the edge of the ditch, into which he descended; then, crawling upon hands and knees up the bank, he looked over into the avenue, and distinguished the glittering raiment of the first sentinel. In the distance he beheld a second, with corresponding pace, moving his "lonely round." Resting his chin upon his palm, Witherspoon took a cool survey of the prospect, and did not even withdraw himself into the hollow when the nearest soldier, having gained his limit, wheeled to retrace his steps.

"I could nail that fellow's best button now with a sly bullet, if 'twas any use, and he wouldn't know what hurt him," was the half-muttered thought of the scout as the sentinel approached. The man came forward until he stood abreast of our scout, who buried himself in the long grass as he approached; then, again wheeling, he commenced his monotonous return. It was now the moment for Witherspoon: he gathered himself up instantly, waited in readiness until the sentinel had gone half of his distance, then, with a single bound, leaped down into the avenue, and sought his way across. His tread was light, wonderfully light, for a man so heavy; but it did not escape the quick ear of the watchful Briton. He turned instantly, presented his piece, and challenged. But the coast was clear; there was nothing to be seen; the scout had already crossed the road, and was sheltered in the thick copse on the other bank of the avenue. The leaves and brush were shaken, and the only response made to the challenge of the sentry was the hooting of a melancholy owl, and a noise like the shaking of wings among the branches.

"What's the matter?" cried the companion sentinel, approaching the challenger, who had remained stationary in the brief interval occupied by this event. "What have you seen?"

"Nothing — it's only an owl. These woods are full of them; the d—d things keep one starting on all sides as if the 'swamp-fox' himself was scrambling over the ditch."

The scout lay close, and heard the question and response. He chuckled to himself with no little self-complaisance as he listened.

"By gimini!" he half-muttered aloud, "what a poor skunk of a fellow I'd be, now, if my edication was no better than that sentry's. Not to know a man's hollow from a blind bird's!"

Waiting a few moments until the guardians of the night had resumed their walk, he at length boldly left the copse, and proceeded without hesitation, though cautiously, still nearer to the house which held the prisoner.

Meanwhile, full of anxiety, the lovers lingered together. This was the night on which Scipio was despatched in search of Witherspoon, and all their thoughts were necessarily given to his successful management of the enterprise. Well might they be anxious; and how natural was the deep and breathless silence which, for protracted hours, overspread the apartment as if with a dense and heavier mantle than that of night. The arm of Mellichampe enfolded the waist of the maiden. She lay sadly, as was her wont, upon its supporting strength; and her cheek, with all the confidence of true and unsophisticated affection, rested upon his bosom. She feared nothing — she doubted nothing—at that moment; for she knew how noble was the heart that beat beneath it.

Her fears were elsewhere. The fate of her lover hung suspended, as it were, upon a thread. He was about to seek a perilous chance for life, to escape from a more perilous, and, as it appeared to them, an unavoidable necessity. Upon the cunning of the slave—upon his successful search after the partisans—and upon their readiness and ability for the adventure, the life of Mellichampe depended. How many contingencies to be met and overcome! how many difficulties to be avoided or surmounted! how many dangers to be hazarded and sought! The accumulating thoughts of these took from her all hope. She was no longer sanguine, though her more buoyant lover, in all the eloquent warmth of a young heart, strove to persuade her into confidence. She lay upon his bosom, and wept bitter tears.

Suddenly there came again to the apartment the faint, distant, but distinct sound—the whistle of the woodman. Mellichampe lifted her head from its place of rest, and his heart increased its beatings. His eye brightened; and, as she beheld its glance, her own kindled amid its tears. Again and again did the well-known notes glide into the apartment, and well did the youth know then that his friends were at hand.

"Hear! hear it, my Janet? He is there—it is Witherspoon—it is his signal—the same that has come to me, and cheered me, night after night, when you could no longer be with me. Do you not hear it?"

The sense of the maiden did not seem so quick as that of her lover. She paused; and, though her eye had caught a glow from the kindled expression of his, it still seemed that she doubted the reality of the sounds when an appeal was made to her own distinct consciousness. She was a sweet dependant—one who could receive consolation from the assurances of another; but, save in love, who could give little in return.

"Is it a whistle, Ernest?—it seems to me little more than a murmur of the wind... Ah! I do—I do hear it now—it is; it is a whistle." And her head sank, in joy, again upon the manly and aroused bosom of her lover.

"It is he, and all's well if Scipio does not miss him. Janet, dear love, we must see to this. Scipio may not yet be gone; and, if not, methinks I can direct him to the very spot whence these sounds come. I know I can. See, dear—hark! To the north—directly to the north—is it not? You hear it now—there, in that direction; and that is toward the little bay that lies between this house and the avenue. That's just the spot in which a good scout would lurk at such a moment, and from that spot he knows that I can hear his signal. He must be there now; and if Scipio passes in that direction, he must find him. If not gone, the fellow must go at once, for Witherspoon can't remain long in one spot while in this neighborhood. The scouts may trouble him. See to it, then, dear Janet—see if Scipio be not gone, and send him on that course: and hold me not burdensome, dearest, that I give you, in these dangerous hours, more employment than affection."

"Speak not thus, dear Ernest," replied the maiden, fondly, as she proceeded to execute the mission—"speak not thus—not thus to me. Are not Love's labors his pleasures always? does he not rejoice to serve? I do, I am sure. I feel that my best pleasures are my labors always—always when they are taken for you."

"Heaven bless you, my Janet," he murmured fondly in reply, as his lips were pressed upon her forehead; "Heaven bless you, and make me worthy of all this devotion."

CHAPTER XLVII.

COW-CHASING.

But Scipio was already gone upon his mission, and the maiden looked for him in vain. The next fear of Mellichampe was that he should miss the person he sought. Scipio, however, though he had left the house, had not yet passed the enclosure. The line of sentinels had yet to be gone through; and a task, like that we have just seen overcome by Witherspoon, had yet to be performed by the negro in crossing the avenue. He had his arts also, and his plan was one after his own heart and fashion.

Creeping along by the fence, which ran circuitously from the house of the overseer to the avenue, and which we have seen employed as a screen to Singleton's riflemen, he reached the entrance of the avenue, though without being able to cross it at the point he made. The sentinels in this quarter were too numerous and close to permit him to attempt it there, and, keeping along the skirts of the copse and under its shade, he moved upward. The soldiers of Barsfield were more watchful without than within; and, though but a few yards separated the negro, in his stealthy progress, from the pacing sentinel, such was the address of Scipio, that he occasioned not the slightest apprehension. But to cross the avenue, and reach the dense wood that lay on the opposite side, was the work of most difficult achievement.

To accomplish this, it was the aim of Scipio to pass through a drain which crossed the avenue, and conducted the waters from the two ditches, when overflowed, into a third, by means of which they were carried off into a hollow bay lying some fifty yards distant in the woods. To penetrate the umbrageous copse on one side of the avenue — to watch the moment when the sentinel's back should be turned — then, dropping down silently into the ditch, to crawl into the drain, the mouth of which was immediately alongside of it, was the scheme of Scipio.

In pursuance of this scheme, he passed on with all the stealthy adroitness of the wildcat — now hurrying, as he found himself too much without the cover of the trees — now crawling forward, on hands and knees, as the clambering vines around him set a firm barrier against undue uprightness — and now lying or standing, motionless, as any warning or occasional sounds reached his ears, from either the camp which he had left, or the woods to which he was speeding. The exceeding brightness of the moonlight rendered increased precautions necessary, and gave bitter occasion of complaint to the negro, to whom, like all of his color, the darkness of the night was a familiar thing, and opposed no sort of obstruction to his nocturnal wanderings when the plantations otherwise were all fast asleep, He penetrated the copse, and, thrusting his sable visage through the shrubbery, looked from side to side upon the two sentinels who paced that portion of the avenue in sight. He duly noted their distances and position, and, receding a pace, threw himself flat upon the bank and crawled downward into the ditch. The mouth of the drain lay a little above him, conveniently open and large; and there could have been no sort of difficulty, when he once reached that point, of making his way through it into the opposite cover.

But it so happened that Scipio, in his progress, gave more of his regards to the sentinel, and less to the path immediately before him, than was either prudent or proper. He did not perceive a slender and decayed pine-limb which lay partially over the route he was pursuing. His hand rested heavily upon it in his progress, and it gave way beneath the pressure, with a crack which might have reached the ears of a sentinel at a much greater distance. With the sound, he turned suddenly in the direction of the negro. The poor fellow had his work to begin anew. He had plunged, with the yielding branch, incontinently into the mire, and in the first moment of the accident his entire face had been immersed in its slime.

However, there was no time for regrets, and but little for reflection. The proceeding of Scipio was that of an instinct rather than a thought. He heard the fierce challenge of the sentinel, who yet did not see him. He saw that, in any endeavor at flight, he must be shot; and to seek to prosecute his scheme would be idle, as the drain lay between him and the advancing soldier; he could not reach it in time to escape his eyes. In boldness alone could he hope to escape; and, in the moment of sudden peril, audacity is frequently the truest wisdom. He rose upon his feet with the utmost composure; and, without seeking to retreat or advance, exclaimed as he rose, in all the gusto of a well-fed negro's phraseology, with a degree of impudence which might have imposed upon a more sagacious head than that of the sentinel before him—

"Looka 'ere, misser sodger, tek' care how you shoot at maussa nigger. Good surbant berry scarce in dis country; and, when gemplemen hab sarbant like Scip, he ain't foolish 'nough for sell 'em. No gould—no silber money guine buy Scip; so take care, I tell you, how you spile you' pocket."

"Why, what the h—ll, Scip, are you doing there?" demanded the gruff soldier, who knew him well.

" Ki, Mass Booram, wha' for you ax sich foolish question? Enty you see I tumble in de ditch? Suppose you tink I guine dere o' purpose, and spile my best breeches? You's wrong. I hold on de branch, and de branch breck, and so I tumble. Wha' more? Da's all."

" And suppose, Scip, that, instead of coming up to you civily, as I have done, I should have sent a bullet into your ribs, or poked you a little with this bagnet?"

" You bin do sich ting, Mass Booram, I say you no gempleman. Nebber gempleman hit nigger if he kin help it; 'kaise a nigger's a 'spectable character wha' can't help heself. Da's a good reason for udder people for no hu't 'em. 'Tis only poor buckrah dat does trouble nigger. Scip has ambitions for gempleman; but a poor buckrah, Mass Booram, he no wuss tree copper."

"All very well, Scipio; but what brought you here, old fellow? Don't you know you have no business in this quarter?"

"Who tell you dat, Mass Booram? He's a d—n fool of a nigger hesself if he tell you so. Wha's de reason I say so? 'kaise, you see, I *hab* business in dis quarter. Let me ax you few questions, Mass Booram, and talk like a gempleman, 'kaise I can't 'spect white man when he lib 'pon gar-broff."

"Go on, Scip," replied the soldier, complacently.

"Fuss, den, you know I hab maussa, enty?"

"Yes, to be sure; if you hadn't, Scip, I'd take you for myself; I like a good nigger mightily."

"'Spec you does, but da's nothing; you hab for ax if good nigger likes you. Maussa want to sell Scip, he gib um ticket look he owner; da's de business. But da's not wha' we hab for talk 'bout. If I b'long to maussa, wha' he name?"

"Why, Mr. Berkeley, to be sure!"

"Da's a gospel. I b'longs to Dick Berkeley—dis plantation b'long to Dick Berkeley—Dick Berkeley hab he cow, enty, Mass Booram?"

"Yes, cow and calf in plenty, and enough of everything beside. I only wish I had half as much, I would not carry this d—d heavy musket."

"Ha! you leff off sodger? You right, Mass Booram; sodger is bad business, nebber sodger is good gempleman. He hab for cuss—he hab for drunk; he hab for hu't udder people wha's jist as good and much better dan heself. I terra you what, Mass Booram, Scip wouldn't be sodger for de world and all da's in it; he radder be poor buckra—any ting sooner dan sodger. A sodger is a poor debbil, dat hab no ambition for 'spectability: I radder be nigger-driber any day, dan cappin, like Mass Barsfield."

"You would, would you? you d—d conceited crow in a corn-field! Why, Scipio, you're the most vainest flycatcher in the country," said the other, good-naturedly. Scipio received the speech as a compliment.

"Tank you, Mass Booram. You's a gempleman, and can comprehend. But wha' I was telling you? ah! Massa hab cow. Wha' den? Now I guine show you wha' bring me here.

Da's some of you sodger bin guine tief de milk, and breck down de gate of de cow-lot. Wha' den?—Brindle gone—Becky gone—Polly gone. Tree of maussa best cow gone, 'kaise you sodger lub milk. Wha' Scip for do? Wha' maussa tell um. It's dat is brin me here. I guine look for de cow. I no bring um home by daylight, maussa say driber shall gib me h–ll."

"And so you want to pass here, Scipio, in order to look after the cattle? Suppose now I should not suffer you to pass, suppose I should send you back to get your flogging?"

"Suppose you does?" said the other, boldly; "suppose you does, you's no gempleman. Da's a mean buckrah, Mass Booram, wha' kin do so to poor nigga. Wha' for you guine let maussa gib me h–ll? I ebber hurt you, Mass Booram? 'Tis you own sodger guine for tief de milk, dat's let out Brindle and Becky. Scip nebber let 'em out. Wha' for you no say — whip de sodger—wha' for you say whip de nigga?"

"It is a hard case, Scip, and you shall pass, though it's agin orders. But remember, old boy, when you bring home the cows, I must have the first milking. You shall provide me with milk so long as we stay here for saving you from this flogging."

"Da's a bargain," said the negro, preparing to depart: "da's fair. Mass Booram, I bin always tink you was a gempleman, dat hab a lub for poor nigga. I kin speak for you after dis."

"Thank you, Scipio," said the other good-naturedly. "Take piece of gunja—he berry good, Mass Booram—my wife make 'em."

The negro broke his molasses-cake evenly between himself and the soldier, who did not scruple readily to receive it. A few more words were exchanged between them, when, passing the avenue, Scipio hurried forward, and found himself, his chief difficulties surmounted, in the deep bosom of the adjoining woods.

Free of all present restraint, the tongue of Scipio, after a very common fashion among negroes, discoursed freely to its roprietor, aloud, upon the difficulties yet before him.

"Well, 'spose I pass one, da's noting. Plenty more, I speck, scatter 'bout here in dese woods; and, ef he ain't tory—wha' den? Some of dese Marion men jis' as bad. He make not'ing of shoot poor nigga, if it's only to git he jacket. Cracky! wha' dat now? I hear someting. Cha! 'tis de win' only. He hab all kind of noise in dis wood for frighten people— sometime he go like a man groan wid a bullet-hole work in he back. Nudder time he go like a pusson was laughing; but I don't see noting here to make pusson laugh. Da's a noise now I don't comprehend—like de nocking ob old dry sticks togedder; 'spose its some bird da's flopping off de moschetus wid his wings. It's a bad place in dis woods, and I wonder wha' make dat Dick Wedderspoon lub 'em so. Whay him now, 'tis like a blind nigga that don't come when you want um. I no bin look arter um now, I plump jist 'pon um. I no hab noting to ax um, he sure for answer. I no hab noting to gib um, he sure for put out he hand for something. He's a—"

At that moment a heavy slap upon the cheek from a ponderous hand saluted the soliloquizing Scipio, and arrested his complainings. The light flashed from the negro's eyes as he turned at this rough salutation.

"Cracky! Who da dat—Mass Wedderspoon?"

"Ah, you rascal—you know'd well enough. You only talked out your impudent stuff for me to hear, Scipio, 'cause you know'd I was close at hand."

"I sway to G-d, Mass Wedderspoon, I nebber b'lieb you been so close. I bin look for you."

"Why, you numskull, you came a great deal out of your way, for I was behind you all the time. You managed that sentinel mighty well, Scip, I heard the whole of your palaver, and really did believe at first that the cows were off, and you were going after them."

"And how come you no b'lieb now, Mass Wedderspoon!"

"Because, you were no sooner out of his sight fairly, but you began to go faster than before—much faster than you ever did go when you went out into the swamp after cattle."

"Da's a trute. But you know, Mass Wedderspoon, wha' I come out for—you know who I looking arter!"

"No—I do not'; but I want to know a good deal that you can tell me, so the sooner you begin the better. How is Airnest, for the first?"

" He mos' well; but here's de paper—read 'em—he tell you ebbry ting."

The scout seized the scrawl, and strove to trace out its contents by moonlight, but, failing to do so, he drew a pistol from his belt, and, extracting the load, flashed the priming in a handful of dry straw which Scipio heaped together. With some little difficulty he deciphered the scrawl, while the negro kept plying the fuel to the blaze. Its contents were soon read and quickly understood. Witherspoon was overjoyed. The prospect of Mellichampe's release, even though at the risk of a desperate fight, was productive to him of the most complete satisfaction.

"Go back," he said, after a while, to the negro; "go back and tell Airnest that you've seen me, and that all's well. Tell him I'll go my death for him, and do my best to git others, though the time is monstrous short."

"You guine git 'em clear, Mass Wedderspoon, from de d——d hook-nose tory?" asked the negro.

"I'll try, Scip, by the Etarnal!"

"Da's a gempleman. But dem little guns—da's jist what Mass Airnest want. He must hab something, Mass Wedderspoon, for hole he own wid dem tory. Put de bullet in de mout' of de pistol, I'll carry um."

"'Spose they find 'em on you, Scip?"

"Enty I fin 'em. I pick um up in de path. You tink dem tory guine catch weasel asleep, when he 'tan' by Scip. No notion ob such ting, I tell you."

The scout gave him both pistols, which the negro immediately lashed about his middle, carefully concealing them from exposure by the thick waistband of his pantaloons.

"Now go, Scip—go back to Airnest, and tell him I've set my teeth to help him, and do what he axes. I'm guine back now to the boys in camp, and I reckon it won't be too much to say that Major Singleton will bring a smart chance of us to do the d—dest, by a leetle; that ever yet was done to help a friend out of a hobble."

They separated—one seeking the camp of Barsfield, the other that of Marion, which, at this time, a few miles only divided.

CHAPTER XLVIII.

REMORSE.

The absence of Blonay occasioned no small annoyance to all the leading parties at "Piney Grove." Suspicious of all things and persons, the tory captain, who depended for the prosecution of his scheme upon Blonay's ministry, began to fear that the half-breed was playing him false. Not confiding to him at first, under a doubt of his integrity, the suspicions of Janet and Mellichampe were duly increased by his absence. Neither of these parties seemed to think of the possibility of evil having befallen him. It was more natural, he was so low and destitute, to think of his evil nature rather than of his human liability to mishap.

But Barsfield made his preparations, notwithstanding the absence of his ally. He had already chosen a certain number of his more resolute and ready men, to whom certain stations were to be assigned, along where the course of Mellichampe lay, under the guidance of the half-breed. The tory, however, had not communicated anything calculated to arouse the suspicions of those whom he employed. That communication was left over for the last moment. He simply prescribed their places of watch, and commanded the utmost vigilance.

There was another order given about this time by Captain Barsfield, which had its annoyances for other parties in our narrative. To Lieutenant Clayton was assigned the duty, with a small escort, of conveying Mellichampe for trial to Charleston, in the beginning of the ensuing week. This order produced some little sensation.

"And you really leave 'Piney Grove' so soon, Lieutenant Clayton?" was the inquiry of Rose Duncan that evening, shortly after tea was over, of the hitherto gay gallant who sat beside her. The old gentleman, Mr. Berkeley — as had been usual with him for some time past — had retired early. His daughter, as a matter now of course, was with her lover; and Rose and Clayton as was much the case since the capture of Mellichampe, were *tête-à-tête*. There was nothing in the words themselves indicative of more than a common feeling of curiosity — nothing, perhaps, in the manner of their expression; and yet the lieutenant could not help the fancy that persuaded him to think that there was a hesitating thickness of voice in the utterance of the speaker, that spoke of a present emotion. His eyes were at once turned searchingly upon her face, as he listened to the flattering inquiry, and her own sank to the ground beneath his gaze. He replied after the pause of a single instant.

"If I could persuade myself, Miss Duncan, that you shared in any degree the regret which I feel at leaving 'Piney Grove' though it would greatly increase my reluctance to do so, it would afford me no small consolation during my absence."

The lieutenant began to look serious and sentimental, and the maiden recovered her caprice. Her answer was full of girlish simplicity, while her manner was most annoying, arch, and satirical.

"Well, I do, Mr. Clayton — I do regret your going — that I do, from the bottom of my heart. Bless me, what should I have done all this time but for you? — how monstrous dull must have been these hours. I really shall miss you very much."

The lieutenant was disappointed. He had not looked for a transition so sudden, in the voice, words, and manner of his fair but capricious companion; and, for a moment, he was something daunted. But, recovering himself with an effort, as from frequent intercourse he had discovered that the only way to contend with one of her character was to assume some of its features, he proceeded to reply in a manner which had the effect of compelling her somewhat to resume that momentary gravity of demeanor which had accompanied her first speech; and which, as it was unfrequent, he had found, in her, rather interesting.

"But I have a consolation in my exile, Miss Duncan, since it is to a city full of the fair; and dances and flirtations every night in Charleston, with the young, the rich, and the beautiful, should compensate one amply for the loss — ay, even for the loss — temporary though I hope it may be — of the fair Miss Duncan herself."

"Treason — treason — a most flagrant rebellion, and worthy of condign punishment," was the prompt reply of the maiden; though it evidently called for no inconsiderable effort on her part to respond so readily, and to dissipate the cloudy expression just then coming over her face again. She was about to continue her reply, and, moved by some uncertain feeling, Lieutenant Clayton had transferred himself from a neighboring chair to a seat on the sofa beside her, when Janet Berkeley entered the room. Her appearance produced a visible constraint upon both the parties, and she saw at a glance that she was unnecessary to their conference. She did not seem to remark them, however; and, though she perceived that a new interest was awakened in their mutual minds for each other, she had no time to give to reflection on this subject; nor, indeed, have we. She left the room after getting what she sought, and returned to the apartment of Mellichampe. She had scarcely done so, when Barsfield joined the two, and offered another obstacle to a conversation which, to both parties, had promised to become so interesting.

So much for the condition of things in the camp of the tory. In that of the partisan, affairs were even more promising. Witherspoon reached it in no long time after his interview had taken place with Scipio. He immediately sought out his superior. Major Singleton was the individual to whom he made his communication: and, through him, the paper sent by Mellichampe, and the facts furnished by the scout, were duly put in Marion's possession. The words of the chief were few — his plans soon laid — his decision readily adopted.

"It will do, Singleton," he said, with a lively air of satisfaction. "The game is a good one, and only requires to be played with spirit. The plan promises better than that of Horry, since we shall now not only rescue Mellichampe, I think, but strike a fatal blow at Barsfield's position. What number of loyalists does Thumbscrew report as in 'Piney Grove' since the 27th?"

"Eighty-six have gone in to him since the 27th — thirty-two before — and the troop which he brought, after all its losses, could scarcely be less than twenty five."

"Making in all—"

"One hundred and forty-three, rank and file."

"Not too many — not too many, major, if we employ the scheme. What say you?"

"I think not, general. Barsfield will concentrate his men, most probably, on the line over which Mellichampe is to be conducted. That direction we know from this paper. The advantage is important which it gives us, since we have only to plan our enterprise so as to avoid this — fall upon other points of his camp, and break in upon his ambush, flank and rear, while avoiding his front."

"True, Singleton — it will be to our advantage in beating Barsfield, I grant you; but not in serving Mellichampe. If he keeps this line, it will be necessary that we strike a moment before he approaches, and just when he has left the house, or he must fall before our help would avail him, coming in from flank and rear. We must confound the ambush in part — we must keep the whole camp of the tory alive by a concerted attack at all points, in front not less than in rear, or we lose Mellichampe, though we gain the fight."

Singleton acknowledged the difficulty.

"If," resumed Marion, "if Mellichampe would only think to avoid the track prescribed by his confederate, and force him to go aside upon another route, however slight the variation, it would yet serve us, and we might save him."

"I doubt not, general, that he will think of this; he is wonderfully shrewd in such matters, though rash and thoughtless enough in others. I think we may rely upon him that he will."

"We must hope for it, at least," said Marion. "The affair looks promising enough in all other respects, and we must drive our whole force to the adventure. We have been cooped up long enough. Go, Singleton, order in your remote scouts. Get all your men in readiness, and send your lieutenant, Humphries, to me. I have some instructions for him. I will lead in this business myself."

Singleton proceeded to the spot where Humphries usually slept, but he was not to be found. Let us account for his absence.

Humphries, secure of his enemy, excited by the trying scene through which he had passed, and scarcely less so by the novel form of death to which circumstances had prompted him to devote his victim, returned to the camp in a state of the utmost mental agitation. It was yet daylight, and sundry little duties in the camp called for his attention. These he performed almost unconsciously. His thoughts were elsewhere. An excitation of feeling, which sometimes moved him like insanity, disturbed his judgment, and affected the coherence and the regularity of his movements. In this state of mind, with just enough of consciousness to feel that he was wandering, and that he needed repose, he made his way about dusk from the observation of the camp, and seeking out a little bank in the swamp, with which he was familiar, where he might sleep in secresy, he threw himself under a tree and strove to forget the past. Shutting his eyes, he hoped in this way to shut out all the images of strife and terror which yet continued to annoy him.

He succeeded in his desire, and at length slept. But his sleep was more full of terrors than his waking thoughts. He dreamed, and the horror of his dreams aroused him. He heard the cries of the victim whom he had buried while yet alive. His dreadful shrieks rang in his ears; and, bursting from their sockets in blood, he saw the goggle-eyes looking down upon him, through the crevice in the cypress where he had last seen them. This was not long to be endured. He started from his sleep—from his place of repose—and stood upon his feet. Had he slept? This was doubtful to him, so vivid, so imposing and real, had been the forms and fancies of his vision. But the night had fairly set in, and this convinced him that he had slept. A faint light from the stars came scattered and tremblingly through the leaves, that complained in the cool wind of evening that fitfully stole among them. The moon was just rising, and gave but feeble light. The heavy trees seemed to dance before his eyes; huge shadows stalked gloomily between them, and, shuddering with bitter thoughts and terrifying fancies, the stout woodman, for a few moments, was unmanned.

"I can bear it no longer," he cried aloud, in his disquiet. "I can bear it no longer."

With the words he picked up his rifle, which lay upon the spot where he had lain himself. He felt for the knife in his belt, and, finding that his equipment was complete, he moved away with the haste of one who has fully resolved; saddled his horse, which he mounted with all speed; and, barely replying to the several challenges of the sentinels, he darted forth upon the well-known road. The relentless spur left the steed no breathing moment. The thoughts of the trooper flew faster than he could drive his horse; and, though going at the utmost extent of his powers, the impatient trooper chafed that the animal went so slowly.

The well-known swamp entrance was in sight; the canebrake was passed; and there, rising up in dreadful silence, white and ghostlike in its aspect under the increasing brightness of the moonlight, stood the tall cypress in which his victim was buried. The steed of the trooper was stopped suddenly—so suddenly that he almost fell back upon his haunches. His rider alighted; but for some moments, frozen to the spot, he dared not approach the object before him. The awful stillness of the scene appalled him. He strove to listen: he would have given worlds to have heard a groan— a moan—a sigh, however slight, from the cavernous body of that tree. A curse—ay, though the wretch within had again cursed his mother—would have been grateful to the senses and the heart of him who now stood gazing upon it in horror and in silence, but with the motionlessness of a statue.

He recovered strength at last sufficient to advance. He reached the tree. The wedges which secured his prisoner had been undisturbed. He put his ear to the rough bark of its sides, but he heard no sounds from within. He drew, with desperate hand, the pegs from the upper crevice, and fancied that a slight breathing followed it—or it might be the soughing of the wind, suddenly penetrating the aperture. He called aloud to the inmate; he shouted with his mouth pressed to the opening; he implored, he cursed his victim: but he got no answer.

What were his emotions as he pulled, with a giant's muscle, the hard wedges from the hollow of the tree below? He had slain his foe in battle: he had killed, without remorse, the man who, personally, had never done him wrong. Why should he suffer thus from the just punishment of a vindictive and a sleepless enemy? He felt, but he did not stop to analyze, this subtilty. He tore away the chunks which had fastened the opening, and thrust his hands into the hollow. The legs of the half-breed had sunk down from the knobs upon which they had rested while he was capable of exertion, and they were now a foot deep in the water which filled the hollow. With both hands, and the exercise of all his strength, Humphries succeeded in pulling him out by them. The body was limber, and made no effort and opposed no resistance. Dragging him through the water, which he could not avoid, the partisan bore him to the bank, upon which he laid him.

As yet he showed no signs of life; and the labor which his enemy had taken seemed to have been taken in vain; but the fresh air, and the immersion which he had unavoidably undergone in passing through the water, seemed to revive him—so Humphries thought, as, bending over him, he watched his ghastly features in the moonlight. He tore open the jacket and shirt from his bosom, and felt a slight pulsation at his heart. Never was joy more perfect than, at this moment, in the bosom of the partisan. He laughed with the first conviction that his enemy still lived. He laughed first, loudly and wildly, and then the tears, an unrestrainable current, flowed freely from his eyes. The half-breed continued to revive; and Humphries prayed by his side, as fervently as if praying in the last moment of his existence, for the mercy of an offended God.

He strove in every known way to assist the workings of nature in the resuscitation of his enemy. He fanned him with his cap—he sprinkled him freely with water, and spared no means supposed in his mind to be beneficial, to bring about the perfect restoration of his victim.

At length he succeeded. The legs of the half-breed were, one after the other, suddenly drawn up, then relaxed—he sighed deeply—and, finally, the light stole into his glazed orbs, as if it had been some blessed charity from the moon, that now glistened over them.

As he continued to improve, and with the first show of consciousness, Humphries lifted him higher up the bank, and laid him at the foot of a shrub tree which grew at hand. He then receded from him to a little distance—placed himself directly before his eyes—resumed his rifle, which he prepared and presented, and thus, squat upon one knee in front of him, he awaited the moment of perfect recovery, which should again, in the consciousness of new life, inform him at the same time, of the presence of an ancient enemy.

Thus stationed, he watched the slowly recovering Blonay, for the space of half an hour, in silence and in doubt. The scene was a strange one; and to his mind, not yet relieved from the previously active terrors of his imagination, an awful and imposing one. In the deep habitual gloom of that swamp region, among its flickering shadows—girdled by its thick and oppressive silence, and watching its skeleton trees until they seemed imbued with life, and, in the ghostly and increasing moonlight, appeared to advance upon, and then to recede away from him—he felt, at every moment of his watch, an increasing and superstitious dread of all things and thoughts, all sounds and objects, that assailed his senses, however remotely, and roused his emotions, however slight. And as the slow consciousness grew, like a shadow itself, in the cheek and eye of the man whom he had so lately beheld as lifeless, he half doubted whether it was human, and not spectral life, that he now beheld. He had believed that an evil spirit had possessed the mangled and deformed frame of the man before him, and was now beginning, with an aspect of anxious malignity, once more to glare forth upon him from the starting eyes of the half-breed.

He shuddered with the thought, and he felt that his grasp upon his rifle grew more and more unsteady, until at length he almost doubted his own capacity to secure a certain aim upon his enemy, in the event of strife. With this fear, determined, as he was, to have a perfect control over the life of Blonay, whatever might be the movement of the latter, he rose from the spot where he watched, and approached so nigh to the slowly recovering man, that the extended rifle nearly touched his breast. At that moment Blonay started, raised his head, and, half sitting up, gazed wildly upon the scene around him. His eye caught that of Humphries in the next instant, and he acknowledged the presence of his enemy by an involuntary start, rising, at the same moment, to a full sitting posture, and answering the watchful glance of the partisan by one of inquiry and astonishment, not less intense in its character than that which he encountered. His eye next rested upon his own rifle, which Humphries had thrown upon the bank, in the full glare of the moonlight, and his body involuntarily inclined toward it. With the movement came the corresponding one of the partisan. The muzzle of his weapon almost reached Blonay's breast, and the lock clicked with singular emphasis, in the general silence of the scene, as Humphries cocked it.

"Stir not, Goggle — move a foot, and I'll put the lead through you. It's a mercy I don't do it now."

Without a word, Blonay kept his position, and his eye met that of his foe without fear, though with the utmost passiveness of expression. Humphries continued—

"You've hunted me like a varmint—you've pulled trigger upon me—I have your mark, and will carry it, I reckon, to my grave. There's no reason why I should let you run."

He paused, as if awaiting an answer; but the stare of his enemy alone responded to his speech.

"What do you say now, Blonay, why I shouldn't put the bullet into you? Speak now — it's only civility."

"Adrat it, nothing," said the other, drawing up his legs.

"You're from my own parish, and that's one reason," said

Humphries, "that's one reason why I want to give you fair play, and it's reason enough why I don't want to spill your blood. Answer me now, Goggle, like a man — do you want mine?"

He paused, but received no answer. He thus proceeded —

"I had you safe enough, but I couldn't find it in my heart to take your life after that fashion, so I let you out. Tell me, now, if you can go without taking tracks after me again? Suppose I let you run — suppose I leave you, without troubling you now with this lead, that only waits till I lift this finger to go through your skull — will you follow me again? will you come hunting for my blood? Speak? for your life depends on it."

"Adrat it, Bill Humphries, you've got the gun, and you say there's a bullet in it. I'm here afore you, and I don't dodge. I ain't afeard," was the reckless and seemingly impatient response.

"That's as much as to say that you wont promise, and it's enough to satisfy me to my own conscience for pulling trigger upon you at once. But I won't. I'll give you a chance for your life. There shall be fair play between us. Take your rifle — there it lies — get yourself ready, and take your stand on the edge of the bank, and then be as quick as you think proper, for the first one to cut away will have the best chance for life."

A visible change came over the features of the half-breed as he listened to this address. His head dropped, his chin rested upon his breast, and, without any other answer, he simply raised the hand which Humphries had mashed so remorselessly with the pine-knot, when its owner had thrust it through the crevice of the tree. He raised it, and in the action showed his enemy how utterly impracticable it was for him to hold the rifle with any hope of its successful use. Humphries was silenced, and his own feelings were strongly affected when he actually beheld a tear in the blear eye of the half-breed, as he looked upon the maimed and utterly helpless member. The privation must have been terrible indeed, to extort such an acknowledgment from one so inflexible. It certainly was the greatest evil that could have befallen him, to lose the use of the weapon on which so much depended; and then, what was his mortification to submit to a challenge from a hated enemy, his weapon and his foe alike at hand, unable to employ the one or to punish the other?

The rifle of Humphries was lowered as he felt the full force of Blonay's answer. He turned away to conceal his own emotion.

"Go!" he cried, "go, Blonay — you are free this time. I must take my chance, and run my risk of your taking tracks after me again. Go now, but better not let me meet you. My blood is hotter at other times than now. I'm sad and sorry now, and there's something to-night in the woods that softens me, and I can't be angry, I can't spill your blood. But 'twon't always be so; and, if you're wise, you'll take the back tracks and go down quietly to Dorchester." -

Without waiting for any answer, the partisan hurried through the canebrake; and, with a motion less rapid than that which brought him, took his way back to the camp of Marion, where he arrived not a moment too soon for the most active preparation and employment.

Bruised, enfeebled, almost helpless, the half-breed slowly returned to the tory encampment at "Piney Grove." He appeared before Barsfield at early morning on the day following that, the circumstances of which we have recorded. His presence quieted the anxieties, as it met the desires, of all parties.

"Your hand — what is the matter with it? why is it bound up?" demanded Barsfield.

"Mashed it with a piece of timber in the swamp," was the unscrupulous answer of the half-breed, who suppressed all the particulars of his affair with Humphries.

"Any luck? — met with your man?" was the further question.

"No," was the ready answer.

"You are ready for mine, however?"

"To-night — yes."

"At midnight. But you must see Miss Berkeley — have

everything well understood, so that there will be no confusion, no delay. She does not suspect—she seems satisfied?"

"Mighty well pleased."

"'Tis well. Thus, then, you will proceed. The sentinel will be withdrawn from the gallery, and you shall have, at the hour, another key to the padlock. Guide him forth as soon as possible after the withdrawal of the sentinel: you know the course?"

"Yes—by the railing, and so on to the avenue."

"Be particular, and do not leave the track for an instant. Go now—I shall be out of the way; seek Miss Berkeley, and conclude your arrangements with her for to-night."

The half-breed left him.

"To-night!" were the only words uttered by the tory as he went toward the outposts, but they were full of import, and his face looked everything which his lips forbore to utter.

CHAPTER XLIX.

ESCAPE.

THAT day was spent in arrangements. Barsfield chose his men for the purposes of assassination; but he did not surrender his secret to their keeping. He was too wary for that. They had their places assigned; and all that he condescended to unfold to them, by way of accounting for the special appointment and the earnest commands which he gave, may be comprised in few words.

"I suspect," said he, "that there is some treason among us. I suspect the scout—Blonay. I have reason to think he purposes, either this night or the next, to betray the camp to Marion, and to escape with the spy Mellichampe. You will, therefore, preserve the utmost watchfulness upon the posts which I assign you; and if you see anything to alarm you, anything worthy of suspicion, act upon it decisively and without pause. If you see the prisoner with the scout, spare neither—put them both to death. To seek to recapture the spy might lose him, and such an event would be ruinous and disgraceful. I trust to you, men—you will do your duty."

In the chamber of Mellichampe, whose fate thus hung upon a thread, the interest, it may be supposed, was not less important and exciting. Concealed in a shawl assumed for the purpose, the maiden carried to her lover the much-desired weapons which Scipio had received from Witherspoon. The message of the trusty woodman was also delivered correctly, and the intelligence strengthened the youth accordingly, and half-reconciled Janet to the experiment which she so much dreaded.

"This is well—this is excellent!" cried Mellichampe, grasping the pistols, trying the charge, and examining their condition—"this is well; both loaded; good flints: I fear nothing now, Janet. At least, I am able to fight—I am not less able to destroy than my enemies."

She turned away with a shudder: but she felt happier and more hopeful as she beheld his exultation.

Not less busy in the camp of Marion, the entire force of the partisans was preparing for the assault. Every available arm was required for the service, as the little squad of the "swamp-fox" at this period barely numbered one hundred and fifty men, many of these only partially armed, and some of them who had never been in fight before.

"Have you had reports from the scouts, Major Singleton?" demanded the general.

"Not yet, sir. I have sent out Humphries and Witherspoon, who will bring us special accounts by noon. We shall have time enough then for our movement."

"Quite—quite. This plan of Thumbscrew's is admirable. If the scouts do handsomely, we can put a dead shot for every sentinel on one side of the avenue. It can scarcely fail, I think."

"Impossible, sir—if the action is concerted, and I think we have time enough to make it so. The firing of the tents must follow the first knowledge we have of Mellichampe's movement; and that knowledge, if I mistake him not, we shall have as soon as he leaves the house, for Witherspoon has sent him his pistols. When the alarm is given by the blaze, I will charge from the lower bay—to which I can get, with all my men, by nine o'clock—moving slowly, and without detection. With proper firmness, we can not help but succeed."

"I doubt not we shall do so, major—I doubt not that we shall defeat the tory, and I hope annihilate his force; but, in that first moment, I dread everything for Mellichampe. The tory, doubtless, will watch every step which he takes, and he may be murdered the moment after he leaves the house."

"But it is on one route only that he puts his guard. Relying on his scout as faithful, he will calculate upon his bringing Mellichampe into his very jaws—"

"And how know we that he is not faithful to his employer? What reason is there to believe him friendly to Mellichampe? This is my doubt. So long as Barsfield can pay this fellow in solid gold, he has his fidelity."

"Yes, sir, very probably; but I scarcely think that Mellichampe will keep the one track. I rely greatly on his sagacity in all matters of this sort, and think that the moment he leaves the dwelling, he will not feel himself bound to follow the lead of his companion."

"I hope not," was the response of Marion to the sanguine calculations of Major Singleton—"I hope not, but I apprehend for him. We must do our best, however, and look to Good Fortune to help us through where we stumble. But no more. See now to your further preparations, for we move by dusk."

The affair on hand impressed no one more seriously with its importance than Thumbscrew. He addressed Major Singleton the moment after his return, bringing the desired intelligence, which he did at noon. He addressed him to solicit what he styled a favor.

"But why incur a danger so great, and, seemingly, so unnecessary? I see no use for it, Thumbscrew."

"No use! There's use for it, major, and satisfaction; as for danger, I'm a born danger myself, and I shouldn't be afraid to stand in the way of my own shadow. But I don't think there's any danger, major; to cross the avenue ain't so mighty hard to a man like me, that's played, in my time, a part of every beast, and bird, and crawling critter that's known to a Santee woodman. I can pass them sentries like a gust from a big-winged bird, and so they'll think me. I can git into that bay without waking a blind moscheto; and, once I gits there, I can do a mighty deal now, I tell you, by a sartin whistle which I has, to tell Airnest Mellichampe where to find me."

The arguments of Witherspoon soon persuaded his superior, and he went alone, long in advance of the partisans, on his individual and daring adventure. He gained the bay with the same ease and good fortune which marked his progress in a similar effort, which we have previously described. There he waited anxiously, but in patience, the events which were at hand.

At nightfall the partisans, the entire force of Marion, approached "Piney Grove"—not so near as to be subjected to any danger of discovery, yet sufficiently so to be in readiness for any circumstance which might suddenly call them forward. In a deep wood, the very one in which Scipio's interview had taken place with Witherspoon, they alighted, and Marion proceeded to divide his men into three bodies. To one, under command of Colonel Horry, he assigned the task of firing the tents and striking at the main post of the encampment. To another troop, acting simply as cavalry under Major Singleton, he gave it in charge to attack the rear by a sudden and fierce onset, the moment that Horry should commence the affair—the firing of the tents being a common signal. To himself he reserved the more difficult, if not more dangerous, task of distributing his men as riflemen, in front, along the whole line of the avenue, prepared to commence the attack in that quarter; and, pressing through the avenue—having first slain the sentinels, each man of whom was to be marked out by a corresponding rifleman—to unite with the other two bodies near the bay so frequently spoken of, where it was their hope to be in time to save Mellichampe from the knife or pistol of the prepared assassins.

This arrangement made, Singleton's troop remounted their horses, and, under the direction of their leader, made a wide circuit around the camp, so as to throw themselves into the thicket lying in its rear. This they gained before the moon rose. The men commanded by Marion and Horry fastened their horses securely out of the reach of danger, and pressed forward on foot to their several stations. The riflemen stole individually from cover to cover, until they ranged themselves along the whole line of the avenue, and looked down upon the pacing sentinels, who walked their rounds all unconscious of the lurking death which lay hovering in dreadful silence, and unseen around them. Each partisan in this way had selected his victim and the "swamp-fox" himself, lying along a little ditch overgrown with weeds half full of water, lay as secretly and still as ever did the adroit animal whose name had been assigned him.

The hour was approaching. Barsfield had set his snare, and was impatient.

"Go now, and bring him forth," he said to Blonay. "The time is close at hand."

The half-breed, obedient to his will, left him on the instant.

"He is mine at last!" was the triumphant thought which the tory muttered at that moment to himself. "The toil will soon be over, and I shall triumph now—I will bathe my feet in his blood."

He went the rounds of the men whom he had stationed on the watch for his victim. Some were immediately around the house, though not known to Blonay. Barsfield anticipated the possibility of the fugitive's taking another direction than that which he had prescribed. For this possibility he had prepared. He was resolved that his plan should not fail through want of due precautions. He saw that all were in readiness; and, not remote, he took a station for himself which would enable him, as soon as the deed was done, to gratify himself with the sight of his murdered victim.

"Hist! hem!" were the sounds that saluted Mellichampe at the door of his chamber. The hour had come. In the next instant the door was unlocked, and with a fearless heart, having his pistols ready in his grasp, he met his guide at the entrance.

"Are you Mr. Blonay?" was his question, as the darkness of the passage-way did not permit him to distinguish features. The reply was affirmative.

"I am ready," said the youth. "Lead on."

"Go not—go not, dear Ernest!" cried Janet Berkeley, who was also watchful: "Go not, I pray you; it is not too late; return to your chamber, for I dread me of this trial. It will be fatal; you can not escape these assassins, and the night is so bright and clear—"

"Hush!" he whispered—"see you not?" and he pointed to Blonay.

"I know—I know; but trust not—risk not, I implore you, Ernest. Mr. Blonay knows—he says that there is danger. He told me so but this moment."

"Nay, Janet; but you are too apprehensive. I know the skill of Mr. Blonay; he can help me through the danger, and I fear it not."

"But, dear Ernest—"

He interrupted her, as, passing his arm about her waist, he bent down and whispered in her ears:—

"Would you prefer to see me hanging from a tree? Remember, Janet, this is my only hope."

"God help me! God be with you, and save you!" she exclaimed.

He folded her to his bosom, and oh! the agony of doubt that assailed both hearts at that instant. It might be the last embrace that they should take in life. A mutual thought of this nature produced a mutual shudder at the same moment in their forms.

"One—one more, my beloved!" he cried, as they parted; and, in another instant, he was gone from sight. She sank down where he left her. Her hands were clasped, and, too feeble for effort, yet too alive to her anxieties to faint into forgetfulness, she strove, but how vainly, even where she lay, to pray for his safety.

CHAPTER L.

THE PINE-KNOT.

It was with conflicting emotions and an excited pulse that Mellichampe hurried away from the embrace of the maiden, possibly the very last that he should ever be permitted to enjoy. In another moment, and the woods were before his eyes; and he now felt assured that every step which he took from the dwelling must be taken in sight of his enemies. Yet he did not the less boldly descend from the threshold, though he believed that with every movement he came nigher his murderer. He did not deceive himself with idle hopes of the forbearance and tender mercy of his foe; yet he was resolute to struggle to the last: he was prepared for anything but martyrdom.

Scarcely had he stepped from the door of the dwelling into the shadow of a little clump of trees that lay before it, when he heard the well-known whistle of Witherspoon. He could not mistake the sounds, and they came with a most cheering and refreshing influence upon his senses.

"Trusty and brave Jack!" he muttered to himself, as he listened, "at least I shall have one true and strong arm to help me in the struggle. I am not alone."

The repeated sounds guided him in his progress. He could not be mistaken now in their direction; he felt certain that they came from the little bay, which he well knew could easily conceal the scout so long as it continued unsuspected. He turned quickly in the direction of the sounds. Blonay touched his arm —

"This way, sir," said the half-breed, in a whisper.

"No, sir, this way!" sternly, but in a similar whisper, responded Mellichampe. "This way, sir, as I bid you; you go with me in this direction, or you die."

"But, cappin—" said the other, hesitatingly.

"No words — I trust you not — on!"

The muttered and decisive language was amply seconded by the action of the speaker. One hand grasped the maimed wrist of the half-breed, the other held in the same moment the cocked pistol to his eyes. Wincing under the pain which the sudden seizure of his injured hand by that of Mellichampe had necessarily occasioned, the fierce savage, with the other, grasped his knife, and half drew it from the sheath. But the momentary anger seemed to pass away before he had fully bared it. He thrust it back again, and calmly replied to his irritable companion—

"You can trust me, cappin; I'll go jist as you tells me, for I promised the gal — she's a good gal — I promised her to do the best, and I'll do jist as you says. Lead on where you wants to go."

"No, no, do you lead on, sir; I will not trust you. To the bay, but keep the trees, and do not show your person unnecessarily. On, sir, the moment you go aside, I shoot you down like a dog."

The words were of fierce character, and uttered with singular emphasis, but still in a whisper. The half-breed by no means relished the manner of Mellichampe, but he muttered to himself—

"I promised her — she's a good gal —"

And thus reminding himself of his pledges, he prepared to go forward.

"Keep close to those water oaks," said Mellichampe to his companion, and he himself sank into their shadow as he spoke. At that moment another whistle, not that of Marion's men, came from the path which they had left. It was answered by another, a few paces distant, on the opposite hand. Mellichampe thrust Blonay forward, and they both moved with increased rapidity along the range of water-oaks, which at intervals afforded them a tolerable shelter. Again the whistle was repeated, and to the disquiet of the fugitives, it was instantly answered by some one immediately in front of them, and on the very path they were pursuing.

"I reckon they've found us out —" Blonay began to speak, but Mellichampe interrupted him.

"Silence, sir, no word, but follow me," and the youth moved hurriedly along, still upon the path he had been pursuing, but looking out for his enemy, and cocking his pistol in readiness. A bush parted and waved a little before him, and with its evident motion Mellichampe darted aside. In the next moment came the shot, and immediately succeeding the report the youth heard a gasping exclamation from his companion, by which he knew him to be wounded —

"Ah! it's me, it's hit me —"

Looking round, he saw the half-breed fall forward upon his face, but immediately rise upon his hands and knees, and crawl towards a little cluster of bushes which rose close at hand; where, with all the instinct of an Indian, even after receiving his death-wound, he labored to conceal himself.

The case was evidently a desperate one. The youth was surrounded by his enemies; and, unless the diversion of the partisans was made promptly, he felt that he must be, in a few moments, in the power of his murderers. The shot had scarce been fired, and the exclamation of the wounded man uttered, when he heard a rush as of several pursuers from behind. He did not wait, but bounded forward, for he knew that his friends were in front, and to perish in the general combat would be infinitely better than any other hazard. But he was not allowed so readily to go forward. With his first movement from the tree which had covered him at the moment when Blonay fell, the assassin rushed out upon his path, with a recklessness which showed that he believed Mellichampe to be unarmed. He paid for his temerity with his life; at five paces, and before he could recover from his error, the youth shot him through the breast. The man staggered out of his path, and fell without farther effort, crying aloud —

"The spy — the spy! he's gone! to the bay! Oh! I'm a dead man!"

While he was yet falling, Mellichampe hurled the empty pistol into his face, and drawing the second and last from his bosom, cocked it instantly for immediate use, and hurried on toward the bay, which yet lay at some little distance beyond him. The rushing and the shouting of the tories, on every hand, informed him of the close watch which had been kept upon his movements. The voice of Barsfield was also heard above the clamor, in furious exhortation —

"The spy has escaped with the half-breed; shoot them both down — let neither escape — but fail not to kill the spy; no quarter to him! five guineas to the man who kills him!"

"He is here!" cried one, dragging the still living but mortally wounded Blonay from the bush where he had concealed himself.

"Ha! where?" was the demand of Barsfield, rushing to the spot where he lay. Without looking he plunged his sword into the body, and felt the last convulsion as the victim writhed around the blade. But he spurned the carcass with his foot the next moment, when he discovered that the scout, and not Mellichampe, lay before him. With a fierce shout he led and hurried the pursuit, impetuously dashing forward with all the fury of one who, having been certain of his victim, now begins to apprehend disappointment.

"Death to the spy! pursue! Five guineas to him who kills him! No quarter to the spy!"

Such were his cries to his men as he himself pursued. They reached the ears of Mellichampe — they aroused him to a like fury. Desperate and enraged, his temper became unrestrainable, and, though imprudent in the last degree, he shouted back, even as he fled, his defiance to his foes. The whistle of Witherspoon fortunately reached his ear in that moment, and guided him on his flight. His voice, meanwhile, had disclosed the direction which he had taken to those who were now clamorously pursuing him. But the pursuit was arrested at the luckiest moment for the fugitive. The tents were now blazing, and wild cries came from the centre of the encampment. Clayton rushed across the path of Barsfield.

"Stand aside, away! The spy—slay him! No quarter to the spy!" cried the fierce tory, as he thrust Clayton out of his path, his eyes glaring like balls of fire, and the foam gathering thick around his mouth and almost choking his utterance.

"What is all this, Captain Barsfield!" cried the second officer, confusedly, to his superior.

"Get from my path! Stand aside, or I hew thee down!" was the desperate answer.

"But the camp's on fire!" said the lieutenant. "The camp's on fire!" was the general cry around him.

Barsfield only answered by pressing forward—selfishly pursuing the one enemy, who, in his sight, took the place and preference of all others. Indeed, at that moment, he did not seem to be conscious of any other object or duty than that of arresting Mellichampe.

"The spy—Mellichampe—he has seduced the sentinel—he is fled—there—Lieutenant Clayton—there—in the bay! Pursue all, and kill him. No quarter to the spy!"

"But the camp—" said Clayton.

"Let it burn! Let it burn!" His words were silenced—drowned in the sharp and repeated shot which rang along the whole line of the avenue. He became conscious on the instant, for the first time; and now, at once, conceived the nature of that concerted combination which was likely to defraud him of his prey. Still he did not conceive the assault to be made by any large force. He did not think it possible.

"A surprise," he said—"a mere diversion to help the spy. To the front, Lieutenant Clayton—send your loyalists to the avenue! Line the front—it will soon be over—it is but a straggling squad. Away—and leave me for the spy. I will manage him with these three men."

The coolness of Barsfield seemed to have come back to him as he gave these orders. But his rage was the greater from having been suppressed so long. He pressed forward to the bay with the three men who were with him. He believed that Clayton would soon manage the foe in front; and he was resolved upon the death of Mellichampe, even if he did not. In another moment, however, he was convinced that it was no random attack, simply for diversion, from a small squad. The clamor was that of a large force, and the repeated and well-known cry of the partisans followed the first volley of the sharp-shooters.

"Marion's men — true blues — true blues! Hurra! no quarter — Tarleton's quarters! One and all, Marion's men!"

"One and all, men!" were the stern, shrill notes that followed the cry.

It was the sharp voice of Marion himself, and it was heard distinctly over the field: the sound was fitly concluded by a second volley and an increasing uproar.

"He is there with all his force!" exclaimed Barsfield; "but no matter. I can not turn now, and, at least, Mellichampe is mine. He is here in this bay. They can not help him in season, and he must perish. That done, I care not if Marion conquers; we can but become his prisoners."

These were the calculations of Barsfield, half uttered as he pursued. Mellichampe was immediately before him. He had heard his shout. The pursuers were now on the edge of the bay which the youth had entered.

"To the gum-trees, Dexter, and watch that point — see that he does not gain the avenue. Keep him from crossing. Put in on the right, Beacham; and you, Mason, go in on the left. Spare him not! Slay him like a dog! No quarter to the spy!"

These were his rapid orders to his men as they rushed into the close but narrow thicket which was called the bay.

"But five minutes! give me that," muttered Mellichampe to himself, "and I ask for no more. But where can Witherspoon be?"

The next moment he heard the whistle of his friend in a denser part of the bay, and he hurried with a new joy toward him.

"There are but three or four; and if we can but join first, we may give them work," cried the youth, pressing forward. But Witherspoon was now already engaged. His voice kept pace in company with his sabre, the clashing of which Mellichampe heard while approaching him. The woodman had encountered one of the pursuers. The affair, however, was soon over. The man had met a sabre where he had looked only for a victim.

"It's one less of the niggers," cried Witherspoon, aloud, as he struck his enemy down with a fatal blow. "Hello! Airnest, boy, where is you?"

But the youth could not answer. He himself was about to become busily engaged. Barsfield was before him, and between him and Witherspoon. Mellichampe had but his pistol, and he determined, as he saw the copse disturbed in front, to conceal his weapon, as he hoped that Barsfield would precipitate himself forward, as if upon an unarmed enemy, when he might employ it suddenly and fatally. Indeed, he had no other chance for life. In part, his plan was successful. The tory leaped forward with a mad fury as he beheld the youth. His sabre was waving above Mellichampe's head, when the latter sank upon his knee and fired—unerringly, but not fatally.

The ball penetrated the thigh of the tory, who sank down upon him. They grappled with each other upon the ground, struggling in a little area where the trees seemed to have been scooped out, as it were, expressly to afford them room for a struggle of this sort. The physical power of Barsfield was naturally greater than that of Mellichampe, and the recent illness of the youth still further increased the inequalities between them; but Mellichampe had succeeded in grasping the neckcloth of his enemy, while the latter had a hold only upon one wrist and part of the dress of the former. They were yet struggling upon the ground without advantage to either, when one of Barsfield's men came to his assistance.

The moment was full of peril to the youth; but his friend Witherspoon was no less prompt to succor and save, than the tory to destroy. He bounded through the intervening bushes in time to neutralize the efforts of the new-comer. A sabre-stroke from the woodman brought him to the ground, and disabled him from any movement toward the combatants; but, raising a pistol, even after he had fallen, before Witherspoon could help Mellichampe or get out of his way, he shot him in the side. Before he could draw a second, the woodman cut him down. He had hardly done so, when a faintness came over the faithful fellow: he leaned against a tree, then sank nervelessly to the ground.

"It's a tough shot, Airnest, and I can't help you. Who'd ha' thought it? Ah! it bites! But hold on, Airnest—hold on, boy; the major will soon come to pull you out of the bear's claws."

"You are hurt, Jack."

"Reckon I am—a bad hurt too, Airnest, if one may tell by the sort of feeling it has."

Without a word, Barsfield continued the struggle the more earnestly, as he now found himself becoming faint from the wound which Mellichampe had inflicted. The youth himself grew momently less and less able to resist his foe, and Witherspoon, who lay but a few feet apart, and saw the mutual efforts of the two, could lend no manner of assistance.

The object of the tory was to keep Mellichampe quiet with one hand, while he shortened his sabre with the other. This, as yet, he had striven fruitlessly to do. The youth, who saw his aim, had addressed all his energies to the task of defeating it; and, when pushed away by Barsfield, had contrived, by the grasp which he still maintained upon the neckcloth of the latter, still to cling so closely to him as to prevent his attainment of the desired object. While the struggle thus remained doubtful, a new party was added to the scene in the person of Scipio, who came stealing through the bushes. He had heard the clamor in that direction which had taken place at first, and the subsequent silence frightened him still more than all the noise of the previous struggle. He came to gain intelligence for his young mistress, whose apprehensions, though unuttered in language or even in tears, were only silent because they were untterable.

Witherspoon saw the negro first.

"Ha, Scip—nigger—is that you? Come quick, nigger, and help your maussa."

"Dah him? wha's de matter, Mass Wedderspoon—you hurt?"

"Ask no questions, you black rascal, but run and help Airnest: don't you see him there, fighting with the tory?"

"Who? Mass Airnest—fighting wid de tory—hey?"

The negro turned his eyes, and stood in amaze, to behold the sort of contest which Mellichampe and Barsfield carried on. The tory first addressed him:—

"Scipio, run to Lieutenant Clayton—"

"Run to the devil!" cried Witherspoon; "knock him on the head, Scipio, and save your master; don't let him talk."

"Only say de wud, Mass Wedderspoon; say de wud, Mass Arnest; you say I mus' knock dis tory?"

"Yes, to be sure," cried Witherspoon, in a rage.

"If you dare," said Barsfield, "you'll hang, you scoundrel. Beware what you do!—fly—go to Lieutenant Clayton—"

The negro interrupted him:—

"You 'tan' fur me, Mass Wedderspoon—you tell me fur do 'em, I do 'em fur true."

"Do it—do it, d—n you! don't stand about it. He will kill Airnest if you don't; he'll kill us all!"

The negro seized a billet—a ragged knot of the heaviest pine-wood that lay at hand—and approached the two where they lay struggling.

"I mos' 'fraid—he dah buckrah—I dah nigger."

"Strike him!" cried Witherspoon, writhing forward in an agony of excitement—"strike him, Scip; I'll answer for you, boy."

"Hole you head fudder, Mass Arnest," cried the negro; "I feard fur hit you."

"Will you dare, Scipio—will you? Strike not, Scipio; you shall have your freedom—gold—guineas," was the supplicating cry of Barsfield.

"I no yerry you, Mass Barsfield: you's a d—n tory, I know. Dis dah my maussa; I hab fur min' um."

While he spoke, he approached and planted one of his feet between the bodies of the two combatants.

"Turn you eyes, Mass Arnest."

The heavy pine-wood knot was lifted above the head of the tory. The eyes of Mellichampe were averted, while Barsfield vainly strove to press forward as closely to the youth as possible, and once or twice writhed about in such a manner, though the grasp of Mellichampe was still upon his collar, as entirely to defeat the aim of the negro.

"'Tan' 'till—I mus knock you, Mass Barsfield."

"Scip—Scipio!" were the pleading tones of the tory, as he threw up his arms vainly. The blow descended and silenced him for ever. The billet was buried in his brains. The skull lay crushed and flattened, and but a single contraction of the limbs and convulsion of the frame attested the quick transition of life to death—so dreadful had been the stroke. Mellichampe had fainted.

"Hurra! hurra! Well done, Scip—well done! you've saved the boy. You're a nigger among a thousand!"

The tones of exultation and encouragement came faintly from the lips of the woodman, who bled inwardly. They fell upon unheeding senses; for the stupefied Scipio at that moment heard them not.

CHAPTER LI.

JACK WITHERSPOON.

The negro dropped the heavy pine-knot with the blow, and, for a moment, stood gazing in stupor upon the horrid spectacle, his own deed, before him. At length, starting away, he dashed out of the bushes, in the direction of the dwelling, crying aloud as he fled, in tones like those of a maniac, and in words which indicated the intoxicating effect of his new-born experience upon him —

"Ho! ho! I kill um — I hit um on he head. He's a dirt — he's a dirt — I hab foot on um — I mash he brains. Ho! ho! I kill buckrah. I's nigger — I kill buckrah! You tink for hang me — you mistake. Mass Wedderspoon say de wud — Mass Arnest no say 'no.' I kill 'em. He dead!"

He rushed into the apartment where the family were all assembled in the highest degree of agitation. The storm of battle, which still raged around them with unmitigated fury, had terrified Mr. Berkeley and Rose Duncan to the last degree. They appealed to Scipio for information, but he gave them no heed.

"Whay's young missis? young missis I want. I hab for tell um someting."

He refused all other answer, and made his way into the adjoining apartment. Janet was at the window — that nearest to the clamor — at which, through another dreadful fight, she had watched unhesitatingly before. She started to her feet as she beheld him.

"Ernest — speak to me, Scipio. What of Ernest? Where is he? tell me he is safe."

"He dead! I kill um?"

She shrieked and fell. The event restored the negro to his senses. He picked her up, howling over her all the while, and bore her to the adjoining apartment, where the care of Rose Duncan in a short time recovered her.

"Speak to me, Scipio," she cried, rising, and addressing him with an energy which despair seemed to have given her, and which terrified all around—"Tell me all—what of Ernest? He is not hurt—he has escaped? You have told me falsely—he lives!"

"I 'speck so, missis; 'tis I's a d—n fool fur tell you he been hurt. He no hurt. 'Tis Mass Barsfield I been knock on de head—"

"Barsfield!—you!" was the exclamation of all.

"Yes—de d———n nigger—enty he been hab Arnest 'pon de ground? he want to 'tick him wid he sword. I take light-wood-knot, I hammer um on he head tell you sees noting but de blood and de brain, and de white of he eye. He dead—'tis Scip mash um."

"You struck him, Scipio?" said Mr. Berkeley.

"Mass Wedderspoon tell me, maussa. Enty he been guine 'tick Mass Arnest? When I see dat, I 'tan look. Jack Wedderspoon cuss me, and say, why de h–ll you no knock um?' Well, wha' I for do? Enty he tell me? I knock um fur true! I hit um on he head wid de pine-knot. De head mash flat like pancake. I no see um 'gen."

The maidens shuddered at the narration, but Janet spoke instantly.

"But Ernest, what of him, Scipio? Was he hurt? You have not said, is he safe?"

"I sway, missis, I can't tell. I 'speck he been hurt someting. I left um on de ground. He ain't git up."

"I will go," she exclaimed.

"Think not of it, Janet, my child, till the noise is over."

But she had gone; while the father yet spake, she had left the room and the house, Scipio closely attending her. The feebleness of age seemed no longer to oppress the aged man. He rushed after the daughter of his heart with much of the vigor of youth, and with all the fearlessness of a proper manhood. In that moment her worth was conspicuous, in his forgetfulness of all fear and feebleness. He heeded not the cries and the clamor, the dreadful imprecations and the sharp ringing shot, which momently assailed his ears in his progress. The fight was still going on along the avenue and in the park, but its fury was abating fast. Mr. Berkeley hurried forward, but soon became confused. His daughter was not to be seen, nor Scipio, and he knew not in what direction to turn his footsteps. While he paused and doubted, he heard the rush of cavalry, like the sweeping force of a torrent coming down the hills at midnight. He could see, in the bright moonlight, the dark figures and their shining white blades. The clashing of steel superseded the shot of the marksmen, and the horsemen now evidently swept the field in irresistible wrath. The tories were flying in all directions, the partisans riding over them with unsparing hoofs, and smiting down with impetuous steel. A group fled toward the house, and came directly upon the spot where the old man's feet seemed to be frozen. Timidly he shrank behind a tree, and, as the cavalry pursued, the tories broke, and dispersed in individual flight. One of them, an officer, sank back slowly, and with an air of resolution and defiance in his manner which soon provoked the attention of a partisan trooper. He pressed forward upon the Briton, who turned gallantly and made fight. The huge-limbed steed of the partisan was wheeled from side to side under the curb of his rider, with an ease that almost seemed the result of an instinct of his own. Neither the steed nor his rider could be mistaken.

"Yield — surrender, sir — you prolong the fight uselessly. Your men are dispersed," were the words of Singleton.

"Never, to a rebel!" was the response of Clayton; "never!" and he struck at the partisan with an earnestness and skill as he replied, which showed him that he was not an enemy to be trifled with. The fierce mood of Singleton grew uppermost as he witnessed the obduracy of the Briton. His own blows were repeated with furious energy, and the retreat of Clayton was perforce, more rapid than before. Backing, and fighting all the while, his feet became entangled in some obstruction behind him, and he stumbled over it without being able to recover himself. He now lay at the mercy of his enemy.

The courtesy of Singleton effected what his valor had not done. His horse was curbed in the instant which saw Clayton fall. The point of his sabre, which had been directed toward, was now turned from his bosom, and he bade him rise. The Briton bowed, and presented his sword.

"Oblige me by keeping it, sir," was the reply of the partisan. "Let me see you to the house in safety."

The only inmate of the house who received Lieutenant Clayton was Rose Duncan.

"I'm a prisoner, Miss Duncan," said the lieutenant, and it did not pain him greatly to tell her so.

"Indeed; I'm so glad of it," was the almost unconscious reply.

Clayton looked grave as she said so, and Major Singleton withdrew, leaving him, however, not so dissatisfied with the general tenor of events as might have been expected. It was surprising how soon he forgot that he was a prisoner, and how readily Rose became his custodier. But this concerns us not.

In the neighboring court the bugle of Marion called his men together. The battle was over. The victory was complete, and the only concern before the partisans was to ascertain the price which it had cost them. This could not be so readily determined.

"But what tidings of Mellichampe?" demanded Marion. "Have you heard nothing, Major Singleton? This was your charge."

"Nothing, as yet, sir; I have dispersed my men in search. It is unaccountable, too, that we have heard nothing of Witherspoon, nor has Captain Barsfield been reported. The command does not seem to have been with him. Lieutenant Clayton is my prisoner."

While they yet spoke, the whistle of Witherspoon—a faintly-uttered note, but well known as that of the woodman—came to them from the bay. To this point they instantly proceeded. But Janet Berkeley was there long before them. She had outstripped even the speed of Scipio; she had heard and been guided by the accents of her lover's voice, as she entered the copse.

"Jack, dear Jack — Witherspoon, my friend, my more than friend — my father — speak to me!"

It was thus that the youth, bending over his prostrate companion, expressed his agony and apprehension at the condition in which he found him. Witherspoon bled inwardly, and could scarcely speak, as he was in momentary danger of suffocation. The next moment the arms of Janet were thrown about her lover, whom she found in safety, and she burst into an agony of tears, which at length relieved her. With her appearance, the strength and consciousness of the wounded woodman seemed to come back to him. He looked up with a smile, and said, feebly, as he beheld her: —

"God bless you, Miss Janet, and make you happy. You see he's safe; and there's no danger now, for I rether reckon, from what I hear and from what I don't hear, that the tories are done for."

"Oh, Mr. Witherspoon! what can I do for you? I hope you are not much hurt."

"Pretty bad, I tell you. I feel all over I can't tell how; and when it comes to that, you see, it looks squally. I'm afeard I've no more business in the swamp."

"Speak not thus, Jack; but let us help you to the house. Here, Scipio, lend a hand."

But the woodman resisted them.

"No! no!" he exclaimed, "this is my house — the woods. I've lived in them, and I feel that it will be sweeter to die in them than in a dark little room. I like the green of the trees and the cool feel of the air. I can't breathe in a little room as I can in the woods."

"But, dear Jack, you can be better attended there — we —"

"Don't talk, Airnest. I won't ax for much 'tendance now. I feel I'm going; my teeth stick when I set them down, and when I try to open them it's hard work. I'm in a bad way, I tell you, when I can't talk — talking was so nateral."

"What can I bring you?"

"Water!" he replied, gaspingly.

But, with the effort to swallow, there came a rush of blood into his mouth, which almost suffocated him.

"It's all over with me now, Airnest, boy. I've done the best for you—"

The youth squeezed his hand, but was too much moved to speak.

"I've worked mighty hard to git you out of the hobble, and I'm awful glad that the bullet didn't come till you were safe out of the claws of that varmint. You've got a clear track now; and oh! Miss Janet, I'm so glad to see you together, lock and lock, as I may say, afore I die. It's a God's blessing that I'm let to see it."

He linked their hands as he spoke, and the tears flowed as if he had been a child. Nor were the two bending above him less moved.

"When you're man and wife, you mustn't forgit Jack Witherspoon. Ah, Airnest, you can't reckon how much he loved you."

"I know it—I feel it, Jack. Your present situation—this wound—"

"I don't mind the pain of it, Airnest, when I think that I saved you. You're safe; and 'tain't no hard matter to die when one's done all his business. Indeed, to say truth, it's high time—Ah! it's like a wild-cat gnawing into the bones!"

The dialogue, broken and interrupted frequently by the sorrow of the spectators and the agonizing pain of Witherspoon, was at length interrupted by the entrance into the area of the partisan-general, with several of the officers. Marion spoke in a low tone to Scipio, who stood at the head of the dying man. The voice was recognised by him.

"That's the gineral—the old 'fox,'" he muttered to himself; and he strove to throw back his eyes sufficiently to see him.

"Stand out of the moonlight, nigger—I wants to see the gineral."

"I am here, Thumbscrew," said Marion, kneeling down beside him. "How is it with you, my friend?"

"Bad enough, gineral. You'll have to put me in the odd leaf of the orderly's book. I've got my certificate."

"I hope not, Thumby. We must see what can be done for you. We can't spare any of our men," said Marion, encouragingly. The dying man smiled feebly as he spoke again:—

"I know you can't, and that makes me more sorry. But you know me, gineral—wasn't I a whig from the first?"

"I believe it—I know it. You have done your duty always."

"Put that down in the orderly book—I was a whig from the first."

"I will," said Marion.

"And after it, put down agen—he was a whig to the last."

"I will."

"Put down—he never believed in the tories, and—" (here he paused, chokingly, from a fit of coughing) "and he always made them believe in him."

"You have done nobly in the good cause, John Witherspoon," said the general, while his eyes were filled with tears, "and you may well believe that Francis Marion, who honors you, will protect your memory. Here is my hand."

The woodman pressed it to his lips.

"Airnest—"

The youth bent over him. The arms of the dying man were lifted; they clasped him round with a fervent grasp, and brought his forehead down to his lips—

"Airnest!" he exclaimed once more, and then his grasp was relaxed. He lay cold and lifeless; the rude but noble spirit had gone from the humble but honorable dwelling, which it had informed and elevated. The grief of Ernest Mellichampe was speechless. And if the happiness of the pair, united in the sweetest bonds by the hands of the dying man, in that hour of pain, was ever darkened with a sorrow, it was when they thought that he who had served them so faithfully had not been permitted to behold it.

THE END.

From the S. Lewis engraving, Plate VIII of the Atlas accompanying John Marshall's *The Life of George Washington* (1807).

EXPLANATORY NOTES

by

Leland Cox

These notes are intended to identify persons, places, events, quotations and obscure or archaic words and terms in the text of *Mellichampe*. Special emphasis has been placed upon Revolutionary War history in the novel, including, when possible, the identification of Simms' sources and his departures from them.

1.4 "that series originally contemplated": Simms probably originally conceived of a trilogy of Revolutionary War novels which was to include the material that eventually went into *The Partisan* (1835), *Katharine Walton* (1851) and *Woodcraft* (1852), centering around the exploits of Robert Singleton and his friend Porgy. After completing *The Partisan*, however, he wrote its sequel, *Mellichampe*, and then concluded the trilogy with *Katharine Walton*.

2.11-12 "the written history": Simms' primary source for material relating to the activities of Francis Marion is William Dobein James' *Life of Francis Marion* (1821). Though very young, James fought as one of the partisans in Marion's brigade, in which his father, John James, was a major. Simms wrote his own biography of Marion in 1844, and used an autobiographical memoir (portions of which have since been lost) by Peter Horry, who commanded Marion's mounted troops. Simms may have had Horry's memoir available at the time *Mellichampe* was written.

2.12, 17 "Barsfield"; "Colonel Brown": As Simms states, the character of Barsfield is partially based upon that of Thomas Browne of Augusta, Georgia. Thomas Browne appears as a character in Simms' *Joscelyn*; see also note 310.36-314.39. There was also an actual loyalist captain named Jesse Barefield whose men operated in the same area as Marion's, and who was responsible for the death of Marion's nephew; see note 187.4.

2.35 "Gabriel Marion": Simms gives an historical account of the death of Gabriel Marion in his *Life of Marion*, p. 161. See note 187.4.

2.38-3.11 "Colonel Tarleton": For the character of Lieutenant Colonel Banastre Tarleton (1754-1833) Simms would have had a number of contemporary sources upon which to draw. In addition to James, there was William Johnson's *Life of Nathanael Greene* (1822), Henry Lee's *Memoirs of the War in the Southern Department* (1812), David Ramsay's *History of the Revolution of South Carolina* (1785) and Tarleton's *History of the Campaigns of 1780 and 1781* (1787). Incidents of kindness on Tarleton's part are recorded in Alexander Garden's *Anecdotes of the Revolutionary War in America* (1822).

3.24 "variation made in the locality": The reference here is to the burning of the Motte house during the siege of Fort Motte; the house stood on a hill on the Congaree River to the southwest of Marion's usual theatre of operations. For a more complete account of this event see note 196.19.

4.24 "One friendly reviewer": Simms probably had in mind the review in *The Knickerbocker*, 1 (January 1836), 91-92, which Simms attributed to William Henry Herbert but which was actually written by Park Benjamin.

[9].1 "The battle of Dorchester was over": A fictitious battle described in the closing scene of *The Partisan* (pp. 517-531). Dorchester was a community located approximately twenty miles northwest of Charleston at the head of navigation on the Ashley River.

[9].9 "Colonel Walton": Colonel Richard Walton, a major fictional character in *The Partisan* and *Katharine Walton*, based primarily on Isaac Hayne (1745-1781).

10.3-4 "the defeat and destruction of Gates's army": General Horatio Gates (c. 1728-1806) was defeated by the numerically inferior force of Lord Cornwallis at the Battle of Camden (16 August 1780). Among the tactical and strategic errors attributed to Gates by Simms was the failure to make proper use of Marion's partisan brigade.

13.23 "Marion's men": A reference to the brigade of partisans led by Francis Marion (c. 1732-1795). Marion had fought as a major in the 2nd South Carolina Regiment at the Battle of Fort Sullivan (28 June 1776) and commanded that regiment until the Siege of Charleston. After the fall of Charleston in May 1780 and the defeat of Gates at Camden, he was made a brigadier general of militia and began what was to become a brilliant campaign as a partisan leader. His experiences in the Cherokee War of 1760-1761 had prepared him well for fighting a guerrilla war.

13.31 "Major Singleton": "Singleton" was a family name of Simms. His great-grandfather Thomas Singleton was a prominent citizen of Charleston who, from September 1780 to July 1781, was held a prisoner by the British in Florida. Simms' grandfather John Singleton served as a captain in Marion's brigade, and he is a possible model for

EXPLANATORY NOTES   435

the novel's Major Singleton. John's brothers Bracey and Ripley also fought with Marion, and, in addition, there were members of a Singleton family from the High Hills of Santee who served in the brigade.

22.9 "Black river": The Black River flows through what are now Williamsburg and Georgetown counties, and empties into Winyah Bay at Georgetown. Williamsburg County includes much of the territory in which Marion most frequently operated in 1780.

22.10 "Williamsburgh . . . Kaddipah": See above. Williamsburg (now Kingstree) was situated on the eastern bank of the Black River and was the second township to be formed in South Carolina. The Kaddipah (a name also used for the Mellichampe plantation) flows south out of the northern part of the state and, turning gradually eastward, feeds into the Greater Pee Dee.

22.37-38 "wait until Lord Cornwallis takes that route": Approximately three weeks after the Battle of Camden, about 7 or 8 September, Cornwallis marched toward Charlotte, North Carolina, and took the town on the 25th. He remained at Charlotte until the news of Patrick Ferguson's defeat at King's Mountain prompted him to retreat into South Carolina on 14 October.

27.5 "borders of the Santee": The Santee River was then formed by the confluence of the Wateree and Congaree rivers. In 1780 it was, generally speaking, the westernmost limit for Marion's partisan activities. It has two outlets to the sea, both of which are situated south of Winyah Bay.

27.25 "Governor Rutledge": Governor John Rutledge (1739-1800), Revolutionary governor of South Carolina, commissioned Marion's activities as a partisan officer following the fall of Charleston. Rutledge appears as a character in *The Forayers*.

27.27 "Charleston": Situated on the peninsula of land formed by the confluence of the Ashley and Cooper rivers. Charles Towne (as it was called until 1783) was the major city in the South at the time of the Revolution. It was captured by the British in May 1780 and held by them until 14 December 1782.

27.28 "Georgetown": Georgetown is located on the western bank of Winyah Bay, at the confluence of the Pee Dee and the Waccamaw rivers.

28.1 "Camden": The principal town of what is now Kershaw County, it is located near the center of the state. It was the site of an important British post during the Revolution and was the scene of two important battles (16 August 1780 and 25 April 1781).

436   EXPLANATORY NOTES

28.21 "'swamp fox'": According to James (p. 63), the name "swamp fox" was given to Marion by Tarleton; see note 275.22-23.

28.24 "the two Peedees": The Greater Pee Dee and the Little Pee Dee rivers flow out of North Carolina and run through the northeastern portions of South Carolina. They merge approximately twenty-five miles north of Georgetown into the Greater Pee Dee which merges in turn with Black River approximately three miles above Georgetown.

28.24-25 "Waccamah": The Waccamaw River flows south through today's Horry County and merges with the Pee Dee River at Georgetown.

28.34 "Snow's island": Snow's Island, one of Marion's principal retreats, lies at the confluence of Lynch's Creek (now Lynch's River) and the Greater Pee Dee. The island, which is described in great detail by James (p. 67), was one of Marion's favorite and most secure retreats.

30.4 "August sun": The correct historical time would have to be early September.

33.37-38 "Thumbscrew": This is Jack Witherspoon, a member of Marion's brigade. He has no identifiable model, though the activities of two Witherspoons, Captains John and Gavin, are discussed in James' *Life of Marion*. None of the recorded activities of these two men, however, parallels the actions of Thumbscrew in *Mellichampe*. Witherspoon also appears in *The Partisan*.

34.3 "Ernest Mellichampe": Although no source for either Ernest Mellichampe or his father, Max, has been found, several persons of this name (usually spelled Mellichamp) lived in South Carolina between 1725 and the opening of the Revolution.

44.1 "Gainey's men": Marion had encountered and defeated loyalists led by Major Micajah Gainey (15 August) prior to the defeat of Gates at Camden. Gainey's men were part of the British force that precipitated Marion's strategic retreat into North Carolina in late August; see note 47.6-7. They were, at this time, in the rear of the 63rd British Regiment under Major Wemyss near Kingstree.

47.6 "Tarleton over Sumter": Lieutenant Colonel Banastre Tarleton surprised and defeated the partisan force of Thomas Sumter (1734-1832) at Fishing Creek on 18 August 1780.

47.6-7 "the supposed flight of Marion": Marion staged a strategic retreat into North Carolina on 28 August and camped near the head of the Waccamaw River, but was back in South Carolina by mid-September.

EXPLANATORY NOTES 437

49.22-25 "Georgia has been long shut up . . . . ": Georgia had been under British control since the fall of Savannah in December 1778.

51.7 "Watson": Colonel Watson, known as a humane loyalist, commanded Fort Watson on the Santee, a small British outpost established to guard the British supply line running from Charleston to Camden.

64.7 "the Yemassee war": The Yemassee War occurred in 1715-1717. The hostile tribes were the Yemassees, the Catawbas and the Edistohs; the Cherokees aided the white colonists.

67.31 "Sir Peter Lely": Sir Peter Lely (1618-1680), a Dutch painter known for his portraits of the court of Charles II.

68.17-18 "four miserable years": Open hostilities in South Carolina had actually broken out five years before in the summer and fall of 1775. Simms treats this period in *Joscelyn*.

74.11 "sand-lapper": This word had a derogatory connotation in Simms' time, comparable to "dirt eater" or "mud eater," and refers to the lowest class of whites, those who supplemented their meagre diet by eating clay.

74.11 "Goose Creek": A reference to both a parish and a stream. St. James, Goose Creek, Parish was situated northwest of Charleston; the stream is an upper tributary of the Cooper River.

75.23 "the dregs of the people": Simms has his loyalists in *Mellichampe* derive predominately from the lower classes, but his other Revolutionary novels portray loyalists from all echelons of society.

78.20 "the smallpox they have in Charleston": Smallpox was prevalent in Charleston in January and February of 1780, just prior to the siege. For this reason it was very difficult to find defenders for the city. Smallpox continued to be a problem in Charleston into the late summer.

83.30 Davis, Baxter, Gwinn: For Davis, see note 153.11-12. Captain John Baxter, later made colonel, was an officer in Marion's cavalry under Colonel Peter Horry. James (p. 94) tells of a young boy named "Gwyn" in Marion's band. He was an excellent shot. In an encounter with Major Gainey near Georgetown around January 1781, Colonel Peter Horry found himself cut off from the rest of his cavalry and pursued by a party under a Captain Lewis. Gwyn shot Lewis from ambush and frightened off the remainder of the pursuing party.

84.11 "'My Lady's Fancy'": Perhaps suggested to Simms by a place called My Lady's Bush located on the eastern bank of Clutters Creek, approximately ten miles north of Charleston.

84.16 "M'Donald": At Nelson's Ferry on 20 August 1780, in his first encounter after Camden, Marion met a British guard with a large body of prisoners taken at Camden, and was successful in retaking all the prisoners. James' *Life of Marion* (p. 55) identifies a Sergeant McDonald as one of the three American soldiers who chose to remain in Marion's brigade. McDonald was killed at Fort Motte in May 1781.

84.23 "Moultrie": A reference to Colonel William Moultrie (1730-1805).

88.7 "hawk hovering over her dovecot": *Hawks About the Dovecote* is the principal subtitle for Simms' Revolutionary War novel *Woodcraft*.

96. chapter title "Scipio": This common slave name is presumably based upon that of Scipio Africanus (237-183 B.C.), a Roman general.

102.26 "Scipio was lifted into air": This incident was perhaps suggested to Simms by Mason Locke Weems, who, in his romanticized *Life of Marion* (1809), describes how a Captain Snipes of Marion's brigade was being sought at his home by a party of loyalists. His overseer Cudjo warned him of their approach and hid him in a nearby clump of briars. The loyalists burned all the plantation buildings, and when they did not find Snipes, they hanged Cudjo three times in an attempt to force him to reveal his master's hiding place, but he did not. A traditional account of one of Colonel William Thomson's slaves, Abram, is similar. He had been entrusted with the protection of Thomson's favorite blooded horse, which the British attempted to take from him. When all else failed they threatened to hang him and finally proceeded to hoist him into the air three times, holding him up until he lost consciousness each time. Each time he regained his senses, however, and refused to betray his trust, through his loyalty and obstinacy managing to preserve both his master's horse and his own life.

114.32-33 "The family estate . . . free grant of our monarch": Barsfield probably gained ownership of Kaddipah plantation as a confiscated estate. The British practice of either confiscating or sequestering whig property during the Revolution was common. A general order of sequestration was issued by Cornwallis on 16 September 1780.

116.6 "Monck's corner": Located approximately twenty-five miles north of Charleston near the head of navigation on the western branch of the Cooper River.

137.19-20 "tories gathering . . . at Sinkler's Meadow": This was actually the Battle of Tarcote Swamp, located at the forks of the Black River, and fought some time in mid-September—shortly after Marion's return from North Carolina. The loyalists of the area had gathered at Tarcote upon the summons of the loyalist Colonel Tynes, who had

EXPLANATORY NOTES   439

brought from Charleston provisions for his new recruits. The details of this short but decisive conflict, especially the element of surprise, are paralleled in the description of Sinkler's Meadow contained in the novel (see p. 276).

141.22-27 "This parchment . . . over his life": This may be a reference to the orders issued by Cornwallis shortly after the Battle of Camden: "'I have given orders that all the inhabitants of this province, who have subscribed and have taken part in this revolt, should be punished with the greatest rigour. . . . I desire you will take the most vigorous measures to punish the rebels in the district in which you command . . .'" (quoted in Ramsay, *History of the Revolution of South Carolina*, II, 157).

144.10 "Meschianza": Usually used as the name of a festivity involving a series of entertainments, in this context the term probably means a series, or medley, of different dance steps.

151.34 "our old acquaintance Tom": Tom first appears in *The Partisan* as Porgy's accomplished cook, and is also a character of some importance in *Woodcraft*, *The Forayers* and *Eutaw*.

153.12 "His force was feeble": Before retreating into North Carolina, Marion had allowed his men to look after the care of their families while awaiting his return, but they took so long in reassembling after he came back in mid-September that he nearly despaired of their return.

153.15-16 "continentals . . . whom he rescued": See note 84.16. Actually, three of the 150 liberated soldiers elected to ride with Marion: Sergeant McDonald and Sergeant Davis, both of whom later distinguished themselves in partisan warfare, and one other man. It is unlikely that this Davis is the model in anything but name for the Lieutenant Davis who is a character in both *The Partisan* and *Mellichampe*. The action at Nelson's Ferry is described in *The Partisan* (pp. 491-496).

154.10 "Lieutenant Porgy": A fictional character who bears some resemblance to a Dr. Skinner described in Alexander Garden's *Anecdotes* (1822), pp. 135-139, and in Lee's *Memoirs* (1812), II, 136-137, 153-154. Porgy also appears as a central character in *The Partisan*, *Katharine Walton*, *Woodcraft*, *The Forayers* and *Eutaw*.

154.20 "those of the Ashley": A reference to Porgy's hunting and dining activities in *The Partisan*.

157.35 "He who sleeps . . . sure of fleas": George Herbert, *Jacula Prudentum* (1640).

159.37 "Jamaica": Jamaican rum.

160.20 "Continental Congress": Created as a voice for American rights, it was formed in the summer of 1774 and began functioning in September. It drew up a Declaration of Rights, and later the Declaration of Independence. Though very weak, it was the central governing body of the states during the Revolution.

160.28-29 "We shall spoil the Egyptians": Exodus 12:36.

169.4 "vinegar and water": In his *Life of Marion* (p. 145), Simms reports that this was a favorite beverage of Marion's; no other source has been found for this fact.

169.12 "Horry": There were two Horrys in Marion's brigade. Hugh Horry was a lieutenant colonel of militia and was for a time the commander of Marion's foot troops. His brother Peter Horry had earlier served with Marion in the 2nd South Carolina Regiment and, in Marion's brigade, commanded the mounted troops.

169.36 "Waccamaw": Probably a reference to the area in and around Kingston township (today's Conway in Horry County), located between the Waccamaw and Little Pee Dee rivers.

169.37 "Williamsburg": This was the place of origin of most of Marion's partisans and of some of the loyalists ("rascals") under Gainey, Tynes, Harrison and other loyalist leaders; see also note 22.10.

170.17 "Captain Melton": A Captain John Melton was in Marion's brigade. It was Melton who fought a skirmish with a loyalist named Barefield either in November or December of 1780, in which Gabriel Marion (Francis Marion's nephew) was captured and then executed. For Simms' fictional account of Gabriel's death see p. 187 of the novel.

171.2-3 "a corps . . . Tarleton's": Having recovered from a fever, Tarleton set out toward Camden by way of Nelson's Ferry across the Santee River in November 1780.

171.4 "Mother Dyson": This may have been suggested to Simms by Tarleton's report that a woman who saw his force before his attempted surprise of Sumter at Blackstock on 20 November revealed his position and strength to the Americans.

171.11 "smite them, hip and thigh": Judges 15:8.

172.15 "Captain James": Captain John James led the men of Williamsburg township in Marion's brigade. Four of his brothers (William, Gavin, Robert and James) and his cousin, Major John James (father of William Dobein James), also fought with Marion.

EXPLANATORY NOTES 441

174.7-9 "British officers": In his *A History of the Campaigns of 1780 and 1781*, Tarleton acknowledges the difficulties caused the British by Marion's harassing tactics. He also quotes a letter to this effect from Cornwallis to Clinton, 3 December 1780: "Colonel Marion had so wrought on the minds of the people, partly by the terror of his threats and cruelty of his punishments, and partly by the promise of plunder, that there was scarcely an inhabitant between the Santee and Peedee, that was not in arms against us. Some parties had even crossed the Santee, and carried terror to the gates of Charles town" (p. 200). Cornwallis also says in the same letter that the locale was so dominated by Marion's presence that supplies to Camden had been virtually cut off.

178.24 "'goods the gods provide me'": John Dryden, *Alexander's Feast*, I, 106.

186.7 "Winyah mud-eaters": A derogatory term equating the loyalists of the Winyah area with the lowest class of white men.

186.37-38 "torn him from his horse": According to James (p. 66), Gabriel Marion had his horse shot from under him.

187.4 "Gabriel Marion": A fictionalized account of the death of Gabriel Marion, Francis Marion's nephew. Gabriel was captured during a clash with loyalists under the command of Captain Jesse Barefield in November or December 1780. When his identity was discovered, he was immediately shot. See note 2.35.

195.37 "Lance": Lance Frampton, a character who has some surface affinities with an actual soldier named Gwyn (see note 83.30). Frampton also appears in several of Simms' other Revolutionary War novels, notably *The Partisan, Katharine Walton* and *Woodcraft*.

196.19 "this bow and these arrows": This is a fictionalized version of a real incident involving Mrs. Rebecca Motte at the siege of Fort Motte (11-12 May 1781)–an action in which Marion and his men were involved. The fort itself consisted of earthworks built around the main house of the Motte plantation. The house was set on fire (but was not completely burned) as a means of forcing the surrender of the British garrison, commanded by Lieutenant McPherson. General Henry Lee (1756-1818) commanded the patriot forces. In Lee's account in his *Memoirs* (II, 77), Mrs. Motte is said to have supplied the arrows used to ignite the roof. James, however, writes that the roof was fired by a private named Nathan Savage with a flaming ball of rosin and brimstone (p. 120). Simms manages to include both versions of the firing in the novel by having Lance Frampton offer to perform the action in the way that Savage is alleged to have done it.

196.21 "gift of a Catawba warrior": This differs from other accounts that the arrows were of a special incendiary variety imported from India and were designed to ignite upon impact. Catawba refers to a Carolina Indian tribe which, with the exception of its participation in the Yemassee War (1715-1717), was noted for its friendly relations with the whites.

201.3 "Tarleton's quarters": This phrase grew out of Tarleton's massacre of Buford's regiment on 29 May 1780 shortly after the fall of Charleston. It meant that no mercy would be allowed to the captured or wounded.

212.10 "the chase we had from the Oaks": A scene occurring in *The Partisan*, pp. 293-303. The Oaks was apparently based on a number of actual low country plantations; it was located near Dorchester. See note 117.1-16 in *The Partisan*.

252.4 "Gum Swamp": Another name for the first battle of Camden (16 August 1780). Barsfield here ironically alludes to Cornwallis' orders for the execution of a number of prisoners after this battle.

252.31-38 "An execution is wanted": Various efforts were made by the British either to pacify or to intimidate the whig element in Charleston. Simms' great-grandfather, Thomas Singleton (see note 13.31), was taken as a prisoner to Florida, along with other prominent Charleston citizens, and the guarantee of their safety was made conditional upon the good behavior of the citizenry. Colonel Isaac Hayne, who serves as the partial model for Richard Walton in *Katharine Walton*, was executed by the British (4 August 1781) as an example to those who had accepted British protection and then had resumed arms against the Crown.

259.19-20 "repulses ... at the hands of Sumter": Sumter's men fought in two engagements in which Tarleton's troops were involved: at Fishdam Ford (9 November 1780), and at Blackstock plantation (20 November 1780). In the earlier battle Tarleton was not personally involved, but a part of his legion was employed under the command of Wemyss, who was wounded and captured and whose troops were defeated. In the latter battle, Sumter was wounded, and the outcome of the encounter was not decisive on either side.

259.21 "Cowpens": The Battle of Cowpens took place on 17 January 1781. Tarleton's legion panicked and was defeated by soldiers under General Daniel Morgan (1736-1802). Tarleton acknowledges this as a great loss strategically as well as militarily since it occurred just as Cornwallis was making his second incursion into North Carolina, this time in pursuit of Greene's newly-formed Continental army.

259.28 "raw militiamen": The forces of Marion, Sumter and other partisan military leaders were voluntary militia and had little professional

EXPLANATORY NOTES 443

military training. After the fall of Charleston in May 1780, there was no sustained presence of Continental troops in South Carolina until Greene took command of the fragmented and disorganized Southern army in December 1780. Therefore the brunt of the conflict during the time when the British had almost complete control of the state was borne by the local militia. However, during and just after the Siege of Charleston, small, independently operating Continental units, such as those under Colonels Abraham Buford and William Washington, were functioning, though without much strength or success, in the interior of South Carolina. The forces of both Buford and Washington were routed on different occasions in April and May 1780.

272.10, 24 "a man something his senior"; "Moncrieff": Colonel James Moncrieff (1744-1793) was senior to Tarleton in age as well as rank. Moncrieff, involved in the war primarily as a military engineer, was the British officer alleged to have carried off some eight hundred Negro slaves during the British evacuation of Charleston in December 1782. See *Woodcraft*, pp. 6-37, in which Moncrieff appears as a central character.

274.4 "my mission": No record has been found of any British attempts to bribe or persuade Marion to desert the American side.

274.12 "baffling Green": Nathanael Greene (1742-1786). This reference to Greene seems to be an error in chronology since he did not assume command of the Southern Continental army in person until 4 December 1780, and did not begin military operations in South Carolina until early 1781.

274.14 "prog-princes": "prog" can mean either to stab or to forage (as for provisions).

275.22-23 "he penetrated the spacious swamp of the Santee": This pursuit did not occur near the Santee River but on Black River. Tarleton was given specific orders by Cornwallis to seek out and disperse Marion's brigade in November 1780. After burning General Richard Richardson's plantation near Camden on 10 November, Tarleton was informed by an American deserter that Marion was planning to attack him. In actuality, however, Marion was staging a retreat across Jack's Creek and down Black River. Tarleton pursued Marion, but lost him due to a poor choice of routes. On finally giving up his chase, Tarleton is reported to have said, "'Come my boys! let us go back, and we will soon find the game cock, (meaning Sumter) but as for this d---d *old fox*, the devil himself could not catch him'" (James, p. 63). This is the source for the popular but probably unreliable legend that it was Tarleton who gave Marion and Sumter their well-known *noms de guerre*.

284.1 "'How sweet the days of Thalaba'": An allusion to Robert Southey's *Thalaba the Destroyer* (1802), in which a young Moslem seeks revenge for the death of his parents.

287.6-13 "'"Aye free aff han' your story tell"'": Robert Burns, "Epistle to a Young Friend" (1786).

288.3-4 "the easy won was but little valued of men": Thomas Paine, *The American Crisis*, no. 1: "What we obtain too cheap, we esteem too lightly."

298.2 "Roscius": Shakespeare, 3 *Henry VI*, V, vi.

298.19-23 "British house . . . began to desclaim": In Britain there was an outbreak of strong resentment against the war after the execution of Isaac Hayne in August 1781. By 4 March 1782 it had become so unpopular that the House of Commons denounced as an enemy to Britain any citizen advising further offensive measures against the Americans and demanded the initiation of peace negotiations. Simms' entire discussion in this passage is anachronistic, however, since *Mellichampe* is set in the late summer of 1780.

298.28 "Rawdon": Lord Francis Rawdon (1754-1826), adjutant general to the British forces in America and later the supreme commander of British troops in South Carolina outside of Charleston, was the opponent of General Greene at the second battle of Camden (Hobkirk's Hill) on 25 April 1781. He left America in August 1781. Rawdon appears as a character in *The Scout* and *Eutaw*.

298.28 "Balfour": Lieutenant Colonel Nesbit Balfour (1743-1823) was in command of the British outpost at Ninety Six during the summer of 1780, but was appointed the commanding officer at Charleston in September. He is a central character in *Katharine Walton*.

299.7-8 "pledged . . . in writing": Following the execution of Isaac Hayne, General Greene received a written proclamation (20 August 1781), urging retaliation upon British subjects, and signed by all the officers of his army except Lee, who was out of the area; see note 298.19-23.

299.23-24 "any of the existing powers": Perhaps a reference to Colonel Balfour or to Colonel John Cruden, the commissioner of sequestered estates.

310.36-314.39 "When this cruel . . . war commenced in South Carolina": The following narrative is based partially on the tarring and feathering of Thomas Browne by Captain Hamilton's Liberty Boys in Augusta, Georgia, about 1 August 1775. Simms treats Browne's story in detail in *Joscelyn*. See also Simms' comments in the Advertisement for *Mellichampe* (p. 2).

339.11 "the thing is a proverb": "Foolish fear doubles danger."

EXPLANATORY NOTES   445

352.29-30 "poor buckrah": Poor whites.

384.29-31 "how he was busy gathering his men": This would be during the period from 4 December 1780 (when Greene assumed command of the Southern army) through at least 20 December, when elements attached to Greene began operating out of a training camp located just above Cheraw. Though he experienced some difficulties with Sumter, Greene soon understood the necessity of taking advantage of the services that an effective partisan force of irregulars had to offer, and so began employing them regularly in all his campaigns from then on.

385.1-3 "The tender mercies": Probably a reference to the execution of Hayne, who was sentenced to be hanged, without being given a formal court-martial, on the joint authority of Balfour and Rawdon; see also notes 252.31-38 and 298.19-23.

410.10-11 "one hundred and fifty men": In the skirmishes fought by Marion during this period, his attacking force seldom numbered more than 150, although he had commanded four hundred at Tarcote Swamp. The size of his force was extremely variable, as his men came and went almost at will.